Assault on CHIMERA

S.A. CARR

First published in Great Britain as a softback original in 2017

All characters and events in this book, other than those clearly in the public domain, are fictitious and any resemblance to real persons, living or dead, is purely coincidental.

Typeset in Dante MT Std

Editing, design, typesetting and publishing by UK Book Publishing

www.ukbookpublishing.com

ISBN: 978-1-910223-97-0

PLANET FALL

A faint humming sound emanated from the holo-projector as it flickered to life, powering up without fail for the third time that day. The device started to beam a sequence of live news events and recordings into the space directly above where it sat, disturbing a large Pyrenean Mastiff that had been asleep on the floor nearby. It also drew the attention of a seated, black-haired youth who eagerly craned his neck to stare up at the videos, adverts and interviews, some of which were now repeating.

The cycle of propaganda continued until a smartly dressed woman appeared holding the projector's remote. She keyed in a series of commands, forcing the machine to display an expanding spherical object instead. This illuminated the room as it grew in size before eventually stabilising, then began to rotate in front of them.

Carmona. Their homeworld.

The aquamarine sphere carried on spinning away as the slender, brown-eyed woman stepped forward, arms folded across her chest. "You weren't watching those awful commercials, were you?" she asked.

Leandro Vela shook his head. His mother smiled mischievously, zooming in on the planet's largest continent and pointed out one of the many sky-cities populating it.

"That's us," she said, pausing to add an expensive-looking purse to the assortment of belongings already packed and assembled close by. "Spire Nara. Twenty billion people on Carmona - most live here in the capital like we do, Leandro. But these places all look the same. It's important to remember where you came from."

The boy sighed impatiently, hoping his mother wouldn't subject him to a late-night history lesson. Learning about the past was boring. When classes were suspended he'd thought whole days would be given over to adventure and play, but his parents had other ideas. Before the academy closed, his teachers had informed them he possessed a 'short attention span', whatever that meant, and as a result they'd opted to continue his education at home. Still, they bought him all the latest toys and allowed him to see his friends whenever he wanted - the two things that mattered most to any eight-year-old boy.

Today had been hard work. Now he just wanted to go to bed and listen to one of Mother's stories about fearless heroes or intrepid explorers.

"Carmona is our home," she resumed, interrupting his thoughts. "But we've seen so little of the galaxy." She moved the star map away from Carmona and panned it left a couple of sectors, finally settling on another world to the galactic west. "Look, Leandro," she said jovially, attempting to enthuse him. "This is Nuevo Córdoba. How would you feel about living here?"

The new planet had none of the soft, swirling greens and azures Carmona did. It was a dull, orange monotone from pole to pole, featureless and barren. Having lived a life of continued stability, Leandro greeted this unexpected revelation with a mixture of angst and defiance.

"I don't want to go there," he complained, standing up and ignoring the resolve behind his mother's words. "I knew this would happen. It will be different and I won't know anyone. Why do we have to go to that place? Why?" He sighed again, loudly, and stared angrily at the floor, unwilling to meet her gaze.

"I-it's only for a short while," she said, hurriedly changing tack. "It'll be like a holiday. You like holidays, don't you darling?"

That doesn't sound so bad, Leandro thought, quelling his own petulant negativity. *I do like holidays. Even if they are to strange planets*. But he still wasn't convinced.

"You promise?"

"I do, I promise." With that, she knelt down in front of her son and embraced him. "Everything will be all right, sweetheart, I promise."

Satisfied, Leandro paid this last remark no heed. Any lingering doubts had been substituted by thoughts of an off-world holiday. But his mother was still talking, half to herself.

"Everything will be all right, you'll see. We'll make it all right..."

She seemed set to continue and most likely would have were it not for his father's sudden return, the man flinging open the front door so forcefully it made both of them jump. He was home early tonight.

Leandro recognised this immediately, closing his eyes tightly in anticipation of the chastisement that would surely follow. He could almost hear his father's scolding remarks now.

What hour do you call this? You should be in bed, young man. Always tinkering around with that infernal contraption. Ignorance isn't an excuse. My father wouldn't have stood for such tardiness. And don't look to her to defend you again.

But the lecture never came. Instead, he elected to say nothing, approaching them with such haste his large frame very nearly went flying over the collection ofbags and cases Mother had been fussing with earlier. Steadying himself with a well-executed half-step, he glanced up and began barking orders at them as if they were his subordinates.

"Ana, get the baby. Leandro, with me. We've got to go, *now.*"

This barrage of directives confounded the boy, who'd fully expected to be on the receiving end of yet another chiding. He'd heard and seen it all before. Father's scowling countenance, his rumbling voice and authoritative, towering stance - yes, they were all there, only this time something was different. Mother obeyed without hesitation, darting off to pluck Leandro's little sister Lola from the warmth of her cot where she slept. Deprived of her comforting presence, Leandro also found himself compelled to acquiesce even as his father gesticulated impatiently, beckoning him over against his wishes.

"Quickly!"

He was obviously distracted by events beyond his control and in a real hurry to get going, his mind elsewhere.

"But I want to go to bed... sir," Leandro grumbled, adding the formal address when he realised he might have pushed too far.

His father stood unmoved and with features unflinching, clearly more concerned with what was going on outside where a terrible wind had started to pick up. Leandro listened too - there were people running around out there, he could hear them even above the howling of the storm. Eventually his father spoke again, this time with composure and steely determination.

"We have to leave, Leandro. We won't be coming back."

...That wasn't what Mother had said.

Father and son ran without stopping through the windswept streets of Nara, glancing back every few moments to ensure Mother and baby Lola were still in tow. Overhead, storm clouds scudded past. The narrow alleyways leading out of the spire's habitation centres offered scant protection from the elements, but father had provisioned them well as he always did. His waterproof coats kept the rain off, though Leandro thought they all looked ridiculous in the oversized green jackets.

They were joined on their journey by ever-increasing numbers of people who had the same idea, spilling forth from their homes and bringing whatever they could carry to the spire's sole spaceport. Leandro wondered how there could possibly be enough room on one ship for everyone.

As if she'd heard his concerns, Mother put voice to them. "Will they be held for us?" she shouted through the driving rain.

Father stopped, shooting her a puzzled look as she caught up.

"Our seats?"

"Of course." He shook his head despairingly. "What do you take me for? They were guaranteed the moment we found out. I've told you this a hundred times, but I see that as usual you didn't bother listening." He lowered his voice to a growl. "There are five ships to help facilitate the evacuation. You'd be able to see for yourself by now were you not dragging those trinkets along. Slows us down. Couldn't you have just left them behind with the dogs?"

Mother hugged Lola tightly to her breast. The rain was heavier now and her long dark hair hung in matted curls around her face. "You'd rather the children forget who they are? Where they came from? They wouldn't be the first."

She sounded upset. Upset and angry. Leandro decided he didn't like it out here anymore and grasped his father's hand tightly. He couldn't understand what his parents were arguing about, reassuring himself it was most likely over something they'd left behind at home. He drew his own conclusions, daring not to interrupt as the row escalated. Leandro tried to count stars, a trick he found helped whenever he felt anxious.

And then he saw it.

There was something up there, far beyond the cloud cover and too distant to fully make out. Something new in Carmona's skies - something he'd not seen before. Any previous apprehensions dissipating, Leandro tugged at his father's arm to try and get his attention.

"Father?"

No response. Undaunted, he pulled a little more forcefully. "What is that?" he pointed. Belatedly, the quarrelling stopped. Father looked up.

"It's just a satellite."

Mother said nothing to contradict him, and after a while her expression softened. No words were exchanged between them, and Father began to nod.

"All right," he said gently.

Before Leandro knew what was happening his father took off, pulling him along as they made for the spaceport anew.

People were running faster now, screaming, shouting, swearing, and discarding the very things they had earlier sought to bring with them. There were thousands of them, hundreds of thousands of people here.

Leandro saw that the perimeter fence around the spaceport was gone, entire sections crushed or swept away beneath a never-ending deluge of desperate Carmonans. They had no choice but to climb like everyone else - climb the great stairway that led to the launch pads and hope they weren't too late.

When they reached the top, Leandro noticed some people who weren't running. The military was here, in amongst the crowd and on the periphery, trying to organise amidst the chaos. High-ranking officers in brightly coloured uniforms barked orders at their subordinates, men and women with guns who brandished them at anyone who came too close for their liking. A squadron of attack jets streaked overhead, fully armed, followed by another. Tannoys and loudhailers blared forth a constant stream of information, telling everyone what to do and where to go.

Father already knew. He'd seen one of the officers wave them over and began to shoulder his way through the crowd towards him, barging people aside like paperweights as he cleared a path for Mother, still holding baby Lola tightly, to follow. It didn't take him long to get there. Appearing impressed, the bespectacled stranger saluted.

"General Vela!" he beamed, a wide grin etched across his face. "You made it!" Then the smile faded. "Most of our unit didn't."

"I know," Father said without emotion. "We can't win this one, Raf."

"We don't need to. Just have to buy some time."

Father laughed heartily as the two men embraced. "Still the optimist after all these years, Raf?"

"Still expecting the worst, General?"

"You know me. We should get moving."

The officer called Raf ignored him, gesturing over in Leandro's direction. "Look who it is! And taller than last we met. How old is he now, General?"

"Eight."

"Eight? Ha! I was fighting alongside your old man eight years before you were born, sonny. What do you make of that? And I'll wager you'll be my CO before either of us knows it!"

Emboldened by these remarks Leandro stood up straight, trying to grow a little taller and mimic Raf's movements. He seemed friendly enough and continued to compliment him as they walked. "We'll need your help tonight, kiddo."

Leandro was relieved to see the fences ringing the launch pads were intact. Raf took out a card from one of his many camo-jacket pockets and held it up in front of a panel on a large steel gate.

"Are you watching, soldier?" he asked Leandro. The red lights on the panel turned green and the gate swung open. "This way."

He motioned for them to proceed through, only following when certain the lock was reactivated and their passage secured.

What a helpful fellow, Leandro thought. *Helpful and brilliant!* That magic card of his had somehow managed to get them inside the spaceport itself - the rockets were right there, waiting!

The installation was massive. An illuminated hub of frenzied activity located near the spire's peak, it served as the capital's gateway to the stars.

Leandro couldn't believe what he was seeing. On each of the five huge launch pads that dominated the spaceport sat an even bigger rocket, their noses pointing skyward.

Planetships.

He'd heard about them in stories but never thought he would actually see one. These gargantuan vessels doubled as self-sufficient cities, originally designed to carry colonists from Earth during the days of the Great Expansion.

Sadly, they weren't quite the awe-inspiring creations of Man that Mother had made them out to be. Instead, the planetships resembled ungainly relics left over from another time that didn't appear capable of flight, let alone operating in deep space.

Leandro heard a noise behind him and looked round at the steel fences. He saw that the military were holding large numbers of people back, but allowing politicians and nobles through.

"Number five!" Raf yelled, pointing at one of the planetships. "That's yours! Go, now!"

Without warning, tracer fire lit up the night sky. The vulture-like jets that were circling overhead banked sharply around the spire's zenith and began to climb, while powerful cannon discharged superheated beams of plasma and explosive rounds into the heavens. Leandro watched in amazement as the display of light intensified, but Father was furious and confronted his friend.

"Whose decision was this? Was it Toldo's?"

"It was the council's decision," said Raf. "The global defence grid is breached - they're hitting the ice caps and northern population centres already. Our ships don't stand a chance against their strike craft unless we engage them, you know that."

"I'll get us by the strike craft," Leandro boasted. "I *always* beat the holo-games. I get three stars on 'expert'."

Raf smiled grimly at this. "We've played our hand, General. Toldo's forces will hold long enough for the fleet to clear the asteroid belt. From there, it's eight days to Nuevo Córdoba. You'll be in charge of overseeing the relocation program. Good luck, sir."

As Raf went to leave, Father reached out a hand and grasped his right forearm firmly. "Don't be a hero, Raf. You get what you can and go. You've done more than enough for us. For Carmona."

Coupled with the magnitude of what was happening around him, Raf seemed to be deeply moved by these words. He tried to say something meaningful back, but could only manage, "Sir." He stood to attention, saluted one final time, turned and then disappeared off into the rain. Father returned the salute before shepherding his family over towards the waiting planetship in the opposite direction.

Number five.

That's what Raf had said and that's where they were heading, up the access ramp of planetship number five. Leandro flinched, thinking he could hear gunshots nearby, but it was just the sound of their footsteps reverberating off the metal floor. It smelled funny inside, and he wondered if things would have been better on one of the other ships. Here, an oily, copperish odour lingered about the interior where a dozen burly soldiers stood watch over the approach. Father marched straight past them and began shouting into the ship's private intercom system.

"This is General Vela. Pilot, why aren't we moving? Why haven't you initiated the launch sequence?"

"Uh... sir... we have several dignitaries unaccounted for..."

"Forget them! They've had long enough. I take full responsibility."

"Y-yes, sir. Right away. Sequence commencing."

Leandro rolled his eyes. Everything was always such a rush with Father. He found it impossible to keep still for prolonged periods of time, even those when they were meant to be doing things together as a family. Recreation remained an alien concept to him. Incompetence was even harder for the general to stomach; number five's pilot becoming the latest addition to a long list of disappointments that started, Leandro suspected, with himself. He'd learned to tread carefully when his father was like this. Nothing good could come of challenging his commands, not that he would have ever summoned the temerity to try.

"Prime engine ignition," informed the ship's computer, sparing the pilot any further unpleasantries. "All passengers please take your seats immediately. Departure countdown underway."

Psh, Leandro thought. He wasn't about to let some computerised voice tell him what to do. How could he when there was a chance to watch the planetship blast off in all its fiery glory?

What a spectacle this would be!

Oh, how he'd laud this over his rich, haughty friends when they got back, for it'd be a memory all their money put together couldn't buy. Who among them could say he or she had been on board such a vessel, watching Carmona recede behind as it drove like a spear thrust towards the stars? There were none!

Jumping around with uncontrollable joy, Leandro pressed his face up against one of the ship's circular viewports.

He recoiled in terror almost instantly.

The military was losing control. As more and more people swarmed against the spaceport's gates they began to buckle, but not before those at the front had already been crushed between the fencing and the weight of the crowd behind. Alarmed at this the soldiers looked to themselves, raising their guns and firing off a couple of warning shots into the air. When these failed to have any effect they pulled back, slapped in higher capacity magazines, switched their weapons to automatic and turned them on the people.

Transfixed with fear, Leandro saw everything. Muzzle flashes lighting up the landing even as the gates came crashing down. Pilots struggling desperately to get their planetships away. Fires burning in Spire Nara's residential towers. And out of nowhere a wall of water thundered towards them like an unstoppable juggernaut, which threatened to devour everything in its wake.

This can't be real, Leandro thought. Some spiteful sap had to be playing a holo-trick on him as he slept. Somehow, though, it had manifested. Somehow, the water which couldn't be there was, and with each passing moment cascading ever closer.

There was no comfort to be found whichever way he looked. Mother had buried her face in Lola's blanket and was mumbling away inanely, trying to hide her tears. Leandro wanted to ask so many questions, but his father's blank expression told him that he didn't know the answer to any of them.

The general put a loving hand on Leandro's shoulder and closed his eyes.

As the huge wave engulfed Spire Nara and everyone within, emergency bulkheads sealed the planetships before they were sent tumbling clear of the spaceport and down onto the newly submerged plains below.

They fell together. They fell for what seemed to be forever. And the places where they finally came to rest grew dark.

ASSAULT ON CHIMERA

1

The *Iron Duke*, an aerial assault transport, cleared the last of the sand dunes and accelerated.

Within her creaking shell, men and women of the regent's enforcer contingent held on for dear life. The *Duke* was flying light with her armature scaled back and rusting gun posts unmanned, a corroded colossus that had once fought in the wars of giants now forced to serve in a more modest capacity. Age made her unsuitable for combat, though the ramshackle craft still laboured under the combined weight of her fifteen passengers - a third of the number she had been designed to carry. But there were no complaints from any on board. Of all the gunboats on Tanis they knew she was the best.

Leo Rossi tightened his grip on an overhead railing as the *Duke* picked up speed, observing the anxious glances that passed between several first timers. He recalled a very different group of individuals from when they'd set out into the arid expanse, neither protesting their bullish comments nor actively dispelling any myths they held as to how elementary it all seemed.

Reality had seen to that for him.

The lessons learnt during this month looked set to shape their futures; some destined to pursue military careers while others would take up alternative challenges.

The gunship's pilot expertly navigated swirling dust storms and crosswinds as she levelled the craft out, always in control of her protesting charge. With the dunes behind, Leo knew it wouldn't be long until they were home. Between here and the great sky-city of

Divinity there was only open desert.

It had taken him two previous campaigns to earn the respect of the senior enforcers who accompanied the rookies on trial. These humourless veterans loathed taking orders from a youthful upstart who, in their eyes, owed everything to his privileged place in society. They cared little for certificates and medals awarded back at the academy - surviving weeks on end in a landscape more unforgiving than they were was the only true test of character here.

The *Iron Duke* shook violently as its pilot fought against the prevailing winds. The initiates huddled together as they had done out in the desert, clinging to whatever they could whilst whispering words of encouragement to one another. Leo understood their apprehension even if the veterans could not.

The enforcers' hostility ensured he'd faced a daunting introduction to leadership, but it was his perseverance and modesty that had finally earned him the right to stand as their equal. Under his instructors' tutelage he'd become a fit and capable young man - his mind sharp and body strong. Having proved himself, he vowed to put those he had the honour of commanding before him, never after. Over the years he'd gained rank and stature, all the more remarkable for a man who'd previously possessed no military training at all.

The planet Tanis was a scorched, inhospitable wasteland. Its solitary bastion of civilisation reached out of the sands bordering the world's equator and climbed ever up, dominating the skyline for miles around in every direction. The royal palaces of Divinity had been Leo's home for twelve years and were all he'd ever known. Records existed that spoke of better times when Tanis had thrived, but he dismissed these as nothing more than the delusions of ancients dissatisfied with their own lives, yearning for the glories of an age long since gone.

He lived on a world like any other; one ruled by a single regent and dominated by a single culture. Yet beneath this simple exterior there were forces at work on Tanis that he struggled to understand. With each passing year Leo found himself increasingly concerned with events beyond his means to influence, events he would have deemed trivial distractions while growing up. He'd thought his father a fool for pursuing his impossible dreams of peace and equality for all, but now realised what an intelligent man he was. Following his example, Leo had grown to comprehend and challenge everything. He resolved to ignore life no longer. Gone were the innocent days of childhood naivety - things could not remain as they used to be. With age came responsibility, and he wished now he'd paid more attention to better men than himself.

From outlying townships to the monolithic residences of her capital, Tanis baked in the oppressive heat of a midsummer's day. It was unnaturally hot here all year round. Those unacclimatised to the world could not stand to be outside for more than a few minutes, while the affluent and privileged lounged about their air-conditioned penthouses. Shimmering amid the haze were the towering superstructures of Divinity, coming into view at last against a yellow sky. The spires would tell great stories of human achievement throughout the centuries if they could; fantastical accounts tempered by equally horrifying tales of suffering and tragedy. A pyramidal metropolis built on tenacious ambition alone, the sky-city was home to countless millions.

Leo's early memories of Tanis were interlaced with resentment. The other children initially did their level best to avoid this strange-looking outsider, calling him *alien* from afar, then *no-name* since he could not remember his own. They would tease him repeatedly, finding it amusing that he didn't know who he was or where he'd come from.

When the regime officials who'd watched from the shadows were satisfied, Leo came to be adopted by Giovanni Rossi, the planetary regent who ruled Tanis in Earth's name. The old man gave him a home, a loving family, a name... all the things he craved. Yet despite his new father's gentle prompting, Leo still struggled to recall the freak meteor shower that had destroyed his homeworld and killed his parents. The doctors had said that the trauma he'd experienced from witnessing such an event had led to a total loss of memory.

But that wouldn't stop him building a new life for himself on Tanis.

He had spent those first years in an education centre alongside Divinity's chosen; gifted children plucked from squalor by wealthy patrons so they might serve them instead. But the regent was kind to Leo, treating him more like an actual son than an adopted one.

Leo cast one final look over the *Iron Duke's* precious cargo, the veteran enforcers to his left preferring to joke amongst their own number rather than converse with the rookies opposite. He would never see any of them again, being of the age that required him to make a choice.

The officer training course was over. Seemingly destined for the contingent's ranks as his father wished, Leo had elected otherwise. As the gunship came in to land he searched for the words to justify his decision. Opting to join the fight against the suffering and injustice that plagued the world was easy. Plucking up the courage to tell the regent would be a different matter. Twelve years ago to the day he'd arrived on Tanis an unwelcome outsider. Now he returned home with a burgeoning reputation as Divinity's most favoured son. Now, as then, the people of the world prepared to celebrate their Landfall Day.

2

Tanis depended upon the output of Divinity's foundries and workshops to survive. Vast industrial zones comprised the city's lower levels, merging together over time to create massive centres of commerce. The factories there belched out an endless stream of pollution, smothering the residential district above in tainted fumes and vapours.

Work in this fiery cauldron was readily available. Impossible deadlines were set, keeping safety concerns down and mortality rates high. Those who cheated the blast furnaces were condemned to serve a brutal shift system, but the money was good and the benefits fair. They laboured away without complaint, as ignorant of the nobility's machinations as the upper classes were of their existence.

The Chimera installation dwarfed all of Divinity's forges, rivalling even the regent's palace in size. One of five new sites commissioned by the ruling regime and located near the city's peak, its presence provoked daily outcry from an elite who argued it blighted their normally idyllic lives. Unique in that respect, many were unsettled at the thought of acknowledging the dreadful conditions there - conditions they could previously ignore. With the complex growing opposite their estates it became much harder for them to do so.

This was as close to royalty as the workers would ever find themselves, short breaks in a demanding schedule being their only time to wonder what could have been were they born higher. Days blended together and escaping the regime's relentless propaganda machine proved impossible. Motivational tannoy announcements broadcast around the site reminded them what they were fighting for, warning of the consequences should they decide not to.

Remain strong of mind. Work hard. Remember you are contributing to a better future for your planet and loved ones.

Thousands had made the journey through the cold void between stars to provide for their families. Others hoped to leave questionable pasts behind or see the galaxy, but all were lured to Tanis under false pretences. The golden land of opportunity they had been promised did not exist.

Laxity will not go unnoticed. Worker absence will be punished. Fulfil your quotas, increase productivity and you shall enhance your standing.

More arrived each day to hasten the site's construction, shipped in on a moment's notice and fast-tracked as additional labour to meet spiralling regime demands. Lacking the training needed to survive in such an environment, most failed to see out the first week. Officials supervised the corpse removal crews as they went about their grim work retrieving the bodies of the fallen. Day and night the crematoriums operated at full capacity, and when one broke down it took several hours to clear the resulting backlog. Every time this happened a claxon would sound, sending the welding teams trudging back down narrow gangways to their allocated living quarters.

They were free to leave at any time. But on a remote desert world far from home there was nowhere for them *to* go. Prisoners without chains, thoughts of escape soon turned to justifying their continued service. They had been given accommodation, food, a job; all the regime asked in return was for them to work tirelessly and meet the quotas. During intervals they would even be let out for fresh air, temporarily reprieved from the searing heat inside. It was a better existence than those dwelling in the squalid depths of undercity eked out.

Kurt Steinsson had been on Tanis for almost two years. Smart enough to see through the masquerade without openly challenging it, his discretion and prodigious workmanship ensured he'd risen quickly to the position of team leader. A compassionate, blond-haired giant of a man, Steinsson's strength made him a dependable asset who could be counted on to motivate others. He led by example, ensuring his team never once missed a quota despite repeated provocation from the Chimera site's overzealous supervisors and discontent workers.

He learned that by telling people what they wanted to hear he would be left largely to his own devices, playing the fool when asked for an opinion on delicate matters. Well-educated, Steinsson was part of a small minority who concealed their true intellect so they might go about their duties unmolested. He busied his mind observing shift protocol instead, becoming aware of seemingly trivial patterns and processes he was convinced meant more.

The six-man outfit he headed had worked the same extensive area every day since their arrival. Steinsson theorised this was common practice for other teams throughout the site but could only speculate as to why. Talk was simpler here, with complaining high on the agenda today. This intensified as a batch of new starters marched past, brimming with naive determination. Steinsson afforded the group a cursory glance, feeling nothing but pity for them.

"Damn fools," a short, bald man piped up, gesturing in their direction. "Where do they find these boys? Fucking forge-fodder. May as well double our workload."

"They already have," his lanky friend affirmed. "We're the mugs who get to train them. Waste of bloody time."

Steinsson groaned inwardly. A minute rarely passed without Saul and Karlsen finding fault with something. Belligerent and uncouth, this bickering pair of malcontents were continually bellyaching, quick to criticise whatever they didn't understand.

Always the first to speak his mind, few of Saul's thoughts stayed private for long. Karlsen would listen and agree or argue with him. Raised in slums on backwater worlds, both men felt society's debt to them was great indeed. Their current predicament deepened this belief, the duo shunning friendship for one another's gloomy company.

Steinsson often wondered where his welding team would be if they worked as hard as they complained.

"To hell with this," spat Saul. "Ain't my job. Supervisors can do it."

"No chance," Karlsen scowled. "Too busy sitting in their offices doing fuck all, arses glued to their damn chairs. We'll be here forever."

Saul's features darkened. "Not gonna happen."

Of the three, only Steinsson knew how close to finishing the project they actually were. The regime's ruthless ingenuity confounded many, but not him. Bringing in off-worlders on temporary contracts was a masterstroke, ensuring quotas were met in short order. They asked few questions and in the event of death or mutilation various clauses meant no benefits would be paid to their families.

"Any idea what they're having us build yet?" Saul demanded. "I bet a day's rations it's one of those fancy new penthouses for some stuck-up noble with more money than we can earn in a lifetime."

"Bollocks to that. Have you seen the amount of industrial piping going into this place? It's a forge, for sure."

"What do you know of forges, Karlsen? Those pipes are for some kind of under-floor cooling system. Think about it. We're near the palace, not the industrial sector."

"I dunno. Maybe."

"Well," said Saul, "I still think the clue is in the name. According to myths a Chimera is a three-headed beast. So whatever we're building is going to serve three purposes."

"It's made up of three creatures, you idiot," scolded Karlsen. "And it breathes fire." Saul looked dubious. "What? Surprised I can read? I know my mythology."

"Never said you didn't. Chances are it's just a random codename. They won't tell us either way."

Steinsson deactivated his welding torch and lifted his helmet's visor, bemused by the nature of their debate. Talking while on duty carried severe penalties, but he was loath to reprimand the pair and destroy what little rapport he had with them at the same time. Jobsworth supervisors were everywhere, intent on pursuing those caught railing against the regime, though Saul and Karlsen had apparently perfected the art of ranting out of earshot.

He preferred to distance himself from these antics and dream of home instead. Steinsson carried a small colour picture of his wife and son in his back pocket and would look at it fondly when no-one else was around. Though he'd promised to return, the picture had begun to fade along with his hopes of ever seeing them again.

Nordica's decline had been sudden and spectacular. Once a thriving outpost of progress, millions had been plunged into poverty overnight as the planet's infrastructure had inexplicably collapsed. The regent had abandoned his people to their fate and fled, allowing the resulting wave of violence to sweep across entire continents unchecked. Many had left aboard regime ships bound for Tanis, a nearby world whose regency promised work for all. After reaching one of the last remaining safe zones, Steinsson too had joined the exodus.

Accepting this had proved difficult for his wife, having just given birth to their son. But she'd known he could no longer support them by staying on Nordica and, tearfully, had endorsed his decision. Memories of her love were all that sustained him through the challenges he faced now. Steinsson was content recalling happier times until Saul noticed he'd stopped working, taking it upon himself to try and include him in their conversation.

"What d'you think, Stein? Reckon you know what they're up to here?"

"Course he does," said Karlsen. "He's team leader."

Steinsson considered his own reply carefully. As they were divided on the subject he could not appear to favour one viewpoint above the other. Nor did he particularly want to divulge his own theories and risk getting drawn into an endless argument with them. However, both seemed to agree the regime was the sole cause of all their misery.

"Hard to say," he remarked after a while, trying to look interested. "Supervisors keep the teams from different areas apart. We've never been relocated since we started working here. They've gone to great lengths to ensure none of us find out what's going on, so whatever it is it can't be of any good."

"Is that right?" Saul retorted. "Give the regime a bad name, will you? What do you know of their motives?"

Steinsson slammed down his visor and reignited the torch almost immediately, not about to lose his cool with two witless dunces who for the mere sake of it now sought to defend the very people they were criticising earlier. Having failed to rile him, Saul returned to squabbling with Karlsen, this time over which of them worked harder.

"My pay's better," he boasted, "so I'm not alone in thinking it's me."

"Really?" Karlsen countered. "I hear those on higher wages have their heads even higher up the supervisor's arse. I ain't kowtowing to anyone - I'll say it how it is. They want to dock my pay, fine. When last I checked it was a free galaxy."

"You what? Who's got his head up whose arse?"

Money mattered as much to Saul and Karlsen as family did to Steinsson. Before meeting his wife he had found work on Nordica securing contracts for several small-time arms dealers, all of which had enhanced his ability to spot potential fraudsters and criminals. Desperate to pay off debts and start again, their love of the material had exposed them then as it did with his present company now. Successfully maintaining the charade created overly defensive personalities, but Steinsson never presumed to tell another how to live. His subtle understanding of their world meant they would only jest with him if they had nothing better to do.

"Well, whatever," said Saul, waving his hand about dismissively. "When I get out I've got plans. Big plans."

"*If* you get out."

"What d'you mean by that, Karlsen? Soon as the contract's done so am I."

"Think they'll honour it, do you?"

"Think they won't? Besides, I need the money."

"Right," said Karlsen. "Except none of us have the slightest idea how long this'll take. It's already been two years. I'm certain old Stanley said we'd be shunted to a new site when we're finished here, just before he got messed up by that buzzsaw."

Saul pulled a face at the prospect of seeing out his days on Tanis. He'd thought himself above such misfortune until witnessing last week's fateful incident.

"Poor bastard never saw it coming," he said of his workmate's demise. "Damn fool shouldn't have tried to get his torch back without stopping the machine first."

"Supervisor would've been pissed if he'd done that," said Karlsen.

"Why?"

"Because of the quotas."

"Fuck him and fuck his quotas."

"Won't happen to me," Karlsen insisted. "If I'm to go then I'll choose how and where. It'll be on my terms, not theirs."

"Like fuck I'd work another site," said Saul. "This lot break the contract and the only place I'm going is off-world, stowed away on the next flight out of this miserable hellhole. Oh... shit. Here comes that wanker supervisor now. Had to mention him, didn't you? He says one thing out of turn and I'll see to it he goes the same way as Stanley."

"Yeah, right. He's regime. Makes him untouchable."

The supervisor that Saul was referring to cut a baleful figure as he stalked along the gangways towards them. Standing no taller than five foot, this stunted individual nevertheless exuded malevolence. His beady eyes were fixed on the three welders, and Kurt Steinsson readied himself for what was to come next. When the vindictive little man wasn't poring over charts and reports he would often go out of his way to belittle the work crews in an effort to demonstrate his superiority. Saul openly despised him and joked that all site supervisors were made from the same mould; arrogant narcissists lacking heavily in people skills.

"I've been watching you for ten minutes," he began, confronting the group. "You know the rules yet continue to break them."

"Yeah, we know of 'em," Saul sneered. "Never understood 'em though."

"Shut up. You off-worlders are all the same. Uneducated. Uncivilised. Your idleness puts my position within the regime hierarchy at risk. We can't be having that. I'm here to remind you what's at stake."

"To try and provoke us for kicks, more like," Karlsen grimaced under his breath.

The supervisor glared at him, unslinging a brown Kevlar bag from his shoulder. He opened it and took out an assortment of paperwork, never once breaking eye contact as he deliberately scattered the many documents all over the floor in front of him.

"Pick them up."

Karlsen didn't move. The supervisor unsheathed his baton.

"Now."

A few seconds passed before Karlsen complied, nearly boiling over with righteous indignation as he set about retrieving the papers. His tormentor smirked and turned to face his next victim.

"Kurt Steinsson. As team leader it's your responsibility to ensure these men are fulfilling their quotas. This means taking remedial action should they fall behind. See that you do, or we shall do it for you."

Steinsson had remained motionless since the supervisor's arrival. He stood firm, head held high and hands behind his back in a defiant pose, seemingly impervious to the man's attempts to elicit a response. The supervisor clocked this and circled him menacingly, rising to the challenge.

"You think you're indispensable, is that it, Steinsson? You're not. You grunts are just cogs in a machine - mine to use however I see fit to get the job done. See those boys who came in this morning? We can get more at your expense and-"

"We've not missed a quota thus far," Steinsson interjected calmly, cutting the supervisor's speech short.

"I don't give a shit. You're not working hard enough and as a result the project risks falling behind schedule." He moved to stand toe to toe with Steinsson, the giant welder's muscular frame towering over him. "Tell me something," he hissed. "Do you care about your family? Want to see that wife and child of yours again?"

"Yes."

"Of course you do. Then perhaps a fresh approach is all that's needed." His voice dropped to a whisper, so Saul and Karlsen could no longer hear him. "I can help, if you'll let me. No-one is questioning *your* ability. But those two... they're incompetent and stir up trouble at every opportunity. You don't have to carry them. Say the word and we can take care of this little problem."

"A kind offer," said Steinsson. "I thank you. But things are fine, really."

The supervisor's snarl grew into a smile. "Are they? Then in that case I think some form of penalty is in order. Let's see how the three of you enjoy going a week without rations. I would have overlooked your insolence and let you all off with a warning until your team leader opened his mouth."

Silence greeted his barbed remark.

With no response forthcoming he turned on his heel and departed, but not before snatching the papers Karlsen had collected and saying, "I'll be watching your performances closely from now on. Oh, and Steinsson? Think about what I've said."

Annoyed by his stubbornness the supervisor strode off in search of easier prey. Saul and Karlsen waited until he had gone before unleashing a tirade of impotent threats, expletives and insults in his direction, improving their moods but achieving little else.

"A whole fucking week?" Saul fumed, furious at what had just transpired. "Wonderful. Brilliant! Sorry Karl, I guess our wager's off. For fuck's sake, Steinsson, what did you say to him? Should've let me do the talking, asshole."

Steinsson still hadn't moved an inch, proud to have emerged from the altercation with his honour intact. The supervisor's plan was clear. They would all have to be careful from now on.

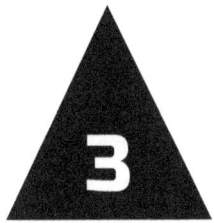

3

Lucas Turilli stalked the corridors of the regent's palace with only his malicious thoughts for company.

Today was his day. While the wretched denizens of Tanis celebrated, he would be putting the finishing touches on a plan that had occupied his twisted mind for years.

The regent-elect was not a patient man. Promises of power and personal gain had eased his frustrations, preventing him from inadvertently unhinging the entire scheme. Ruthlessly ambitious, Turilli judged an idea not on its merits but to what extent it benefitted him.

And this one had been well worth pursuing despite the wait.

He snarled threateningly at a young servant-girl who dared cross his path. She retreated into a side room and locked the door behind her, trembling with fear. A wicked grin spread across Turilli's face. It had always been his destiny to rule. Everyone else existed purely to serve great men like him.

Now he made for the council chamber, keen to ensure the day's events unfolded exactly as he'd envisioned. Having called a session, he intended to arrive long before any of Divinity's ministers so he could prepare. Clerks and menials swarmed like vermin all around him, scurrying aside to avoid his malevolent stare as he passed.

Turilli dreamt of a world free from tedious debates, one where he ruled alone. He imagined the expressions of sheer terror etched on his ministers' miserable faces when that day finally came. With any luck, it would come sooner than he thought. There were dark forces at work on Tanis, and Turilli was glad they were working in his favour. Should he fail, he knew they would not hesitate to turn on him.

The new recruits leapt to their feet as the *Iron Duke* touched down, chattering away excitedly as they prepared to disembark. The veterans looked on as they practically forced the exit ramps open, racing clear of the gunship's hold and back into civilisation's stifling embrace. The sudden drop in air pressure caught many by surprise; those who didn't start retching collapsed to the floor inelegantly. The grim-faced enforcers followed after a while, strolling leisurely behind, offering belated words of wisdom to the young ones.

Leo was the last to leave, ensuring all of his company were accounted for. Even at this late stage he remained vigilant, determined to see out his duties to the end. He exchanged words with the *Duke's* pilot, thanking her for bringing them home safely, then went about checking on the distressed rookies.

"They'll be fine, Leo. But what of you? Still putting others first?"

Giovanni Rossi stood nearby, his ornate royal cloak fluttering in the breeze. Leo smiled at the sound of the regent's voice. Dressed from head to toe in pure white and gold finery, the old man was always there to welcome him back from his adventures. That would never change even if he did.

"Am I wrong to do so, Father?" he asked in swift reply.

"Wrong? No. Never. You have a good heart. Now, enough of that. Let me look at you."

Embarrassed, Leo tried to avoid his gaze. A month in the desert had left him with an untidy beard and greasy black hair. More heavily tanned and taller than most, he was a far cry from the refined young noble he sought to present himself as. The regent observed his son's reaction and attempted to boost his spirits.

"The sands have forged you a fearsome look. Yet so thin! You could do with getting some proper food. Hmm. Maybe a shave, too."

Leo felt the whiskers on the side of his face. "That first!"

His father laughed in agreement before leading him away from the gunship and towards the city. From where the *Iron Duke* had landed it was only a short walk to the marble halls of the regent's palace.

Though it had been only a month, Rossi appeared to have aged considerably since Leo last saw him. His hair blended with the apparel and he now wore a pendant around his neck that displayed the regime's pyramidal crest. Leo wondered what he despised more - wearing the trinket or being made to dress in such grand attire.

But expectation had a way of rendering personal desires irrelevant.

"You must tell me of your trials," the regent said as they walked together. "The names of those enforcers who excelled along with any who require additional training. I need not ask about you; your courage and tenacity are unmatched. Yes, yes. You always do well regardless..."

His speech gradually tailed off into incoherent mumblings and Leo found his father talking to himself once more. He thought the elderly man's eccentricities endearing but there were those within the palace who argued otherwise, calling into question his ability to rule Tanis as regent. For a man who had done so much Leo found this wholly unacceptable, getting into trouble on more than one occasion for so fiercely defending his father's honour and making his own feelings known. While Rossi insisted such things didn't bother him, Leo couldn't help but speak out against them.

The palace itself was a labyrinth of myriad corridors, chambers and guest rooms. Situated at the city's peak, some five miles up into the sky, its immensity never ceased to amaze him. Imposing statues of past regents lined both sides of the entrance, avatars of the regime's puissance, cutting dramatic poses or pointing to the stars. Massive solar installations brought power to the world all year round. Fine art galleries adorned every stately room, far from the chaos of life below. As a boy, Leo would spend hours wandering the palace's pristinely maintained gardens. He felt he'd no need to ever leave Tanis - everything he ever wanted was right here, all within his very own paradise.

"You've made it back just in time," Rossi said suddenly, his words now clear. "The Landfall preparations await. I suspect young Marcus has already been making a nuisance of himself. He's been asking after you, of course."

Leo was glad to hear his best friend hadn't forgotten about him. For some, Landfall Day would be spent celebrating the world's only public holiday, while others honoured the names of those interstellar visionaries who had first arrived on Tanis, this day, five millennia ago. Leo and Marcus saw it as an opportunity to create mischief instead, either by deceiving some unfortunate noble or embarrassing an overly proud patrician, much to the delight of everyone watching. The regent went on to explain that while Leo was away in the desert Marcus had worried what to do without him, their antics having become a key fixture in the palace's own festivities.

"You'd better run along if you want to help," Rossi suggested. Leo was strangely subdued. When it became clear he was in no hurry to leave the regent softened, bidding his son sit beside him on the artificial grass before the palace steps. "Can you tell me what's troubling you?" he asked, even though the wise old man already knew.

Leo sat down slowly, glad to rest his tired legs. He wondered if it was selfish of him to burden others with his own trivial problems.

"Father," he sighed, "for three years I've been committed to the enforcer program."

Rossi nodded. "Unconditionally. Your selflessness and devotion are admirable qualities - qualities that I am deeply proud of. A father could wish for no more than to see his son join the contingent's prestigious ranks, be it here or another world."

"Yes, I know. But something's changed, something I can't make any sense of. Maybe I'm not meant to."

"Maybe I can?" the regent offered. He studied the uncertainty in Leo's eyes as he fidgeted about, trying to make himself comfortable. The carefree boy he'd taken in was gone.

"I don't think so," Leo said dejectedly. "Coming back to the city, tomorrow being Landfall Day, all of this... nothing felt the same. I can't explain it, what was missing or different, if anything. I've no answers, and I'm afraid people won't like it - won't be willing to accept me when I can no longer be who I was."

"Leo, listen to me. Now that you're older it's perfectly normal to occupy your mind with greater concerns. I know what this is about. It's easy enough to learn right from wrong, but what sets one apart is their ability to think and act for themselves. The bravest of us cry out against fate, while most meekly accept their lot in life. You're only just beginning to understand your place in this world and how you can influence it, but all of us have to face the same challenge at some point in our lives. The places you know seldom change, only the people within. Others will understand what you are going through, even if you don't at this moment.

"I still recall your desire to grow up and start putting the world to rights. Perhaps you seek a return to simpler days. Perhaps now you can see why I implored you to cherish your childhood. It was because I never did. Yes, believe it or not I was once young, like you! And had the same questions for my father. We didn't know then that it wouldn't last forever, did we? I've always been honest with you, Leo, as he was with me. I'd ask you not to look upon the past with a hope to revisit older, happier days, for that way lies disappointment when they fail to live up to the expectations of memory. Instead, focus on what you have here and let your actions define you, rather than words.

"Marcus has been your friend for many years. He understands what you've been through. All the initiates look up to you, the enforcer veterans respect you. The people love you, and we still have time for each other, don't we? Oh, you have happy memories, we all do, but what's stopping you from making new ones?"

"I don't know how," Leo conceded.

"I do. It's within your power alone to embrace life and make the most of the people around you while they're still here today. Not everyone on Tanis has the luxury of being able to make a choice. Do you regress, fearful of what others think and become who they want you to be, or fight for your future?"

"I want to be someone," said Leo.

"Who doesn't? When you first came to us you were only eight years old, but even then I knew one day we would have this conversation. My son, still so full of self-doubt and indecision! You owe me nothing, Leo. I'm not your father and have never pretended to be, but my time and advice are yours should ever you need them. In return, please heed an old man's assurances when he says everything will be as it should. Your best years are still ahead of you while mine are all but spent."

"I want to help," Leo asserted. "I can't forget the suffering I've seen below in undercity. I think I could make a difference and improve the lives of the people there."

Rossi's expression grew sterner. "Growing pains for a city this size are natural. I've given my whole life that you may do as you wish with yours. I would caution against pledging yourself so readily to a thankless cause when you've the potential to do such great things."

Leo couldn't decide whether his father meant this or was merely trying to inspire him. "You do," he challenged. "Help the people, I mean."

"This is my duty, as regent and the regime's representative. I believe yours lies elsewhere. Work hard and you shall reap the fruits of your labour, but in trying to please everyone you'll only end up failing them all."

"I don't want that."

"No. There are none who do. I'll be proud of you regardless of what you decide. You don't need my approval anymore. You are blessed with a brilliant mind and kind heart, though I fear others may seek to exploit these traits and use them to further their own ends."

"Others like Lucas Turilli?"

Rossi fell silent. He shared his son's negative feelings towards the man who was destined to replace him. A man with questionable morals and no code of honour, hand-picked by the ruling regime on Earth to be his successor. Unpredictable and violent, Turilli lacked the empathy required to effectively govern this office. Yet instead of speaking his mind, the regent said what he needed to.

"Give him a chance, Leo. There's no point speculating. What's certain is that he *will* be regent and I'm sure you'll serve him as well as you've served me. In turn, he could be of great counsel. Together, the two of you can only benefit Tanis. He knows this, though is too proud to say. When the war ravaged our world we trusted those on Earth to intervene and end the conflict. Now I urge you to trust them again in making this appointment.

"Remember how you willingly adopted our culture, won over all who doubted you and overcame challenges lesser men would have baulked at? All people need sometimes is an opportunity. Stop worrying about what might happen. Wait and see what does."

"I will."

"Good. Then I suggest you go enjoy one final Landfall feast without these cares. For your father's sake. Oh, and do be sure to let Marcus know you're back."

Leo didn't need asking a second time. His eyes lit up, filled with newfound optimism. Rossi watched him go as he ascended the palace steps, ashamed at having lied to his son again. Tired though he was, it remained his responsibility to protect Leo from the evils of a world he was still largely ignorant of. A world he'd wronged years ago. Fate had presented him with one final chance to make amends, so some things were going to have to remain unsaid. For now.

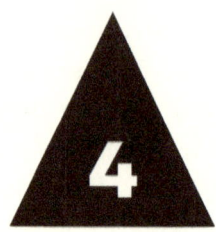

4

While the tortured heart of undercity beat on, the sector's soul had been crushed out of it by continued upheaval centuries ago. Murderers roamed streets once home to thriving market stalls, the blood of their victims mingling with the city's waste and excrement to create a rotting, fetid cesspit.

Crimelords vied for dominion over a blasted hellscape at the very foot of Divinity, free to engage in heinous activities and impose their own laws. On occasion, a particularly ruthless individual would emerge from these bitter struggles to unite the gangs of undercity behind them. When this happened the regime would send their enforcers into this lawless realm en masse, forcibly reminding the people dwelling there just who ruled Tanis either by dispatching the ambitious warlord or publically butchering their supporters. The resulting power vacuum ensured a swift return to years of infighting, leaving none strong enough to challenge the status quo.

Each time the denizens of undercity endured - waiting, hoping for things to change even though they never did.

Feared for the atrocities he'd committed against this society, yet respected for his later attempts to become part of it, William Marshall's plight perplexed those around him. Men and women who put every ounce of their being into gaining favour with the regime could not fathom why one who had previously enjoyed their boons so readily spurned them and chose to live among Divinity's gutter scum.

But Marshall never expected anyone to understand.

Initially, he'd hoped redemption would come through repairing the lives of those he'd once destroyed. Now, he knew this wasn't to be. The memories of horrors he'd unleashed still stalked his dreams and haunted every waking minute, and while the people grew to forgive him he never could.

Consumed by self-loathing, Marshall had opened a trader just below the industrial sector. Though there were easier options, he wasn't about to give those who gossiped the satisfaction. Devoid of all emotion, an animated husk of a man unable to forget, Marshall accepted he would never know peace. These hollow days served as punishment enough for a lifetime of evil.

He recalled the moment he'd learned that his application to the enforcer contingent on Tanis had been successful. He remembered the teary expressions of heartfelt pride on his parents' faces when he'd told them.

Tanis. A world of wonders.

Utopia.

Such illusions that captured the minds of those on the outside looking in.

Young and impressionable, Marshall thought he could make a difference. The honeyed words of praise lavished upon him by the regime fed his willingness to perpetrate dark acts against the populace in their name. He did so without question, trusting in everything he'd been told; that a small number of souls must suffer for the rest of them to live. The whores and gangsters gnawing away at Divinity's foundations had to be eradicated - he shouldn't have any qualms about putting an end to their debauchery. But the warnings he shouted at such people soon gave way to beatings, then summary executions. Too far gone to turn back, there was but one option left.

Commit.

Anything less would have prompted his superiors to declare him unfit for duty. The shame of this alone was not worth bearing. Though his hardened exterior belied the turmoil within, Marshall repeatedly told himself that sacrifices had to be made to keep the world's exploding population down. After a while even he started to believe it.

Another poignant scene filled his mind. He lashed out at the woman, sending her sprawling to the ground like a flogged cur. Sobbing, she tried to crawl away from him on her hands and knees. Marshall stepped forward and pressed down hard on her back with his boot. He raised his baton, ignoring the pleas for mercy which escaped her bloodied lips. He didn't care who she was or what she was trying to say.

To the left, something caught his eye. Frightened faces looked on from behind a broken bench. He hesitated, turning his gaze from the cowering children to their mother, then back again. Marshall sensed the departure of his soul. He dropped the baton and ran.

Deserters were hunted down by their former comrades. They were weak, traitors to the regent they had sworn to serve. Interrogated by agents searching for any hint of dissent, in private Marshall reflected bitterly on what the regime had done to him. What they had turned him into.

No longer a man at all, instead a heartless tool of destruction enslaved to equally callous puppeteers.

He searched for a better memory. After five decades of servitude, he was free. Honourably discharged along with the rest of his unit, the day passed unmarked and uncelebrated. One by one they filtered out of the barracks, soulless automatons drifting into a life of opulence provided at the expense of their humanity. He could have gone with them and buried his past forever. Letting the discharge papers fall from his hand, Marshall left without a word, disappearing into the night a wretched creature with no idea who he was anymore.

Deservedly so, he thought.

The familiar sounds of the city woke him from his reveries. A trio of intoxicated youths swaggered past his storefront, spitting and talking loudly as they went.

Marshall barely recognised the area from when he'd first made his home here, establishing a business that prospered through the sale of on and off-world artifacts. Victoriam Plaza was seen as a relatively stable place back then, trouble-free and tolerant. But the boom years couldn't last. A victim of change, the plaza underwent a hideous transformation into a neglected, out-dated fortress of ignorance. His mind free to wander, Marshall watched on from the confines of his dingy trader as the district plunged headfirst towards its ruin, trapping him inside a self-piteous web of stoic remembrance.

In the wake of so much death it was a twisted miracle or perhaps fate itself that had decreed undercity live on when by all rights it should have destroyed itself. The distant spires of Divinity's palaces appeared to grasp at Gethsemane, the world's solitary moon, in the hope of latching on and wrenching themselves free from this depravity. Having served the elite long enough, Marshall knew there were some who actually wished for this to happen.

There was a point when he had.

Fifty years of practice made it easy to act as if the problems and people there didn't exist at all, acknowledging them only when he was sent to suppress yet another food riot or murder innocents on regime orders. Five miles were all that separated the regent from the poorest of his people, though it might as well have been several star systems. Divinity was no natural creation, and the full extent of a planet's troubles were crammed into a single sky-city circumscribed by a four hundred metre high stone wall. To the ignorant, Tanis' capital was a marvel. Those who really understood knew that it was nothing more than a glorified ghetto.

Like a mirage amid the dunes, Divinity beguiled and misled. A world within a world, its rulers could claim that it was everything good about the planet Tanis.

And everything bad, too.

Millions lived within the city whose name itself was a lie, for there was very little divine about this place. Life was fleeting, dreams crushed beneath the boots of the regent's private army of enforcers or failed to flourish in the face of an overly critical society where anything new was seen as suspicious and frowned upon. Crumbling structures and temperatures that exceeded those of the desert expanse added to the multitude of ever-present threats the people of undercity faced, which kept them from aspiring to achieve anything greater than everyday survival.

How convenient for some, Marshall mused.

Those who managed to best these tribulations often did so through nefarious means. Over time this miserable existence became the accepted norm; that staying alive was as good as it got, tolling the death knell of progress, reason and ambition. On Tanis there was nothing save the eternal struggle that winnowed the ruthless from the meek, and each day this tragedy played out anew, here and on a hundred other worlds.

A barren rock orbiting its parent star, Icaria, all that marked Tanis out among the cosmos was the blistering heat it experienced as a result of its closer-than-normal revolution. Though the terraformers of old could work wonders - a planet's biosphere could be altered and conditions made ideal for humanity to thrive - those days were now consigned to history. The light breeze that graced the spires from time to time never permeated through to the lower levels, which remained shrouded in perpetual darkness, further amplifying undercity's woes.

A consequence of this was the inadvertent alienation of the people living there. All worlds in the galaxy were dominated by an overriding culture, but on Tanis a new, fiercely independent group had begun to emerge, openly hostile towards outsiders and reliant on none but themselves.

Off-worlders such as Marshall were the exception, never needing to be accepted as regular citizens did. Barring the sons and daughters of noble houses, enforcers weren't recruited locally, allowing them to visit violence on whoever they wanted without fear of reprisal. Swearing loyalty to the regent and given the regime's best equipment and training, these arbitrators were then granted free rein to maintain order in whatever manner they deemed fit. Their number sufficient to keep control of the planet they policed, restrictions imposed by Earth prevented contingents growing strong enough to either overthrow their regent or help them secede. An autonomous organisation with near-limitless authority, it was ironic that the lawless were the ones set to enforce the law.

Stifled by draconian edicts and dogma, Divinity suffered at the hands of power mad autocrats with little or no concept of life's true hardships beyond their own narrow-minded vision. A single pen stroke could put entire worlds to the torch, and those who wielded these deadly instruments did so with all the restraint of an irritable child. Promises of a bright future served to placate the middle-classes, while regime deviants quietly hoarded away technology meant for all and coerced the planet's best minds into working exclusively for them.

One final step needed to be taken, then absolute power would be theirs.

The regime that William Marshall once served had now changed beyond recognition, limiting his ability to anticipate their wild schemes. Something was very wrong in Divinity, he'd known this for some time, though the question over *what* remained.

Unable to think clearly, Marshall stepped outside of his trader to gaze up at the regent's palace and the highest levels of the city. Work continued on several sites there, one much larger than the others, and the cacophonous sound of construction rang out across the city as it had done every day for the past two years. Higher still the gargoyles and chimeras slumbered on undisturbed, their expressions constant, transfixed where they stood with gaping maws for all eternity.

5

As Leo slept, his mind played host to terrible nightmares.

The young noble had decided against attending the Landfall Day preparations and returned to his chamber, fatigue having forced him to take a mid-afternoon siesta instead. He lay down on the fresh sheets of his bed still in full military dress, reasoning that at least he would be ready for a wild evening of feasting, festivity and folly before tiredness overtook him.

His dream took on a terrifying form. Leo stood alone on the ashen plains of Tanis, fighting hard just to breathe. His clothes were torn and he could taste metal. A warning siren wailed against a ruinous backdrop, but nothing was there save the charred, lifeless husks of people all around and the burnt-out shells of once proud starships before him. Divinity loomed large in the distance, barely recognisable from the wonder he knew as home. Leo staggered forward, battling starvation and thirst in a desperate bid to reach the city's brooding spires. His skin simmered, peeling loose as he walked.

Then the dunes were gone and a sprawling urban wasteland reared up in their place. Leo realised he was back behind the great stone walls of Divinity, but could only look on in horror as the fortifications shook violently, crumbling down into the sand. The blackened city still stood, balancing precariously upon the shoulders of thousands of men, women and children whose destruction in turn fed its own survival. People barged past him, appearing to know neither where they were going nor what they were doing.

Amid the bedlam, Leo heard someone calling out. He saw all of his friends standing safely at the peak, waving for him to join them. Driven by hope he started climbing, but a sudden deluge of water stalled his progress. When he looked again they seemed further away than before, their smiles gone, replaced by stares of contempt and derision.

"Ungrateful brat," snarled an enforcer captain. "Should've left you in that pit to rot along with everyone else."

"You don't belong here," jeered a stony-faced marquise. "You're not one of us. Never will be. See all of this? It's a facade."

Hurting, Leo felt more alone now than he did in the desert. There was nowhere left for him to go. The taunts continued from above while below Divinity's oppressed had risen and tore furiously at his heels, eager to bring the man they deemed responsible for their suffering to justice. He cried out in anguish, shattering one illusion and supplanting it with another.

A raging red sky bore down on him. Lightning struck as warships swarmed about the maelstrom, their weapons tracking. As one, they locked on and fired.

The shock jolted Leo awake, his heart pounding and eyelids heavy. He lay still for several minutes, staring up at the ceiling as if paralysed, watching a million dust motes dance in the light that filled his chamber. Slowly, reality became distinguishable from dreamscape once more. The vision was gone, only fragments remained. Details faded as he tried in vain to recall them. *Did it mean anything?*

The palace counsellors certainly wouldn't have thought so. Their diagnoses rendered any other explanation irrelevant. Curtly dismissive of his previous concerns, these apathetic scientists branded dreams dangerous delusions or fancies fabricated by a weak mind. Such imaginings were not meant to be taken seriously, but this one had been so vivid, so lifelike... he could feel the water's icy touch even now.

What if they were wrong?

Leo scoffed in annoyance upon realising this 'water' was nothing more than beads of sweat on his brow. He wiped them away casually, angry at being so easily duped. As usual, he'd seen only what he wanted to see.

It was late afternoon in Divinity, the waning sunlight still strong enough to keep air conditioning units working overtime. Nobles and servants alike hastily prepared for the celebrations which were soon to begin. Leo contemplated getting ready himself, managing a smile as he remembered past Landfall Days.

Magical days.

The one time of year when all stood together. Status no longer mattered. Rank was forgotten. High or low, all played their part. Gifts were exchanged as families sat down to give thanks for what they had. Banquets would be held to the sound of raucous laughter and music. Drink flowed freely and fireworks burst across the sky. Father's annual Landfall speech was delivered with its usual eloquence; the regent toying with his audience's emotions in a display of fiery rhetoric that left them sitting in silence, enthralled. He had such a way with words Leo could never understand.

As the night wore on, those who remained gathered closer to hear stories of an era when giants bestrode the stars. Expeditions from Earth carried Mankind's hopes and aspirations, colonising worlds and ushering in a new golden age of discovery. Tales of heroism and self-sacrifice warmed the soul. Leo wished he could have been there to stand alongside such fearless individuals. Now the fires of conquest had cooled, and their like would never again walk the galaxy. The time of legends was over.

A loud knocking at the chamber's door brought him to his senses. Leo sighed wearily, rising at last, wondering when he might next be able to spend a moment in quiet reflection or daydream. Doing little to alter his bedraggled appearance, he at least made an effort in tidying away some of the military attire lying strewn across the floor. He stumbled about this way and that, throwing clothes into cupboards and bags under the bed, keen to establish a modicum of external neatness.

Few others would have gone to these lengths or been so accommodating. Executors - personal adjutants to the nobility - seldom troubled their masters, least of all Lucas Turilli who had been rumoured to fly into fits of rage so maniacal he would beat whoever disturbed him.

Leo tried to make time for everyone. Satisfied with his work, he activated the room's external security camera via remote, then walked over to a small monitor next to the door to see who it was.

Staring back at him wasn't an executor, but a tall, well-dressed man about his age, whose imposing physical presence seemed entirely at odds with the white senatorial tunic he wore. Had Leo not known this burly individual then the Royal Guard would have been called immediately, such was the visitor's strident demeanour and brash mannerisms.

Marcus Rathen went from striking a stern, sullen pose to ensuring what little hair he had was immaculately presented, then returned to eyeball the camera once more. He did this several times until it became clear to Leo he wasn't going away, leaving him no choice but to open the door.

"So, you're back. Well rested?" Marcus asked sardonically, stepping inside. "You look it. I hope the desert wasn't as taxing as letting me know you were home."

Leo attempted to explain, but his friend interrupted before he had the chance.

"No, I understand. Really. You don't want to be seen with the wrong people now you've a reputation to uphold. Must be hard, not giving a damn anymore. Prancing around saying one thing, doing another. Pretending to care about those closest to you. We were brothers, once."

"We still are," Leo insisted, baffled by Marcus' overreaction.

"When it suits. Why else not bother telling me? Too tedious? No servants around to deliver a message?"

"No, nothing like that..."

"Then what?" Marcus demanded.

"I was tired, is all."

"Tired? This time last year we'd already tricked Cyrus into believing someone had made off with his tributes *and* seen to it that Turilli would be surrounded by beautiful women all night."

A big grin spread across Leo's face. "I doubt we'll be seeing much of our regent-elect this year," he joked, convinced his forgetfulness hadn't been the only thing to upset Marcus today. Leo knew he had to keep him talking in order to ascertain what the problem was, though it wouldn't be easy.

"Don't change the subject," Marcus ranted, "and don't make excuses! I'm not stupid. You sound exactly like my father, lying through your teeth that what you do is for my own good, all smiles and pretence while spitting venom behind my back. If I had something to say I'd tell you straight. Is it wrong to expect the same in return, or are you all too spineless to be honest now?"

"Look, I'm sorry," Leo apologised, still no closer to discovering what had triggered Marcus' ire in the first place. "I wasn't thinking."

"Only of yourself."

"Maybe, but comparing me to your father? What did you mean by that?"

"Nothing."

"No, tell me." A hint of frustration played over Leo's features.

"Doesn't matter," said Marcus. "You'd never listen anyway."

"I am now, aren't I?"

"Apparently."

Leo shook his head. This approach wasn't getting him anywhere. "I always do. What makes you think I wouldn't?"

"Forget it."

"Go on," Leo pressed. "Either say what's on your mind or you can go somewhere else to mope. This isn't a counsellor's office and I'm no psychologist."

Marcus appeared surprised at the resolve behind this statement. "Fine," he mumbled. "It's clear you don't care. You've changed, though not for the better."

"Of course I've changed!" Leo snapped, a rare note of anger in his voice. "People change, they grow up! Were you expecting things to stay as they were forever? They can't. What did you think would happen - we'd never take on the same responsibilities nor carry the burdens others do? Never have decisions to make? Whatever the issue is you're not out there confronting it, you're skulking about here feeling sorry for yourself. You say I've changed, yet when did Marcus Rathen turn down a challenge?"

Leo's words hit home with the force of a sandstorm. The resentment that had eaten away at his friend began to subside, and he looked on as Marcus shuffled over to the room's panoramic bay window, his head bowed and anger spent.

"You're right," he admitted eventually, ashamed of his childish outburst. "And one of the few I could count on to speak the truth, even if it wasn't to my liking."

"We all deserve that," said Leo.

"I know. And I'm glad; it's something my parents are incapable of."

His assumption justified, Leo now knew what had Marcus so vexed. His friend seldom talked about the past, having once alluded to an enforcer raid into the undercity district where he and his family lived. The soldiers had fallen upon them without warning, wilfully slaughtering any who resisted or couldn't get out of the way quickly enough. He would have perished too were it not for the actions of strangers who'd followed in the destruction's wake, pulling him from the ruins and into another world, adopting him as their son.

Only later did he find this wasn't done out of love, but the desire to acquire a living status symbol typically befitting those of noble rank, his very existence affirming their generosity and compassion, not to mention wealth. For affluent couples unable to conceive or poorer families unwilling to pay the tax on having children, adoption proved a viable alternative. Marcus however suspected cruder motives behind his salvation; personal gain and control chief among them.

His foster parents denied this of course, even while limiting the choices and options a child should have been given, then removing any remaining liberties altogether. Certain the boy's best use lay in politics they forced him to enter public life, acting as an extension of their will and manipulating him into thinking every decision he made was his own. And yet Marcus never yielded nor believed anything they said, for he knew from that day in undercity what people were capable of without feeling the need to explain themselves to anyone. Had he finally ended the charade, or maybe said something forcing his parents' hand? Leo could imagine any number of scenarios that might have provoked such a fierce reaction.

"How was it then?" Marcus ventured, hoping to make amends by expressing an interest in his friend's exploits.

"It?"

"The training."

"Oh," said Leo. "You know. Same as always."

"I don't know, and I wish you'd say. There's got to be more to it than that. Being away from the palace, not knowing if or when you're coming home. Holding on to the memory of that first deployment while craving the next, recounting stories of the campaigns you've fought and things you've seen."

Leo's heart sank in disappointment at this overblown, romanticised vision of life in the contingent. He'd only joined to see his father happy, not because he agreed with the organisation's ethics and morals.

"Aren't you excited?" Marcus pressed, growing in confidence. "You're a trained officer now. You'll be out of here and moving into the barracks or going off-world the moment your application hits the regent's desk. Need any help finishing it? Then we can work on mine."

"What?" Leo spluttered.

"I picked up a form this morning, right before telling my parents. They didn't think I'd follow through, making a point of reminding me how dangerous it was anyway. I went there spoiling for a fight but sat down and heard their concerns, believing they might actually care after all."

"Wait, so they approved of your decision?"

"Not exactly. I felt bad, seeing them worried. Nearly changed my mind. Then I asked myself what if this was their goal all along, and the only thing they were afraid of losing was their control over me." He paused to keep his emotions in check, repressing any trace of hatred or sorrow before saying, "Somehow I already knew the answer."

Leo nodded admiringly, but said nothing. He could tell Marcus meant every word and now possessed the grit to openly question those who had monopolised him for so long. Why then did *he* baulk at making his own feelings known? The regent was not an unreasonable man and would almost certainly support him, regardless of the choices he made. He'd spent years helping initiates find their courage and Marcus the strength to stand up for himself, yet had failed to hold his nerve when it mattered most. He felt like a hypocrite, and it showed.

"I know what you're thinking," Marcus continued, mistaking Leo's trepidation for qualms over his plan. "Don't worry, I've got it all figured out. I'll join a contingent on another world so no-one can block my application; only the regent there can approve or reject it."

"Sounds good," said Leo.

"Can you help me fill in this form?"

"Sure." Leo took the papers and started reading through them.

"Not now!" Marcus laughed, finding his business-like approach highly entertaining. "We should be at the party. Leave it till later. Won't take us more than a few minutes, since you've already done yours."

Leo carried on scanning the document, paying him little attention. Certain words stood out more than others: *education, experience, accomplishments*, and he visualised the life he'd spurned in favour of a dream.

"You *have* done yours, haven't you?" asked Marcus.

Sidestepping questions and procrastinating for days on end were what had led to this sorry pass in the first place. "No," Leo answered, without hesitating. "I've not, nor will I."

Marcus took the revelation in his stride, gleefully pointing out that both of them were doing what they wanted with their lives. Guessing

Leo hadn't yet told the regent, he assured him that his reaction would depend upon the manner in which he raised the subject. "You can't be this cold," he said, "after everything the man's done. Rossi cares, perhaps too much, so consider his feelings when you tell him. Just wait for the right moment."

"There'll never be a right moment," said Leo.

"Then lie."

"And make things worse? No."

"Only if he finds out. Look, in politics you'll face these tests every day. It's tough and brutal and can corrupt the best of us. The fairest proposal sparks uproar because there are people here who can't stomach the thought of anyone being happy and get off on the hurt they cause others. He's not like them. But one man or woman alone won't change Tanis; it's too big. Why stay? Come with me and we'll make a difference on a world that has a future."

"Leaving Turilli free to do as he pleases? I've seen the suffering and chaos his vanity will bring. We'd be responsible for whatever fate befell the millions we left behind, no better than the patricians who pretend such things aren't happening now."

"Well, when you put it like that..."

"I can't do it alone," said Leo. "I need your help."

Marcus swelled with pride, his skills and talents recognised at last. "I'm game if you are," he beamed, seizing the opportunity to repay Leo's faith in him. "I'll stick around until my application goes through. Anything I can do in the meantime?"

"There is one thing."

"Name it."

"Divinity's changing," Leo stated glumly. "Turilli may be capricious, but his schemes are predictable enough. I hear he's already demanding the nobility's allegiance, and is doubtless searching for ways to strengthen his rule when he becomes regent. Those building sites we've been watching appear all over the city could be one - not even my father knows what's going on there."

"I suspect you'd like to, though."

"The nearest is a level down from the spire's peak," said Leo, outlining his intentions. "They're always recruiting, so pose as a worker and join one of the groups. Keep your head down and do what they say when they say it. Gain their trust, find out which regulations are being broken and how, then slip away at the earliest opportunity. If you can find evidence that'll implicate Turilli, all the better. When I make my report to the regent, no amount of flattery will stop him putting an end to the illicit practices I'm certain are occurring there. Either way, it's visible proof someone is fighting for the people and provides a means of checking Turilli's ambitions discreetly without openly challenging them."

Marcus listened intently, impressed by Leo's attention to detail but secretly unnerved at the antipathy driving him. He pushed those negative thoughts aside, focusing fully on the task ahead. Out of the two he was by far the better suited for such an enterprise, less conspicuous than his illustrious friend and easily able to talk his way out of any situation, a skill Leo hadn't quite yet mastered.

"Any idea who handles security?" he asked, aware any information of this nature might give him an advantage.

"Enforcers," said Leo. "Maybe even the Phalanx, the contingent's elite."

"Right. I'll make up a story and leave within the hour," Marcus declared, heading for the door.

Leo found it hard to contain his amusement. "Where are you going?" he shouted after him. "Have you forgotten what day it is tomorrow?"

"But I thought..."

"I didn't mean now! Get yourself to the party! I'll meet you there."

Marcus smiled as he left, determined to make their last Landfall Day together the best yet.

6

The greatest disaster to ever befall Tanis wasn't the war, but a man. Administrator Luther arrived at this conclusion the moment he entered the council chamber, astonished to find obscenities and dark utterances flying where once there had been civilised debate between equals. Hate burned in the eyes of the world's finest politicians, many reduced to spewing forth outrageous accusations at their rivals and thereby turning their democratic stage into a scene resembling an undercity tavern brawl.

Lucas Turilli sat tall in a magnificent golden throne atop a seven-stepped dais in the centre of the room, gleefully presiding over the pandemonium. Wielding the royal sceptre and garbed in an embroidered purple toga, he was known and feared by all. A short brown beard framed his face, accentuating his rugged jawline and sharp, craggy features. A banquet was laid out at his feet and he kept an ancient bust of some great regime leader beside him. Occasionally, he would make what he thought to be a witty remark and glance over at it, as if expecting the sculpture to marvel at his words.

"Come, brothers and sisters of Divinity! Present your motions before I, Lucas Turilli, and receive my merciful judgement!"

The chamber rang with the buzz of lies, over-elaborate schemes and malice, every statement dripping with insincerity. Luther watched the man destined to become regent aggrandise himself at the expense of councillors who disagreed with him, issuing bizarre threats in their direction before covering his ears and pretending he couldn't hear their responses. Easily distracted, the mad regent-elect would quickly find fault with something else, stand up and screech his displeasure at that, too. With enforcers stationed all around, few dared speak against him.

Luther took his seat next to Cyrus, a well-nourished, educated man and Divinity's minister of commerce and trade. Though they rarely agreed with one another, this sudden change in protocol had stunned them both. Giovanni Rossi never needed armed guards inside the chamber - no regent had - but Turilli's arrogance and paranoia ensured decades of tradition were ended just in time for today's council session.

The balance of power on Tanis was shifting. Rossi no longer headed the council and made fewer appearances at public events, readily granting his successor these opportunities instead. Many embraced the new regime not fully understanding it, casting reason and honour aside so they might further their own agendas. Luther let old memories comfort him, quietly reflecting on the years of service he'd given his world while facing up to the prospect of continuing alone without its brightest star.

"Pretentious idiot," Cyrus hissed under his breath. "Rossi wouldn't have stood for such flagrant vulgarity. I'm done."

"Be quiet," said Luther firmly, straightening his tunic. "Smile. Applaud. Cheer as if your life depends on it, because it does." The minister took his rival's advice and started to clap meekly.

Though not of noble birth, Luther's prodigious intellect meant he excelled in the role as Divinity's senior statesman. Determining the purpose of Turilli's second council long before anyone else, he'd set about helping others pass the test secretly set for them. Most had responded positively out of respect, and while the more cavalier elements had ignored him, they soon ended up grovelling before the dais in a desperate attempt to prove their loyalty. His madness matched by flashes of brilliance, Luther often wondered which of Turilli's personas would win out in the end.

By contrast, Rossi ruled with dignity, a pure, radiant light amidst a sea of darkness. He and the old man were close, having worked together for what seemed a lifetime. The regent had elevated him from humble beginnings, instilling virtues and principles where there were none, even introducing him to his future wife, Elena. He owed Rossi his life and career, convincing himself that for all their triumphs over the years they could still achieve so much more. But the world had turned, and things he thought couldn't change did.

If only he'd known and treasured each step of their journey, looking forward instead of back at what had been and could never be again.

"Yes, let us sign your petitions! Be quick! With this very pen I can make your endeavours succeed!"

Turilli's rasping voice dragged Luther back to reality. He strutted about like some heathen god, surrounded by sycophants championing his strength, roaring with laughter at any quip he made, agreeing with every assertion. The court had fast become a breeding ground for such behaviour.

Gathered here today were representatives from all the noble houses and major organisations within Divinity, thronging the chamber at the vice-regent's behest. Envoys jockeyed with architects, ministers with accountants, making for a chaotic spectacle in which proposals could be heard or lost amid the tumult.

Turilli passed those he liked the sound of on a whim. Rejecting calls to end council early, the raging regent-elect made it clear his business came before any celebrations being held that night, and as the evening wore on Luther found himself increasingly preoccupied with thoughts of Elena.

"My lord regent!" an elderly man called Dietrich cried out above the din. "Kastor, prefect of house Mercurio congratulates you on your ascension. It is long overdue. As my lord knows, Kastor ardently supports regime construction within the city, but fears progress has stalled on this latest project and would like assurances-"

"Treachery!" Turilli screamed, spilling wine and knocking food all over the chamber floor. The mewling lackeys gathered about his feet were forced back, cowering even lower in abject submission as their master shook with uncontrollable rage. "Kastor talks, talks, talks, yet does nothing! Where is he today? Servicing his whores, perhaps, or slinking off to one of those vile Landfall parties!"

"Indisposed, my lord."

"Ha! He spends more time worrying about the view from his estate than backing me."

"All the same," said Dietrich, "he wants to know how long-"

"Wants?"

"Uh, requests."

Turilli eyed him suspiciously up and down. "Kastor forgets himself," he fumed. "I made him, and can un-make him just as easily. This project has been approved by the highest authority on Earth - his opinion is immaterial. Does this answer your question, whelp? Good. Now be silent and hound me no more."

Rebuked, Dietrich sat back down with the taunts of Turilli's minions ringing in his ears. The vice-regent's changeable disposition unsettled Luther, who knew only dangerously unstable individuals would agree or disagree with others depending on what mood they were in. He'd made a habit of avoiding such people and resolved to spend as little time around Turilli as possible.

Easier said than done, he thought.

Over the course of several hours the stone chamber slowly emptied. Dignitaries departed having aired their motions, a majority heading straight for the palace's own Landfall festivities. Turilli's closest advisors remained, and if the prolonged bout of politicking had riled either Cyrus or Luther, then they didn't show it. A regent traditionally entertained delegations before discussing private state matters, though Turilli did this purely because there existed an opportunity for personal glorification. He didn't value the opinions of councillors and cared even less about them as individuals, but tolerated his ministers if only to pass off their ideas as his own.

Eventually, Turilli grew tired of playing the wish granter. He began shouting commands from atop the dais, ordering the room cleared with his usual decorum.

"Enough babbling! Get out! These affairs do not concern you, nor will they ever. Go, or I'll find more competent emissaries!" He glared impatiently at the enforcers, who unsheathed their batons and started herding people towards the chamber's great wooden doors. "Not you!" he growled, noticing some of his advisors making to leave. "I require your counsel."

Ministers shuffled anxiously in their seats, unsure what would happen next. Turilli rose, gesturing for the doors to be sealed, his movements calm and regal. He smiled wryly, prowling the stage like an apex predator, emotionless eyes searching out any signs of weakness. No-one held his piercing gaze for long, men and women recoiling as if they'd seen something within those bottomless pits, something that told them what he was capable of and how far he'd go to achieve it.

"Make your reports," he rumbled, his words echoing around the chamber. "So we may complete our business." The twelve ministers exchanged worried looks upon realising Turilli's enforcers were still inside with them.

Another test.

Luther had anticipated this, but he wasn't expecting Cyrus to meet the challenge head-on. Clearly amused by his peers' sudden loss of form, the outspoken politician stood, confident that he alone possessed the nous to handle any question thrown at him.

Let that be enough, willed Luther, trying not to think of the consequences should he fail.

"My lord," he began, "as minister of commerce and trade, I have drafted plans aimed at renewing our resource-sharing agreement with Gethsemane. Talk of independence persists, however this deal will ensure our economy remains strong regardless."

Turilli looked pleased. "Good. I trust its terms are heavily weighted in our favour. The thought of Tanis being dictated to by an overreaching, insignificant speck of a moon disgusts me."

"With respect, we do rely on imports from Gethsemane more than-"

"For now!" Turilli boomed. "*We* are the regime's powerbase in the sector. You'd do well to remember that, minister. Their accomplishments are mere footnotes next to our glories. Had I the means I'd wipe them from the sky, but not before burning my name into the minds of all who dared resist." Turilli's brown eyes flashed with anger. He teetered on the brink of madness, unable to control his emotions. Staring ferociously at Cyrus, he composed himself by taking a number of deep breaths then asked, "How goes our drive for self-sufficiency?"

"A work in progress, my lord," the minister replied, unflustered. "The noble houses possess enough revenue and land to sustain it, although there is no guarantee they will. I fear raising taxes again might end any chance of cooperation-"

"Nonsense," said Turilli. "You speak as if these bigots have a choice in the matter. They don't. Forever finding fault with everything I say, each law passed. No. Increase taxes immediately then demand their compliance, at gunpoint if necessary. Should any refuse, call it treason. We'll soon discover who can be trusted."

"Yes. On a related note, output in the construction industry is up eight per cent on last quarter," Cyrus announced, hoping to distract Turilli with better news.

"So there was no truth behind what Kastor's man said? Progress hasn't stalled and we are, in fact, ahead of schedule?"

"My lord, I don't-"

"Yes or no, minister."

It dawned on Cyrus that he had no control over the situation whatsoever. Construction wasn't his area of expertise - did Turilli know that? Did he care? What was the vice-regent hoping to gain by asking him questions he couldn't answer? Anxiously scanning the room, the beleaguered minister found none willing to support him. "Forgive me," he stammered, thinking quickly and motioning towards Lady Chiara, the director of engineering. "I believe my esteemed colleague can deliver a more thorough analysis."

"I asked *you*," Turilli snapped, secretly revelling in his discomfort. "You took leadership of the discussion, so lead."

Cyrus sensed everyone in the room was staring at him. His pulse quickened and he started to sweat, realising he couldn't talk his way out of this. "My lord honours me," he said, determined to avoid embarrassing himself completely. "But I need more comprehensive data. The recent rise in output may be influenced by several factors. Without knowing I can't possibly comment on the project's status."

"Then let me enlighten you," said Turilli. "An increase in output tends to happen when jobs are filled. The only openings on Tanis are in construction, as they have been for the last two years. Targets haven't changed, menials aren't suddenly working harder and there hasn't been a technological revolution. Is that comprehensive enough? I'll ask you again, minister. Where do we stand?"

"We're on schedule," Cyrus blurted out, Turilli's relentless manoeuvrings having proved too much for him.

"Really?" The regent-elect spoke as if he already knew the answer and had just been toying with his minister all along. "I was told we were a month ahead."

Cyrus didn't know for certain, but felt sure that if this were true then he would have been told. His ring of executors were industrious and reliable in their espionage. Newly completed forges likely accounted for the increase in output, while he'd heard and seen nothing to substantiate Kastor's claim.

Right or wrong, he figured Turilli wanted to prove some sort of twisted point by humiliating him anyway. No amount of arguing could have ever altered his fate, he saw that now, and realised whoever spoke up first was always going to be made an example of. Worse still, Turilli had somehow known it would be him. With nothing to be gained by contradicting himself, Cyrus upheld his original assertion.

"We're on schedule, my lord," he repeated, noticing Lady Chiara looking at him imploringly from the corner of his eye. "Not ahead, nor behind. On schedule."

"So I'm misinformed?"

"I didn't say that."

"Well, either you're lying or my informant is," said Turilli.

Cyrus held up his hands, through with the interrogation and Turilli's accusations. "I'm no liar," he thundered in riposte. "Construction doesn't fall within my remit. All of the ministers present before you will guarantee my integrity."

"Not all," Turilli snarled, turning away and casually waving the enforcers forward. "We stand upon the precipice of change. The old ways will die with Rossi. I'm building a new world here, a better world. One where loyalty is prized and rewarded, because a loyal subject is a truthful subject. You, unfortunately, are neither."

Batons drawn, the soldiers made their way over to where Cyrus was standing. He faced them bravely despite their reputation, adrenaline coursing through his veins. The lead enforcer, a hulking, armour-clad brute of a man, pushed him aside effortlessly and continued on, took hold of Chiara's plaited hair and dragged the helpless minister screaming from the room. Cyrus stared at Turilli in disbelief, overcome by a mixture of gratitude and fear in the wake of what had just happened.

He'd manipulated proceedings to expose Chiara's lie, his harsh response ensuring no other would dare deceive him again.

The vice-regent whirled around to address his council.

"I do not require your love, just your loyalty," he said. "You may hate me as long as you serve me. Forget the past, look to the future. Fail me, lie to me, and I will destroy you. Is this clear?"

Their silence told him he had been understood.

"That is all. You can go." The ministers eagerly complied, falling over one another in their haste to leave. Turilli felt satisfied with his evening's work, but still had one final thing to take care of.

"Luther," he called, beckoning his administrator over. "Come with me. We have much to discuss."

7

As midnight approached, an air of excitement and anticipation began to build throughout Divinity. The electric atmosphere was palpable from the ramshackle slums of undercity to the gleaming spires of the regent's palace, intensifying as Landfall Day drew nearer. In great mansions, squalid abodes and isolated communities nestled amid Tanis' dunes, those native to the world embraced their sole holiday without any worries or fears. This was a night for the rich and poor alike, and it would be another year before they had reason to celebrate anything again.

Divinity's elite were gathering beneath an enormous white pavilion which had temporarily taken over the palace grounds. They danced and laughed, their appetites sated by a constant supply of food and drink brought forth by the regent's innumerable servants. Spoilt children rank amok, gorging themselves on cake or knocking over the beverages of irate politicians as they played.

Leo had showered, shaved and donned his finest clothes, confidently mingling with councillors and military officials. Many went out of their way just to comment on how smart he looked, though he appeared rather bemused by all the attention. Others kept a wide berth, mindful of the young noble's penchant for mischief. Equally comfortable in a royal tunic as he was his enforcer armour, Leo drew admiring stares from envious lords and captivated noblewomen wherever he went.

The pavilion was so crowded Leo could barely move without bumping into someone. He couldn't see Marcus but recognised his father's voice. The regent was serving drinks to new arrivals, his warm smile and gentle manner making everyone feel at ease. Old age hadn't prevented him from enjoying the occasion, for while he politely rebuffed the few ladies who asked him to dance, he talked with them at length about their hopes for the coming year.

Never had there been a more beloved regent.

Leo felt a tug on his arm and turned to find a curvaceous young woman standing beside him. Tall, lithe and graceful, she wore a blue silk dress that highlighted the healthy glow of her chestnut skin. Her golden hair, parted in the middle, fell in waves about her shoulders. Leo was mesmerised by her indigo eyes and self-assured demeanour. Oddly, he hadn't noticed her exquisite beauty until tonight.

"You're a lot like him," she remarked, her tone soft and earnest.

Luna was the headstrong daughter of Arturo and Maria van Dyck. She'd befriended Leo the day he'd arrived on Tanis, shielding him from the cruel taunts of the other children who'd never seen an off-worlder before. Like Marcus, she was tenacious and genuine. Her parents were wealthy aristos from one of Divinity's oldest royal houses, renowned among the nobility for being ruthless schemers and deceivers, as vicious and egotistical as Luna was kind.

"He's a good teacher," Leo replied, thinking himself unworthy of her praise. "And I'm grateful, even if I don't always show it. I've much to thank him for - he's the reason I'm here today."

Luna smiled broadly. Though their temperaments were different, she and Leo had lots in common. Being of the same age, they'd attended the royal academy together. They shared a passion for history, his natural intellect complementing her innate knowledge and understanding of the world.

"You're here because he saw something within you," she said. "Something other than the potential to merely do his bidding. He chose you because he recognised you have the humility and virtues to act as a force for good. Anyone can learn the skills necessary to succeed in life, but how one goes about achieving their dreams is more important. In any case, his decision not to adopt a child from Tanis served as a damning indictment of this world's 'talent'."

"I don't believe that," said Leo. "There are many people here smarter and kinder than me."

"Name one."

"You."

Luna blushed. "Then it's a good thing I was born so high and the nobility can't put their children up for adoption! Listen, I'm going out into the desert later," she said, changing the subject. "Why don't you join me?"

Leo contemplated his response. He wanted to, but remembered what Marcus had advised earlier. "Thanks, but I think I'll stay," he said after a while. "I need to speak with my father. Tell me, what exactly do you do out there anyway?"

"Come along and you'll see. There is a world outside of the palace, you know."

"Why do I find that hard to believe?" Leo asked sarcastically.

"Because you've seen so little of Tanis? Or you're a pessimist," Luna chuckled.

"I'm not! And I've seen more than enough open desert in the three years I've spent with the contingent. The dunes are where we train. There's nothing out there but sand."

Luna fixed him with a mischievous stare, as if to say she knew otherwise. During periods of downtime at the academy she would disappear for days, returning with strange trinkets and artifacts, never saying where she got them. Leo had struggled to hide his interest, asking her repeatedly without success. He was loath to pass up the chance to find out, but there were more important matters that required his attention tonight.

"Well, as long as you're sure," Luna sighed, sounding disappointed.

"I am." Leo considered explaining why he'd really turned her offer down, but found himself distracted by a conversation between a group of nobles nearby.

"Then at least have a drink with me," said Luna, her voice insistent.

Leo wasn't listening. He had overheard an intoxicated man saying less than complimentary things about his father. Locating the cretin, he felt a red-hot rage build inside as he started walking, fists clenched, with retribution on his mind.

He'd barely taken two steps when he felt someone holding him back.

"Don't," Luna pleaded with him.

Leo met her gaze, looking into her soft, blue eyes. "Don't what?"

She nodded in the man's direction.

"I was only going to have a little chat with him," said Leo, his livid expression and aggressive tone betraying his true intent.

"Right. The last person you 'talked' to ended up with a split lip."

"Because he deserved it," Leo spat contemptuously. "I won't let these people think they can get away with insulting a great man."

"But react with violence once too often and you'll soon gain an unsavoury reputation. Do you want to be respected or feared, like Turilli? Don't let it bother you. Rossi doesn't."

Still seething, Leo allowed Luna to walk him away. Her words, however true, failed to pacify him. Who would defend his father's honour if he couldn't?

"None dare speak ill of Turilli in public," Leo mumbled through gritted teeth. "Maybe he's onto something."

"Maybe he is. And if you want to be like him then that's your choice. The nobility have always used fear and force as means to maintain their power, so no-one would care if you did likewise."

"Good," Leo said bitterly, his anger threatening to overtake him.

"You can't, though, can you? Such wanton behaviour is against everything you stand for, everything you know to be true and good. Divinity doesn't need another Turilli. It needs someone who has the heart and courage to stand against monsters like him. Rossi won't ever say this because he's afraid - not that you'd be unable to cope with the responsibility but what might happen if you did. Confrontation and violence are anathema to him. He'd have you leave Tanis and escape what is coming rather than fighting it."

"I should go, then." Leo felt torn between his duty to his father and doing what he knew was right.

Luna reprimanded him sharply. "How much longer must we pretend you've not already decided to stay? You can change everything, but not as an enforcer. Don't waste time feuding with tyrants and don't commit assuming praise and success will immediately follow. They won't. Help those who are struggling to help themselves because you *want* to. One day they will thank you for all you've done, though you may not be around to hear it. Even if all you achieve is improving conditions in undercity it'll be more than anyone has done for those poor people in centuries. Myself, I foresee you'll do great things but only if you believe you can."

Her concise appraisal of the situation helped calm Leo's mind. Thinking clearly once more, he finally realised that the decision to join the contingent or follow his heart had always been his own. He'd spent months worrying how the regent might react when he could have told him and started making plans for the future. For all his brilliance and despite Marcus' reassurances, it had taken the words of a soft-spoken yet remarkable woman to make him see that his father loved him dearly, and would be proud of him regardless.

Leo hung his head, embarrassed. "What about now?" he frowned. "You must think I'm an indecisive coward."

Her answer surprised him. "No. You stop to consider the feelings of others before your own. In a self-centred, material world, that is a rare quality. You're kind and protective of the people you care for, which is why it's so hard for you to ignore slights against them."

"I can't win either way," Leo conceded. "If I say nothing I'm seen as heartless and cold. Speak out and I'm overreacting. The nobility talk and act as if their regent is already dead, too preoccupied with winning the favour of a madman when they should be fighting for their world. I don't understand why Rossi doesn't do something to stop it or at the very least challenge those responsible. His inaction vexes me."

Leo was so perturbed he didn't see the worried glance Luna shot him.

"Turilli isn't regent yet," he fumed. "The bureaucrats on Earth are just as much to blame for appointing him in the first place. He squanders our wealth on construction sites and vanity projects to inflate his ego, surrounding himself with idiots like Cyrus who tell him only what he wants to hear. He'll destroy Tanis if given half a chance, and my father is letting it happen. A part of me thinks he's given up caring and-"

The sound of someone deliberately clearing their throat stopped him mid-sentence. Caught off-guard, Leo spun around only to be confronted by Giovanni Rossi, who stood before him looking decidedly unimpressed with what he'd just heard.

"Given up?" the regent questioned, more upset than angry. "Do you really think so little of me, Leo?"

"No, of course not," came the apologetic reply.

"Let's you and I have a talk, shall we? You've obviously got more to say. I'm sure Miss van Dyck wants to enjoy the party and not spend her whole evening mired in tedious conversation."

Excusing herself, Luna headed over to the bench where her parents were sitting, leaving Leo to face his father alone. Though the old man was patient and forgiving, she observed a sudden change in his usually calm disposition as she left. This both frightened and intrigued her, for it appeared he was hiding something and had been suffering from the strain of doing so for a long time.

She quickly banished the thought from her mind, having no desire to meddle in the affairs of others.

"It's a clear night," the regent remarked as he accompanied Leo out of the pavilion and into the palace gardens.

The searing heat of the day had gone, leaving a soft, warm breeze in its place, and a million stars glittered like tiny diamonds in the sky above them. Old satellites, relics from Tanis' heyday, still circled the world in their decaying orbits, and the brightly illuminated cities of Gethsemane seemed close enough to touch.

As they walked, Rossi reflected upon the true meaning of Landfall Day. Around this time five thousand years ago, the ship bearing the first colonists was beginning its descent to the planet's surface. He could only imagine how different Tanis looked back then, and how the hundreds of men and women who made the journey must have felt upon arriving.

The regent sighed quietly to himself. People didn't make history anymore, they just studied it.

Leo's thoughts, meanwhile, were fixed firmly on the present. He'd made his point and was now prepared to argue it, tired of keeping his opinions to himself.

"I meant everything I said about Turilli," he declared defiantly. "The way he swans around thinking he's regent is reprehensible and insulting. How can you tolerate that? Don't lecture me just because I'm the only one who has the guts to say it."

"I'm not going to," Rossi said flatly.

"Oh. Well, good."

"I admire your honesty. You hold nothing back, but sometimes you must tell people what they want to hear rather than what you think they need to."

"Why?"

"Because the truth is a weapon," said Rossi. "One so powerful it can make or break a man. By exposing an individual's flaws so candidly, you risk provoking a heated reaction. Few will accept it without compromise, but those who do you can trust with your life."

"Like you?"

Rossi smiled. "Like me. Leo, the path you've chosen is not an easy one. We all believed we were capable of changing the world at some point in our lives. Perhaps, with the lure of power or promotion, some still do. But in reality little changes, and most give up when events conspire to keep them down and rob them of their dreams. We're only as great as our hearts will allow. Please don't lose the belief and desire to succeed that I once had, or let the fire within you go out like I did."

"Wait, what path?" Leo inquired suspiciously.

"It's all right," the regent affirmed. "I support your decision."

The casual manner in which he'd raised such an important issue took Leo aback. He wondered how Rossi could have learned what he intended to do with his future when he hadn't directly discussed it with him. Speculating wildly, it didn't take him long to reach a conclusion.

"Did Marcus tell you?" he demanded, angry at the thought his friend had betrayed his trust.

"No. Though I'm unsure why you felt you could tell him and not me."

"Because I knew you'd be disappointed," Leo replied. "It isn't what you want."

The regent placed a reassuring hand on his son's shoulder. "All I've ever wanted is for you to be happy. I'd never interfere with your choices, nor presume to make them for you. Truthfully, I don't know why you're even seeking my approval on this private matter in the first place."

"But it's *not* private," Leo insisted. "I'd like you to be involved in my life and instead all I've done is cut you out of it. I've let you down when all I want is for you to be proud of me."

Rossi was overjoyed to hear Leo still valued his guidance. He'd felt increasingly redundant as Turilli had assumed more power, but the fact his son needed him made up for that. Having watched him mature into a kind-hearted, thoughtful young man, the regent now only needed to add steel and resolve to his many qualities. If he didn't, less scrupulous individuals would try to take advantage of his good nature. In putting others first he'd neglected himself, and Rossi knew he had to make him aware of how harsh and unforgiving the world could be before it was too late.

But not here, and not now.

"I've no reason to be disappointed with you," he said, recognising the importance of easing Leo's fears, not deepening them. "You're out there making something of your life, not throwing it away. Stop concerning yourself with what other people think and don't worry about the potential consequences of your decisions before you've even made them. For once, act on impulse and do whatever makes *you* happy."

Leo shook his head. "It's not that easy."

"Easy? I didn't say it would be. Nothing in life ever is."

"Then will you help me?"

"No. This is something you must do on your own."

"Why?"

Rossi sighed. "Because I'm old, Leo. The demands of my office have worn me down over the years and all I want to do now is rest. My door's always open, but I'm not about to go charging off with you on another adventure. This old man's time for that has long since passed. These days are yours - embrace them."

"I'll try," said Leo.

"Good. It's for this reason I'm handing Turilli more responsibility. I can no longer rule Tanis with the same vigour and surety I once did. A regent needs to be sharp of mind and tongue. Do you understand?"

"I think so," Leo replied, glancing over at the pavilion. Rossi saw this and smiled.

"I'll not detain you any longer," he said, laughing lightly. "I'm keeping you from your friends. If you've the time, perhaps you can stop by my office a little later when the party's over?"

"Yes, of course."

"It's nothing that can't keep, so don't rush," said Rossi. "I've some bills to approve and require your input. Now, off with you. Enjoy tonight and remember what I said."

Leo gladly complied, suspecting the regent wanted to share a celebratory drink with him instead.

Rossi bowed his head and trudged back towards the palace, relieved his son lacked the ability to read and interpret facial expressions like Luna could. He paused to gaze up at the stars then out over the city he once ruled, knowing twelve years of preparation ultimately came down to this one moment. It didn't matter whether Leo was ready or not. He'd invested far too much time in him to fail now.

8

Luther didn't say a word as he followed Lucas Turilli into the palace's inner sanctum. He'd walked these marble corridors once before, years ago, when Giovanni Rossi had asked him to serve as planetary administrator. The sights and smells assailing his senses seemed hauntingly familiar, and in remembering the moment he let present fears subside in favour of an old memory. Ahead, Turilli pushed open a door with intricate patterns carved into the wood. The regime's insignia featured prominently, as did a more recent engraving of what appeared to be Divinity, overshadowed by a peculiar-looking monolith atop the city's peak.

Beyond lay the royal residence, an area of the palace few knew existed and even fewer had seen. A regent was expected to live here in absolute luxury along with any immediate family, waited on by a small army of servants whose own quarters were cramped by comparison. This had grown over time as each regent had strove to outdo his or her predecessors, resulting in a sprawling complex of stately rooms and immense chambers, all furnished by the finest materials and décor available.

Turilli had started making some changes himself. Hand-painted portraits of the regent-elect hung from every diamond-studded wall, golden frames glittering in the light cast down by countless crystal chandeliers. Mosaics adorned the floors, murals the ceilings, with handmade rugs made of pure silk arranged carefully here and there. The west wing was designed to be the ultimate expression of regime power and wealth on Tanis, with only the most illustrious visitors permitted to gaze upon its magnificence.

"Rossi's problem," Turilli said as they turned down another corridor, "lay in frugality. He never utilised the tools at his disposal to their fullest extent. Why hide things away or hold people back? Moderation? No. This was an old man's weakness, nothing more."

"He has his principles," Luther stated politely. "You have yours."

"Indeed. But I didn't bring you here so we could spend hours bandying words, administrator."

"Then what *did* you bring me here for?" Luther asked.

Turilli stopped and looked him dead in the eye. "You'll see. This way."

Luther stayed alert as they continued on. Though alone, he refrained from saying anything that might rouse the vice-regent's anger, wary of his volatile temperament and capacity for violence. He'd already endured a difficult day, and matching wits with a deranged tyrant would require all of his remaining strength and resolve.

The great hall, where regents received high-ranking regime officials, was their destination. An ancient law forbade any major structural enhancements, meaning the hall's appearance had changed little since its creation millennia ago. Given the frequency with which old edicts were amended or conveniently lost, Luther wondered why this one had been so strictly adhered to.

"Remarkable, isn't it?" Turilli crowed as he crossed over the threshold. Luther nodded stoically in agreement.

All those fortunate enough to be allowed inside were instantly overwhelmed by the craftsmanship of the hall's artisans. Many had stood in awestruck silence without even noticing the room's centrepiece - an exquisite wall-mounted tapestry depicting Tanis' history. But this was only half the experience, for the domed room's essence resonated with echoes of the past and could affect people in different ways. Luther felt himself drawn to the tapestry, noticing several key events missing from the timeline.

Selective remembrance, he thought. *The many triumphs of Man have been enshrined, though in forgetting the hardships these were born out of so do we ultimately forget ourselves.*

He took a step back, aghast, as if he'd stumbled upon a terrible secret and greatly feared what he now knew. Were regime scholars falsifying records and erasing those they couldn't? What if this archaic hall wasn't a testament to how far they as a species had come but how far they'd fallen?

Behind him, Turilli basked in the moonlight flooding in through the hall's high arched windows, utterly oblivious to his administrator's reaction.

"I would see our glory days restored," he declared. "See Tanis rise again and take her rightful place as the jewel of Carina."

"It'll come at a cost," said Luther, unnerved by the scale of his ambition.

"I accept that. But immortality can only be achieved through sacrifice."

"There are other ways," said Luther. "Our ancestors-"

"You're wrong," Turilli interrupted, shaking his head. "Horrors lurk between the lines of every story. We just choose not to see them. Do you think our idols weren't monsters who built their legends atop the bones of those they purported to love? And yet who do we remember - the hero or their companions? *What* do we remember - the struggle or its eventual outcome?"

Luther felt inclined to agree. "People have always needed heroes," he said. "Even presented with the truth they would wilfully look beyond it."

"Precisely. The end result is everything. How we achieve it doesn't matter. Should we do things right, our names, and thus our legacies, will live forever." Turilli perched himself on one of the windowsills, glaring expectantly at his administrator. "So how would you begin?" he asked nonchalantly.

Luther hesitated and ran his fingers through his cropped black hair. If Turilli had correctly gauged his character, he may well have deduced the best way to bring him onside was through a tailored approach. Fear and force were his trademarks, but he'd surely realised they were useless here. Then again, the scheming regent-elect could just be trying to engage him in another of his myriad games. With a coolness rivalling the coldest night, Luther responded by playing along, set on finding out.

"I'd levy new taxes against the nobility," he said. "Coerce or threaten them into compliance and secure their loyalty, but respect their limits."

"Good. And then?"

"Sign the agreement with Gethsemane, increase the flow of raw materials into Divinity."

"Yes, yes. What else?" Turilli pressed.

"Close down the construction sites."

Turilli's face contorted into an angry scowl. "Oh? And why's that?"

"Too costly. Casualty rates among the work crews are unsustainable."

"And this is your solution?"

"The only one I can think of," Luther shrugged.

"Then I suggest in future you leave such matters to me. Your advice is welcome, but ill-informed judgements are not."

"You asked me what *I'd* do," Luther remarked haughtily, hoping to goad Turilli into revealing what had riled him so. "Why not shut them down?"

"Because I don't have a choice! You answer to me, as I answer to Earth. *They* chose Tanis over a hundred worlds, trusted us with the planning and realisation of their most ambitious project yet and I must do everything in my power to convince them they made the right choice. All other considerations are secondary."

"Even the human cost?"

"Like I said."

Luther pretended to look confused. "Then it's an undertaking of great importance?"

"Obviously," Turilli scoffed, visibly irritated by his persistence. Usually it was him asking the questions. "I don't expect you to understand the pressures placed on a regent," he smarted. "It's an office few can fill. If it helps assuage your fears, we're free to bring in additional manpower as and when we need from neighbouring sectors."

Luther smiled inwardly. Belatedly realising their importance, in one minute he'd learned more about the construction sites than anyone had done in years. A mandate clearly existed granting Turilli far more power than most regents, though Earth's desires saw him placed under enormous stress. He may have been the greatest disaster to ever befall Tanis, but someone had chosen him for a reason. Weighing the merits of uncovering more against analysing the information he already had, Luther displayed great self-control in choosing the safer option. The vice-regent was smart, and he wouldn't underestimate him like Cyrus and Chiara had earlier.

"Forgive me," he said apologetically, feigning contrition. "My lord is right. I spoke out of turn."

"Of course I'm right," Turilli sighed. "It doesn't matter. You serve me now, not Rossi. Share his scruples if you wish, but remember that for the duration of my regency they count for nothing."

"Yes."

"You're an able man, Luther. I see potential, which is why I retained your services. Like me, you want what's best for Tanis. I'm not wrong, am I?"

"No."

"Then tell me how else I might best proceed."

"The growing population poses all kinds of problems," said Luther, brushing a hand over the stubble on his jaw. "We must act, and soon."

"Then you've arrived at the same conclusion I have," Turilli remarked, lying so he didn't appear incompetent and glad someone was thinking for him. "Another purge is overdue. I'll send the enforcers, keep up the pretence of maintaining order in undercity. As a more long-term solution we'll implement a one-child policy and up the cost of adoption. The nobility can still buy their bastards after the enforcers are finished, though will pay handsomely for the privilege. We can also use technology," he said, a wicked grin spreading across his face. "I hear there are ways to identify defects in unborn children. Forced terminations will ensure our society remains strong and healthy, while those unable to contribute should be expunged."

Luther's icy blue eyes narrowed. "Expunged?"

"Don't look so morose, administrator. It's my responsibility to make tough decisions, not yours. People are living longer and there invariably comes a point when they cease being useful and become a burden. What would you do in my stead?"

"The same," Luther admitted grimly. "My lord is most ingenious."

Turilli lapped up the praise, confident he'd gained a new ally. Unlike the sycophants who fawned over him at council, here was one whose creative ideas could prove invaluable. The loyalty he owed Rossi would be his just as soon as the old fool passed, making for a more pliable servant open to his schemes and machinations.

"I am," Turilli said, feeling mightily pleased with himself. "Now let me show you why you're really here."

The vice-regent sauntered over to one of the hall's adjoining side rooms, producing a small brass key along the way. Luther followed, delighted to have gained his trust so quickly. Perhaps in time he could manipulate Turilli into unknowingly advancing his cause and bring the regency's considerable power against the few enemies he had.

"What lies beyond this door is real," Turilli continued. "Places like these shouldn't exist. It's our fault they do." He passed the key to Luther and said, "Not all of our history is buried out there beneath the sands."

Luther hesitated.

"It's perfectly safe," Turilli soothed, crossing his arms over his chest. "Open it."

The administrator stepped forward. He put the key into the lock and turned it, forcing the door open on its rusty hinges. He blinked as a blast of cold air hit his face.

The room was dark, dusty and windowless. There were no lights, only lanterns hanging from hooks embedded in the wall. Turilli struck a match and lit one, allowing Luther to see a little clearer. The faint outlines of objects emerged from the blackness, some no larger than a pen and others that towered above him.

Luther felt his heartbeat quicken as he reached out and picked up what appeared to be an unremarkable item from a nearby shelf. He let it rest in the palm of his hand, fascinated by its sleek, sturdy design and simple yet aesthetically pleasing appearance. Upon closer inspection he saw there was a cracked screen on one side and a logo he couldn't quite make out on the other. Had he understood the device's purpose then he might well have appreciated it more, but he didn't know what it was. He didn't know what anything was in here.

Turilli's voice cut through the silence. "There are many gaps in our past. All we can do is try and fill them."

It dawned on Luther that something momentous was happening. "No games," he stammered. "What is all this?"

"Your heritage. Relics from another time and technology the like of which is not in the world today." Turilli raised the lantern, its light revealing shelves filled with books, paintings and ornaments. "The war was fought without regard for treasures such as these. Here they are protected and preserved."

Luther stared in wonder at the vast collection of priceless artifacts arrayed before him. Were there clues to his own past hidden amongst the archives of old? If so, answers to his many questions lay tantalisingly within reach.

"Stay true to me and it's yours," Turilli promised, demonstrating his powers of persuasion. "I can help fill these gaps."

He knew the administrator was curious. People with no memory of their parents often were. If Luther felt there was a chance to find out where he came from then he would surely seize it. Taking advantage of his continued silence, Turilli pressed on.

"I ask little in return. Serve my office and your rewards shall be great indeed. But don't make the mistake of abusing my trust and overreaching yourself as our former director of engineering did.

Believe me when I say you wouldn't want to share her fate."

"My lord is most generous," Luther replied, tiring of Turilli's repeated attempts to secure his loyalty. He wasn't cowed by his threats - the worst Chiara could expect was to be temporarily relieved of her duties - but he found it hard to refuse the vice-regent's offer. "If you can get me unrestricted access to this room," he said, "I'm at your disposal."

"Then we're agreed," Turilli declared triumphantly, allowing a small smile to creep across his features.

It seemed everyone had a price after all.

9

Years from now, Leo believed he would look back on this day and remember the moments that had defined him.

He'd spent the last few hours surrounded by his friends, unable to recall a more enjoyable Landfall feast or think of a time when he'd been happier. Though his life was about to change forever, knowing he had the support and approval of those he loved helped him embrace the change, not fear it. He'd lived with fear in his heart for far too long.

Tired but keen to show willing, Leo departed the celebrations and made his way back to the palace. His father had requested he stop by, and if the regent had a mountain of paperwork to tackle then the least he could do was offer to help.

Expecting Rossi to be hard at work or waiting with a drink and some kind words for him, Leo found the office unlit and his father's chair empty upon arriving. As he was often called away on state business, Leo thought nothing of it, happy to sit and wait for his return.

The regent's office was tidy and clean. A large mahogany desk dominated its interior, flanked by bookcases filled with ancient texts which reached to the ceiling. The only other items of furniture present were three brown leather chairs, two facing the desk and one behind it, with none of the vanity on show that was so widely displayed throughout the rest of the palace. Leo admired his father's frugal nature. Despite being one of the richest individuals on Tanis, he'd never felt the need to flaunt or exhibit his wealth.

"Humility is its own reward," he'd said.

Leo switched on the light and walked over the patterned burgundy carpet towards the desk. Its surface was largely unmarked. Books and stationery were neatly arranged on a green placemat which protected the smooth, dark wood from damage. Unsure how long his father would be, Leo opted to recline in the regent's chair while he waited. It was old and worn but surprisingly comfortable. He yawned wearily, not noticing that the room's internal security camera had activated.

Leo willed himself to stay awake. Needing to keep his mind busy, he began looking around for things to do. He knew where the power button was for Rossi's holo-computer, but not its password. His gaze shifted to the bookcases. The regent's works were controversial and thought-provoking, but he'd read them all at least twice. Frustrated, Leo stared dumbly at the desk then leaned forward and tried opening its drawers. They were all locked.

All but one.

Leo pulled the bottom left drawer open with some force, thinking it would be locked like the others. The young noble let out a cry of dismay upon realising it wasn't, so surprised by the complete lack of resistance he overbalanced and very nearly ended up on the floor. Bracing himself against the desk, Leo rose to check if anyone had witnessed his moment of foolishness. He'd left the door ajar, but luckily the corridor outside was empty. Feeling relieved and a little embarrassed, he slowly made his way back over to the regent's chair.

The drawer he'd pulled out had stuck open, its contents a mess. Leo sighed in annoyance and bit his lip, knowing he would have a damnable time trying to put everything back as his father had left it. He sat down in the chair and smiled, having inadvertently found something to do after all.

Because the drawer hadn't been locked, Leo didn't feel guilty about going through it. The regent was not a careless man; all of his private files were stored away safely on the holo-computer. Leo doubted he would find anything of interest within, though he did spot several photos buried beneath an assortment of pens and other stationery. His curiosity piqued, he reached in and carefully retrieved them.

Most were pictures of Leo and his father at Landfall feasts and various awards ceremonies over the last twelve years. Others were more informal. Rossi was reading to him in one, and in another they both stared up at a massive regime starship hanging over Divinity. Supply ships from Earth made routine stops at the capital every six months, but Leo had never seen one like this before. He turned the photo over, wondering if this was the ship that had brought him to Tanis. On the back was a note, written in the regent's hand, which read, 'close observation, second day'.

Intrigued, Leo continued leafing through the five remaining prints and it soon became apparent that these had all been taken before his adoption. He recognised his father straight away but not the petite, grey-haired woman who appeared next to him in every picture. Leo thought for a moment. The regent had never mentioned a wife, if that's who she was.

One of the photos was dated twelve years ago, almost to the day. His father stood in full military dress, his arm around the same lady. They both looked happy. Overhead loomed the same colossal starship he'd seen in the other photo. Leo felt humbled to have had a small glimpse into his father's past, but had been left with more questions than answers.

Had Rossi adopted him out of love or pity? What did "close observation" mean? Who was the woman in the photos and where was she now?

Only the regent would know. Leo resolved to ask him, then had second thoughts. None of this really mattered. Their bond was strong now, regardless of what may have gone before. He shuffled the photos into a neat stack in his hands and reached over to put them back in the drawer. It was then he noticed that they had been sitting on top of a thin black file folder. The folder was labelled 'Carmona'.

On seeing this, Leo froze. Aware the regime kept comprehensive records of all things, he dreaded to think what it might contain.

Likely a hundred detailed accounts describing his homeworld's final hours, all from different perspectives. There would be countless graphic images of the devastation the meteor shower wrought. A complete list of measures the world's leaders took to try and prevent it, and transcripts of desperate calls for help to nearby systems when they knew they would fail. His father had told him everything - what more did he want to know? Leo slouched in the chair until curiosity got the better of him. He discarded the photos and opened the folder.

Inside was a single sheet of paper. Leo saw that it was a printed log of transmissions sent from one of the rescue ships back to Tanis. His father was listed as both sender and fleet commander. Feeling his stomach tighten, Leo took a deep breath and started reading.

The words cut into his heart.

First transmission, one day out.

The fleet is underway. Our regime liaison informs us that we are to travel to Carmona - a temperate world in system fifty-eight that has gone dark. Primary objectives are to investigate and re-establish communications. Due to my previous 'hands-on' experience I have been selected as the mission's commander. Captains Mayer and Paulus will provide support from their vessels, the Restitution *and* Deliverance, *respectively. Tanis might be behind us, but you are never far from my thoughts, Lina. I... apologise for sounding so formal, but even a regent's broadcasts are monitored.*

Leo paused. *Lina?* His father might well have married at some point after all. Hoping to find out, he read on.

Second transmission, three days out.

New orders. There might be more to this than I first thought. Our liaison has just finished briefing the captains on a meteor shower that was reported to have hit Carmona six days ago. We are the rescue mission. It is not my place to question the regime, but I fear we have neither the ships nor personnel to mount a successful relief effort. Our vessels are warships, and we've room for a thousand civilians between us. Estimates put the population of Carmona at twenty billion. When I raised my concerns with the liaison he calmly dismissed them without explaining himself. What is our purpose there if we're not in a position to help? Are more ships coming or are they really expecting us to find so few survivors? The next briefing is in five days. I trust that by then I'll have some answers.

Third transmission, eight days out.

The fleet is now in-system. Owing largely to my efforts, our liaison has requisitioned another ship, the Reckoning, *which will join us on final approach. Mayer and Paulus were as relieved as I was when we heard that. I've studied her blueprints and it appears she is a newly launched Salvation Ship, the largest in her class and outfitted with the best medical equipment available. I expect us to enter orbit within the next eleven hours. All crews have been briefed and are on standby. Are they loyal, brave and committed? Yes. Are they ready? We'll know soon enough.*

Leo paused again, preparing himself for what he knew would come next.

Fourth transmission, nine days out.

We've been unable to establish any form of communication with Carmona. Yet all of our long-range scans are coming back negative and the world's major population centres seem to be intact. It's possible the meteor shower has disrupted interstellar broadcasts, though we will continue to try and raise them. Shuttles are being readied to deploy rescue teams planetside if needed, though landing at the capital's spaceport could prove difficult. Scans show it is at capacity, and there's something else. This doesn't look like a world affected by the war. It's thriving. A living relic from humanity's golden age. I wish you were here with me to see it. Carmona is what Tanis was... and could be again.

Leo shook his head in disbelief. This wasn't how it had happened. Carmona had been devastated several days before his father arrived... or so he'd been told.

Fifth transmission, encrypted.

If the regime are listening, I expect my life will soon be over. I've taken every precaution, but even that might not be enough. Regardless, someone has to speak the truth and someone has to hear it. Mayer is dead, and Paulus arrested. Our liaison has assumed direct command. He lied to us, and like a trusting child I believed him. There was no meteor shower, nor any need for a rescue mission. We were never here to try and save Carmona, but destroy it.

Why? Because they refused to be bound by regime law. For wanting to be free. When Mayer objected he was killed, and Paulus relieved of his command soon after. I was only spared because I managed to convince the liaison I agreed with the regime's sick plan.

There's more. The Reckoning *is not a medical ship - she's a planet killer. The blueprints I saw had been doctored, meaning someone on Earth has gone to great lengths to ensure this mission's secrecy and success. I'm afraid, Lina. Afraid of what they'll do to Tanis if I refuse to partake in this genocide. To save one world I've no choice but to condemn another. Do you see? I don't have a choice. I never did.*

Final transmission, encrypted.

It's over. The fleet has already departed. I've been given leave to stay and search for survivors, but there's little chance of finding anyone alive. Carmona is gone. They fought, but the liaison had anticipated they would. I stood by and watched him murder twenty billion people. There was nothing I could have done to stop it. I dared not try. I've seen what the regime are capable of - what they would do to Tanis if I faltered. I've not slept for days. Without sleep I can't think. Forgive me, Lina. Forgive me for what I've done, because I can't.

Leo threw the blasphemous document to the floor and stood up. It couldn't be true. His father was a good man, not a murderer.

The confusion and anger he felt after reading such hurtful lies briefly threatened to overwhelm him. Every word had surely been fabricated by vindictive wretches bent on destroying them. Wretches like Turilli. Only the vice-regent was depraved enough to play such an underhand trick.

Leo shook with unbridled rage and clenched his hands into tight fists at his sides, knowing he could not let this pass. He wasn't afraid of Turilli or his lackeys and vowed to make them pay for the insult. Leo hadn't even thought about what he was going to do when the tidal wave of emotions he was drowning in triggered a long-repressed memory. He remembered another time when he'd believed an equally cruel trick was being played on him.

"I'm sorry you had to find out like this, Leo."

A familiar voice pierced the silence. Its tone was cold and level. Leo looked up but no longer recognised the man standing before him.

Giovanni Rossi stood impassively in the doorway of his office, expressionless, arms folded across his chest. He'd wanted to tell Leo the truth every day for the last twelve years, but had always convinced himself he wasn't ready to hear it. Now he had no choice. He'd lived a full, remarkable life, and couldn't leave those he loved with lies in his heart.

Leo didn't say anything. The words fell like hammer blows, destroying all of his childhood preconceptions and naiveties in an instant. His world, once filled with light, was falling into darkness.

"I've no right to ask your forgiveness," the regent continued, "but if you'd let me explain..."

"Explain?" Leo's voice was charged with emotion. The man he called father wasn't sorry at all. He'd beguiled him to this juncture for reasons unknown, allowed him to find the folder and have a sheet of paper do what he could not. Leo took an involuntary step back, appalled to learn he'd grown up idolising a coward. A coward and a murderer.

"Yes," Rossi insisted, making no attempt to hide his self-disgust. He knew who he was, *what* he was, and what he had to do.

Leo struggled to contain himself. "Why should I?" he spat, his voice rising with each word. "There's nothing you can say to justify what you've done. To think I loved you, defended you! How does it feel to have slain billions? I hope you suffered for it and die afraid and alone like they did."

"I've suffered, but I don't expect you to understand. You weren't there."

"I was," said Leo.

Rossi shook his head. "You've no idea what would have happened if I'd refused. You'll never understand what I can never forget. I watched a planet die and the only word they could think of to describe it was 'victory'. I made a choice and relive the consequences every time I close my eyes. I wish things could be different but they can't, though if I had to do it again I would."

"You... you don't regret this?" Leo stammered, unable to quite believe what he was hearing.

"You're not seeing the bigger picture! One world died but another lived. Put yourself in my position and tell me you'd have done otherwise. Consider the alternative. There were agents on every ship. They'd have killed me, lain waste to Carmona then turned their guns on Tanis. I wanted my people to survive, not fade quietly into the void. I saved them all and in return lost everything."

"Are you done?" Leo growled through gritted teeth. "Just answer the fucking question."

The regent flinched at his harsh tone. It was the first time he'd ever demanded anything of him.

"I regret so many had to die," he said solemnly, "but not the choices I made that day. I did what I had to do to save my world... and save you."

"And Carmona? What about everyone else?"

"There was no-one else."

His words stunned Leo into silence. The thought of being the last of his people was too much for him to bear. How could he continue their traditions when he didn't remember anything about them? Who would honour their accomplishments, their history? An entire civilisation had been wiped out and all that remained was a mass grave lost among the stars. He wanted to close his ears and call Rossi a liar, but the regent wasn't finished.

"I saw the bombs fall. No-one could have survived the storm that broke upon Carmona, but you did. Improbable as it sounds, I'd like to believe I was *meant* to find you and raise you as my son."

Something inside Leo snapped. "I'm not your son. And you're not my father. You killed my father. My mother. Maybe a brother or sister I never even knew existed. I was just a pawn in your quest for redemption, adopted to ease your guilt. You let this happen and all you could think about was how best to use me. You should have tried stopping it!"

"And ended up like Mayer? Dead, with my family killed? I didn't knowingly place myself in that situation, Leo. One day you'll be forced to make a choice, destined to be damned whichever way you turn. We are, all of us, at the mercy of others."

"Not me." Blinded by his anger, Leo dismissed the regent's argument out of hand. The reasons he gave were excuses, and excuses were the refuge of the weak. "Why not fight them?" he demanded, convinced Rossi had made the wrong choice. "You'd gained their trust. All you had to do was shoot down the other ships."

"You make it sound so simple. But it wasn't. Another fleet would have followed, and another if that had failed. I had one ship, not an armada. I led a four hundred-man crew, not an army."

"There was an army on Carmona! Twenty billion people would have fought and died for you, but you didn't even give them the chance. You could have been their saviour, not their destroyer. They'd have followed you to Earth and the heart of this cancer if you'd asked. Even if you'd fallen short, far better to have died free, fighting for what you believed."

Rossi felt a searing pain in his chest but ignored it. "I was afraid and in no mind to lead anyone. But you can."

The regent knew Leo had it within himself to right his wrongs, though convincing him he could was another matter. His passion and willingness to confront injustice filled him with hope. Humanity's future looked a little brighter.

"Afraid?" Leo fumed, entirely unaware of what Rossi wanted. "You're a spineless coward, too proud to admit the folly of your actions and too weak to tell me yourself."

"Would you have believed me if I had?"

"I..."

Rossi snapped his fingers. "Exactly. You'd have thought me a senile old fool and taken my words no more seriously than the delusional ravings of a madman. This was the best way. The only way. I had to warn you what atrocities the regime are capable of because I didn't want to see you forced into committing one like I was. You deserve to know the truth."

"And what am I supposed to do with it?"

"Act."

"I don't want to act," said Leo. "I want to know who issued your orders and why you made me join the contingent if you hate the regime so much."

"I promised I would."

"Promised who?"

"The woman I loved."

"Stop speaking in riddles!" Leo shouted, furious Rossi was still trying to evade his questions. "Who?"

Rossi didn't respond immediately. He was gripped by anxiety and struggled to breathe. It pained him to revisit the past and reopen old wounds he'd thought healed. "My wife," he said after a while. "You already know her name."

"Lina?"

The regent nodded. "Angelina. I told her everything and didn't even consider the effect it would have on her. I realised this too late, returning to Tanis as quickly as I could, but my actions had already claimed another life. Hers, by her own hand. I made the nobility swear they would never speak of it to you or anyone else. She couldn't live with what I'd done, but before the end made me promise to care for you and prepare you for the trials ahead."

Leo's eyes narrowed. "What trials?"

"Someone has to put an end to this regime's tyranny. Someone has to fight them."

"You're deluded," Leo scoffed, finally grasping the magnitude of what Rossi was asking him to do. "Deluded and arrogant to think I'd let you use me in such a manner."

"So you'll do nothing?"

"Don't you dare lecture me about morality."

"Leo, please, just listen," Rossi pleaded. "Maybe their intentions were pure to begin with, but at some point the message got lost. Power can corrupt those you believe to be incorruptible. The regime feed off our ignorance and willingness to accept there can never be anything better. We're so mired in our fight to survive we overlook their broken promises and unjust laws. They say taxes are necessary and that population control is for our own good, but I've seen what came before and how far we've fallen."

"Your point?" Leo asked when the regent did not continue.

"The point is that people have grown accustomed to it. It'll take an unprecedented event to open their eyes and an even greater force to unite them."

Leo scratched his forehead. "You mean Carmona?"

"No. They're far too clever to be undone by something so routine. Manipulation is an art they've perfected over many years. When a planet dies at their hands they rewrite its history, and Carmona was no exception. The records list a meteor shower as the sole factor behind your homeworld's destruction."

"If they went to that much trouble, why risk keeping me alive?"

"They didn't risk anything," said Rossi. "Several agents were sent here to observe you and see how much you remembered."

"I remembered nothing."

"Only the name of the world you came from. The doctors said your memory loss was trauma related and likely to be permanent. The regime seemed content enough with that to let me take you in."

This simple remark seemed to infuriate Leo further. His face glowed with anger and he fixed the regent with a stare that would have made lesser men crumble. He suspected very different motives behind his adoption. The regime weren't likely to let him live unless they stood to gain from his survival, and what better way to profit than use him to convince the people of their mercy and compassion? They had saved him, after all. Leo couldn't bring himself to listen to or trust another word. He made for the door, ashamed to have played a part in this deception and incensed he'd not seen through it.

Rossi moved to stop him, the pain in his chest now unbearable. "Leo, when I die Turilli will be regent. If you care about these people then you must protect them. You'll know how. But you can't stop with Tanis - there's too much at stake. I've left a file in your room. Please read it. Act."

Still reeling from the shock of what he'd discovered, Leo barged past him without a word. He stumbled out into the corridor and ran. He ran without looking back as if all the demons of old were after him.

In the regent's office, Giovanni Rossi fell to the floor clutching his chest and whispered his adopted son's name one final time.

10

Marcus Rathen had never seen the streets of Divinity so deserted. The usually bustling plazas at the city's peak were empty, and the glittering emporiums that served the nobility around the clock stood closed. They would remain so until Landfall Day had passed, monuments in darkness devoid of people or purpose. Though the pounding energy of a million parties and galas pulsated throughout the city, Marcus felt a degree of sadness at the surreal scene laid out before him. Without those who made Divinity what it was, it had been transformed into a hollow, soulless place.

Marcus moved with a speed and grace that belied his imposing stature. Though tall with a solid broad-shouldered build, he'd always prided himself on his ability to move quickly and quietly. As he traversed the avenues and winding passageways around the noble residences, his thoughts strayed from the mission he was currently undertaking to the day's events.

This year's Landfall feast had been a quiet but thoroughly enjoyable affair nonetheless. He'd spent most of it reminiscing about old times with Leo, then danced with several of the palace's noblewomen after his friend had left. Having quickly tired of the party and missing Leo's company, he'd slipped away and resolved to make good his earlier promise to him.

Realising the Phalanx could be out patrolling the area, Marcus slowed his pace to a leisurely stroll so as not to arouse suspicion. Though an enforcer would never directly challenge the adopted son of a noble house, all incidents, however minor, were recorded in detail and promptly investigated. His parents might not care, but an overzealous executor would, and he knew Lucas Turilli had plenty of those roaming the city at all hours.

Marcus checked his watch. He'd wanted to arrive at the installation designated *Chimera* before sunrise, yet for all his enthusiasm found he had miscalculated how long it would take him to get there. Refusing to dwell on the error he pressed on, never doubting he'd succeed despite this momentary setback. Instead of being disheartened he embraced the situation, having learned to adapt, believe in his abilities and trust his instincts. Those who didn't were doomed to fail. Luna had taught him that.

He'd admired the youngest daughter of the van Dyck house from a distance for some time, envying the friendship she and Leo shared. She was spirited and earnest, not to mention beautiful, and if Leo had intended to court her then he would have surely done so by now. It was obvious they cared for one another, but no more than a brother and sister did. Now he came to regret his wild youth. How could he convince her he'd changed and put his philandering ways behind him? He didn't want to ask for Leo's help regarding the matter, but his nervousness around her might well leave him with no choice. All the other nobles his age were engaged or married, and Marcus had decided it was time for him to settle down as well. They could leave Tanis together and start a family on a better, brighter world.

Marcus sighed wistfully. His dreams were just that - quixotic fantasies destined to remain unrealised. Putting thoughts of Luna aside, he refocused his attention on the mission Leo had given him.

The Chimera site was a level down from the palace, in a zone classified as 'unsafe' by the regime. This made Marcus curious. The noble houses had prevented alterations to their beloved cityscape for years, so why relent now? Either the regent had managed to convince them or there was some other factor behind their abrupt submission. Marcus knew there were many who wished to see the project flounder, so suspected it had been forced upon them rather than agreed. He chuckled quietly, remembering his parents' initial reaction. The discomfort felt and voiced by the frustrated nobles was a source of perpetual amusement for both him and Leo.

It was a warm, clear night, and nothing escaped Marcus' heightened senses. He could hear the gentle humming of the city's air purification units, and the sound of raised voices approaching him from behind. He continued walking, unwilling to risk even the quickest of glances for fear of drawing attention to himself. He hoped that whoever it was would turn off down some side street or alley, but the three voices grew louder and the irregular tread of footsteps dragging on marble became audible.

Thinking quickly, Marcus left the main street and descended a flight of stairs between two mansions. He rounded a corner and stopped, waiting in the shadows until he'd heard the footsteps recede and the voices subside. Though a skilful fighter and more than able to handle himself, he had no time to brawl with drunks.

Marcus let another minute elapse before resuming his journey. He'd planned his route carefully, and walking was the safest way to travel.

In Divinity, walking was the *only* way to travel.

Rusting metal frames supporting miles of track and cables were dotted all over the city, but the shuttles that once ran on them had long since disappeared. Marcus had heard stories of automated carriages and pedal-driven transports - he'd even seen the contingent's gunships flying off into the desert - and wondered if Leo was right.

Were these just the melodramatic lamentations of bitter individuals, or had a golden age of technology and progress really once existed? And how had Man come to Tanis if it hadn't?

Yes, he'd seen the gunships. And longed for the chance to join the contingent like Leo. The more his parents tried to dissuade him, the more determined he'd become. It was his future, not theirs. Tonight he'd prove them wrong and prove to himself he was ready.

Four marble stairways linked the city's highest level to the one below, and Marcus knew all of them would be unguarded. The nobility were free to move about as they pleased, their luxurious estates occupying eighteen levels in total, and safeguarded by a minimal enforcer presence. They were shielded from the middle-classes by a huge concrete wall, complete with sentry towers, electric fences and redoubts, and the elite operatives of the Phalanx ensured no undesirable ever set foot above the nineteenth. Marcus imagined security at the Chimera site on level two would be equally formidable.

The stairway he'd chosen was the one closest to the installation and furthest from the palace. Its proximity to the site put many off using it, and this meant Marcus could expect to encounter far fewer people than on the other three. Indeed, by the time he'd reached the bottom he'd passed two councillors and a menial, none of whom appeared the least bit interested in his presence. Nevertheless, he remained wary and would stop on occasion to see if he was being followed, taking advantage of the brief pauses to plan his next move.

Half an hour passed and Marcus kept walking. The Chimera loomed up ahead of him.

Whatever the regime were building he'd never seen anything like it before. The site alone was massive, and the domed citadel that rose up out of it rivalled the regent's palace for size. He'd watched it grow and take shape from his chamber, but only now did he truly appreciate its enormity, along with the hands and minds behind this staggering feat of engineering. It might well take more than a change of clothes and pair of wire cutters to get anywhere near the superstructure, but they were all Marcus had brought with him and would have to do.

As he neared the site's perimeter, he noticed the entire area was bathed in a luminous red glow. Safe zones such as the one he was about to leave were lit by a more natural blue hue; the different colours helping Divinity's more illustrious residents avoid dangerous or unsightly districts.

He'd been tasked with infiltrating one.

Manors and penthouses provided him with ample cover as he made his approach. A mesh fence ringed the installation, but there were no enforcers in sight. Marcus couldn't believe his luck. Ducking down behind a wall some thirty yards from the fence, he removed his tunic to reveal a baggy shirt and black trousers. His politician's garb had served its purpose. From here, he'd adopt the persona of a poor, downtrodden outcast seeking work. He discarded the tunic in an artificial hedgerow, burying it deep among the plastic leaves and branches. A grin eased across his lips as he inched closer to the site. His parents wouldn't be happy, but they'd just have to buy him another.

Marcus moved from cover to cover, trying to make as little noise as possible. At last he reached the fence, surprised to find it completely unguarded. Then he saw why.

The colossal size of the Chimera made it appear much closer than it actually was. The superstructure sat at the centre of the site behind another, taller fence - this one protected by enforcers, metal detectors, motion sensors and a fully armed gunship for good measure. Marcus cursed silently. He'd anticipated a substantial military presence but hadn't reckoned on the two fences being so far apart. His heart sank as he realised he wasn't quick enough to cover the distance without getting spotted. If he was lucky he might have got a little over half way, but no further. The entire site was too well illuminated and patrolled. To compound his problems, the first signs of dawn were beginning to appear in the eastern sky.

Skirting the perimeter fence trying to find a weakness wasn't an option. The area was far too large to get around in the limited time he had. He could have turned back, but the thought of admitting defeat did not sit well with him. On top of that, he'd then suffer the indignity of explaining to Leo why he'd failed. *But only if he found out...*

Marcus stopped himself before he went any further. Deceiving his best friend would make him no better than Turilli and his ilk.

There had to be another way in. Surely there were outflows or vents - maybe even smokestacks. Maybe...

The sound of an approaching gunship instantly caught his attention. He searched the sky but couldn't see anything. The noise intensified and after a few seconds the buildings around him started to shake. Whatever was coming sounded much bigger than a gunship.

Marcus strained to get a better view of the city, then flung himself to the floor as a large bulk freighter passed overhead. The ungainly-looking ship slowed as it came in to land - almost exactly half way between the two fences.

Grumbling profusely, Marcus struggled to his feet. Though unhurt, his instinctive dive had been unnecessary; there being little chance anyone had seen him. He retreated back to the shadows, complaining as he went, and watched the freighter slowly descend. Upon landing, its cargo bay doors swung open and out poured a mass of people instead of the building materials he'd presumed were aboard.

Leo was right. All the equipment needed to complete the project was likely already here, but the demand for workers remained.

More were emerging all the time. It finally dawned on him that he could use the freighter's arrival to his advantage. Some of the enforcers had left their posts to shepherd the workers inside, while others lined up to process them. Seizing his chance, Marcus took out the pair of wire cutters and began to cut a hole in the fence. He worked as quickly as he could, opening a gap without removing any of the wire mesh. That way it would spring back into position when he was through, concealing the breach from all but the keenest eye.

Crawling inside on his hands and knees, Marcus waited, fearing he'd tripped a silent alarm. He lay still, ready to run at any moment, listening out for panicked cries or the wailing of a claxon. A minute passed, then two. The enforcers continued to bark orders at the new arrivals, splitting them into groups. Marcus determined it was best to try and join an established team and discreetly quiz the workers for information. Those stepping off the freighter would know as much as he did - nothing.

Feeling certain his presence had gone unnoticed, he stood up and made for the ship. He moved cautiously at first, then broke into a sprint across the tarmac. From here he had to act like he belonged.

Marcus approached the freighter from behind, using its gargantuan hull for cover. With the enforcers distracted, none of them questioned him as he casually joined the tide of workers streaming towards the Chimera.

There were equal numbers of men and women in the crowd, some as young as ten and some much older. One or two made disparaging remarks about the site, but most said nothing, trudging forward in silence. Marcus wondered if they were here by choice, and whether the regime had lured or strong-armed them into coming to Tanis. Either way, he was puzzled as to why so many workers were still needed when the Chimera looked close to completion.

Leo had speculated it was a terraforming machine. The building was painted a dull grey and resembled an observatory, but the regent owned three and they were seldom used. *A museum, then?* Marcus shook his head. No, this was something else, and before he'd finished he intended to discover what.

First, though, he'd have to come up with a story. One that would convince the clerks and supervisors he was meant to be there when he wasn't. He didn't need to maintain the charade forever, just long enough to complete his mission. Marcus knew the moment an over-efficient bean counter started making enquiries he'd be forced to make a quick exit.

Taking stock of his surroundings, he spied a group of workers milling around away from where the freighter's passengers were being processed. He broke rank and headed straight for them, breathing a huge sigh of relief when none of the enforcers challenged him. Marcus tried to avoid making snap decisions, but had he waited any longer they could well have gone back inside.

The team consisted of six men in total, but his attention was drawn towards two bickering individuals and the curly-haired giant who watched over them. Marcus hoped this man - who he assumed was their supervisor - would accept him and thereby quash any complaints that might arise from the others. Confident and full of self-belief, he marched up to them without giving his introduction any real thought.

"Good morning," he offered, somewhat awkwardly. "I'm-" He got no further before one of the unsavoury-looking men interrupted him.

"Good fucking morning? Well, I've heard it all now. Look here, Karlsen - some posh prick reckons it's a good morning. Are you lost, mate? Can't tell a penthouse from a building site?"

"Shut it, Saul." The tall man took one step forward and his quarrelsome colleague fell silent. "You'll have to excuse our resident lout," he said, his stern gaze shifting to Marcus. "Every site has one, but here there are two. Lock either of them in a room alone and they'd start a fight with themselves. Now that's done with, I believe you were about to introduce yourself."

Marcus cleared his throat, cringing at the inadequacy of his opening remark. "The name's Lucas," he said, thinking quickly. "I've been assigned detail on your team. It's a pleasure."

The giant shook his hand warmly. "Likewise. I'm Kurt Steinsson, team leader. You must be Stanley's replacement."

"Yes," Marcus replied, without hesitating. "Though I wasn't told what happened to him."

Steinsson grinned. "No matter. Welcome to the Chimera. I'll show you the ropes, get you started. There isn't much time, so let's go."

As Steinsson showed him inside, Marcus disposed of the wire cutters in an unattended toolbox.

He was in.

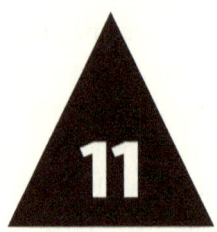

11

It was mid-morning when Lucas Turilli entered the regent's office. At first he stood and stared in disbelief at the sight that greeted him, then allowed himself a smile. His time had come at last. Giovanni Rossi was dead.

Nothing could stop him now. He began to chuckle, amused by the demise of the man who'd sought to deny him his dream. He'd waited years for this moment and was going to savour every second - even if it meant temporarily relaxing his guard.

Rossi had lived to help the people. He was going to exploit them.

Drunk with power, Turilli strutted about the office plotting his next move. Those loyal to the old regent would be given the chance to swear fealty to him. Many already had, but there were still some dissenting voices.

Turilli looked forward to silencing them personally.

Having decided on his next course of action, the mad regent's attention wandered back to Rossi. Any normal person would have immediately alerted the palace's medical staff and undertakers, but Turilli wasn't normal. He stood over his rival's lifeless corpse, trying to figure out how he'd met such an ignominious end. He inspected the body from a safe distance, not wanting to get too close.

After failing to find any injuries or signs of a struggle, he concluded Rossi's death had been the result of a heart attack. Satisfied with his diagnosis, he turned away. There was no need for an autopsy to tell him what he already knew. Turilli smirked, betting himself he'd be a far more adept doctor than the overpaid, arrogant dolts who attended the nobility.

With Rossi gone, Turilli could do as he liked. The thought warmed him as he lounged back in the regent's chair. *His* chair. Earth would hear of his succession in due course, but not before he had removed all traces of the old regency from Tanis.

He'd start with the office. Its current condition did not befit a man of his status. Menials would have to redecorate and furnish it with all the pomp and splendour a regent deserved. Rossi never made use of the power available to him, but Turilli would. He planned to advance the careers of those who did his bidding, surrounding himself with a cadre of loyal and devoted individuals. Any who challenged him, dared to disagree with him, would find promotion nigh on impossible to achieve.

Luther had been one of Rossi's closest advisors, but showed promise. He could have replaced him easily enough, but had decided against this when considering the time it took to train a new administrator. He was prodigiously skilled and hard-working - the perfect servant in Turilli's mind. The regent hoped to turn him into a more willing, obedient subject. Most importantly, he wanted to prove to himself that he could. Now Luther had enjoyed a taste of what the new regime offered, Turilli anticipated he'd crave success and power all the more. Now he had something to lose he would do just about anything to hold onto it.

Turilli revelled in his triumph, amazed at how easy it had been. He reflected on how quickly one's priorities shifted when exposed to a radical idea or emotion they'd never experienced before. In time it would occupy their thoughts and consume them. Soon enough they'd find they could not live without it. Leaning back in the chair, Turilli put his feet on the desk and closed his eyes. Though there was no-one on Tanis capable of appreciating his brilliant schemes, maybe one day someone would.

And yet for all his genius, one thing gave him cause for concern.

Several high-ranking ministers had taken it upon themselves to meddle in his affairs. Now the Chimera project was nearing completion, interest in it had begun to grow. The eyes of the nobility were fixed on the construction sites, and Luther was asking questions. Chiara knew too much. As director of engineering, she'd become obsessed with discovering what was going on there. Whether she'd found out or was merely trying to impress the regent by exaggerating the project's status, Turilli couldn't take the chance. Apart from him, only Rossi had known the truth about what they were hiding, and he intended to keep it that way. Security was tight and there had been no leaks thus far, but the possibility Rossi may have told someone before he'd died unnerved him. Turilli's masters on Earth demanded absolute secrecy be maintained, and he dreaded to think what might happen if he failed them.

Hopefully the way in which he'd dealt with Chiara would dissuade others from interfering.

But what if Rossi had told Leo? He couldn't cow the saintly boy into submission like he'd done his ministers. Equally, promises of power or material gain were pointless. Turilli feared Leo was smart enough to see through his lies and might even seek to replace him as regent.

Turilli pulled at his hair in frustration. He despised Leo yet admired his purity. He was young, opinionated and highly intelligent. But Rossi's brat also had a strong sense of right and wrong, and the regent knew nothing he said or did would ever convince him to see things his way. Turilli decided Leo was an obstacle on the road to glory, and intended to deal with the upstart as he did all who opposed him.

His plan was simple. A heart attack hadn't killed Rossi. Leo had.

Having learned he wouldn't be regent, the resentful boy had murdered his father and attempted a coup. He'd gathered his supporters and moved against Turilli, but the Royal Guard had stopped them before they could reach him.

This was perfect!

Turilli would pretend to be as shocked as everyone else upon hearing of Leo's betrayal. Those who refused to believe his version of events would indirectly be calling him a liar. The regent cackled in delight.

Someday he'd have to think up a new punishment for insubordination.

To ensure success, Turilli thought it best to keep his sordid scheme to himself. That way there would be no leaks. He didn't want any traitorous nobles running off to warn Leo and ruin the surprise he had planned for him. The boy might have been smart, but he was determined to prove himself smarter.

He'd not see this coming.

Turilli mused for a moment on why Rossi had adopted Leo. The regent supposed he'd found raising a child a rewarding experience, but couldn't for the life of him figure out how. What were children but unwelcome distractions from life's true pleasures? They cost time and money, both of which would surely be better spent on him. A child's purpose, it seemed, was to perpetually torment those who'd brought it into the world. Turilli nodded as if to affirm what he was thinking. He'd worked tirelessly to build up his fearsome reputation and was not about to let some mewling infant destroy it overnight.

He swivelled round in the chair and stood up, pacing about with his hands behind his back as he contemplated the future. He'd convert or crush those loyal to Rossi, bring Gethsemane to heel and oversee the completion of the Chimera project in short order. Promotion would swiftly follow, and with the success of his plan a mere formality, Turilli couldn't help but laugh. He laughed long and hard until his sides hurt and he had tears streaming from his eyes.

It was then he realised he was no longer alone.

A nervous-looking executor stood trembling before him, trying in vain to hide the fear on which Turilli fed. His unexpected appearance startled the regent, sending him over the edge and into madness.

"What do you want?" he snarled, furious to have been caught off-guard. "It better be important. I'll cut out your heart and feed it to the dogs in undercity if you dare waste my time!" The poor executor struggled to respond, his eyes fixed on the dead body. "Speak!" Turilli roared, marching up to him. "Stop snivelling and start talking!"

A moment passed before the executor regained his composure. "My lord," he managed eventually, "forgive my intrusion, but-"

Without warning, Turilli slapped him across the face. "Shut up. You're lucky I'm in a forgiving mood. I told you not to bother me unless you had important news."

"But my lord, I do," the executor insisted. "We've received a transmission from Earth. They request you contact them immediately."

This simple statement evoked a sudden change in Turilli. His usual bluster and self-confidence evaporated, leaving behind a pallid, expressionless shell. A hundred questions, none of which he knew the answer to, raced through his tortured mind.

Why had Earth made contact now? His reports on the project had all been thorough and accurate. Didn't they trust him? Perhaps that wasn't the reason at all. Maybe they were already aware of Rossi's passing. But how could they be?

Fearing the worst, Turilli stormed out of the office and headed back to his chamber. The executor watched him go, relieved to have escaped with only a stinging cheek this time, then went back to worrying about what to do with Rossi's body.

Turilli cursed out loud as he went. Leo could wait. Before taking a life he may first need to save one.

12

As the sun reached its zenith in the summer sky, Divinity began to stir. Landfall Day had dawned at last, and an air of optimism hung over the city as it did this time every year. While the nobility followed up the previous night's festivities with lavish banquets, the poor sought to make the most of this one day they had to themselves. Many would spend it in the relative comfort of their own homes, surrounded by friends and family, and plan for a better future. But no sooner had the day arrived than it was gone for another year, the call of the forges turning hopes to fears and denying millions the chance to ever live their dreams.

Leo sat on the edge of his bed, staring into space. He'd exhausted himself reliving the previous night's events, unable to get any sleep as his emotions careered between grief and anger. The young noble had been dealt a blow from which he would struggle to recover. He couldn't forgive or forget anything Rossi had said, let alone ever trust him again. The regent's revelation had thrown his world into turmoil, leading him to question everything he'd once thought to be pure and true.

Hate filled his heart. An all-consuming need for vengeance was tempered only by Leo's desire to preserve the memory of his people. The ghosts of Carmona cried out for justice, for someone to expose the lie and bring those responsible to account. Leo swore to find the faceless cowards who'd condemned his homeworld and pursue them until either he or they were dead.

The idea of an emotional, revenge-driven crusade against the regime initially appealed to him. But the more Leo thought about it, the more he came to accept that there were better ways of honouring the lost. They wouldn't have wanted him to lash out in anger, to kill or die for them, and he knew it. The galaxy had seen enough death already.

Leo showed great restraint when presented with the truth. He confined his vengeful thoughts to the prison of his mind, refusing to let emotions get the better of him. It hurt to admit Rossi had been right about anything, but the regime was far too strong for any one man or woman to face alone. Leo intended to use what he'd discovered against them, though until the day their fleets lay broken and their armies scattered he would have to divert his energy elsewhere. There was work to be done on Tanis, and he remained in a position to help those far less fortunate than himself. Through selfless gestures and small acts of kindness his people would live on.

Instead of obsessing over what had happened, Leo decided to move out of the palace and into one of the estates bordering the residential zone. He didn't know how he'd feel when he saw Rossi again, and believed all things pointed to the time being right to strike out on his own. To him, it made perfect sense. With the population of undercity feeling persecuted and powerless, he couldn't well command their respect if he remained in the palace. The move would take him away from a superficial, pampered lifestyle but not his friends, meaning there was no danger of an over-imaginative nobility spreading rumours of a rift between him and the regent.

Leo managed a half smile, recalling his adoptive father's disdain for gossip. The old man had been an inspiration - one of the few regime officials he'd both admired and adored. Now everything had changed. Their relationship was characterised by mutual trust and honesty, or so he'd thought, which is what had made the betrayal particularly hard for him to take. Leo could neither condone Rossi's actions nor forgive him for what he'd done, electing to rebuff the regent's excuses and face the future without his guidance.

Seeing no reason to delay, Leo gathered his thoughts and stretched his legs. He sighed mournfully, then pulled two large camo holdalls out from under the bed. They were all he needed to pack what little he owned.

A noise in the corridor distracted him before he got any further. Someone was trying to deactivate the room's security system. Leo had no time to react as the door to his chamber was prized open and an enforcer stepped inside.

"We need to get out of the palace." The enforcer's face was partly obscured by a military cap and pair of shades, but Leo recognised her voice immediately. "I don't know how long we've got," she continued, walking over to him, "but we have to leave, *now*."

Luna looked completely different garbed in the black armour of the contingent. Her golden hair was tucked neatly under the cap and the smile she had worn last night was gone. Leo tried to hide his surprise at the ease with which she'd been able to break in, annoyed to discover the system protecting him was anything but secure. Bemused by her behaviour and unable to figure out why she'd turned up unannounced, he took the initiative and asked.

"Rossi's dead," she replied flatly. "We can't stay here - there's no-one to stop Turilli now. Throw us one of those bags and I'll help you pack."

Leo reluctantly complied as he mulled over her words. Turilli was a devious, savage man - regent in all but name - and didn't need to use Rossi's death as an excuse to crush his enemies. He'd be off planning his succession ceremony the moment he found out, unless circumstance had presented him with the means to eliminate one of his rivals. Luna's appearance told him that not only must such an opportunity exist, but the threat to his life was genuine.

"Why Turilli hasn't acted is beyond me," Luna said suddenly, stuffing some of Leo's clothes into the holdall. "He'd arranged an audience with your father for earlier this morning, so he surely knows. Whatever the reason, we should be grateful."

"Or wary." Leo frowned. "How did you find out?"

"Rossi wanted a report on the academies. My parents sent me to deliver it."

"On Landfall Day?"

Luna nodded. "They're hosting Kastor and his cronies and-"

"Wanted you out of the way for a couple of hours," Leo finished for her, worried Turilli's inaction was merely a ploy to ensnare them both.

"Something like that. I'd have made myself scarce anyway. There's not enough room in our suite for all those obnoxious people and their egos. I took the report, went straight to the regent's office and that's when I found him."

Leo raised an eyebrow. "Was it Turilli?"

"I don't know. He's certainly capable, but why not do it sooner? Regardless of what happened, he's now in a position to accuse whoever he wants of murder."

"No-one would believe I killed my own father," Leo scoffed, trying to piece everything together.

"The nobles will believe anything Turilli tells them. They might not like him, but they're far more scared of him than they are of you."

Leo knew she spoke the truth. If Turilli declared him responsible for Rossi's death, none would dare argue otherwise. The majority of Divinity's elite were passive hypocrites, more than happy to lambast their new regent behind closed doors but too afraid to publically challenge him. Had Rossi gone peacefully in his sleep, then the palace doctors would have announced his passing right away. But he'd died under suspicious circumstances, meaning whoever found him first could either dutifully report his death or use the situation to their advantage.

Leo didn't need to think twice about what Turilli intended to do. "I wasn't aware he saw me as a threat," he said, still finding it strange the mad regent would want to come after him.

"Maybe not," said Luna, "but are you willing to take the chance? Turilli's a paranoid psychopath whose thoughts and actions defy logic. You can't predict a man like that. He's just as likely to wage war on a servant who spoke ill of him once as he is an outspoken critic. With Rossi gone he might try to implicate one of the houses or focus his efforts on destroying an individual. Any with the strength to resist him - those with dignity and honour - are now in danger because they represent the opposite of what he stands for. There's the possibility he'll leave you alone today, but what about tomorrow? You're one of the few nobles he couldn't touch before and I'm not going to sit back and wait for him to strike now."

"So why hasn't he? It could be a trap," Leo pressed.

Having filled the holdall, Luna zipped it shut and laughed lightly. "I wouldn't worry. Turilli lacks the restraint to plan or think things through in such detail. He'll charge headlong into exploiting any opportunity that comes his way, so I'd wager something else has distracted him."

Leo wondered what could possibly be more important to the regent than the chance to dispose of a hated rival. He started to pack the remainder of his belongings into the second holdall, noticing for the first time a thin grey folder on the bed behind him.

Luna had spotted it too. "Are you going to bring that or just stare at it?" she asked, frustrated by Leo's lack of urgency.

"Huh? Oh, sorry..." he mumbled, picking up the folder and throwing it into the bag. "That's everything."

"You sure?"

"Yes. So where to now?"

Luna shook her head slowly. "Get changed."

"What?"

She motioned towards the cupboard where Leo's enforcer armour was hanging. "We'll be harder to find. Fewer questions. If Turilli wants you dead he'll send the Royal Guard, and you'll stand no more chance of outrunning them in that tunic than I do in a dress." Leo grinned and did as she asked. "My parents have a private estate on the fifth level," she continued, keeping watch by the door while he changed. "They never use it. Every year my father buys a newer, bigger mansion just to flaunt his wealth or outdo another noble. I don't think he's lived in any of them, but he didn't even have a security system installed in this one." Sensing Leo was looking away, she stole a quick glance at him and whispered, "not that it would've been a problem if he had..."

"All right," said Leo, wrestling with his armour and unaware Luna was now eyeing him intently. "We go to your parents' estate. Then what?"

Luna shouldered the heavier of the two holdalls. "We wait for Turilli to show his hand. I just hope I'm wrong and this is all over quickly, because if it isn't... well, I haven't really thought about that."

Leo finished dressing, took one final look around his room and followed her out into the corridor.

They ran as fast as they could down winding passageways and flights of stairs, never needing to pause or catch their breath. An enforcer's armour appeared cumbersome, but was designed to allow for maximum movement and flexibility. Hidden power units enhanced the wearer's strength, and the interlocking ceramic plates were robust enough to deflect bullets. While Leo was allowed to keep his for as long as he remained in the contingent, he guessed Luna had either appropriated hers from the palace armoury or one of her sisters.

They made it all the way to the main lobby before Luna stopped, but it wasn't because she was tired.

"What is it?" Leo asked, glancing around nervously.

"I'm not sure."

There was a hint of excitement in her voice which Leo found strange given the circumstances. "Well, at least one of us is having a good time," he remarked off-handedly.

"We could always stop by the archive," Luna retorted. "Isn't that your idea of fun?"

"No..."

"Then I must have heard wrong." Knowing how easy it was to wind Leo up, she couldn't resist teasing him a little more.

"What did you hear?" he asked.

"Oh, nothing. I wouldn't let the opinions of my friends and parents worry you."

Leo's face turned red with embarrassment. "They talk about me? To you?"

"All the time. Say, are there any emporiums between here and the fifth?"

"Several, why?"

"I can buy you a sense of humour on the way."

Despite himself, Leo laughed. "Thanks." Luna's good-natured, playful banter had helped allay his fears and ease his mind. She had the uncanny ability to remain positive whatever the situation. It was her gift. "At least it looks like you were wrong about Turilli," he said, casting his eyes around the deserted lobby. "Maybe we can-"

"Quiet!"

Now she sounded serious. Leo scowled. He still couldn't hear or see anything out of the ordinary. Frustrated, he left himself open to doubt. Turilli *was* unpredictable, and Luna had every right to be concerned, but the regent had obviously decided to pursue a more worthwhile target. He started to think she'd overreacted and they were out here for nothing.

That was until a dozen royal guards entered the room in full battle dress.

The regent's soldiers advanced towards them in two lines of six, emerging from a chamber at the far end of the lobby. Distinguishable by their long black cloaks and visored helmets, they were among the most highly trained and dangerous enforcers on Tanis. Upon recognising Leo they fanned out into a single line and drew their batons. Their orders were to capture, not kill.

It was clear to Leo that he and Luna were heavily outmatched. Royal guards could not be reasoned with or bought. A skilled enforcer with luck on their side might be able to best one, but twelve? They had no choice but to run.

The wall of steel marched forward.

Leo turned to Luna, but instead of panicking or telling him what to do she calmly bent down as if to tie her bootlaces.

A fine time for that, thought Leo. Now it fell to him to save them. He was so fixated on the advancing soldiers he didn't see Luna take a small silver sphere out of one of her pockets. She primed the device and rolled it along the marble floor towards the enforcers. Spotting it at the last moment, Leo just had time to look away before the stun grenade detonated.

The blinding flash was followed by a pulse which disabled the enforcers' radios and heads-up displays in their helmets. Black-clad figures stumbled about in a daze, disoriented. His ears ringing, Leo reached out and steadied himself against the wall. The next thing he knew, Luna had grabbed him by the arm and pulled him back into the inner palace.

"Go!" she yelled.

"Go? Go where?"

She took off without a word. Leo followed, unsure what she had in mind but secretly impressed by her audacity.

The enforcers quickly recovered from the effects of the grenade and pursued them. Damn, they were fast! Luna was relieved she'd had the foresight to plan ahead; if they were unable to make it to her parents' estate then she was counting on a well thought-out contingency to see them safe instead.

Menials and politicians dived out of the way or stood bewildered as they sprinted past with the Royal Guard not far behind. Luna attempted to widen the gap by cutting through private staterooms and taking shortcuts not even Leo knew existed, but their pursuers were relentless. When they reached the area of the palace that was home to the van Dycks' luxury residences and storehouses, the enforcers were only a few metres behind.

The majestic grandeur was completely lost on Leo, who was straining every muscle and sinew just to keep pace with Luna. She'd risked her life to help him, whereas he'd been anything but grateful.

He cast a glance back down the corridor then turned just in time to see Luna disappear into one of the suites. The enforcers were close but slow to react as he dived inside after her. She slammed the door shut behind them and bolted it. The Royal Guard began hacking away with their batons, the sound of steel crashing against iron continuing for about a minute before it stopped. The door held firm, but Luna knew Turilli's soldiers had only paused to look for other ways to get in.

"That won't stop them for long," she said, flicking a switch. The windowless room was suddenly bathed in light.

Leo gawped in amazement. The room wasn't a suite at all, but a storehouse for the van Dycks' countless family heirlooms and precious artifacts. Luna pulled the dust sheet off what looked like a small two-man spaceship and threw him a helmet.

"What am I supposed to do with this?"

"Put it on," she demanded.

"Is that thing safe?"

Luna rolled her eyes. "Of course it's safe."

"What is it?"

"An airspeeder." Luna removed her cap and shades. "Still flies true."

Leo heard a noise behind him and spun around. The enforcers were using grenades to try and blow the door open. Three detonated in quick succession but didn't make so much as a dent. Not to be denied, they next attempted to cut their way in using thermal lances. The iron door began to warp and buckle.

"Father won't be too happy about that," Luna mumbled with a wry smile. She turned to Leo. "Ready?"

"No, of course I'm not ready!"

"Good. Shut up, put that helmet on and get in. Now!"

Leo muttered something about sending Luna to charm school as he walked over to the airspeeder. "Aren't you going to show me what to do?" he asked, hesitating.

"You want to fly it? Alone? That's a good one." She took the pilot's seat and donned her helmet. "Come on!"

"You're not serious. What about your parents? Your friends?"

Luna didn't reply.

"Have you thought any of this through? If you come with me you'll lose everything."

Luna sighed and said, "I already have."

Before Leo had the chance to ask what she meant, the ceiling of the room began to retract. Luna punched a button on the airspeeder's dashboard and it spluttered to life, then started to gain height.

Leo jumped in. "You're mad."

The moment they were clear of the palace, Luna gunned the speeder and the two of them jetted off into the unknown.

13

William Marshall was having a productive day. He'd completed a count of all his stock and found very few discrepancies, making some good sales to boot. Most of his customers had been regulars, though he'd seen one or two new faces which gave him cause for optimism. With any luck they would tell others of his varied assortment, boosting profits and contributing towards the funds he needed to fix up his storefront. It was near the end of the month, a tradesman's busiest time, and he'd done so well today that he contemplated closing early.

Few traders stuck to their opening hours any more, but Marshall was a strict adherent to the old ways. He'd built his reputation on punctuality, arriving at the same time each morning to prepare for the day's trade and would only leave when satisfied his store was tidy. Marshall didn't entertain many customers until his clientele had received their monthly paychecks, though opened up daily if just to keep his mind busy. He enjoyed talking to anyone who came to peruse his collection of trinkets, impressing them with his knowledge before invariably making a sale.

A popular topic for discussion today had been the change of regent. Marshall found it hard to appear interested in something he cared little about, for what did it matter who ran Divinity as long as he was making enough money to live comfortably? If his stock failed to arrive or the regime increased taxes he might have something to say, but until then he felt he had no need to concern himself with such trivia.

Marshall was about to start tidying away when he heard the door creak open. He'd been making space in his stockroom for future deliveries, but returned to the counter in the hope of finishing the day on a high.

His customer was browsing the *pre-war* displays, among which were some of his most expensive artifacts. Her dark brown eyes darted this way and that, coming to rest on a shelf filled with antiques from Earth and the Home System. Marshall's pulse quickened. No thief or petty bandit carried themselves the way she did, and only the affluent could afford such treasures.

Marshall regarded his customer from behind the counter. She wore her short black hair in a ponytail and was carrying a leather bag over her shoulder. He'd never seen her before, but it was fairly obvious she didn't live locally. In fact, he doubted she came from undercity at all. Her face was too pure and clothes too clean for her to be of lower class. This was a woman of great status and power, and though Marshall felt no threat from her, he sensed there was something dangerous about her.

He had to remind himself that she was just another customer, and he was there to assist her in making the right purchase.

"Is there anything I can help you with, madam?" he asked, noticing the woman glance over at him. She nodded and Marshall walked stiffly towards her, his joints aching from the rheumatoid arthritis that racked his body.

"I'm looking for a gift," she said. "What do you suggest?"

Marshall clasped his hands together to stop them from shaking. "Depends on the recipient and the occasion."

"It's for my husband."

"On or off-world?"

"What?"

"The type of artifact."

"Oh. Off, I suppose. Whatever you recommend. Money's not an issue, just tell me what you have."

Her defensive tone bordered on arrogance, and Marshall quickly deduced she was not only incredibly wealthy but keen for everyone else to know it. "A relic from Earth would certainly be well received," he said, sensing she had come in an adversarial mood.

The woman raised her chin. "Show me."

Marshall guided her over to a display stand where a number of pendants were hanging. He picked one out and allowed her to handle it.

"This belonged to the first emperor of an ancient civilisation on Earth. Nations, rulers and even his own people burned in the wars his legions made. These men of iron subjugated or enslaved whoever they considered inferior, claiming dominion over all Europa."

"Spare me the history lesson, shopkeeper. Is it authentic?"

"Of course. I have the paperwork to prove it." Marshall folded his arms across his chest. "All my stock is checked by the regime. They'd close down any trader found to be selling fakes and replicas."

"Rightly so," the woman remarked, handing the pendant back. "My husband won't wear that. It's small and unspectacular. He's a man of refined taste."

Marshall bristled at the rebuke. "It belonged to an emperor," he repeated. "I think it'll be more than good enough for your husband."

"I'll be the judge of that. What else do you have here?"

The tradesman gestured towards a tall glass cabinet to their left. Inside were several paintings, all in mint condition. One in particular - an oil on canvas depicting a starry night - stood out.

Again, the woman appeared unimpressed. Marshall turned away from her, asking himself what more he could do. Blinded by their own self-importance, Divinity's elite failed to appreciate true beauty even when it was laid bare before them. They'd sacrificed their humanity for wealth and land, more concerned with how their peers perceived them than fighting poverty and injustice. This woman, he decided, was no better than the egomaniacs he'd served during his time in the contingent, but that didn't mean he was going to give up on trying to make a sale. If these moneyed types had one weakness, it was their compulsion to make vanity buys, and Marshall believed he had just the right product for his customer.

"This way, m'lady," he said, leading her back to the counter. "We'll find a suitable gift for your husband, I'm sure of it."

"Not if you've only more pendants and paintings to show me."

Marshall chuckled. "No. No more trinkets. There isn't enough room for me to put all my stock on display, and even if there was, I wouldn't."

"Why's that, then?"

"Victoriam Plaza is a dangerous place. One can never be too careful these days."

The woman shrugged. "Seems alright to me."

Spoken like a true aristo, Marshall thought. *People like you live in another world - one where the average person's problems don't exist because you can't see them, or choose not to.*

Younger traders might well have said out loud what he was thinking, but Marshall never let ego get in the way of making a sale. Resisting the temptation to verbally spar with his customer, he retrieved a long brown box from underneath the counter and fought to stand it against the wall.

A look of surprise spread across the woman's face, but she said nothing. Whatever it was stood almost six feet tall - the same height as the shopkeeper.

Marshall took a penknife from his trouser pocket and cut the four packaging straps one by one. "This was recovered from the ruins of Denver. It was part of an exhibition at the city's museum round about the turn of the third millennium."

"I've heard of Denver," said the woman, showing a little more interest. "And the super eruption that destroyed it."

"An event that brought a once-great nation low," Marshall remarked. "But we've always been a reactionary species. Still are. We wait for tragedies to occur before thinking about how we might prevent them or lessen their impact in future. Only after Earth was threatened did we take to the stars in earnest."

With the last strap cut, he removed the front of the box and let it fall to the floor.

The item inside was obscured by wads of bubble-wrap and polystyrene sheets. Marshall began to pull the packaging away, gradually revealing an ancient relic from a forgotten time.

The woman saw that it was a claymore sword, estimating the shaft alone to be nearly four and a half feet in length. "Impossible," she whispered under her breath. "To wield it you'd have to be-"

"A good foot or so taller than me," Marshall offered.

His customer glared at him expectantly. "Well?" she pressed when he did not continue.

"Well what?"

"Aren't you going to tell me a little about it?"

"If you are willing and able to endure another history lesson," Marshall retorted.

"I am."

"Very well." He disposed of the packaging behind the counter and said, "It's a Scottish claymore. Thirteenth century. Unusual in that there's no record of who it belonged to. My supplier believes it saw action during one of many campaigns fought between two rival kingdoms."

"Why were they fighting?"

"Our ancestors fought over many things, m'lady. Land, money, resources... women. In truth, I don't know. The records are incomplete."

"How did you come to have it?"

Marshall hesitated. "I've a supplier who works for the regime on Mars. He can source anything."

"Don't give me that. The regime hoard artifacts like it's nobody's business, so either they're unsure of the sword's authenticity or you acquired it through underhand means."

"I operate with their blessing," Marshall said, remaining calm despite his customer's provocations. "They check all my stock thoroughly before letting me have it."

"Then I have my answer. But I really don't care. My husband doesn't own a sword, nor do any of his peers. You can repackage it now - I'll take delivery tomorrow."

Marshall felt the aches and ailments that plagued him recede. This had been his biggest sale for years. His persistence had paid off, and all he needed to do now was negotiate a price. But the woman had no intention of bargaining with him.

"How much do you want for it?" she asked, fumbling around in her bag.

Marshall thought about overcharging her, but honesty was what set him apart from Divinity's other traders. He took payment and made a note of the sale before asking her where she would like it delivered.

"Bring it to the nineteenth level as soon as you can. You'll be met by someone at the wall who will take it the rest of the way."

"Understood."

"I appreciate your advice, shopkeeper. I must admit, you've proved me wrong."

"Wrong? How so?"

"I thought undercity was full of nefarious, immoral types."

Marshall smiled. "Oh, it is. Similar to how the palace is overflowing with spiteful, self-serving sycophants. But there are good people to be found in both."

The noble houses of Tanis were in a state of shock and mourning.

United by grief, they all came to pay homage to a man who'd spent much of his life trying to better theirs. Even Giovanni Rossi's detractors wept for him, filtering past as he lay in state, ashamed they'd never made the effort to apologise for their vicious insults and slights. The change many of them wanted was finally here, though only now did they understand that it wouldn't be for the better.

Rossi's death affected everyone from the politicians he'd made to the servants whose lives he'd touched, but the news that his adopted son was responsible had been particularly hard to take. The nobility loved Leo as much as they had his father, and away from the ears of

Turilli's spies the new regent's implausible revelation was ridiculed and rejected. Some even suspected Turilli, though they lacked the courage to confront him. Fearful of losing their wealth and titles, the nobles reluctantly accepted what they'd been told - much to the regent's delight.

Turilli spoke at length about Leo's betrayal and subsequent capture, going on to declare he would work tirelessly to restore Tanis to her pre-war splendour. Those who attended the regent's ascension speech didn't doubt he meant it, but having witnessed his fanatical zealotry wondered if he was planning to first break the world before remaking it in his image.

Fear permeated every room like a thick, noxious gas. Several households suddenly decided they had spent too long in the palace and needed to tour their estates, leaving Turilli to do as he pleased. Unsure of the regent's true intentions, the popular belief was that he couldn't be trusted and more purges would almost certainly follow in the coming months.

Sure enough, an edict was swiftly passed granting the Royal Guard special powers to help cement their master's rule. An official communiqué from Earth endorsing the new regent was broadcast throughout the city, and all enforcers were recalled to pledge their allegiance to him. Keen to impress, the servants arranged to hold a grand banquet in Turilli's honour. But when his aides arrived to escort him there, he was nowhere to be found.

The executors conducted an immediate search of the regent's private staterooms while Turilli's supporters fought to keep his disappearance a secret. But the truth could only be suppressed for so long. Without the regent, Divinity's political processes ground to a halt. It fell to administrator Luther to run the city in Turilli's absence, though this was only after repeated requests from desperate ministers for him to do so. Thrust into a role he had no desire to take on permanently, Luther deployed enforcer patrols throughout the palace to try and locate the missing regent.

It took them three whole days to find him.

Turilli had locked himself in Leo's room and refused to come out. He tried to hide from the enforcers at first then screamed at them to leave him alone, muttering dark words none could understand. Again the ministers called on Luther to intercede, but the calculating administrator sent one of Turilli's menials instead. When the man emerged half beaten to a pulp, it was clear Turilli would only return when he was ready.

The politicians and nobles remained on edge, well aware of Turilli's ability to appear weak when he was strong. They speculated that this was another of the regent's tests; that he wanted to see how his enemies might respond if he were to be incapacitated. But no coup was attempted and Luther followed regime protocol to the letter, performing the duties of a regent without declaring himself one. The ministers deliberately refrained from holding sessions and passing any new laws, but they need not have worried.

Turilli had been informed of Leo's escape and reacted the only way he knew how. He'd flown into a rage and berated the Royal Guard for their failure, vowing to hunt Leo down himself. Stumbling out of his office in a near-catatonic state, he made for the palace armoury only to find it locked. Unwilling to summon executors or enforcers for fear they were conspiring against him, something in Turilli's mind snapped. He had to vent his terrible anger, and went to Leo's room to do it.

After destroying everything the boy had left behind, Turilli proceeded to beat his fists bloody against the wall until he no longer had the strength to lift a hand. A sudden change then came over him and he sat amongst the wreckage with no idea what to do next. He felt uncharacteristically weak and powerless - human. Having been taught from birth that he was better than everyone else, these strange new emotions both confused and terrified him. When the nobility found out that Leo had escaped he'd look a fool - more so as he'd already announced his capture. Worse, the damage to his reputation could prove irreparable if they discovered he'd had help. He swung between despair and euphoria, ranting to himself for three days, but on the morning of the fourth he rose again with renewed purpose.

Leaving the palace with a train of enforcers in tow, he made the short journey over to the estate where the van Dycks were residing. They were in the middle of breakfast when the regent descended upon them in an eye-popping, vein-throbbing state of apoplectic rage.

"Arturo! Where are you? Show yourself!"

Turilli commanded the enforcers to wait outside while he dealt with Luna's parents. He watched in amusement as Arturo van Dyck came running, followed by his young wife, Maria. It was clear from their panic-stricken expressions that they hadn't been expecting him, and this pleased the regent immensely.

"What a charming place," Turilli snarled, looking around. "Not sure I agree with the choice of décor, though. A little bland for my taste."

The regent went from madness to the very picture of composure in the space of a few seconds. His rapid transformation rendered Arturo speechless, prompting Maria to deputise for her bewildered husband. She fared little better.

"My lord, we had no idea you would be coming! You honour us. How long can we expect the pleasure of your company? Goodness, where are my manners? I'll have the servants bring a chair. Can I get you anything? A drink or-"

"Calm yourself, my lady," said Turilli, raising his hand. "A glass of water would be lovely. Forget the chair."

Maria bowed her head and disappeared, glad to be away from the changeable regent even if it was only for a minute or two.

Turilli turned to face Arturo. "You look awfully pale, prefect. Are you unwell?"

"N-no, my lord."

"No?"

"Overworked, maybe. It's been a busy few days."

"Yes, of course," Turilli smiled. "Divinity is a complex machine. Your efforts are to be applauded."

"Thank you, my lord."

"Perhaps now the work I do will be appreciated. Can you imagine if I was to take but the briefest of holidays? The whole city would collapse!"

Arturo laughed uneasily. "Administrator Luther has been managing state affairs in your absence."

"So I hear."

"Alas, he is not you, my lord. He's done well enough I suppose - for a man of low birth. But the speed with which he assumed power... no sooner had he learned of your disappearance than he was issuing orders and amending laws. I fear he means to take the regency for himself."

Turilli batted away the prefect's concerns. "Your fears are unfounded, Arturo. Luther is a trusted friend and ally. His decisiveness shows initiative, not disloyalty. Need I remind you that he chose to remain in the palace when everyone else deserted me?"

"Ah, my lord, now, we only left because..."

Turilli listened to the man's bungling excuses, paying particular attention to the names of any nobles he mentioned. Arturo was a coward, but that didn't mean he couldn't learn anything from him. The nobility would often blame others for their mistakes, but in the regent's experience these individuals were far more worthy of his trust than their accusers. At the same time he was finding out who Arturo secretly envied or despised, and made a mental note of this for the future.

Maria returned and handed Turilli his glass of water. He took a sip and said, "I'm not interested in your reasons for leaving. I'm here because I need you back at court. I need my allies around me. Gethsemane and the sector as a whole must see Tanis is united and strong. I trust I can count on your continued financial and political support, Arturo?"

"Naturally, my lord."

"Good. You will return immediately. We can then set about bringing Rossi's murderer to justice." Turilli kept his expression bland but a note of anger entered his voice. "Though the Royal Guard outdid themselves in thwarting Leo's attempt on my life, it was their incompetence that allowed him to escape."

"*Gross* incompetence, my lord," Maria added, sweeping a dark strand of hair behind her right ear.

"Quite. But I've heard some alarming reports. It appears your youngest, Luna, may have helped him."

Maria and Arturo were instantly put on the defensive. They'd learned of Luna's involvement from one of her sisters whose enforcer armour had gone missing. Arturo hesitated a moment, recognising the regent wasn't making so much a statement as an accusation. He had to word his response carefully. The Royal Guard would have told Turilli everything, so there was no point denying Luna's actions.

In the end he decided that he wasn't going to let one wayward daughter bring him down. She'd forced his hand, but he had plenty of other children who were far more pliable than she ever was. Maria wouldn't be happy about it, but Luna's position was indefensible.

"I can't understand why she'd betray us," he sighed, shaking his head. "After everything we've done for her. She had the best education and a good upbringing - the same as all her siblings."

"A senseless act of defiance," said Turilli, setting his glass down on a nearby table. "You can rest assured that her irrational behaviour will not detract from the years of service you and your family have given me."

"Thank you, my lord."

"Though it would be unfortunate if any of your other children were to now have doubts about where their loyalties lay."

"Of that you need not worry," said Arturo. "They will do as I say. I cannot answer for Luna, but we remain your true and loyal subjects."

"You aren't going to tell anyone she helped him, are you?" Maria asked Turilli.

"No. If this debacle ever came to light then it would damage both of us. My reputation would be tarnished and your name forever dishonoured. You see, the nobility can accept Leo escaped because he was part of the contingent and a competent soldier. He chose to run and this confirms his guilt, benefiting me. But if they were to learn he had help, questions would be asked. Why did the daughter of a respected noble house choose to aid a murderer? I can't say she was part of his plan without publically shaming you. Worse, it'd be known that an unskilled girl was able to outsmart the regent. If the nobles think the Royal Guard aren't as brutally efficient as they've been led to believe, they would begin to question my competence and take more liberties."

"I can see where this is going," said Arturo. "What do you suggest?"

"I understand she wasn't politically active, nor that well known at court. No-one will notice her disappearance, and if they do, lie. There are many young nobles choosing to leave Tanis in order to further their careers elsewhere. She can be one of them."

"And what of Leo?"

"I haven't thought about that yet," said Turilli. He had, of course, and knew he faced a difficult decision. If he went after Leo then he'd be derided as the regent who was afraid of a boy. But do nothing and his inaction would be perceived as weakness. He hoped the van Dycks had a solution and also wanted to see if they were really prepared to disown their daughter. Arturo would do almost anything to remain in his good graces, but Maria was renowned for valuing family over power. Much to Turilli's surprise, it was she who spoke first.

"A token gesture should suffice, my lord."

"Explain," the regent pressed, keen to find out what she meant.

"Let it be known that you are sending out gunships to search for Rossi's killer. Deploy a squadron or two, no more. Allow the nobility to see you upset, not angry, and pressing ahead with other matters."

"They'll think I've gone soft."

"Far from it. They will see a bereaved regent determined to hold Leo to account for his crime. Your measured response means no-one can accuse you of ignoring the issue or obsessing over it."

"A flight of gunships stands little chance of finding two traitors who could be anywhere," Turilli scowled.

"What does it matter if they succeed or not? You've ordered a search; the onus is on the pilots to locate them. If they can find Leo then all the better - it'll be a weight off your mind."

"And if they don't?"

"Then the sun will do your soldiers' work for them. It's all desert out there. He has nowhere to go."

"*They* have nowhere to go," Turilli corrected her. "Luna's fate will be the same as his. Doesn't this bother you?"

Maria shrugged. "She's made her choice. All traitors to the regent deserve to die."

"Excellent." Turilli was impressed by Maria's callousness. He'd searched her words for a hidden agenda but couldn't find one. She must have finally recognised the benefits of putting the regent before her own family - that or she was simply scared of him. He had that effect on a lot of people. "Thank you, my lady," he continued, fixing her with his most charming smile. "If you would be so kind as to leave us for a few moments, I wish to speak with your husband alone."

Sensing her suggestion had been well received, Maria retreated with a swagger in her step and confidence high. Turilli waited until she had gone before he turned to Arturo and said, "I've neglected you and your house for far too long, and for that I apologise."

"My lord?"

"You've supported me from when I was but a mere minister. Even then you saw what no-one else did - that I was marked out for greatness. In return I have failed to give you the recognition you deserve. A reward is long overdue."

"To continue working alongside you would be reward enough, my lord," said Arturo.

"Yes. Your modesty and selflessness do you great credit." Turilli looked away for a second then grabbed Arturo by the front of his tunic and slammed him against the wall. "But if you or anyone associated with you ever betrays me again then I'll bring your whole debauched world crashing down far quicker than the time it took you to build it. Do you take me for a fool, prefect?"

"No, my lord, never!" Arturo blurted out. "Forgive me."

Turilli wasn't listening. "It is a poor excuse for a father who cannot control his children. Or should I be blaming your pretty little wife instead?"

"Having one rebellious daughter does not mean the rest of my family are traitors!"

Turilli hammered Arturo into the wall again. "But that daughter's actions could destabilise my city! I hope you are able to bring the rest of your spawn into line and this lesson isn't lost on you. For your family's sake."

"I won't forget it, my lord," Arturo whimpered.

The regent released the man from his thrall and straightened up. "Then we're done. I expect to see you back in the palace by tomorrow at the latest. You'll want to get started on the paperwork that accompanies your new role."

Arturo stared at him, confused. "My new role?"

"Yes. I've decided to make you vice-regent. Report to my office for the brief. That's all."

Turilli departed feeling satisfied with the outcome of their exchange. He had no reason to doubt Arturo's loyalty but liked to motivate his allies with a mixture of threats and incentives. They would pursue whatever rewards he dangled in front of them with little regard for anything else, blind to the bigger picture, and currently nothing was bigger than the Chimera project. Earth was supplying Tanis with vast amounts of raw materials, but he still needed the noble houses to help finance it.

If they ever discovered what it was before its completion, two troublesome children would be the least of his problems.

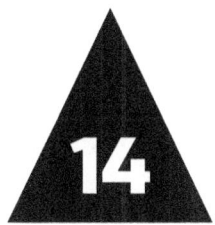

14

The battle for Tanis had been fought and lost almost three hundred years ago. In his hubris, Man had thought himself the victor - that he'd beaten back the great deserts and dunes of this bright new world forever - but just as technology had been instrumental in his rise, so did it help bring about his fall. Ancient weapons of terrible power were unleashed upon Tanis and a hundred other worlds, undoing centuries of progress in a single day. Few knew it, but Divinity and a handful of far-flung settlements were all that remained of a once proud colony.

From his seat in the speeder, Leo gazed out over a flat, yellow vista, broken only by the occasional dune. He'd briefly considered asking Luna where they were heading, but her stern expression told him any questions were best left for later. She hadn't needed to stop once since leaving Divinity; a feat Leo found quite remarkable given that was near eight hours ago. Temperatures were falling along with the light, but he trusted her to find them a place to stay.

Luna's continued silence had given him time to think. He wondered what Turilli was planning to do next and how his chaotic schemes might affect the people, fearing Marcus and those he cared about would be made to suffer in his place. Leo hoped they'd managed to escape Turilli's wrath or convince him of their loyalty, but knew there were some too stubborn to do either.

Leo spotted a formation of dunes up ahead and assumed that was where they were going. To survive out here they had to find shelter for the night, or risk falling foul of the sandstorms that swept the open desert. Then he noticed they were slowing down.

Gradually, Luna brought the speeder to a halt. She looked over at Leo and said, "Lucky for us I know about this place."

"What place?" asked Leo, bemused. "So you've found some dunes. Are these ones any better than those closer to Divinity?"

Luna chuckled. "You think they're dunes? Look again."

Squinting, Leo saw they weren't. What he took to be a natural formation was something else entirely.

"Is it possible?" he asked himself, his voice almost a whisper.

"Yes," said Luna. "Once there were six. Six cities, each making Divinity look like a pauper's hovel. This was the capital." She checked the speeder's dashboard readings then accelerated, leaving Leo sitting in stunned silence as they raced towards the ruins.

With the speeder back to full power, it took them no more than a few minutes to get there. The skeletal remains of skyscrapers towered over them, even after centuries of exposure to the elements. Though but a fraction of its former height, the ruined city still stood at least half a mile high. Luna stopped the speeder just outside and powered down, then jumped out and shouted for Leo to follow. Removing his helmet, Leo grabbed the two holdalls he'd brought with him and hurried after her.

"Suppose you want to know what happened here," said Luna.

"It's pretty obvious. Many worlds were left shattered by the war."

"But few reverted to their natural states after. The bombing of Tanis was so intense that it levelled cities and all but reversed the terraforming process. This was once a rich and fertile place, Leo." Luna's expression grew bleak, filled with deep sorrow. "We'll never see a return to those days."

"So how come Divinity survived? And Gethsemane?"

Luna swept a golden lock of hair behind an ear. "This sector saw some of the fiercest fighting because of its strategic importance. It lay on the borders of two great spheres. One attacked the other, but the fleet sent to devastate Tanis and the surrounding worlds was driven off."

"You're speculating," Leo scoffed. "No-one knows what really happened."

"I do."

"How?"

"You think that airspeeder is the only relic locked away in the palace vaults?"

"I-"

"It was a rhetorical question," Luna smiled. "Of course you do. You believe exactly what you're told, but me, I dig a little deeper."

Leo glared at her, more embarrassed than offended. "I'm quite capable of thinking for myself," he insisted.

"Perhaps. Leave the bags and help me take a look around. I want to make sure we're alone."

Leo followed Luna into the ruins. Now it was clear where she'd been disappearing off to when they were at the academy. He initially wanted to challenge her accusations or make some witty remark, then thought better of it. After everything she'd done for him, the least he could do was let her comments slide. Starting an argument with her would have been in poor taste, partly because she'd just saved his life but also because he knew she was right. These past two days had helped put things into perspective, and Leo resolved to focus on more important issues than his pride.

"It's clear," said Luna after a thorough sweep of the immediate area. "Make yourself at home. There's no-one here but us."

Leo returned to where he'd left the holdalls, while Luna went to check on the speeder. She retrieved a small black bag of her own and opened it. Seeing this, Leo grinned.

"Is there anything you haven't planned for?"

"Only rain," said Luna, producing a torch.

"Rain. I think it used to rain on Carmona."

"Where?"

"Carmona. My homeworld. I don't remember anything else."

Luna seated herself in the sand next to him. "Are you sure you want to?"

"Of course. Why not?"

"Because it's done with. Even if you knew, who's to say you wouldn't go mad thinking about it - what you did or didn't do, what you could've done differently, what's been and gone and won't be coming back irrespective of how much you yearn for it."

Leo sensed there was a hidden meaning behind her words. He decided it was best to tell Luna everything - everything from his homeworld's destruction to Rossi's hand in it - even the argument they had prior to the regent's death. He wasn't looking for sympathy, but rather hoped this move would encourage her to open up about her own past and whatever it was that troubled her.

"So you weren't being cold at all," said Luna, relaxing a little. "I didn't know what to expect when I told you about Rossi. I must admit you had me worried for a moment."

"How so?"

"Your reaction. It wasn't you. You just seemed so..."

"Heartless?"

"I was going to say distant." Luna smiled. "Thought I'd have to drag you out of the palace kicking and screaming."

"I was about to leave anyway. I've seen the regime for what they really are."

"So have I," said Luna.

Leo cast his mind back to their conversation in the storehouse. "Want to tell me what happened?"

"May as well since we're on the subject."

"Only if you're ready."

Luna sighed. "Ready? I guess we'll find out soon enough. Tell me, have you seen the moons of Orar?"

"No."

"What about the garden worlds of the Lyran system?"

"Can't say as I have."

"My parents took me to Lyra for my eighth birthday. Father paid well above the odds to charter a ship there. Two weeks in paradise, no brothers or sisters, just us - I couldn't turn them down. Who in their right mind would have? At that age all I ever wanted was to be the centre of my parents' world; to feel loved and appreciated. I don't expect you to understand - you didn't grow up with four spoilt siblings. I was always treated differently, like I didn't belong, but never knew why until Lyra.

"I still remember it, Leo. Golden beaches stretching for miles. Glass cities and clear blue skies. The seas were pure and unspoilt. Every day more perfect than the last until the regime came."

"And did to Lyra what they'd done to Carmona," said Leo.

Luna nodded, her features darkening at the memory. "I'd heard Mother crying the night before we were meant to leave. Later on she read me a story and told me she loved me - something she never did. I used to have trouble sleeping, but that night got off just fine. When I woke, it was like a thunderstorm had suddenly sprung into existence, and the ground shook as if the planet was tearing itself apart. I'd no idea of the danger I was in, but knew I couldn't stay put. I went looking for my parents. They'd gone, taking their bags and all their possessions with them. I tried to get out but the door was locked. I thought that if I could scream loud enough or cry for long enough someone would come. No-one did. They were all trying to save themselves."

"So how did you escape?" asked Leo.

"We were staying at a resort just outside Lyra's second city. I saw it take a direct hit and had to turn away, the fireball was so bright. When I looked again it was a smouldering ruin, and the door to our room stood open. Back then I thought it to be a miracle. Now I know the power failed. That strike must have taken out the entire grid, and all the door locks were electronic.

"I managed to get out. I'd this mad idea that if I could steal a speeder I could find somewhere safe to hide. But everyone had left - everyone apart from a young couple and their two children. One of the women looked at me and I at her, then she turned to her partner. I can only assume she was pleading for my life. Eventually, she came over and held out her hand.

"I've no memory of what happened next. I must have passed out, and when I came to I was on a ship bound for Tanis by way of Orar. Many of the refugees from Lyra had homes there, including the women who'd saved me. For them the nightmare was over - or so they'd thought. The moons of Orar were aflame, destroyed by the same fleet that had burned Lyra to ash."

Luna shook her head at the barbarity of it all. "Carmona, Lyra and Orar. How many more worlds shared their fate, and for what? Unpaid taxes? Transgressions against the regime? No, this was something else, and it'll keep on happening unless someone acts."

"Rossi's words exactly," said Leo, sounding suspicious.

"Because it's true."

"Be that as it may, you and I aren't going to change anything."

"Why not?"

"Look at us," said Leo. "Hiding away out here while a madman ruins what's left of this world."

"Who says we're hiding? We're considering our next move, that's all. You just relax and leave the planning to me."

"Relax..." Leo grumbled, half to himself. He looked over at Luna, wondering if he actually knew her at all, then began taking her words a little more seriously. "I think I know why the regime targeted those worlds," he said after a while, a moment of sublime recognition surfacing.

"Because they're genocidal maniacs?" Luna snorted.

"Because Carmona and Lyra weren't touched by the war, and I'll bet Orar wasn't either. It's been three hundred years - have we rebuilt or regressed? The regime's strength lies in our willingness to accept there can't be anything better. Those worlds were proof there could."

Luna's blue eyes narrowed. "They wanted to start again? By wiping the slate clean?"

"What better way to build an empire?"

"Do you think-"

"I know what you're going to ask," Leo interjected. "That line of thought could take us to a dark place. I'm not even considering it. We need to focus on the here and now."

"Alright." Luna relented, pleased that Leo was coming round to her way of thinking. His eyes, closed for so long, were beginning to open at last, and she remained hopeful he would act when the time came. Leo wasn't one to spend days or weeks wallowing in self-pity, but Luna knew she had to first make him believe in himself before expecting more. He'd endured a torrid couple of days, and the last thing he needed was pressuring into something he wasn't ready for.

Luna found herself staring at Leo once more, thinking back to the day they'd first met. He was a lonely, troubled boy back then who wouldn't talk to anyone. Curious, she'd gone to see the adopted son of the regent and befriended him, learning they were alike in more ways than one. Since that day they'd grown ever closer, their playful debates masking an unbreakable friendship born out of mutual respect. For Luna this was never enough, though her belief that Leo was destined for greatness meant she'd always stopped short of asking him *that* question.

She was about to bid Leo goodnight when he requested she continue her story.

"So what did your parents say when they saw you again?" he asked, eager to find out more.

"Say? They didn't say anything." Luna laughed. "The look on Father's face said it all. His eyes were full of fear and regret - regret that he hadn't finished the job himself. But he daren't, not now we were back on Tanis."

"Job? What job?"

"A few weeks later I hear Turilli bragging about this new policy he'd implemented. Families with more than four children had to surrender half their estate or risk sanctions - all to fund some new regime project. There's a law preventing the nobility from putting their children up for adoption, so my parents felt they'd only one way out. Apparently I was worth less to them than their material holdings. As the youngest, I'd drawn the short straw without even knowing it.

"Of course, I'd already confronted Father about what'd happened on Lyra. He said I was confused and had imagined everything, going so far as to blame me for leaving the resort. I've been pushing my luck with him ever since - he thinks I've accepted his lies and that I'm just a problem child - but I never forgave and never forgot what he did."

"I'd no idea," said Leo, leaning forward.

"Why do you think so many choose to adopt? There are no incentives to have children of your own anymore. The taxes are astronomical."

"Population control at its finest."

"Adoption," Luna scoffed. "How kind and generous of the nobility to step in and save the world's orphans. Just like they did with Marcus."

Leo arched an eyebrow at her. "You're saying the enforcer raid was planned?"

"The noble houses won't adopt street urchins," said Luna. "They look for healthy, well-bred children - those who've had good upbringings - and take them. If anyone stands in their way... well. That's what the enforcers are for."

"Does Marcus know?"

"He's as unaware of the truth as you were."

"Then let's keep it that way. He might do something rash if he were to find out."

Luna laughed lightly. "Glad I'm not the only one who thinks that." She sat up and stretched her arms, then rested her head on Leo's shoulder. "I won't sit back and watch Turilli bleed Tanis dry. I can't."

"You really care about this world, don't you?"

"There are good people here. I care about them."

Leo shuffled uneasily. "Do you truly think we can make a difference?"

"I think we'd surprise ourselves. Pithy words and promises will only carry you so far. We've spent our lives putting things off, mired in self-doubt, but relying on others to do what you yourself can isn't how change happens. When people look to you for answers - the day your hand is forced - then you'll know the truth."

"So why not act yourself?"

"I was wondering when you'd ask. It'll take a better mind than mine to save Tanis. I know my limitations, but you... you have none."

"Everyone has limits," said Leo.

Luna frowned. "The people love you, Leo. Why can't you see that, or at least acknowledge it? Your visits to undercity meant so much to them. You gave them food, gifts - *hope*. I've never seen so many people so happy."

"And why was that?" Leo's expression tightened. "Because the enforcers threatened to shoot any who didn't smile or applaud? If someone was waving a gun in my face then I'm pretty sure I would have done, too. They were there for the hand-outs, nothing more."

"They were there for *you*, just like I was. Their smiles were genuine. Believe what you like, I'm done trying to convince you. It's late - I'm going to try and get some sleep." Luna took a sheet out of her bag and placed it on the sand. "I never had you down as a cynic. Guess I was wrong."

"Guess you were." Leo stood up and started walking, taking his holdalls and Luna's torch with him. He stopped a respectable distance away from her, seated himself and began to organise the bags' contents. Eventually he came across the file Rossi had left him and decided to read it, if only to take his mind off things.

His day had been full of surprises, but there was one more revelation still to come.

15

Construction at the Chimera site proceeded apace. Those who had arrived on the freighter were assessed and put to work, with the team leaders and other experienced hands expected to train them. The supervisors would delegate, detached from all reality, demanding they meet ever-increasing quotas and impossible targets from the comfort of their offices.

The regime had recruited workers with little or no knowledge of the construction industry, for it cost them far more to employ a skilled labourer than an unskilled one. Those with any relevant experience were never fully utilised; a welder would be asked to drill while a surveyor would end up joining one of the corpse removal crews. In overlooking their skillsets and assigning workers to areas they were unfamiliar with, the regime could get away with paying the majority of the workforce no more than the minimum wage.

An outsider might have regarded this process as counterproductive, but the regime weren't just out to save money. New workers would be fit and enthusiastic - at least for a few weeks - and able to meet targets in the short term. The strong would survive the Chimera site's many hazards and go on to become useful assets, while those who fell by the wayside were simply replaced.

Many were unprepared for the horrors of site life. Appalling conditions and the schemes of ruthless overseers turned every day into a desperate fight for survival, but all one could do was obey and endure. This soon became apparent to Marcus Rathen, and when he'd raised his concerns with Steinsson, the team leader had smiled and said, "People talk about leaving, but there isn't anywhere else for them to go."

Marcus had adapted to his new role with ease, impressing Steinsson and his fellow welders, though Saul and Karlsen continued to grumble. He'd already tried various tactics to try and win them over, learning that by offering to do some of their work they would leave him alone. Marcus relished the challenge but was careful not to overexert himself, all the while finding out what he could about the Chimera.

Having been starved of meaningful conversation for the past two years, Steinsson was pleasantly surprised to discover Marcus was an educated man. They'd become fast friends, looking out for one another and debating a range of topics from the regime's policies to humanity's place in the universe. Though Marcus was reluctant to take advantage of their newly forged friendship, the nature of their discussions meant that it was inevitable one of them would mention the Chimera before long.

"I don't know what this place is," said Steinsson, "but there are four other sites that are being built to power it." He was keen to hear Marcus' opinion, explaining how these installations - codenamed *Gorgon, Hydra, Manticore* and *Basilisk* - were so large they could support the entire city.

"Might be a terraformer," Marcus suggested, dreading to think what else might require so much power. "Or some kind of weapon."

Steinsson shook his head. "The regime have no enemies. There are none with the will to oppose them. But your theory about a terraforming machine is an interesting one. If you're right, it would allow them to remake the world as they see fit."

"A new order of the ages," Marcus mumbled, quoting the regime's motto.

"Precisely. If they've altered the technology to suit their own needs then I'm afraid that doesn't bode well for the rest of us."

"What do you mean?"

"I'm referring to the later years of the Great Expansion. The rich and famous would cordon off whole worlds to avoid the masses. Their lust for perfection and pursuit of pleasure pushed us perilously close to species doom. They genuinely believed they were superior beings, sustained by the ignorance and misplaced adoration of billions. Real heroes with real accomplishments were forgotten. Now I'm worried the same thing is happening again. The regime already pretend we don't exist, but what if we didn't and it was just them alone in their little paradise?"

Marcus pondered this as a flight of gunships left the city.

"Where d'you suppose they're going?" asked Steinsson.

"No idea." Marcus knew the iron birds were most likely ferrying enforcers to their training grounds in the dunes, but couldn't say so. He'd managed to convince the welders he'd come from another planet like the rest of them, so had to feign ignorance whenever they discussed events on Tanis. Steinsson and the others had bought his act thus far, but he'd yet to be formally assessed by the team's supervisor. With paperwork taking up much of the man's time, Marcus had prepared a story he hoped would convince him. If the things Steinsson had told him about the supervisor were true, then it needed to be watertight.

Marcus stifled a yawn and scratched the stubble on his chin. The sun beat down on Divinity with increasing ferocity, telling him that it was just past midday. This was the first time he'd been outside since arriving five days earlier. Reprieves and extended periods of rest were awarded to any team that met their quotas, and Steinsson's unit had a reputation for exceeding theirs on a regular basis.

This in itself was considered a remarkable achievement. The regime granted workers two ten minute breaks and four hours sleep each day, but the physical stresses they had to endure were immense. Those who failed to adapt were far more likely to suffer lapses in concentration, and many either fell to their deaths or sustained terrible injuries - injuries the regime had no obligation to treat.

"Safety," Steinsson had said, "comes second to profit."

Marcus looked over to where Saul and Karlsen were playing cards. *So does work*, he thought.

The two welders squabbled and swore, perched on empty crates turned upside down, using the occasion to air their many grievances. Marcus sensed that while outwardly hostile and lazy, they had it within themselves to be good people if they chose to be.

Or maybe I just see the best in everyone.

He was so preoccupied with trying to figure them out that he didn't see the supervisor walking across the tarmac towards him. Kurt Steinsson turned to face his diminutive nemesis while Saul and Karlsen stood up, alerting Marcus to the man's presence. Now came the first true test of his resolve. If the supervisor uncovered his deception then he'd have to think fast, and something told him he already had his suspicions.

The welders watched him warily as he approached. Marcus went over his story once again, but still worried he'd overlooked some minor detail or flaw.

"Haven't you all got somewhere you need to be?" the supervisor spat, eying the welders contemptuously. "Break's over."

"Like fuck it's over," said Saul. "I reckon we've got another ten minutes."

"More like fifteen," added Karlsen.

"You think so? I say you don't. I say it's time you got back to work and set about justifying your paychecks." The supervisor drew his baton and said, "This can go one of two ways."

"I'll take a third option," hissed Saul.

Steinsson stepped between them. "Enough. We'll go, but I expect those ten minutes to be added on to our next break." His firm tone brokered no argument.

Faced with the prospect of a physical confrontation, the supervisor had little choice but to accept Steinsson's terms. "Fine," he snarled, already plotting his revenge.

The welders gathered their belongings and started walking back towards the Chimera. Marcus went too, but the supervisor moved to block his path. "Wait a moment," he said, raising his hand. "I've some questions for you."

Saul and Karlsen disappeared inside, still chuntering away, while Steinsson waited at the site entrance. He'd already warned his new friend of the supervisor's methods, but wanted to ensure no harm came to him.

"You've not been formally assessed yet, have you?" the supervisor asked Marcus.

"No, sir."

"Sir? Well, it's good to see at least one of you runts recognises authority. I presume Steinsson's already gone through the site rules and regulations with you?"

"Yes, sir."

"Good. Do as you're told and we won't have a problem. But if you allow the bad habits of others to rub off on you then I can make your time here extremely unpleasant. Understand?"

"I do."

"Then let's make a start, shall we?" The supervisor took a pen and scrap of paper from his pocket. "Name?"

Again, Marcus gave his name as Lucas. This would prevent his adoptive parents from finding him if they went looking. Leo had advised him how sites like the Chimera functioned, but while the supervisors didn't know the names of new recruits in advance, they kept a comprehensive roster of all workers that anyone with the relevant clearance could access.

Marcus wouldn't allow himself to be caught out that easily. The supervisor continued to ask him questions, and he answered in an assured, articulate manner. His self-belief was unshakeable, but he'd every right to feel confident given his familiarity with regime protocol. He'd also learned more about the site and its shortcomings from Leo, who'd overheard a heated discussion between his father and the director of engineering three months earlier.

It had surprised him to discover the regime's security checks were not as stringent as he'd first thought. If a worker misplaced their papers then there was no way of proving who they were or where they came from. Verifying their identity took weeks, and only a handful of supervisors felt obliged to do this. While the regent could make contact with Earth in a matter of seconds, low-ranking officials relied on an outdated system to submit requests which were often ignored. Marcus had anticipated the supervisor would ask to see his papers, but claimed he'd lost them while en route to Tanis. The little man glared at him and muttered something under his breath, but left it at that.

Marcus figured the regime were relying on a show of strength to deter interlopers, and eagle-eyed supervisors to help catch any who slipped through the net. Though a sound strategy in principle, this was undermined by a combination of arrogance and laxity. Site officials left the enforcers in charge of security, believing that no sane man or woman would willingly risk their lives to infiltrate a construction site. Over time they'd grown complacent, prioritising quotas so they might gain favour with their superiors, leaving one or two of their more industrious colleagues to do the work of many.

Making things even easier for me, Marcus thought.

"Homeworld?" the supervisor asked, continuing his interrogation.

"Meridian. System twenty-seven."

"Occupation?"

"Painter."

"A painter?" the supervisor scolded. "No wonder you ended up here. There's no money to be made from painting. What a pointless thing to do with your life."

"It's a hobby," said Marcus.

"Of course it is. Anything to avoid getting a proper job, eh? You off-worlders are all alike. Coasting along until one bad decision forces you to get up off your arse and find work. What was it? Gambling? Debts? Got some daft tart knocked up and need to start paying your way?"

"Suppose so."

Marcus knew the supervisor was looking for weaknesses he could exploit later on. His questions - though innocuous enough - would have caught him out if he hadn't been prepared, and were clearly intended to unsettle and provoke. The supervisor had a malicious streak to him like Steinsson said, but Marcus ignored his jibes and gave nothing away.

"I'll leave it at that for now," the supervisor growled, sounding almost disappointed not to have riled him. "If you see or hear anything out of place then it's your duty to let me know. I want you to pay particular attention to Saul and Karlsen. Those two half-wits are nothing but trouble. They'll snipe away and drag you down to their level if you let them."

"I'll bear that in mind."

"I'm sure you will. I expect the new regent to set more challenging quotas than his predecessor, so if any of you ingrates are slacking it'll be up to me to find someone who can get the job done properly."

Marcus felt a chill run down his spine. "New regent?"

"That's right. Maybe now I'll get the promotion I deserve."

Having completed the assessment, the supervisor marched off to belittle whoever he came across next. Marcus wandered over to where Steinsson was waiting, furious he'd put himself in a position where he couldn't warn or help Leo. With Rossi dead, there was no-one left to protect him from Turilli's machinations, and Marcus knew that even if he managed to escape the Chimera there was a good chance he'd be too late.

"What was that all about?" asked Steinsson, sensing that something was wrong.

"My assessment," said Marcus.

"And?"

"Everything's okay. Not looking forward to working these new quotas, though."

"I don't think anyone is. No-one's told Saul and Karlsen yet."

"I'm guessing the supervisor has left that honour to you?"

"Naturally." Steinsson snorted a laugh. "Everything's black and white to them. They'll see me as the enemy, not him. He might be a coward, but he's a smart coward. Maybe this will prompt them to leave after all. They talk about it often enough."

"People can leave?"

Steinsson raised his chin. "See that gunship over there? Workers who quit get a one way ride out of here."

"Where do they go?"

"Where indeed. The choices are undercity or the desert. Now do you see why so few go through with it?"

Marcus nodded, considering his next move. If what the supervisor had told him was true then he needed a way out, and Steinsson had just informed him of one. He was desperate to discover what had happened to Leo, and if there was anything he could do to help.

"Say if Saul and Karlsen wanted to leave," he said, accompanying Steinsson back inside. "Do they need to tell anyone?"

"Just the supervisor. He's the one who's got to replace them."

Marcus thought for a moment. "I suppose he deals with all leave of absence requests, too."

"No, they go through me," said Steinsson. "Not that anyone bothers with that sort of thing."

"Why not?"

"You've read the contract. We're all permitted one leave of absence, but it has to be taken outside of work hours. The regime aren't stupid. They know we need that time to get some shut-eye, and if that doesn't put you off, the amount of paperwork will."

"But it's within site rules and regulations?"

"Yes," said Steinsson. "A legal requirement, apparently."

Marcus smiled. "Then I need to ask a favour."

16

The recently refurbished regent's office now lay at the heart of Lucas Turilli's domain on Tanis. It had taken an army of builders and decorators the best part of a week to get it right, but the work had finally been completed to a standard the regent deemed acceptable.

Jonas Hauser, Turilli's chief executor, had looked on in horror as his master's latest creation took shape. Gone were the bookcases and old mahogany desk, along with all traces of the room's previous occupant. The carpet had been ripped out and replaced by marble flooring, while the four wall-lights that glowed a warm orange were dismantled in favour of a gem-encrusted chandelier.

Having served the nobility long before Turilli came of age, Hauser felt that the regent's disregard for history and tradition masked something far more sinister, though he couldn't quite put his finger on it. He'd long since given up trying to advise or reason with Turilli, who liked to remind him that it wasn't his place to have an opinion. Where Rossi listened with a keen ear and open mind, Turilli would descend into madness whenever someone had the temerity to disagree with him.

Hauser watched the temperamental regent go about his business. Broken bones, bruised ribs and a fractured eye socket had taught the elderly executor the virtue of silence. He checked Turilli's schedule, noting it was clear for most of the day, then rechecked it just to be sure. He stood alone in a corner of the office, head bowed, while his master sat and conversed with two fierce-looking men dressed all in black.

He'd spent the past hour or so watching them, trying to listen in to what was being said whilst feigning indifference. Turilli himself seemed unusually subdued, letting the strangers do most of the talking, which was enough to make Hauser curious. They had claimed to be special operatives of the Royal Guard, with Turilli hastily confirming this before he could question them further. The regent had gone out of his way to accommodate these men despite the fact they'd arrived unannounced, and while they certainly looked like military operatives, Hauser had his doubts because he knew no such rank existed - at least not on Tanis.

He was so intent on eavesdropping that when Kastor - one of Divinity's most influential noblemen - suddenly appeared, he was powerless to stop him from storming inside.

"Turilli!" Kastor shouted, his fists clenched and dark eyes burning with anger. "You'd better have a damn good explanation for this outrage." He glared suspiciously at the two men then turned his baleful gaze upon Hauser. "Get out. This is a matter for the regent and I, not you..."

He searched his vocabulary for a word that could articulate his loathing.

"...Insects," he said eventually.

Alexis Kastor was not only older than Turilli, but considerably taller, too, and cut an imposing figure as he confronted the regent. Weaker men with more fragile hearts might well have recoiled in fear, but Turilli's movements were calm and unhurried. The regent rose slowly from his chair, bidding the operatives leave and for Hauser to wait outside. The room was cleared in a matter of seconds, leaving Turilli face to face with a man who looked ready to do him some harm.

"Of what 'outrage' do you speak, Kastor?" the regent asked nonchalantly. "And what makes you think I'm responsible for it?"

Kastor snarled, curling a lip to show some teeth. "Don't play ignorant with me. You know full well why I'm here, just like I know you're the one behind these new taxes. If your plan is to ruin Tanis and isolate the nobility, then congratulations - you've succeeded. This ends now,

Turilli. We're not paying."

The regent seated himself with a sigh. "Sit down, Kastor."

"I'd rather stand, thank you."

"As you wish."

"This smacks of arrogance," said Kastor. "I know you passed that edict. Are you going to deny it and call me a liar? See what happens."

Turilli chuckled and held up his hands. "No, I'm not denying it. Quite the contrary. And you're right; I *do* owe you an explanation - of sorts."

Thinking he was making progress, Kastor pulled up a chair. "Then explain."

"It's good to see you out and about again, Kastor. You've been sorely missed at council. Your man Dietrich informed me you were unwell. I trust you're feeling better now?"

"I am," said Kastor, trying to keep the irritation from his voice.

"Good. I've nothing but respect for the work you do. I understand that a prefect's job is never done. Trying to keep so many people happy all of the time can be stressful at best."

Kastor rolled his eyes. "Stressful? It's proving nigh on impossible given the taxes you've imposed on us. Have you no shame? No restraint? I'd hate to see what you do to your enemies if this is how you treat those closest to you."

"This affects every noble," said Turilli. "I've not singled anyone out for special treatment. No-one is exempt. The cost of maintaining our construction sites must be borne by all."

"Must? Why?"

"For reasons far beyond your understanding."

"Try me."

"Because I promised those on Earth that we'd the means to sustain such an endeavour," said Turilli. "They're using Tanis as a testing ground for their latest invention, and I had to fight long and hard for this great honour."

"If that's what you call it," Kastor scoffed.

"Look, I was offered the chance to win great renown for this world - for all of us - and I took it. Think of the rewards that await us if we succeed! Would you have turned them down, Kastor? Will you tell them now that we can't hold true to our word when we're so close?"

"I'd have asked my peers what *they* thought. You don't think though, do you? That's your problem. You just go ahead and do whatever you like without considering the consequences."

"One of the many perks of being regent." Turilli kept his expression bland. "This agreement was signed years ago. We can't renege on it now."

"I never signed any agreement," said Kastor. "Nor was I invited to air my views on this - what did you call it? - 'endeavour'. As far as the money's concerned, you can go whistle for it."

"Well, I'm sorry to hear that, Kastor. I must say, I'm surprised and disappointed you feel like this. You're the only one who's taken issue with the edict. Everyone else is happy to pay. Maybe it's because they can see how much this enterprise will benefit Tanis."

"And maybe they're just afraid to say 'no'. But I'm not one of your lapdogs, Turilli. I'm not someone you can threaten and cow so easily. You've gone too far this time."

Turilli smiled and shook his head. Far from being unsettled or intimidated, the regent appeared rather amused by Kastor's outburst. Unlike the rest of his peers, he wasn't even trying to hide the real reason behind his complaint - the cost. *Nobles*, Turilli thought, smirking inwardly. They could dress their arguments any way they liked, but it was only ever about money.

"Everyone misjudges me, you know," said the regent. "If I was the tyrant you perceive me to be then I'd have summoned the Royal Guard the moment you got here. But I welcome your opinion, Kastor. These taxes aren't permanent, so you and your house can sleep easy tonight."

Kastor stood up. "You're a clever man, Turilli. Others might not see it, but I do. You just keep pushing and pushing until you find our sticking point. Now that you have, you're showing remorse. I'm not one of your lackeys, so don't you dare treat me as such."

Turilli rose as well. "Speak plainly, prefect."

"Alright. You say we need to fund this project - why? If our masters on Earth can afford to send shipments of building materials and resources our way then surely they can finance it. Unless..." Kastor paused for a second to gather his thoughts. "Unless you told them *we* could."

Turilli allowed himself to laugh. "Oh, don't look so surprised. Someone has to pay the workers. The noble houses are monstrously rich - far better to put their wealth to good use than just sit on it."

"We 'sit' on that wealth to secure our futures," snapped Kastor. "That money's for our children."

"Some of it, perhaps. Do stop pouting, Kastor, it doesn't become you. If I'd have hesitated then the contract would've gone to another world and the chance for glory lost forever."

"What glory? And where are these rewards you speak of? What have we to show for your folly other than empty treasuries? Enough is enough. We're not paying."

"And I'm not going to force you to," said Turilli. "In fact, I'm rather glad you told me. I admire your honesty. If more people spoke out than sat on their feelings then Tanis would be a better place. Come, walk with me a moment." Turilli gestured for Kastor to join him by the room's tall bay window overlooking the city.

His point made, Kastor sauntered over to where the regent was standing. "I'm pleased you've seen sense. Maybe house Mercurio can find a way to contribute after all."

"It's entirely your decision," said Turilli. "Any funds you can spare would be gratefully accepted."

"The size of these donations could be increased if we were to learn what the money was being spent on," Kastor ventured.

Turilli smiled. "Look there, Kastor. The Chimera is nearing completion. In less than a year this'll all be over, and the galaxy changed forever. Come closer. If you look hard enough, you can see what it is we're building. You've a keen eye, so you'll soon spot what others have missed."

Kastor's curiosity was instantly piqued. He'd not only more than held his own against Turilli, but had somehow managed to convince the regent to give up the Chimera's secrets as well. His bold, aggressive display had paid off and put him firmly in charge. He was so intent on solving the mystery for himself that he failed to see Turilli take a silver object from his desk.

"I can't see it," Kastor complained.

"Top of the dome," said Turilli.

Kastor's eyes widened. "What in the name of-"

It was the last thing he ever said. In a blur, Turilli unsheathed the knife he was holding and plunged it into Kastor's neck. The regent stepped back, watching excitedly as he fought for his life. Kastor fell to his knees, trying desperately to stem the bleeding, but his struggles were in vain. Turilli circled the dying prefect like a hunter, electing to taunt him from a distance.

"My poor, naive Kastor. Your first mistake was thinking you had a choice at all. A regent does not barter for the loyalty his subjects owe him. You come here, to my office, and dare lecture me? You forget your place. I'm not about to tell Earth we're behind schedule because of one intransigent noble. Have you any idea what would happen if we failed? No, of course you don't. The finer points escape you, just like they do everyone. But fear not. Your troubles are almost over."

Turilli continued to rant for several minutes before he realised Kastor was dead. The regent retrieved his knife and wiped it clean on Kastor's tunic, annoyed to see blood all over his brand new flooring.

"Hauser!" Turilli roared at the top of his lungs. "Come here. Make yourself useful for once."

The executor came running, afraid he'd unwittingly provoked his master's ire. During his time with Turilli he'd seen some disturbing things, but nothing could have prepared him for the sight of Kastor's bloodied corpse.

"My lord?" he stammered, trying to stay focused. "You called for me?"

"I did," said Turilli, motioning towards the prefect's lifeless form. "Dispose of it."

Hauser looked unsure. "How, my lord?"

"What?"

"How do you want me to-"

"I don't know!" Turilli screeched. "Get a mop for starters. I can't have that lying there. Look at it - there's blood all over the place. Idiot. Learn to think for yourself! Oh, and don't forget to sanitise everything when you're done."

The regent watched as Hauser set about his grim task. Kastor's death would send a message to the rest of house Mercurio - pay or die. In time they'd choose a new prefect, but Turilli wasn't worried. They had their weapons, and he had his. He was about to draw up a list of suitable candidates when he noticed another executor lurking at the door.

What surprised him the most was that this one didn't show any fear. She was smartly dressed and attractive - for a servant-girl. Her red hair was her most striking feature, and Turilli immediately recognised her as one of Luther's executors. Only the administrator treated his staff so well.

"What news from Luther?" Turilli demanded, beckoning her inside. "It appears your master has been avoiding me of late."

The executor bowed politely. "I assure you, my lord, that is not his intent. He works hard and without pause to ensure Tanis continues to thrive. He asked me to convey his gratitude for being allowed to continue on as administrator."

"Did he?" Turilli scoffed.

"Yes, my lord. He seeks your counsel on a number of important issues."

"Though clearly not important enough to come see me himself."

"He's held talks with the nobility," said the executor. "He fears that if taxes continue to rise you'll lose the support of the houses. Talk could lead to action. He urges moderation, and asks you to consider relenting."

The thought of Luther worrying about his safety amused the regent. "His concerns are duly noted," said Turilli. "Now tell me, what do *you* think?"

"My lord?"

"Your opinion, my dear. Do you think I'm being overly harsh on the nobility? Should I - as Luther suggests - relent?"

"That depends," said the executor, keeping her tone level. "Would you rather I speak the truth, or tell you only what you want to hear?"

Turilli laughed aloud. "Ha! Very good. Luther has trained you well. It's as if I'm speaking with him now. He is right, of course. You may tell him that this latest rise was the last. Was there anything else?"

"As requested, five gunships now search for the traitor, Leo. Luther would like to follow this up with additional mobilisations."

Turilli shook his head. "We've more pressing matters to attend to. Tell your master to ready the Phalanx. We move against undercity in the morning. Is that all?"

"One final thing, my lord. Luther wants to procure some ships in advance to take the workers home. He assumes we're to honour their contracts as soon as the building work is complete."

"He is wrong to assume!" Turilli shouted. The regent's mood changed in an instant. "I've thought of a better way to cut costs, and it doesn't involve spending time and money on relocating half a million people. I've already told Luther to leave the important decisions to me. Must I repeat myself?" He sighed loudly, then dismissed the executor with a wave of his hand. "You can go. The day wears on and there's much to do."

Not wanting to push her luck, the executor retreated, thanking Turilli for his time as she went. She waited until she was well away from the prying eyes of the regent's servants before deactivating the video recorder in her watch.

Luther was playing a dangerous game, but his executors were under no illusions as to who would make a better regent.

17

Sitting comfortably at his desk, administrator Luther sipped a glass of orange juice as he pored over innumerable regime files. His quest for knowledge had taken him into the early hours of the morning, and while he'd learned much, this wasn't enough for the administrator to deem it a success.

"I'm wasting my time," Luther complained as his wife entered the office, not noticing the scowl on her face. "Maybe I'm missing something."

Elena looked at him impassively. "You've been in here all day. How about spending some time with me?"

Luther put the file he'd been reading down and sighed. "Not now, woman. This is important. I won't be long."

"Uh-huh. That's what you said nine hours ago." Elena released her raven hair from its ponytail and folded her arms. "What are you looking for?"

"Doesn't matter," said Luther, straightening his tunic.

Elena reached over and took one of the files for herself. "Must be *really* important if it's keeping you away from me."

The administrator protested, but Elena ignored him. Luther leaned forward, his concentration broken, and rested his head in his hands. Elena could be infuriating at the best of times, but he loved her and wouldn't have changed anything about her - even if he had the chance to. She was a rare beauty, a daughter of starlords, and could trace her heritage all the way back to the founding of Divinity. Standing barely shorter than he was, she exuded power, and Luther found it very seductive.

"Files on Turilli?" Elena scoffed, leafing through the pages. "You're right - you *are* wasting your time. What more can they tell you about him that you don't already know?"

Luther rubbed his eyes and sat up. "He's unwell."

"I think the word you're looking for is 'unstable'."

"Yes, but-"

"I know what you meant," said Elena. "He's a hype. So what? We all take a little something to get by."

Luther activated his holo-computer and dimmed the lights, noticing for the first time the striking red dress Elena was wearing. It fitted her form perfectly. "I'm trying to understand how he thinks. Look at this." The administrator played a recording that one of his executors had taken earlier. "There," he said triumphantly. "Look at the way he reacts when she starts using words like 'wants' and 'assumes'."

Elena appeared bemused by her husband's scheme. "And you're making these recordings because...?"

"Because the camera Rossi had me install in his office was removed."

"Well, I still don't see the point of whatever it is you're doing."

"That's easy for you to say. You don't have to work with the man." Luther pressed his hands together, fingertip to fingertip. "I need to learn more about what I'm dealing with. How to act, what to say. He's only unpredictable when things don't go his way. I can use these recordings and thereby use him to further my own cause - in time."

"It all seems terribly long-winded," said Elena. "Why not simply remove him from power and take your rightful place as regent? It's the least you deserve. Far better to rule yourself than be enthralled to that raving lunatic."

"This again," Luther sighed. Though content enough with his current station, Elena's ambitions for him went far beyond the rank and title of administrator. Her hatred of Turilli had only intensified since Rossi's death, and she'd often insinuate that a stronger, fairer individual should move to usurp him.

"If you don't, someone else will," she'd insisted.

Elena claimed this would be for the good of Tanis, but after fifteen years of marriage Luther was wise to her tricks and knew what she really wanted. He'd no desire to be regent himself, but as Turilli had lurched from one disaster to another, he'd begun to consider the possibility of moving against him - not for the power Elena craved, but to preserve what was left of Rossi's legacy.

"You'd make a fine regent, my love," Elena declared. "With me at your side."

"The nobility would never allow it," said Luther. "Neither would Earth. I just want an easy, quiet life. No complications. Besides, Turilli's helping me with a private matter. All things considered, he's not actually that bad - just a lot of work."

"Not that bad? He's insufferable. The way he talks down to me - me of all people. I've more royal blood in one finger than he does his whole body. And I don't know what you're smiling at, you're not much better, letting him fob you off with false promises and niceties."

"Then maybe you should do it," said Luther.

"Do what?"

"Kill Turilli."

"Don't be ridiculous," Elena scoffed. "I'm royalty."

"Whereas I'm not," said Luther.

Elena perched on the edge of his desk and shook her head. "I didn't mean it like that. I just think you deserve better - Tanis deserves better."

"You don't give a damn about Tanis," Luther snorted. "You could oust Turilli yourself if you really wanted to. But you're afraid, aren't you? Afraid of failing, and afraid you'll have no-one to hide behind if things go wrong."

"Which is exactly what you're doing now," said Elena. "Cowering behind Turilli because you're scared you'll be a worse regent than he is."

"I wouldn't be and you know it."

"Then why continue like this?"

"Because we have to." Luther assured her that his inaction owed nothing to cowardice, but legitimate concerns over what Turilli's masters might do if their vassal was to be displaced. He argued the ruling council had only promoted Turilli because he was easy to control, and that Earth's kingmakers would never tolerate a free-thinking regent. Elena listened intently, silently agreeing with everything her husband said, and it wasn't long before she'd devised a plan of her own.

"We can keep on talking," Luther continued, "but it won't change anything. Tanis doesn't elect a regent; Earth chooses one. All yes-men and women - it's the same on every world."

"Rossi was hardly a regime stooge," said Elena. "He was chosen too, was he not?"

"Yes, but Rossi never said any more than he needed to. He never gave the regime cause to doubt him. I think that everyone - those on Earth in particular - underestimated just how clever he was. A mistake they realised they'd made far too late, and one they aren't likely to make again."

Elena stood and moved gracefully around the desk towards Luther. "We can't be alone in thinking they chose poorly. There's bound to be someone on Tanis who hates him as much as I do. It shouldn't take much to convince them that removing Turilli would be for the best."

"Who do you have in mind?" asked Luther.

"No-one in particular. A pliable character, or one who wouldn't suspect what we were about. Use this pawn to unseat Turilli, then step in to restore order when he's gone. A coup that looks genuine; one we'd orchestrate, then crush. We'd be hailed as saviours, and the regency would be our reward."

"Leo certainly fits the bill," said Luther after a moment's thought. "He's naive and impressionable, easy to manage, and must be aching to get back at the regime. He has a strong motive for wanting Turilli dead, and no connection to us. He's perfect."

"You forget, dear husband, that he's also a murderer."

"I'm open to suggestions," said Luther, "but I didn't hear you mention anyone. And only a fool would believe what Turilli said. Leo's no murderer - I've got a recording that proves it. A recording I can use to ensure he does our bidding."

Elena's expression sharpened. "And how do you intend to find him? He could be anywhere by now, if he isn't dead already."

"Don't worry, I've a feeling he'll resurface sooner or later."

"Well, if you say so. I'll find you someone better in the meantime."

"No you won't."

What surprised Elena was not what Luther said, but the way he said it. Elena had expected his tone to be full of anger and mistrust, and for him to take umbrage over her remarks. Instead, the administrator's rebuke came as a matter-of-fact comment, and his voice carried the slightest hint of mockery.

Luther shook his head. "I've read his file. Perfect scores in all his tests. He's the most naturally gifted enforcer the contingent has ever trained. An officer in his third year. I didn't think that was even possible."

"It isn't. Or shouldn't be. Rossi must have put him on the fast-track."

"I'd agree, but that's something regents can't influence. Earth has the final say in who goes where and when."

"So he bribed them," said Elena.

"Now you're just clutching at straws. Leo's a thinker, just like his father. A survivor."

"His father? They weren't related. And how do you intend to manipulate him if he's so smart? You know what I think?"

"No, but I've a feeling you're about to tell me," Luther mumbled.

"I think you admire the boy. I think you'd rather make Leo regent and rule through him instead."

"Would that be such a bad idea? Rossi raised him to be a good person. That's what Tanis needs right now."

"You aren't listening!" Elena snapped. "*You're* a good person. I know it, and so did Rossi. He never wanted Leo to replace him - if he'd had a choice he would have chosen you."

Elena turned away in frustration. Only Luther vexed her this much.

She loved him, but hated how stubborn he could be. He'd pursue his ideas doggedly, preferring to take the longer route to success over the shortcuts she offered. She accepted her scheming was more to blame for this than his pride, and often reflected on the years she'd spent putting her own interests first, thus making him wary of every word she said.

Luther rose from his chair. Elena felt his hands on her shoulders and allowed him to turn her around.

"We wait," he said, his voice soft and silky. "Can you do that for me?"

Elena wrapped her arms around his waist and leaned against him. "I suppose so." Luther held her like a child, strength flowing from his grip, and Elena let her body relax. Nothing would be decided today, but she was a patient woman and content to play the long game. "Are you coming to bed?" she asked, suppressing a yawn.

"No. I've business in undercity."

Elena pulled away from him. "What business?"

"Enforcer business. Turilli wants me to lead the Phalanx against the crimelords."

"That man. And what am I to do with you gone?"

"I'm sure you'll think of something," said Luther. "But let's have no more talk of the regency." The administrator returned to his desk and retrieved the file he'd been reading previously. "Don't wait up for me."

Elena knew there was little point in arguing. Luther was a kind, attentive man, and would come to her just as soon as his work was done. She pretended to be hurt by his flippant behaviour and stormed out, looking forward to the apologies and expensive gifts that would follow.

Before she left, she caught a glimpse of the file her husband was holding. On the front was written a word she'd heard mentioned before, a word she'd ignored and thought very little of until now.

Chimera.

18

Leo and Luna had made slow progress. Incessant sandstorms swept the barren plains of Tanis, turning their drive across the desert into a protracted, arduous affair. Luna's plan to strike out had suffered a setback when the airspeeder - its engine and vents clogged with sand - finally ceased to work. Continuing on foot, she chose this moment to tell Leo where they were going; a secluded township called Arcana.

The two outcasts half expected Turilli to come after them, but knew the regent's gunships would remain grounded until the weather cleared. A brief lull between storms allowed Leo to share with Luna what he'd learned from Rossi's file, shaking her confidence to the core. Luna feared that unless they acted soon, her devotion to Tanis wouldn't be enough to save those she loved from the regime's murderous intentions.

Luna took two bottles of water out of a holdall and passed one to Leo. She watched him drink, looking back on everything he'd done for her homeworld, and ahead to all the things he had yet to do. Though they'd be safe in Arcana, Luna didn't want to feel safe. Out here, with Leo, she felt alive.

Arcana was a remote, sparsely populated settlement hidden amongst the dunes. It sat within a dusty valley three hundred leagues north of Divinity, home to a hardy people who lived short but free lives. From above, Leo watched them in their daily struggle against the encroaching sands. He understood why they'd chosen this way of life but also recognised the futility of their gallant efforts. It hadn't taken him long to work out that if the great dunes continued migrating,

Arcana would be gone in less than forty years.

"There's always been a settlement here," said Luna, unwilling to entertain the possibility that this could happen in her lifetime. "And there always will be."

Leo deduced she'd formed an emotional attachment to the people of Arcana - one that had blinded her to the terrible reality facing them. "One that started the day you found the speeder locked inside your parents' vault."

"How could you possibly know that?" Luna scoffed incredulously.

Leo realised he'd been thinking out loud. "Because I know *you*," he said with a smile. "The academy wasn't challenging enough - you were always looking for things to do and places to go."

"Simpler times," said Luna.

"The vault was a test," Leo continued, "but that wasn't going to stop you. You can break into anything. So you took the speeder and found something you weren't expecting - something you deemed important enough to keep going back to. I bet it came as quite a shock when you stumbled upon Arcana."

"Naturally." Luna started walking towards the town and motioned for Leo to follow. These were her people, and she wouldn't let anything happen to them. Leo was wrong about Arcana's fate.

He had to be.

The road into Arcana was flanked by a series of unmanned watchtowers, half submerged beneath the sands. Leo concluded that Arcana was once a single district within a much larger town, and that this settlement's layout was not unique. The design was symmetrical and well executed, the buildings all alike, suggesting its creators had been copying a template - a constructor's guidebook that all colonists would have been expected to follow and not deviate from.

Leo and Luna proceeded inside. With no sentries or lookouts, their arrival went unchallenged but not unnoticed. The townsfolk were delighted to see Luna had returned and stopped working, welcoming her as if she was one of their own.

They were far more cautious around Leo. "Who's this?" one of the women asked. The children of Arcana surrounded him, putting forward their own theories.

"A traveller."

"An enforcer."

"A spy."

"Luna's boyfriend."

This last remark provoked a chorus of chirrups, whistles and laughter. Playing along, Luna took hold of Leo's arm and led him away. As they walked together, she looked back at the group and winked suggestively, reducing many of the children to hysterics.

His face red with embarrassment, Leo tried to avoid making eye contact with anyone. Sensing no threat from him, the townsfolk relaxed. Luna was an exceptional judge of character. If she trusted him, so could they.

Leo pressed ahead, determined to see as much of Arcana as he could. He hadn't got far when he stopped in front of a tall white sandstone building with a small cross on top.

"The people meet here occasionally," said Luna, noting his interest. "There's room enough for everyone."

"Can we go inside?"

"Sure." Luna didn't know if he was hoping to find something or just wanted to get off the streets.

Leo entered first. A flicker of disappointment crossed his face. Save for the rows of pews and a lectern, the building was empty. The odd window let in some light, but there was nothing spectacular or unique about it.

"Has it always been an assembly hall?" he asked Luna.

"As far as I know."

They walked along the nave towards the lectern; an unremarkable wooden stand from where countless sermons and eulogies had been delivered over the years. Luna recalled the speakers' impassioned rhetoric, the people who hung on their every word, and all the good that had flowed from this place and into the world. She was eleven when she'd heard her first sermon. The building was full, and many of the townsfolk had to stand. Nine years on, and there was now a seat for everyone.

Leo knelt and laid his palm flat on the tiled floor. "Terracotta," he murmured. "Cheap, but built to endure." He closed his eyes and wondered if maybe this building had served another purpose in the past.

"Let's find you a place to stay," said Luna from behind him. "And a change of clothes."

Leo stood up slowly. "A shower would be nice."

"We're in Arcana, not Divinity," Luna smiled.

"Oh, right. Sorry."

"There's an underground lake you can use," said Luna. "Arcana lies directly above it. They've managed to get the old water purification system working, but don't expect any of the luxuries you're used to."

Leo laughed. "At least no-one's trying to kill me here." He was about to follow Luna back down the nave when he heard the tramp of feet and sound of voices from outside.

The doors opened and a tall, blonde-haired man appeared holding a book under his right arm. He glanced briefly at Leo then turned to shut the doors behind him, closing them softly and with care.

"They told me I'd find you here," the stranger said, and Leo couldn't tell whether he was addressing Luna, himself, or the both of them.

The man was scruffy and unshaven, his skin tanned from a life spent outdoors. Leo estimated him to be a little older than he was, and noticed he walked with a slight limp as he approached them. Though the stranger wore a welcoming smile, Leo sensed bitterness and anger lurking beneath his placid exterior, like a rabid dog on the end of a slowly fraying rope.

"It's not safe out there," the man said to Luna as he leaned casually against one of the pews. "The sands are shifting again."

"So I've seen," Luna replied.

"Yes. The Season of Storms has broken early this year. Still, at least you didn't make the journey alone this time." The man turned to Leo and said, "Aren't you going to introduce us?"

Looking distinctly uncomfortable, Luna put her hands in her pockets and mumbled, "Leo Rossi, a friend of mine from the academy. Leo, this is Martin Kruger. Arcana's first citizen."

Leo thought it strange that one so young occupied such an important position. He extended his hand but Kruger refused to shake it, the man electing to fold his arms and fix him with a cold stare instead.

"Yes, I've heard all about you," Kruger sneered, drawing himself up to his full height. "Leo Rossi. *The* Leo Rossi. Why didn't you tell us you were coming? We'd have held a great feast in your honour had we known. Put on a show. That's what you nobles like, isn't it? As it is, I imagine we're something of a let-down."

Leo found himself at a loss for words. Kruger's tone was aggressive and heavy with sarcasm, and Leo struggled to understand why he'd reacted so angrily after learning his name. Had he slighted or offended him in some way? Maybe he'd broken one of the town's laws or failed to observe a long-standing custom. Keen to try and defuse the situation, Leo thought it best to clarify his position and apprise Kruger of recent events.

"I don't really care who sits on some golden throne in some far-off palace," said Kruger. "Turilli strikes me as someone who'll end up destroying himself - or everyone around him. Still, there's nothing more he can do to us that hasn't been done already. Your father saw to that."

"You should be proud of these people," Leo offered, doing his best to stay positive. "Their spirit and resilience do you great credit."

"Oh, I am. But do not presume to know my people better than me. You and your kind have done nothing to help them."

"We're not all alike," said Leo. "We do what we can."

"Save your excuses," Kruger scolded. "They're meaningless. What do you know of suffering - you've never had to work a day in your life. I'll bet none of you have. You wouldn't last five minutes out here because you've inherited your wealth and think you're entitled to a life of luxury, just like you think our sole purpose is to break our backs for the privileged few. We fight to live and live to work - what do you do?"

Leo shuffled uneasily. "We could have done more. *I* could have done more."

"You're not in a position to help," said Kruger. "You never were. It's the regent and his lackeys who hold power - the same hypocrites who lie and cheat and ask your opinion when they've already decided what to do. Turilli might be many things, but at least he's blunt, speaks his mind and doesn't bother maintaining the pretence of democracy. You've seen for yourself how bad things are. The regime are destroying the townships of Tanis, and people like you are letting it happen."

"I don't understand," said Leo, confused. "They let you live here in peace. If you're so concerned for the future, why not move to Divinity?"

"Because that's what they want! The people of Tanis all together in one place, all under regime control." Kruger shook his head. "You really didn't know your father at all, did you? He started the process. A campaign of extermination against the towns that refused to bow. He'd have succeeded there and then were it not for the questions his own ministers were asking. But this minor setback didn't stop him; if anything it inspired him to try harder. He saw it as a challenge. By cutting ties with the villages he deprived us of vital aid and the means to halt the advancing dunes. He'd saved the townsfolk from destruction only to doom them to a slow death. Too slow for his liking, as it turned out. Now each year the regime take the fittest men and women to work in the factories and palaces of Divinity, with some even training to become enforcers."

"I was close to the regent," said Leo. "I heard nothing of this."

"Then you heard only what you wanted to. That, or he did a good job of keeping you in the dark."

Leo fell silent, wondering how many more secrets his adoptive father had suppressed. An overwhelming sadness gripped his heart. He remembered precious little of his childhood, and the rest of his life had turned out to be nothing more than a lie.

Seeing Leo upset, Luna, who'd been standing quietly listening to Kruger's rant, decided to speak up. She lambasted Kruger for his harsh remarks, reminding him that Leo had done more for Tanis than most of the nobility, and that she herself was the daughter of one of Divinity's noble houses.

"That's different," said Kruger. "You help us willingly. He's here because he's got no other choice."

"I'm here because of Luna," Leo retorted, finding his voice at last. "I want to help, not whine about my lot in life and how good things used to be a decade or two ago."

"More talk," said Kruger. "That's all you people do. There's no-one left to speak out and fight anymore because they've all been slaughtered or paid off by the regime. Look, I appreciate the offer, but if Turilli wants you dead then the best thing you can do is leave. Don't give that tyrant the excuse he needs to destroy us, because he's certainly looking for one."

"If Leo goes, so do I," said Luna, her eyes ablaze. "Cast us out and you're no better than Turilli."

Leo looked past all of Kruger's bluster and saw a kind, caring individual who'd been subjected to a lifetime of hurt and broken promises. It would have been easy to label him a cynical, bitter man, but the depth of feeling and passion behind his words told Leo everything he needed to know about him.

"You're wrong, Kruger," Leo said suddenly, interrupting the argument that had followed in the wake of Luna's statement. "The regime haven't silenced everyone. You still have the courage to speak your mind, as do I."

"And I," said Luna.

"What'll that change?" Kruger spat. "You want to talk them into submission?"

"Nothing like that," said Leo. "But we can work together to save your people. You could use my skills, so what's stopping you from accepting my help? I thought you had Arcana's best interests at heart? Don't let pride get in the way of progress."

"Pride? I've given this town my life - done everything I can without complaint or need of praise - are you saying it isn't enough? Who are you to pass judgement? You don't know anything about me."

"On the contrary, I know you very well. For a start, your name tells me that while you might be native to this world, your ancestors weren't. It's fairly safe to assume you've had military training judging from your quick reflexes and how in tune you are with your surroundings. Even the way you move - a dead giveaway. But I don't recall a Martin Kruger ever having served in the contingent. So where were you assigned? The Royal Guard, perhaps? The Phalanx?"

"Wait a minute," Luna interjected, "Kruger was never an enforcer."

"Wasn't he? He said so himself that some of the townsfolk go on to join the military. He'd have been ten when they took him, old enough to begin basic training but naive enough to be successfully indoctrinated. And yet here he is, back in Arcana. How? We all know what happens to deserters, and he's far too young to have completed a full tour. The only way out - other than suicide - is to try and convince them you're more of a liability than an asset. Layabouts are disciplined, so he must have suffered serious injury in the line of duty. Look at the way he's holding his leg. That's not recent, it's long-term. I'm guessing friendly fire or accidental discharge."

Kruger pretended to itch his leg and cleared his throat.

Leo smiled and addressed Kruger directly. "When you came back to Arcana, the village wasn't how you remembered it. You felt guilty, blamed yourself for what had happened and wanted to make amends. Now every day you're not just fighting the dunes but the weight of the past as well. Your quest for redemption is personified by Arcana's ongoing fight to survive. Here you're needed and loved - you have a purpose until such time as you decide you've done enough. But we both know that day will never come, don't we? You feel that a lifetime isn't long enough to right all the wrongs in the world, and it's the fear of failing those you love that is destroying you."

The tone of Leo's words sent a shiver down Kruger's spine. He glared at Luna, not knowing whether to be angry or impressed. "Did you tell him all this?" he demanded.

Luna shook her head. "I didn't even know half of it."

"I'm not saying I can change the world," Leo continued. "Just the lives of these people for the better. We don't have to be best friends, just work together. Don't worry about all the things you can't do. Focus on what you *can*."

Again, Leo offered his hand. This time, Kruger shook it firmly. "I've something here that might help," Kruger said, handing over the book that he'd been holding on to.

Leo retrieved Rossi's file from his holdall and passed it to Kruger. "And this could be of use to you."

Kruger took the file, turned and departed without a word.

"Well," Leo said to Luna. "I think that went rather well, don't you?"

Luna laughed aloud. "He didn't hit you or swear once. I call that a result."

19

Saul and Karlsen were hatching a plan. Like all of their schemes it was simple and reckless, with progress hindered by day-long debates and disagreements over the most minor details. These petty disputes would have typically resulted in one or both men backing out before they'd agreed where to begin, but on this occasion they persevered, determined to rid themselves of their hateful supervisor once and for all.

"People die here every day," said Karlsen. "We can make it look like an accident."

Saul was less optimistic. "And if we succeed? What then? They'll just replace him with another."

"But that'll take time. A week or two, maybe more. Besides, whoever we get can't be any worse."

The two welders learned to compromise, directing their repressed anger towards the supervisor instead of each other. Heated arguments still flared up at the slightest provocation, but Saul surprised everyone by letting Karlsen have the last word. This in turn prompted Karlsen to support his friend whenever he expressed doubts over their enterprise, reminding him of all the grief the supervisor had caused them in order to keep him focused.

"This vendetta against us ends now," he declared boldly.

Though unanimous in their contempt for the supervisor, neither man particularly relished the idea of murdering their nemesis in cold blood. Saul wanted to frame him for pocketing regime funds, while Karlsen suggested enlisting some of the other welders to do their work for them. Unable to find any incriminating documents, Saul reluctantly approved Karlsen's idea.

It took them a few seconds to agree on who they could trust. Their peers were either too dense or too passive, and Saul suspected that Steinsson was secretly working for the regime. Only one met their standards, but how he felt about them was anyone's guess. Undeterred, Saul and Karlsen decided to ask him if he wanted in.

Their campaign of flattery took Marcus by surprise. Saul's offer to share the workload and Karlsen's repeated attempts to befriend him seemed genuine, but Marcus wasn't fooled.

"I'll think about it," he said, hoping he'd be long gone before they forced him to make a decision.

Marcus pretended to empathise with them whilst planning his escape. Giovanni Rossi was dead, and all around Divinity there were signs Turilli's reign of terror was gathering momentum. Though he feared the mad regent had already done his worst, he wasn't about to give up on Leo so readily.

His focus had switched from the Chimera to the regime's elite cadre of gunship pilots. They were supposed to relocate any workers who quit the site, but Steinsson warned him that few of them followed protocol.

"You're not thinking of leaving, are you?" Steinsson asked, worried he might be about to lose a good friend.

"My sister's in undercity," said Marcus. "The regime have gone in with everything they've got."

"Why?"

"It's a sanctioned cull of the lower classes. Population control. I have to make sure she's alright."

Moved by Marcus' devotion to his family, Steinsson agreed to help. He arranged for one of the more honest pilots to meet with Marcus - a professional he didn't need to bribe or deceive in order to secure their services.

"This one won't ask questions," Steinsson assured his friend, "but you won't be going anywhere today. These pilots need at least three months' notice. All outbound flights from the Chimera have to be approved by the administrator first."

Though tired and tense, Marcus stuck to his task. He didn't like lying to Steinsson, but couldn't tell him the truth for fear that the supervisor might be listening. Steinsson thought he was signing off a legitimate leave of absence, but Marcus hadn't the heart to tell him he wouldn't be coming back.

Unaware of Marcus' true motives, Steinsson accompanied him outside. "Two minutes," he said, pleased to see the pilot waiting for them. "I'll stall the supervisor should you need longer. Saul and Karlsen will tell you what happens if he catches you coming back late from your break."

Marcus headed over to where the pilot was standing and introduced himself.

"Lucas, you say?" she remarked, inspecting him intently. "I'm Kara. Steinsson said you need a pilot."

"That's right," said Marcus. "I want out."

"Can't say that I blame you. You're not the first. Won't be the last, either."

Marcus blinked. "How many?"

"I've taken several hundred. Men, women, children. All sorts. All thinking they'll be safe the moment they walk out those doors."

"Aren't they?"

Kara looked up at him. "Depends on the pilot. Just because I've got morals doesn't mean the rest of my unit has. They'd drop you out in the desert and leave you to die - or come back a day later and hunt you for sport. It's disgusting. Gives honest people like me a bad name. Why, if I was regent I'd-"

"No time for that," Marcus interrupted. "Is there anywhere on Tanis that's actually safe? The Chimera's a death-trap, undercity's starting to resemble a warzone and there are gunships flying off into the desert at all hours."

"Probably not." Kara grinned. "It'll quiet down in a couple of days. I don't know what's happening in undercity, but you needn't worry about the gunships. We've been given orders to search for two murderers, that's all."

"Seems to me like someone's gone to an awful lot of trouble just for two murderers. Think you'll catch them?"

"Not a chance. CO wants us to sweep the planet with five gunships. We'd need five hundred. I'm telling you, whoever's in charge of this balls-up has no understanding of the distances and logistics involved. Damn pencil pushers keep telling us how to do our job, think they know best. Murderers, my arse. If I found them I'd pretend I hadn't, and I'm pretty sure the others would too."

"What do you mean?"

"One of them used to serve in the contingent. Kindest man I've ever met."

"And the other?"

"Some girl from one of the noble houses." Kara shook her head. "Murderers. The nobility don't go around butchering one another. They have slaves for that sort of business. You want my opinion? It's a set-up."

Marcus thought for a moment. If the man the enforcers were hunting was Leo and Luna had gone with him, then he'd an idea where they might go. Though he'd no proof and very little to go on, he had to start looking somewhere.

"So," Kara continued, "where to?"

"The desert," said Marcus. "A place called Arcana. Heard of it?"

"Yes, I know it. I'll get you there. When would you like to go?"

Marcus remembered what Steinsson had said but thought he'd try his luck anyway. "Today. Now, if possible."

"No can do. Need approval from the administrator first. Don't look so worried - I'll get it. Just takes time."

"How much time?"

"About three months." Kara paused. "Actually, I'd wait a little longer if I were you. There's a forced recruitment drive set for Arcana and the northern villages that week. You could end up back where you started if the enforcers find you. We'll go when it's over."

"Don't worry about that," said Marcus. "Just get me there as soon as you can."

"Alright," Kara huffed. "No need to be rude. I'll file the flight plan and see you in three months."

"Count on it. And don't tell anyone but those you have to where we're going. The fewer people who know about this, the better."

Leaving politics to her husband, Elena basked in the late afternoon sun. She sat on the rim of a fountain somewhere on the fourth level, watching the nobles and councillors strut about while she plotted and schemed.

The sun's rays touched the highest towers of the regent's palace, and around them the air seemed to shimmer. Elena leaned back, gazing up at her destiny. Small water droplets splashed against her skin, glistening like jewels in the sunlight, and she welcomed their cooling touch even though she was accustomed to the heat.

With Luther hard at work and a construction site on her doorstep, she would often leave the palace during the day and look for things to do. The views her penthouse offered were spectacular, but she wasn't able to fully enjoy them until the building work was complete.

Elena closed her eyes and sighed contentedly, mentally rehearsing the intricacies of her latest plan. The fourth level was home to Divinity's most prestigious retailers, and while she made a habit of going shopping there at least once a week, she wasn't here for clothes or jewellery today.

A company of enforcers trudged past, disturbing her contemplation. Weighed down by weapons and armour, Elena didn't envy them in the slightest. The Royal Guard might have had it easy patrolling the air-conditioned corridors of the palace, but the rest of the contingent weren't so lucky. Underpaid and overworked, Elena pitied those stationed in undercity the most.

She checked the time and stood up, her eyes fixed on a marble stairway over to her right. Sure enough, the person she'd been waiting for appeared just like she knew he would, proceeding across the plaza towards the shops. Elena waited until he'd passed by before setting off in pursuit, keeping her prey in sight at all times.

Jonas Hauser had no idea that he was being followed. His responsibilities had doubled now that his master was regent, forcing the elderly executor to work around the clock. Starved of sleep, Turilli's constant demands had sapped his strength and made him careless. Afraid to ask for a day's respite, he had instead requested a transfer to Luther's office, enraging Turilli to the point of violence. Hauser had argued that a younger, fitter executor could better serve him, but no amount of reasoning could sway the regent, who'd responded by striking him repeatedly and calling him a traitor. Elena had watched the drama unfold from a distance like she always did, but this time decided to act and turn the situation to her advantage.

Hauser put on a sudden burst of speed but Elena hung back, happy for him to widen the gap between them. She'd spent weeks watching him and learning his routine and knew exactly where he was going.

All the components of her plan were now in place. Ahead, the enforcers had set up a temporary checkpoint and were stopping people at random, acting on rumours that Leo had returned to the city. Elena figured that Hauser knew all there was to know about Turilli's secret dealings, but she had to decide whether to try and extract this information from him or convince him to part with it. Fortunately, his desire to join Luther's staff had provided her with an edge. If she played this right then she'd gain a useful ally. Fail, and Hauser could tell Turilli everything.

One of the enforcers moved to intercept him, but Hauser carried on walking without noticing the checkpoint.

"Papers," the enforcer demanded, raising his baton and using it to block Hauser's path. "Let me see some identification."

"What?" Hauser snapped. "I'm the regent's chief executor. If you know what's good for you then you'll step aside and let me pass."

His haughty response didn't go down well with the enforcer. "I don't care if you're the regent himself. There are dangerous criminals abroad. Murderers. Show me your papers or I'll be forced to detain you."

It wasn't in Hauser's nature to argue or pull rank, but he was tired and in a foul mood. "Who carries their papers with them?" he spat, realising he'd left his back at the palace. "Damn military drone. Go ahead and detain me. Then you can explain to the regent exactly why his afternoon meetings didn't happen."

Just as the enforcer was about to retaliate, Elena made her move. "Wait. I know this man," she declared, interceding on Hauser's behalf. "I can vouch for him. Check my papers instead."

The enforcer hesitated, unsure how best to proceed. He turned to his commanding officer, but she had her hands full with a rowdy minister and his litter-bearers. "I believe they're in order, my lady," he said after a while, affording them only the most cursory of glances. "Carry on."

Elena put her arm through Hauser's and led him away from the bemused enforcer. "My husband speaks very highly of you," she remarked, "but I'm yet to be convinced. Taking on a company of soldiers isn't the wisest thing to do now, is it?"

Hauser hung his head. "No, my lady."

"Brave, yes," she continued, "but reckless. Turilli's enforcers are a law unto themselves."

"They could have easily turned on you," said Hauser. "Why help me?"

Elena smiled. "We've not spoken at length before, have we?"

"Just the once, my lady. At Rossi's wake."

"Yes, I remember. Turilli sent you in his stead because he was having one of his moments. It's a pity he doesn't appreciate his executors. Ours are acknowledged and rewarded for the work they do."

Hauser frowned, silently cursing the day he'd sworn to serve Turilli. He'd seen how well Luther treated his staff and wanted out of the regent's madhouse, but Turilli had slammed the door firmly shut. With his transfer blocked, he could no longer see an exit and had resigned himself to the fact that his master would never let him go.

Elena was well aware of Hauser's predicament. "I can have Luther force the issue if you like," she suggested. "Turilli's taken quite a shine to him. Your application hasn't been rejected, and I'm certain the regent will reconsider. Turilli blocking it tells me he needs you more than he lets on, but he might see his way for my husband."

"You'd do that for me?" Hauser scoffed, stopping abruptly. "Why? What do you want in return?"

Elena tutted. "So suspicious! Can't a woman help someone realise their potential? I ask for nothing - it's Luther who needs your assistance."

"Luther?"

"Yes, though I suspect he wouldn't be too happy if he learned we were having this conversation. Male ego and such."

"How can I help?"

"Well," said Elena, "that's easy. Luther can't do his job because Turilli doesn't tell him anything. The city's funds and resources aren't being fully utilised - he just expects Luther to know what to do with them. But how can he without being accused of second-guessing him? The noble houses are just waiting for Luther to make a mistake so they can replace him with one of their own. Eventually we'll reach a point where Divinity grinds to a halt and Turilli takes his anger out on those around him as a result. It won't be pretty. But if you can inform Luther of Turilli's dealings then it might help him and in turn placate your master."

Hauser pulled a face. "You want me to spy on Turilli?"

"I want you to try and make Luther's life a little easier. He's so caught up in his work that I hardly get to see him. I'm not demanding you break your oath to the regent, nor am I trying to bribe you. I would, however, ask you to help us."

"How?"

"Pass on to me anything you think could benefit Luther. If you do this, I can guarantee he will get Turilli to reconsider your request. My husband can be very persuasive. Do we understand each other?"

Hauser nodded. "I should tell you that I work faster if there's an incentive, my lady."

"What incentive?"

"With Turilli it's all stick. I prefer carrots. Carrots in the form of cash."

Anger sparked in Elena's eyes. If any of Luther's executors had spoken to her in such a brazen manner then she'd have had them flogged on the spot. "Blasted impudence," she muttered under her breath, then turned to address Hauser directly. "That won't be a problem."

"Excellent. I'll get started right away. Is there anything you want me to pay particular attention to?"

Elena folded her arms and looked up at the Chimera. "That monstrosity, for one. Luther's worried the workers are cutting corners and I want to know what my money's being spent on. We can't sleep for worry the infernal thing will collapse and take half of Divinity with it."

Hauser thought for a moment. His master talked about the Chimera all the time. "I've seen the plans," he said, "but they're all designated low priority. Are you certain this is worth the effort? It looks fine to me."

"Luther seems to think so," said Elena. "Get me those plans if you can. I want to see them."

"I'll get them, my lady." Hauser was still puzzled as to why she and Luther were so interested in the Chimera. It was just a building, and an oversized, expensive one at that. "Is there anything else you'd have me do?" he asked, confident he'd be able to retrieve the plans.

"In time, perhaps. Let's call this a trial run. We'll see how you do then take it from there."

"And payment?" Hauser pressed.

"Upon completion. You have my word. Bring me the plans and anything else that might be useful. You know where to find me."

Hauser took off, as eager as a little boy being given his first bike.

While he looked forward to working for Luther, Elena was already planning ahead. She decided she'd equip him with a voice recorder the next time they met. If Turilli spoke openly about the Chimera in Hauser's presence, it must have been because he believed his executor was too stupid to understand what he was saying.

But she might.

With Hauser long gone, Elena went back to the checkpoint, exchanged words with the commanding officer and departed with the enforcers in tow.

20

It was the hottest day of the year so far, and Martin Kruger was out looking for Leo. At Luna's urging, he'd got to know his illustrious guest a little better, and it wasn't long before he'd realised there was something different about him.

Great events had started happening in Arcana - events that Leo alone had the brilliance to envision and the will to follow through - and Kruger couldn't help but think he'd judged a good man too rashly.

But he still had his concerns and felt compelled to voice them.

Leo was standing atop Arcana's new perimeter wall. He'd been working on the town's defences all day and showed no signs of slowing.

"Have you got a moment?" Kruger called up to him. "We need to talk."

Leo waved him over. Kruger ascended a rickety wooden ladder and dusted himself off, casting his eye over Leo's army of volunteers. They never used to turn out for him in such numbers.

"We've done well today," said Leo, wiping the sweat from his brow. "Another day, maybe two, and Arcana will be safe."

Kruger nodded thoughtfully. "From the sands, at least."

"But not your pessimism," Leo laughed. "What's wrong?"

"This file of yours," said Kruger, folding his arms. "You say the old regent intended you to have it?"

"That's right."

"So maybe he was hoping you'd have used it by now..."

Leo shrugged. "Maybe." The hurt of his adoptive father's betrayal still cut deep.

"There's no 'maybe' about it," Kruger scowled. "I've read the file. A keen mind can decipher it, but a great one might be able to exploit it."

"You're more than welcome to try."

"Credit me with at least a modicum of intelligence," said Kruger. "I've not spent the last three months with my head in the sand waiting for you to act. Neither has Luna. Now we know the regime's plan it's up to us to stop them, or at the very least warn the people what they're up against. Turilli and his minions can continue to persecute us, but they haven't won yet. You know what it is they're building, but *I* want to know what you're going to do about it."

Leo was tempted to tell Kruger what he wanted to hear just to avoid another argument. He'd already clashed with Luna over the same subject earlier that day and was tired of fighting. Leo had hoped the three of them could agree on a measured, practical response, but Kruger didn't look like he was in the mood to compromise. He'd read the file and reacted as any sane man would, but while his anger was justified, it blinded him to the moral dilemma Leo had spent days agonising over.

Attacking the regime head-on was madness. Their enforcer battalions, though small in number, had weapons and training, and any war Kruger started would end badly for all the innocents involved.

But do nothing and they'd be abandoning the people to their fate.

"It's not as simple as that," Leo said eventually. "What *can* we do?"

"Well, I've already decided," said Kruger. "You can join me if you like or stay here - it's your choice. I thought I'd ask, though, just in case you had any ideas of your own."

"No, but I'm guessing yours involves rallying enough people to try and take Divinity in a straight fight."

Kruger nodded. "There's no point training them. Numbers will make up for our lack of weapons."

"And how do you plan on getting inside? Those walls are four hundred metres high."

"We'll breach them."

"Say you do. Say you make it all the way to the nineteenth level. There's another wall there, only this one has its own garrison of enforcers and gunships. Next, you'll have to face the Phalanx, the Royal Guard and whatever other nasty surprises are lurking beyond."

"We'll beat them too. Like the heroes of old we'll march on Divinity, smash the gates and win our freedom."

"It'll be a massacre."

Kruger looked at him, his eyes ablaze. "Then we'll just have to take as many of them with us as we can."

"This is your plan?" Leo blinked with surprise. "You wouldn't get anywhere near Divinity. Turilli's gunships would make short work of any uprising." He sighed and said, "You don't know the man like I do. He's utterly convinced of his own divinity but ruled by an inordinate fear of his masters on Earth. He'd sooner destroy his city than lose it to you."

"So what if the odds are against us?" Kruger snapped. "You think our ancestors would have hesitated as you do? Think they'd have stood by and let a tyrant win? History shows they didn't."

"No, history shows revolutions to be short, bloody and often unsuccessful. Your heroes of old are just that, Kruger. They exist in your mind and in stories, not the real world. Everyday men and women who've been made greater than they were by an adoring public, whose deeds have been exaggerated by centuries of lies and the passing of time. Now there's just you, me and a handful of decent people trying to do the right thing."

Kruger felt his optimism drain away. Leo could inspire or crush a man with just a few select words, and now Kruger began to realise the hopelessness of their situation. He'd always believed they stood a fighting chance and that one day he'd be able to emulate the feats of his idols, but Leo was right. The days of freedom fighters and the glorious uprisings they'd sparked were consigned to history. Within months the regime would have the means to ensure they never returned.

"Let me tell you a story about a young peasant girl," said Leo.

"Her country was riven by political instability and falling to a ruthless enemy. Demoralised and desperate, the lord she had sworn to serve asked her to lead his armies in battle. Trusting a girl with no concept of war and military tactics might sound like folly, but the lord's list of allies was short and he'd already exhausted every rational option. This remarkable girl won a series of stunning victories against all the odds, driving the invaders back and uniting her country, giving her lord the lands and support he needed to crown himself king.

"The invading armies were so disheartened that the men who led them sued for peace, fearful they'd lose the war to an illiterate peasant girl. She warned the king that it was a ruse - a ploy to buy time - but he didn't listen. When the aggressors renewed their offensive they got lucky by capturing her when she came to the aid of a besieged town. They didn't kill her immediately - they had to make her pay for defying them. Only after humiliating her and a politically motivated trial did they grant her the mercy of death. Her king made no attempt to secure her release, for her popularity and influence were now seen as a threat to him. The war was lost soon after and her name faded from history."

Kruger frowned. "I see that you were fed the same lies I was while at the academy. But I did some further research. Her people went on to win the war, not lose it. Yes, she was tried and executed, but later revered as a martyr and inspiration for countless generations after. The regime didn't tell you what really happened because they don't want people like you following her example. You're no fool, Leo, but it seems their tactics have worked."

"The point is that she died before her time," Leo remarked, continuing as if Kruger hadn't said anything. "She drew the gaze of malevolent forces that ultimately destroyed her. We should try to stay small because if history's taught us one thing, it's that powerful regimes crush the life out of those they notice."

Kruger opened his hands. "You overestimate this regime's power. No-one's tested or challenged them before."

"And no-one's going to."

"*We* could. The three of us, together. I've seen the way the people look at you - that Luna looks at you. They know you're capable of so much more."

"And you, Kruger?" Leo asked. "What do you think?"

"I think I misjudged you."

Leo smiled. "I know what it is you all want from me. I'm aware of the consequences of doing nothing."

"Then help us. Fight."

"I'll think on it. But I'm not promising anything."

Kruger straightened up and posted his fists on his hips. "Not good enough. That's a politician's answer."

"It's an honest answer and the only one I can give you right now. I-" Leo stopped himself abruptly having heard the familiar hum of a distant engine. He turned away from Kruger and scanned the horizon for movement.

Kruger had heard it too - a sound he immediately recognised from his time in the contingent and one that to this day instilled fear in the hearts of his people.

The sound of the regime's harbingers of death. The sound of gunships.

Jonas Hauser strode leisurely down the darkened corridors and passageways of the regent's palace. His chores complete, Hauser had been given leave to run several errands while Turilli enjoyed a late-afternoon siesta. Waiting until his master was asleep, Hauser swiftly located the drawings and blueprints pertaining to the Chimera, copied them, then set off to deliver the schematics to Elena.

Hauser allowed himself a smile, imagining the praise Elena would heap upon him for bringing her the plans so promptly. He'd listen at first, then exaggerate the complexity of what she'd asked him to do. With Elena in awe of his exploits, his reward would be even greater.

Knowing Turilli would sleep for at least an hour, Hauser sauntered along clutching a folder that contained all of his own files as well as the plans. While it wasn't his intention to keep Elena waiting, he walked with his chest puffed out and a swaggering gait that reflected his newfound confidence, drawing bemused stares from menials and councillors alike.

Success had made him bold. Now that he'd tasted it, he wanted more.

Hauser was about to enter the administrator's quarters when he sensed something wasn't right. He turned to see two enforcers approaching him with their batons drawn. His first instinct was to run, then he remembered who he was and resolutely stood his ground.

"Is there a problem?" he demanded, trying to mask his concern behind a vacant expression.

The soldiers towered over him. "This way," one of them growled, moving off. The other remained to ensure Hauser followed, which he eventually did.

They led him back to the regent's suite, ignoring his questions along the way. His consternation palpable, Hauser feared Turilli had uncovered his treachery and was going to make him pay for it in the most bloody and humiliating ways imaginable.

The enforcers stopped outside one of Turilli's private staterooms and bade Hauser enter. Mustering his courage, the elderly executor opened the door and stepped inside.

The first thing Hauser noticed were the drawings. Hundreds of sketches littered the floor - concepts and paintings of fantastical, futuristic-looking buildings. His gaze shifted to a table at the centre of the room. On it sat a model of Divinity, but the balsa wood creation looked nothing like the city he knew. Lucas Turilli was standing nearby, so intent on the model that Hauser wondered if the regent had seen him.

"I couldn't sleep," Turilli complained after a while. "There's so much to do."

Hauser approached his master cautiously. "Can I help with anything, my lord?"

"Look what Luther's designed for me," said Turilli, still captivated by the model. "What do you think of it?"

"It's beautiful."

Turilli slammed his fist down on the table, causing Hauser to jump. "Isn't it? I knew you'd like it." His face glowed with pride. "Luther's been working on this for days. The man's a genius. Can you believe he was worried I wouldn't like it? How can I not? It's magnificent."

Hauser inspected the model, finding it hard to share his master's enthusiasm. "I didn't know Luther was an architect," he remarked churlishly.

"*Chief* architect now," Turilli corrected him. "I don't trust Chiara's man. He looks at me funny. Luther shares my dream and says he'll work with me to help make it a reality."

"Dream, my lord?"

"A new Divinity. A city so grand it will eclipse all others. We'll build spaceports, trains, museums and stadia, all of the things they have on Earth only bigger and better. It'll be the cultural and technological centre of this sector and in time, the galaxy." Turilli smiled wickedly. "When we're strong and self-sufficient, we won't need Earth anymore. That day will come sooner than they can imagine, to their regret and my great joy. A shame, then, that you'll not live to see it."

Hauser took a step back. His heart began to beat faster. He checked the table for weapons and the room for enforcers but saw neither.

"This is not some short-term project," Turilli continued, folding his arms across his chest. "Luther's best guess is sixty years. You're what? Ninety-seven?"

"Ninety-eight."

"Time," Turilli sighed. "It catches up with all of us."

Hauser realised he'd been holding his breath and exhaled slowly. "That it does, my lord."

"Time won't defeat me," said Turilli. "If I have to get every man, woman and child working then so be it."

Hauser stood and listened to the regent outline his grand vision.

Like Luther, he lacked the nerve to tell Turilli his dreams were just fantasies - and with good reason. His master could turn in an instant, and common sense told Hauser to nod and agree with everything he was saying.

"I didn't see undercity on the model," said Hauser, trying to make conversation. "What'll become of it?"

Turilli shrugged. "If my city is to grow then there has to be sacrifices."

"And the people living there?"

"People? There are no people in undercity. The Chimera will take care of that particular infestation."

"I see. But what if someone discovers your plan and tries to stop it?"

Turilli looked at him dismissively. "We both know that's not going to happen, don't we?"

"Yes, my lord," said Hauser, still clutching his folder tightly. "We do."

21

The gunship came in low and fast over Arcana's south wall, its rotors roaring and the sun's rays reflecting off its windscreen. The pilot made two more low passes before circling around and coming in to land - right on top of a small house at the centre of the village.

Kruger watched the senseless act of destruction from atop the wall. He turned to Leo, his fists clenched, anger and frustration flaring in his eyes. "Go find Luna," he ordered. "Look after her. I'll handle this."

Leo obeyed, sprinting off towards the shelter where Luna was staying. He felt like a coward, but his instincts told him otherwise.

The gunship continued to descend, its pilot using his craft's considerable bulk to demolish the structure beneath it. The beleaguered occupants saved what they could and fled, looking on from a distance as their home was flattened by the gunship's skids. Touching down, the metal monster disgorged its deadly cargo - a squad of ten enforcers - into Arcana. Their commanding officer remained behind, shouting orders and gesturing wildly at his subordinates, who loped off into the village in pairs.

Leo ran as fast as he could, following the wall around to the shelter. Luna had said she'd meet him there when the regime returned, but that didn't stop him worrying about her.

The enforcers set about detaining the first able-bodied youths they ran into, beating any who resisted with their batons. Leo avoided them easily but risked several glances to gauge their competence. Their brash, reckless behaviour told him that these enforcers were likely fresh out of boot camp - maybe even on their first deployment - more interested in impressing their commander than conducting a thorough search of the village as a seasoned soldier would have.

The absence of any veteran enforcers puzzled Leo. He'd been expecting a bigger show of strength than this. The Season of Storms was over, and Turilli free to deploy the full might of his aerial armada whenever he pleased. Sending one squad to do the work of three made no tactical sense. A single gunship couldn't take the combined weight of the enforcers and all of their captives, so they were either going to have to make several trips or wait for reinforcements.

It was the latter prospect that worried Leo the most. If more enforcers arrived and found both him and Luna, the people would suffer for having helped them. The regent's soldiers would drag the two fugitives back to Divinity and before their master, then return to wipe Arcana off the map with Turilli's blessing.

Leo couldn't allow that, but neither could he spend his life looking over his shoulder. He asked himself why he should be the one running when he hadn't done anything wrong. His friends were right. He had to find the strength to break the cycle of repression or they'd never know peace. Changing direction, Leo made for the building where he'd left his helmet and armour.

Pleased with how the operation was going, the enforcer captain steeled himself before disembarking. He was immediately confronted by two irate villagers who had noticed the enforcers weren't just taking youths, but infants and newborns too.

"So what?" the officer sneered. "What are you going to do about it? We can take as many of your runts as we like. Ten, twenty, a hundred - you've no say in the matter. You'd do well to keep your mouths shut and your opinions to yourselves in future."

He went on to threaten violence unless the men backed down, and it fell to Kruger to lead them away. The officer continued to mock them as they withdrew, demonstrating nothing but contempt for them and their way of life.

It took Leo less than a minute to don his black enforcer armour. He marched out of the building, helmet in hand, afraid but determined to stand up for himself. Heading straight for the gunship, he found his way blocked by Luna. He tried to sidestep her but she matched his every stride, refusing to let him past.

"I count ten enforcers," she said, meeting his gaze. "One commander. Think you can take them alone?"

"I was just going to talk to them," quipped Leo, and Luna smiled.

"No helmets. No firearms. Twin-linked autocannon on the gunship but it isn't loaded."

"Rocket pods might be," said Leo.

"Then hit the gunship first. You get a look at the pilot?"

"No. But it takes some skill to pull off a landing like that."

"One gunship," Luna scoffed. "Nice to know what Turilli thinks of us."

"He thinks we've no backbone," said Leo. "That the villages won't fight."

Luna folded her arms across her chest. "Care to prove him wrong?"

"Only if I know you're safe."

"The safest place is right beside you."

Leo knew better than to argue. If he was to succeed then he needed all the help he could get.

The enforcers returned to the gunship, parading their captives before the commander. "On your knees!" he roared, his soldiers forcing those who hesitated down. He stepped forward to inspect them, keeping a watchful eye on the crowd that had started to gather behind Kruger. Irked by the villagers' presence, the commander couldn't resist goading them a little more. He walked right up to Kruger and pushed him aside, daring the townsfolk to strike him.

"I thought so," he said when it became clear none of them were going to. The commander smirked. "You've got five seconds to get the fuck out of my sight or-"

A loud bang cut him off mid-sentence. He turned to see thick white smoke billowing from the gunship's cockpit. The pilot stumbled out, overcome, then collapsed on the floor.

"Sound off!" the commander barked, trying to figure out what had happened. "Anyone see anything?" The dazed enforcers shook their heads. A few of them started to look like they really didn't want to be here. The commander motioned towards the pilot's prone form. "Go check on him," he growled, glaring furiously at the nearest soldier. More afraid of his commander than the unknown, the man started to inch forward but froze when he saw movement through a rift in the smoke.

The enforcers instinctively unsheathed their batons. Bold as brass, two civilians stepped out from behind the gunship. Their faces were hidden by strange-looking helmets, and while they wore the contingent's armour, the regime's insignia and identifying name-tags had been defaced.

None of the enforcers could quite believe what they were seeing. The civilians drew their own batons and took an aggressive stance, prompting worried looks from the regent's soldiers.

This wasn't how they'd been told their first mission would go.

The commander goggled in thunderstruck silence at the audacious rebels. When he finally came to his senses, his voice was a strangled yell: "Seize them! Bring them to me!"

Three enforcers advanced automatically. Two more followed after briefly composing themselves, the rest staying back to guard their captives.

Leo turned to Luna. "You should have taken more of those grenades."

"Overkill," she grinned.

The lead enforcer sprang forward, brandishing his weapon. Leo struck out with his baton, serpent-swift, a single well-aimed blow to the man's head sending him to the floor.

Undeterred, the other enforcers continued to advance. Leo ducked beneath a baton swing and caught one of the soldiers squarely in the ribs, causing him to double over. He brought his knee up into the man's face and, as he fell, lashed out at another enforcer to his left. The soldier groaned and went down.

Ignoring his unprotected back, Leo failed to see two more enforcers stealing up behind him. They came forward, batons raised, but before they could strike, Luna had interposed herself between the soldiers and Leo. She wasn't as strong as him, but had the speed and agility to more than hold her own in a fight.

Luna managed to stagger one of the soldiers with a precise kick to his temple. She spun low on the spot and swept his legs out from under him, raising her arm just in time to block an attack by the second enforcer. The strike clanged off Luna's armour, but the unexpected force of the impact drove her to her knees. Refocusing, she rolled back, out of the enforcer's reach. He snarled and went after her, swinging his baton wildly. Out of the corner of her eye, Luna saw the man she'd knocked down was trying to get up.

A flurry of punches ensured he didn't. Leo left the stricken enforcer where he lay before catching up with Luna's assailant, dispatching him with contemptuous ease. Luna sprang back to her feet, as spirited and determined as ever.

"Six to go," she smiled.

Enraged by his soldiers' inability to capture the rebels, the maddened commander prepared to lead the rest of his squad against them. He was so fixated on Leo and Luna that he completely forgot about the people behind him. He'd barely taken two steps when a mighty blow struck him at the base of the skull, knocking him to the ground. All reason evaporated from his brain as stars exploded before his eyes. He somehow managed to roll over onto his back and saw Kruger standing over him, his fist raised.

There were plenty of men who would have hesitated and thought about what they were doing at this point.

Kruger wasn't one of them.

Inspired by their defenders' acts of bravery, the villagers surged forward. They fell upon the remaining enforcers, many of whom elected to throw down their weapons and surrender without a fight, while those who didn't were beaten into unconsciousness by the vengeful crowd.

Leo removed his helmet, contemplating the magnitude of what they'd accomplished. It had been three hundred years since the regime's soldiers last tasted defeat. Kruger was about to go over and thank him when another gunship thundered past, scattering the townsfolk like dust in the wind.

They ran over to Leo, counting on him to save them from this new threat. Looking out over a sea of frightened faces, Leo refused to panic. He spoke forcefully, as if tapping into a hidden reserve of power, convincing the people to stand beside him and fight.

Then he realised the gunship wasn't firing on them. It was coming in to land.

Shielding his eyes from the sun, Leo squinted at the approaching craft. The regime's insignia was emblazoned on its fuselage, but there didn't appear to be any enforcers on board. It touched down close to where the first gunship had landed and a tall, scruffy-looking man jumped off.

Leo couldn't hide his relief when he saw it was Marcus. He went over to embrace his friend, amazed he was still alive and had known where to look for him.

"A lucky guess," Marcus beamed. "Luna mentioned this place once before. It's funny what you remember." He paused to survey the aftermath of the battle and smiled. "What did I miss?"

"The first step," said Leo.

"Step?" Marcus threw him a questioning look. "Are we going somewhere?"

Leo took a deep breath and said, "Let's find out."

All eyes were on him as he climbed up on top of the downed gunship. In awe of his exploits, the entire population of Arcana turned out to hear him speak. Even Kruger allowed himself to be caught up in the mood of optimism that was sweeping the village. His people were daring to dream again. Maybe they could fight the regime and win.

Maybe Leo was the one to drag them out of darkness and into the light.

The crowd hushed in anticipation, but Leo hesitated. Hundreds of people were now relying on him. What would happen if he failed them? They wanted him to tell them what to do. What if he couldn't find the right words?

Showing courage and maturity beyond his years, Leo directed his thoughts away from any doubts he had and focused solely on what he wanted to say.

Words came easily to him. The people roared their approval. He wasn't studying history anymore, he was making it.

22

Watching the sun set through an open window, William Marshall waited anxiously in the reception room of the local administrator's office. The man had requested his presence at short notice, forcing him to close early, then had the cheek to keep him waiting half an hour for a supposedly urgent meeting without any explanation.

Tired and frustrated, Marshall comforted himself with the thought that he had nowhere else to be. He could return home an hour late or not at all - no-one would care. The only time people did was the instant he fell behind with his taxes or when *they* wanted something, and since all of his payments had cleared, Marshall wondered what the administrator was going to ask of him now.

The sound of the reception room's door opening interrupted his thoughts. The local administrator - a silver-haired, bespectacled man - cleared his throat and glared at Marshall from across the room, mumbling something that sounded like an apology. Rising painfully from the chair, Marshall followed him out into the lobby and down a short corridor, ending up in another room where the administrator liked to talk shop with the level's traders.

Having spent most of the day on his feet, Marshall eased himself into a comfier seat than the one he'd vacated. His host sat opposite, behind a black metal desk, his weathered face drawn and pale.

"It's been one thing after another today," the administrator began, and Marshall felt bad for expecting to be seen immediately. There was one local administrator for each of the city's five hundred and nineteen levels, and all of them worked long hours in a poorly paid, thankless job. Marshall had known his regime representative for the best part of ten years, and while he couldn't say that he was best friends with the man, he certainly didn't feel any animosity towards him.

The administrator reached into his desk and removed a tall green bottle and a pair of pewter tumblers.

"Drink?" he asked, and Marshall nodded. The administrator poured dark red wine for the two of them and sat back in his chair, regarding his guest over the top of his tumbler. "I'm glad you could come," he sighed, taking a sip. "I don't like discussing the subject of change in a letter. It's a cold and insensitive way of doing business."

"And I don't like change at all," said Marshall. "Why fix something that isn't broken?"

"It's how we move forward."

"Or backwards," Marshall scoffed.

"Nevertheless," said the administrator, "change is inevitable."

"Only if enough people get behind it," said Marshall. "I presume that's why I'm here. You want to raise taxes and bribe or strong-arm the traders into supporting you like you did last time. It won't work. We can't convince the people to stay quiet and compliant if it keeps on happening. They're already at breaking point. If you up taxes again then you'll have a full-scale insurrection on your hands. That's not a threat, it's just friendly advice."

The administrator took another sip of his drink and said, "No, we're not raising taxes. You won't have to convince or deceive anyone. This change affects you, and only you. *That* is why you are here."

"How?" Marshall demanded.

"You're the only trader on the level who deals in antiques."

"I didn't ask why, I asked how."

"They're closing you down, Marshall. Next week. I've done my best for you but it's out of my hands."

Marshall sat in stunned silence, letting the words sink in. "I don't understand," he stammered. "They want to take my shop away from me? It's all I have."

"I did try telling them that," said the administrator, "but this comes right from the top."

"Have I done something wrong?"

"Let me be clear with you: this has nothing to do with your business setup and level of service. Both are first-class. You pay your taxes on time and turn a tidy profit. The city's administrator knows you are beyond reproach."

"Then why?" Marshall exclaimed.

"They didn't say. It's not really my place to ask. They want all of your stock and files - records of sales, those sorts of things - packed and ready to go. They'll be sending a team to collect it all five days from now."

"I can't..."

"Can't or won't? Look, the regime are willing to compensate you if you play ball. You can retire a wealthy man, which is something I'll never be able to do."

"I don't want or need their money," said Marshall. "I have my health. My independence. I'm not some money-grubbing Shylock looking for a payout."

The administrator placed his tumbler back down on the desk and held up his hands. "No-one's saying you are. But the fact is they've made you an offer when they didn't have to give you anything. You'd be a fool not to take it."

"Sell myself out, you mean? They think everyone's got a price. Think they can throw enough money at a problem and make it go away."

"You want to fight them?" the administrator asked, surprise evident in his voice.

"I would if I thought they'd listen," said Marshall. "But I know better than to pursue a lost cause."

"You could always partner up with one of your fellow traders," the administrator suggested.

Marshall's face twisted into a snarl. "I want nothing more to do with those pompous layabouts."

"So I'm guessing that isn't an option..."

"You're damn right it isn't!" Marshall spat. "That shop is my life. I've worked hard every day to make it a success and now you're telling me the regime want to close it? They're the ones who gave me my license in the first place! What's changed?"

"I don't know."

"You must know something," Marshall pressed. "Doesn't a man in your position hear things?"

"People talk," said the administrator, pouring himself another drink. "I listen."

"And what exactly have people been talking about?"

"The regime, of course. I seldom hear of anything else. Word on the grapevine is that you're not the only one getting shut down. On this level, yes, but Divinity's a big place. Other traders on other levels are in the same boat as you."

Marshall's eyes narrowed. "What trades?"

"Those who deal in antiques, books and art."

"What about the hundred odd gift shops on this level alone?"

"They're unaffected."

"Why do you suppose that is?"

The administrator shrugged. "Could be that the regent wants to move high value stock somewhere safe."

"Safe from what? His own enforcers?"

"Who knows. I'm sure there's a perfectly good reason for it. I've every confidence they'll explain why this is happening in due course."

"It's good to see blind optimism is alive and well," Marshall remarked sarcastically.

"There's nothing wrong with hoping for the best," the administrator countered. "And the best thing you can do is take the money. They won't ask so nicely next time."

"There won't be a next time." Marshall stood and sighed, angry with himself for having capitulated so readily. The regime had won, just like they always did. Before he left, Marshall reached over and grabbed the bottle of wine from the administrator's desk. He'd turned to drink once before, years ago, and now he'd no purpose in life he was free to do so again.

23

As daylight died, Arcana came alive with the noise and energy of a rejuvenated people. Many of the younger residents had never stayed up all night in their lives, and to those who'd known nothing but the daily struggle against the dunes, the town looked like something out of a dream. The villagers laughed and danced under the stars, lost in the moment, and none of them wanted the night to end. They celebrated well into the early hours, telling stories and exaggerating the feats of their saviours, not noticing they'd slipped away from the festivities when no-one was looking.

Leo and Luna found sanctuary from the praise and adulation that accompanied their newfound status in the village hall. They sat opposite one another on the front pews, deep in conversation. While the townsfolk revelled in their victory, Leo and Luna were trying to determine how best to capitalise on it.

They were joined after a while by Kruger, who stumbled into the hall with a bemused look on his face. He slammed the doors shut behind him and paused to catch his breath, having decided the best way to deal with fame was by running away from it. Surprised to find he wasn't alone, Kruger recovered from his initial shock and seated himself on another pew, keen to join in the discussion.

"We can't afford to hesitate," he insisted, "because the regime won't. When Turilli learns what's happened here he'll either send his armies against us or go after those unable to defend themselves."

"Someone in the high command will have realised one of their gunships is missing," said Luna. "They'll be out looking for it come first light."

"What I want to know is who in their right mind would pack rookie enforcers off into combat with no equipment," Kruger continued. "I don't like it. I don't like it one bit. What's Turilli playing at?"

Leo listened and waited patiently for his moment, careful not to interrupt. "It's safe to say they weren't expecting any resistance," he said eventually. "If no-one's ever stood up to the regime before, they'll have come to view the villages as soft targets. Turilli's strategists spend weeks planning these operations. They'd have known exactly how much manpower was needed to achieve their objectives, so sending in one gunship isn't actually that surprising. Had the three of us not made a stand, it would have been enough."

"Economy of force," Luna added.

"The regime won't waste their resources," said Leo, "but neither will they spread them too thinly. If they're pressing newly trained enforcers into service then all other units must be committed elsewhere."

Kruger rolled his eyes and feigned a yawn. "This is all very fascinating, but I fail to see how any of it helps us. Do either of you have a plan? What's our next move?"

"What would you do?" Leo asked, encouraging Kruger to take the lead and air his views.

"Me? I'd get that gunship working, fly it back to Divinity and strike at Turilli. Kill the regent and this is over."

Luna smiled and shook her head. Kruger saw this and scowled, then looked to Leo for approval.

"A bold strategy," said Leo, "but would Turilli's death really end the Chimera project or just stall it?"

"Neither," Luna interjected. "Turilli's masters are the real force behind this. They'll promote another puppet to replace him and we'll be back to square one."

"We have the element of surprise," Leo continued, "so I say we use it. Tanis would be better off without Turilli, no question, but I don't think there's anything to be gained by killing him."

Kruger frowned. "Fine," he mumbled. "What do you have in mind?"

"A revolution," said Leo. "Rally the townships and march on Divinity. Sound familiar?"

"Of course it does. It's my idea. An idea that you dismissed, if I remember correctly."

"That was before any of this," said Leo. "The people have shown they're willing to fight. All it takes is a spark."

"And what of Turilli?" Kruger demanded. "You're as mad as he is if you think he'll surrender his city without a fight. He'll retaliate the instant he discovers what you're doing, and we all know what that means. Those are your words, Leo, not mine. You're the one who warned me how hard this would be. We can't beat the regime in a pitched battle. They've got tanks, enforcers, the Phalanx... and a fleet of fifty gunships."

"Forty-nine," Luna quipped.

"Half of which don't fly," said Leo. "The rest belong on the scrapheap. Turilli's enforcers can't leave their posts unless he wants chaos on the streets, and the Royal Guard are confined to the palace. His tactics are doubtless the same as previous regents - crush threats as and when they arise within Divinity - but there's no strategy in place to deal with an armed uprising beyond the wall. He can't risk contacting Earth for help because he'd lose face. The only force Turilli is able to call upon is the Phalanx, and mobilising a unit that size takes time."

Kruger snorted lightly. "Or he could just weld the city's gates shut and not send anyone out at all."

"Unlikely, but we've salvaged two rocket pods from the gunship. Both were loaded."

"Even that might not be enough to breach them," said Kruger. "And what about the regime's armoured divisions?"

"A few dozen APCs at most."

"The spy satellites, then? The electric fences and motion sensors?"

"Inoperable."

"And the guns on the city walls? I suppose they're just cardboard cut-outs or inflatables, right?"

"Haven't worked in years." Leo thought back to the time Rossi had asked him to look for weaknesses in Divinity's defences. He'd delivered a comprehensive report that identified several shortcomings, which the regent noted but kept locked away. Leo had believed the whole thing to be a test, but now he wasn't so sure. Had Rossi been genuinely concerned about security, or was there some other agenda behind his request? That was two years ago, and nothing had been done to address the problems since then.

"You're forgetting one thing," said Kruger. "The regime have guns. We don't."

At this, Luna reached down and pulled one of her holdalls out from beneath the pew she was sitting on. She unzipped it to reveal a small arsenal, including a high powered bolt-action sniper rifle. Leo smiled, not surprised at all, while Luna glared at Kruger. "You were saying?"

"Where did you get those?" he asked.

"Let's just say the palace armoury isn't as secure as the regime thinks."

Kruger turned to Leo. "She's lucky she didn't get herself caught. You wouldn't be laughing then, would you?"

"Oh, lighten up you miserable sod," Luna huffed. "Live a little."

"Like you?" Kruger said in his most sarcastic tone. "Might be hard since I don't have a death wish."

"That's enough!" Leo snapped, ending their exchange before it could escalate any further. "We don't have time for this. If either of you have a better idea then I want to hear it." Silence answered him. Leo changed tack. "Well, can anyone think of a reason our plan might not work?"

"Yeah, I'm looking at one," Kruger mumbled.

Luna was itching to continue trading insults with him, but held her tongue out of respect for Leo. He knew far more about the regime's modus operandi than she did, having been close to a regent and trained by the finest minds in the contingent - minds he'd ultimately surpassed. If Leo believed that rallying the townships was the best way forward, then so did she.

Kruger, on the other hand, was warming to Leo but still seemed unhappy. "This would have been easier," he complained, "if you'd kept hold of that file. You say you can trust this Marcus character, but I don't know him. Why does he need it? We have the one thing that could topple the regime in our possession, and you go and send it back to Divinity. If I didn't know better, I'd say that you're wilfully squandering our advantage. How are you going to persuade the people to get behind you now?"

"That's where you come in," said Leo. "You're a man of influence out here; known and respected among the townships. Whenever you speak, people listen. Maybe they'll listen long enough to hear what I have to say, but I need you to convince them to take me seriously. To them, I'm just another outsider. You can say otherwise. These villages have been repressed by the regime for so long it won't take much to bring them onside."

"And Marcus? What's his role in all this?"

"I can't tell you," said Leo. "We're risking our lives in different ways, and I've already asked far too much of him. When he's safe, we'll talk. Until then, you're going to have to trust me."

"Why should I? Trust has to be mutual, and clearly you don't trust me enough to tell me anything."

"I trust you enough to know you won't ask me to reveal something that could put a friend in danger. The regime have eyes and ears everywhere. The slightest slip and this could end badly for all of us."

Kruger's face lit up. "You mean the prisoners? I've a simple solution, then - let's kill them."

"We can't do that," said Leo. "We're not the regime - we're a league fighting to liberate this world and others like it. Our humanity is what makes us different. Just because the regime would doesn't mean we should."

Kruger stood and glared defiantly at Leo, frustrated by his overly cautious approach. "You've not listened to a single word I've said, have you? I don't know why we're even having this conversation - you've already decided what you're going to do regardless of what we say. Well, if that's the case, go ahead. Do what you like, just don't come running to me when you fuck it up and need someone to bail you out. Luna might, but I won't."

Ignoring Leo's protestations, Kruger left the hall with many of his questions still unanswered. Luna dismissed his behaviour as nothing more than a bout of petulance, explaining to Leo that Kruger found it hard to keep a lid on his emotions - especially when he didn't get his way.

"He'll come around," she assured him. "Just don't expect an apology."

"He's only speaking his mind," said Leo. "I wish everyone was as honest as him."

Luna smiled. "No you don't."

"Was he always like this?"

"From day one."

"He must have been through so much."

"No more than us." Luna leaned forward, resting her elbows on her knees. "He did have a point, though. About the captives. It doesn't benefit us to keep them alive. In fact, it's a huge risk when you think they might escape and warn Turilli."

"Far likelier to wake in the night and find me dead," said Leo.

"Well, that's one way of looking at it..."

"They won't go anywhere without supplies," Leo continued, "and it would take hours to empty the silos. Try to think like an enforcer - one being held against her will at that. You've dishonoured the regent - who'll destroy you himself if he learns of your failure - so how best to make amends if you manage to get free? Killing the man who wishes your master ill, of course, then taking control of the village. Think of the glory, imagine the gifts and titles Turilli will bestow upon you."

"Gifts and glory? The only thing coming your way would be a hail of bullets from Turilli's firing squad."

"But they don't know that," said Leo. "They don't know Turilli. They've just sworn an oath to protect him, so they're honour bound to try to escape whenever an opportunity presents itself."

"Good to know. I must say, you're not doing much to reassure me at this point."

Leo stifled a laugh and said, "Killing unarmed prisoners would set a bloody precedent. We're liberators, not murderers. The people would never accept us if they thought they were just swapping one oppressive regime for another. But neither can we bring them with us; if even one enforcer escaped then people would start to question our chances. We'd be looking over our shoulders as we go from town to town, and that's not how you win a war. The only option is to leave them here in Arcana. There's enough food and water to survive indefinitely, and it's to our advantage that both are underground."

"That's brilliant," said Luna, standing up. "I'll ask the guards to move them now."

"Have the people take what they need before you do. Enough for a five-day march through the desert. We'll reach the nearest village in two, but there's no harm in being prepared." Leo hesitated for a moment, mulling a point over, then decided to address it in a way he thought Kruger would approve of. "When you're done, bring me three batons, a rocket pod and two of the most badly damaged suits of enforcer armour. I'll get that gunship working and crash it a mile or so south of Arcana - make it look like an accident. Any search party will likely assume pilot error or system failure, and that's what they'll tell Turilli. He'll want answers the same day and won't wait for a full investigation - the regime don't have the resources to mount one anyway."

"Why you?" Luna asked, her voice tight. "Why not get Kruger or one of the townsfolk to do it?"

"Because they don't know how to fly a gunship."

"Neither do you." Luna turned away from Leo and closed her eyes. She knew this was something he had to do - the people would shun him if he asked another to go in his place - but his willingness to face danger made her realise just how much she cared for him. In her mind, a future without Leo was no future at all, and she had to tell him how she felt before he left.

It could well be her last chance to.

Leo stood and went over to her. "There's a perfectly good guidance system on board," he said, gently brushing her golden hair back off her shoulders. "I'll set the autopilot and jump before it goes down."

"Well, here's something you haven't considered," Luna declared, spinning around. "How people feel about you. Not just me, but the enforcers you've trained and all those you've helped. If you marched on Divinity with an army at your back the city would rise, and a good number of regiments would have to decide where their loyalties lie. None of us command that kind of respect. What chance do you think we'd have without you leading us?"

"Don't sell yourself short," Leo said with a smile. "If I'd have died on Carmona then it would have been you."

"If you say so."

"You're telling me you'd have stood by and done nothing?"

"I wouldn't have known what to do," said Luna. "What to say. Where to find the strength to make any of this possible."

"You'd have found a way." Leo looked into her eyes but could only guess what she was thinking. A braver man would have asked - would have told her he wanted to spend every minute of every day with her - but he couldn't find the words. "We should go," he said, and the moment passed. His own happiness was very much a secondary concern now.

"Okay," Luna nodded. "So we're a league fighting to liberate this world."

"What?"

"Something you said earlier. I like it."

"Like what?"

"The *Liberation League.*"

"Well, in that case," said Leo, "so do I."

24

Sandstorms raged across the desert as Kara guided her gunship back to Divinity. Garbled transmissions from the city filled the airwaves, but the panic in her commanding officer's voice was clear. The regime's fleet of gunships had been recalled, and the city was on lockdown. Something had the senior officers of the high command worried - something they could not immediately explain.

Alone in the gunship's main hold, Marcus Rathen sat reading the file Leo had entrusted him with. It was a disgusting, despicable document that reflected the malice of those who had penned it, with pages of graphic content exacerbated by a single, chilling statement:

Demonstration and casualties essential.

Earth's own unique seal was printed alongside the regime's insignia on every page, quashing any doubts Marcus had over the file's legitimacy. Corruption and madness had taken root at the very heart of the galaxy. If the regime succeeded here, more worlds would follow Tanis into darkness.

The vile document had the potential to whip quiet indignation and dissent up into a storm of vengeance, but its complexity meant that out of those who tried, few could hope to understand it. Even Marcus was at a loss until Leo explained the Chimera's true purpose, and still he struggled to grasp the depths of the regime's depravity and the scale of what they were trying to do.

Things like this only ever happened in the books he'd read as a youth. Fictional stories intended for hungry, impressionable minds - stories that inspired but were never meant to be taken seriously. Yet these books had been written millennia ago. The future their authors described was now history. Had they, in fact, been warnings that no-one had heeded?

"Two minutes!" Kara shouted, snapping Marcus out of his trance. Divinity filled the gunship's forward viewports, and now began his toughest test. He rolled his right trouser leg up to his knee, removed his belt and strapped the file to his leg, concealing it from unfriendly eyes.

The gunship climbed quickly, and Marcus went over his mission one last time. He had hoped to stay with Leo, but his friend had other ideas. By returning to the city, Marcus could use his position within the Chimera workforce to aid him, and his story about a sister in undercity would still hold up. Leo seemed especially interested in Steinsson, and was counting on Marcus to get the file to him.

Cleared to land, Kara set her gunship down within the Chimera site's perimeter. Marcus stepped out of the hold and onto the tarmac, bidding her farewell. She nodded once but said nothing, silently cursing her weakness and the position she'd put herself in because of it. If Turilli moved against Leo then she would almost certainly be in the vanguard of the force sent against him. She'd have no choice but to fire on those she respected the most - unless she managed to find a way out.

Kara watched as Marcus disappeared inside. Arcana called to her from across the dunes. If she'd had the courage to remain there then she knew she wouldn't be facing this dilemma now.

Marcus made his way past the sleepy-looking enforcers stationed at the site's entrance, trying his best to stay calm. The soldiers stared vacantly into the distance, unperturbed by his presence, tired and fed up of waiting around for their relief to show. Just as Marcus started to think he'd avoided the Chimera's guardians, one of them stepped into his path, his baton held across his chest.

"And where," the supervisor snarled, "have you been?"

"Out," said Marcus.

"I can see that. Don't try and be smart with me, boy."

"I'm not being smart," Marcus retorted, his composure beginning to waver. "You asked me a question, I answered it."

The supervisor lowered his baton. The team's newest recruit wasn't his usual calm, controlled self. He sensed that if he continued to press him he might learn something that could speed his promotion to director - or at the very least gain fresh ammunition to use against Saul and Karlsen. "Not sufficiently," he said, watching Marcus closely. "It's in your interest to comply fully with site rules and regulations. Nowhere does it state that you can go gallivanting off into the city whenever you feel like it."

Marcus shrugged. "Where does it say I can't?" He knew what the supervisor was trying to do, but found it hard to keep his composure given the circumstances. Just how much did he know about the Chimera and what was going on here?

"You'd better watch your tone when addressing me," said the supervisor. "I've already warned you about the dangers of falling in with the wrong crowd."

"It says in the contract that workers are permitted to leave the site," Marcus stated.

"And yet here you are."

"I've broken no rules. These four hours are my own. If you're that bothered about where I've been, go ask Steinsson."

"I'm asking you."

"Divinity," said Marcus. "Not that it's any of your business."

"That's where you're wrong, boy. You see, I own each and every one of you, and that makes it my business. The gunships aren't your personal taxi service. Workers leave all the time, but as a rule they don't come back. You have, so either you've spent the last four hours whoring your way through the city, or you're trying to smuggle something inside." The supervisor stepped back, took a small canister of pepper spray from his belt and said, "Turn out your pockets."

Marcus did as he was told, concerned by the supervisor's persistence. The man's ambitions were well known, and he would have no qualms about destroying one or more workers in his quest for promotion

- if they gave him reason to do so. Finding nothing of interest, the supervisor put the canister back and glared at Marcus, disappointment lining his wrinkled face.

"I suppose you'll want to strip search me next?" Marcus scoffed.

The supervisor shook his head. "Not me. I don't know where you've been." He gestured towards the enforcers. "But these men have no such concerns. You'll tell me what you were doing or I'll be forced to conclude that others have influenced you to the detriment of the project."

"Fine," Marcus sighed, not wanting to land his fellow workers in trouble. "I went to see my sister. She's the reason I'm here. I had to make sure she was alright otherwise there's no point in me staying."

A mirthless grin spread across the supervisor's face. Maybe he could use the threat of violence against this peasant's sister to have him do his bidding. "Do anything for your family, would you?" he smirked, confident he'd soon have another worker passing him information from inside.

"I would," said Marcus.

"Glad to hear it." The supervisor stepped aside and said, "I think we're done here. You'll work on reduced rations until I'm satisfied you've got that temper of yours under control. Off you go."

Marcus scowled and turned on his heel. If the supervisor suspected he was lying then he didn't show it, but Marcus knew better. He had to move quickly, as something told him his time here would soon be at an end. Yawning wearily, he returned to his quarters just as Steinsson and the rest of the team were getting ready to start another shift.

"Well?" Steinsson pressed, taking him aside. "Did you find her?"

"I did," said Marcus. "She's fine."

"And you?"

"I've been better." Marcus rubbed his eyes and said, "Might I have a word with you in private?"

"Sure."

Marcus waited until only he and Steinsson remained before

retrieving the file. He handed it to his friend, who immediately recognised some of the drawings and blueprints.

"What's this?" asked Steinsson, eagerly leafing through the pages.

"Why not have a read," said Marcus, "and maybe you can tell me."

Stony-faced and silent, William Marshall looked on as regime officials cleared the stock from his store. He sat slouched against the wall of the building opposite, his eyes flitting from the enforcers to the bottle of wine he was holding, then back again. The soldiers loaded everything into two waiting transports, watched by an irritable curator who would occasionally berate them for their heavy-handedness.

As the enforcers finished loading boxes and moved on to paintings, Marshall took the bottle, unscrewed the cap and lifted it to his lips. The wine's sweet aroma leapt out at him and a memory stirred in his mind, a memory he had no desire to recreate in the present. Marshall hesitated, lowering the bottle to rest it on his thigh.

A sudden gust of wind whipped past him, battering at his skin and blowing grains of dirt and sand into the enforcers. Marshall stood and stared up at the regent's palace, surprised to see dark clouds forming overhead. A storm was coming down from the north, and there was nothing the regime could do to stop it.

"Little early to be out drinking, don't you think?"

Marshall turned to find the beautiful, raven-haired woman who'd bought the Scottish claymore standing before him. She was dressed in the same utilitarian clothes she'd worn that day, but her hair was down and her tone more serene, almost jovial.

"What's happening here?" she asked, her concern genuine.

"Take a wild guess," Marshall snorted. "Looks like you've had a wasted journey."

"Only if I wanted to buy something."

Marshall's eyes narrowed. Though in no mood to accommodate anyone, the old shopkeeper was at least a little curious about his wealthy customer's intentions.

Who was this woman and why had she returned if not to make another purchase? Maybe she was here to chase a refund, or simply wished to bask in his misery.

"I need your help," she continued, "if you've a mind to hear me out, that is."

Marshall looked dubious. "Alright..."

The woman reached into her bag and retrieved a scrappy piece of paper. She passed it to Marshall and said, "Do these numbers mean anything to you?"

Marshall glanced briefly at each of the four numbers, but none of them stood out. "No," he said after a while, unable to find a pattern. "They don't."

"They don't?" The woman sounded disappointed. "Well, it was worth a shot."

"In all fairness," said Marshall, "you've not given me much to go on. Did you find that scrap of paper or just copy those numbers onto it?"

"I copied them."

"Then perhaps if I could see the original document-"

"Why?" the woman exclaimed, taking a step back.

"Context," said Marshall.

"Oh. Yes, of course. One minute." The woman turned her back on him and rummaged through her bag, pulling out a handful of creased and wrinkled pages. From these she selected four to show Marshall, carefully storing the others away. "Here you go."

Marshall started reading, drawing on his vast knowledge of antiques and his experiences as an enforcer. After the contingent he'd both sold and appraised hundreds of documents, and if this one was worth something then there were few better placed to say than him.

"Have you any plans for your retirement?" the woman asked, looking around. Marshall didn't answer. "It's rather nice here, isn't it?" she continued. "Clean. Quiet."

"As you say," said Marshall.

"Not at all how I'd imagined. You know, I was half expecting the rumours about this place to be true."

"What rumours?"

The woman shrugged. "That the lower levels have risen against the regent. That people are dying in the streets for want of food."

"They're not just rumours," said Marshall. "You should go to undercity. See for yourself."

"Isn't *this* undercity?"

Marshall smiled. "A common misconception, particularly among the nobility."

"Then enlighten me."

"We all define it differently. The ten lowest levels could all be considered part of undercity, but so could the next ten, or twenty. The nobility think it's everything south of the wall, while the term itself was actually coined on Earth to describe a city's subterranean levels."

"It all looks the same to me," said the woman.

"Hence the confusion. If you asked one person from each level to show you where undercity starts, they'd all point to the same place. Ask them where it ends and each will tell you different. I guess there's no right or wrong answer these days, but any self-respecting citizen will tell you that undercity ends before their level. No-one wants to be associated with a place whose name has become a byword for death and misery."

"And how do *you* define it, might I ask?"

Marshall straightened up. "I don't," he said, sidestepping the question. "But the high command use the term to classify the lowest fifty levels. They refer to it as the 'killzone', not undercity. They need somewhere to keep the undesirable elements of society contained, and where better than the levels furthest from the palace? The people do a wonderful job of killing each other over food and amenities, but sometimes the enforcers are needed to speed things along when births start to outstrip deaths."

"Maybe," said the woman, "if they stopped breeding like rabbits then I might have some sympathy for them."

"What else have they to do? Turilli has overtaxed the people and left them with nothing. Even his predecessor understood the importance of making token gestures and concessions. Rossi would offer hope where Turilli offers violence - a smart regent gives with one hand, not takes with both. If it weren't for his agents and enforcers, I'd wager they'd have already strung Turilli up from the nearest spire."

The woman blinked. "Are things really that bad?"

Marshall shrugged and handed the pages back to her. "Don't worry yourself. For now there are more than enough soldiers and gunships to keep order. Every time the people rally behind a figurehead, the troops go in and murder that individual along with their closest supporters. The regime are right to fear a popular man or woman because that's what the people are looking for. They're tired of living like this and just want someone to believe in - someone who's prepared to fight for them." Marshall's face hardened as a note of warning entered his voice. "One day soon there'll come a reckoning. I might not be around to witness it, but I'll bet my life that you will."

The woman's eyes flashed for a second, then widened. Marshall took this as a sign of confusion, but the confidence remained in her expression and she smiled coldly, as if she'd somehow spied an opportunity to profit from the suffering of others.

"What do you make of the document?" she asked, changing the subject.

"Intriguing," said Marshall, "but completely worthless."

"Can you tell me anything useful about it?"

"Appears to be schematics for some sort of fire control system. To say it's an ambitious design is an understatement. The wording is beyond me; either it's a language I'm not familiar with or code. The numbers are clear, though, and the four you identified are all prefaced by letters. I'm surprised you missed that."

The woman flicked through the pages and saw he was right. "Does that change things?"

"Dramatically," said Marshall. "Alone, they're just numbers. Add the letters and you're looking at elements; plutonium, hydrogen and uranium. I don't recognise the fourth."

"A philosopher *and* a scientist," said the woman, impressed. "I knew I'd come to the right place."

"A place that history will soon be done with."

"Yes. The reward for trying to earn an honest living: forced retirement and no way to pay Turilli's taxes." The woman opened her hands. "Maybe there's some way in which I can help. I do have a great deal of money after all."

"The only way you can help is getting me my shop back."

"I can't do that, but at least let me pay you for your services and help today."

Marshall shook his head. "Valuations are free."

"That, then." The woman gestured towards the bottle Marshall had set down earlier. "My husband has a particular fondness for wines. How much do you want for it?"

Marshall reached down, took hold of the bottle and handed it to her. "Just don't tell him where you got it."

25

When word of rebellion reached Lucas Turilli, the paranoid regent at once flew into a terrible rage. Hurling a plateful of fruit at the poor agent who had brought him the news, Turilli began frantically searching the palace for Luther - the one man he felt he could trust.

Barging menials and enforcers aside, Turilli searched every room, growing angrier with every second his administrator hid from him. Surrounded by incompetent, self-serving lackeys, Turilli believed that only Luther's cool intellect could save him from the myriad of problems he was facing.

Earlier, the regent had learned that the riots in undercity now threatened to spread to other levels. Worse, the freak sandstorms that battered Divinity and kept his gunships grounded showed no signs of abating. Earth's power brokers quizzed him about the Chimera project incessantly, and now there was talk of unrest among the townships.

Overwhelmed, Turilli tried at first to ignore the situation, but the thought of a planet-wide revolt gnawed away at him and ultimately destroyed what little sanity he had left. By the time he found Luther - at a private dinner for Divinity's ministers - Turilli was foaming at the mouth and had worked himself up into such a state that he could barely string two sentences together.

His expression alone was enough to clear the room in a matter of seconds.

"Out!" he roared, his eyes blazing with anger. "Now!"

As the ministers fled, Turilli fixed Luther with a hard, contemptuous stare. His reputation was at stake, and all the administrator could think about was filling his belly.

Luther cleared some plates and invited Turilli to join him, but had to duck to avoid a goblet thrown by the seething regent in response.

"Bumbling idiot!" Turilli shrieked. "Do you think I haven't noticed how you've deserted me?"

Luther looked at him, confused. "I serve my lord in all things. I obey without question."

"Then prove it! Prove to me that my faith in you is not misplaced." Turilli pulled up a chair and drummed his fingers on the table impatiently. "Tell me what's to be done and you might yet live."

Luther sighed and sat back in his seat. He'd learned early on that Turilli didn't make empty threats, so spent the next few minutes massaging the regent's ego while assuring him of his loyalty - afraid he'd end up like Kastor if he didn't. Over time, Turilli's behaviour had become ever more erratic and unpredictable, and many nobles now went out of their way to avoid him. Luther couldn't, so had been forced to come up with a new strategy; namely one where he'd dispense with the truth and tell the regent exactly what he wanted to hear. As Turilli fell further into madness, so had Luther found himself more open to Elena's whispers and suggestions, secretly plotting with his wife to usurp him and free Tanis from his destructive grip.

"Those are fine words," Turilli ranted, "but your actions show otherwise. I'm fully aware of your political manoeuvrings, Luther. Watch and wait for your enemies to destroy one another. Never commit until the outcome is clear. I'm right, aren't I? Yes, yes, you see, I know you better than you know yourself. So very careful to ensure you always end up on the winning side, only this time you got it wrong!"

"Was it wrong of me to back you, my lord?" asked Luther. "I've already chosen my side - you were there when I swore to serve you and no other. If you need proof of my loyalty, ask yourself: have I ever failed you? Ever given you cause to doubt me? I'd like to think not. If people are choosing sides, then you'll find me by yours, as always."

"A touching speech," said Turilli, "but your words ring hollow, administrator. You stay because you're afraid that if I fall then you'll come tumbling down with me." The regent pressed his hands together, satisfied Luther spoke the truth and that he'd unsettled him enough. "Still," he continued, "you've a calmer head than most, and I need you. I need to start hearing solutions. You are my advisor, so advise me."

Luther nodded slowly, pondering how he might turn the situation to his advantage. "I suggest we prioritise," he began. "Your forces can't be everywhere at once."

"True enough."

"It would be prudent to secure the city before worrying about what may or may not be happening outside of it. Say the word and I can deploy additional battalions to stop these riots in their tracks."

"Then do it," said Turilli. "I wonder it took you this long to come up with a fitting strategy in the first place."

"Well, my lord did say to leave the important decisions to him..."

"Yes, yes. And where are these reinforcements going to come from?"

"The upper levels," said Luther. "Or we could ask Earth for help."

"No!" Turilli screeched. "They cannot learn of this. I'd be the laughing stock of the galaxy - the one regent who couldn't even keep his own people in line. No, we'll have no more talk of that. I won't let a swarm of riotous plebs sully my name with their thuggery."

Luther ran a hand over his mouth, masking a smile. He knew Turilli would never do as he suggested, but seeing the regent panic amused him. "I'll inform the high command immediately," he said. "Give it a month and your enforcers should have things under control."

"So long?" Turilli queried.

"It might well be longer. Military actions only succeed if there's adequate planning beforehand. If you want order in undercity, every street must be pacified. Curfews have to be implemented, the ringleaders made an example of, executions sanctioned and so on."

Turilli's eyes narrowed. "You have some other notion you wish to discuss?"

"Just a thought," said Luther. "Your subjects are fickle, but they're easily pleased. Ignore them and they grumble. Persecute them and they will rise. A riot is the language of the unheard. Rossi advocated compromise - he'd visit undercity at least once a year and let people look him in the eye. By handing out clothes and gifts he'd placate the masses and give them something to lose. His enforcers seldom saw combat because the mere thought of having these trinkets taken away kept the people in line. I would advise my lord to either follow his lead or negotiate and-"

"Negotiate? I'm going to eat their fucking hearts! Lucas Turilli does not compromise, not now, not ever. You've much to learn about leadership, Luther. Violence must be met with violence - only then will people think twice about rising against you in future. The moment your enemies sense weakness, they'll pounce. They won't hesitate, so neither should we. Don't forget that these fickle subjects outnumber my enforcers a hundred to one, and if they're ever allowed to unite against me then there's no force on Tanis capable of stopping them."

"I appreciate that," said Luther, "but Rossi-"

"Rossi's strategy was flawed," Turilli snapped. "The old fool didn't realise that if you give people something for nothing, they'll just ask for more. Euphoria turns to expectation, requests become demands. The real miracle here is that he managed to hold onto power for as long as he did with the misguided policies he adopted. Visits to undercity? I couldn't bring myself to walk among those filthy vagrants let alone meet with them - who knows what I might catch."

Luther smiled and nodded while Turilli continued to rant about conspiracies and phantom plots against him. By dismissing the more practical of the two solutions he'd proposed, Luther saw that the regent was barrelling down the path to destruction with only one goal in mind; the extermination of anyone he deemed to be inferior.

Turilli's arrogance blinded him to everything but his own prejudice. The mad regent believed himself infallible, and where Rossi would have listened to counsel, Turilli only pretended to. Even when those trying to help him were wiser or had a better handle on the situation than he did, Turilli would still shut his ears and delude himself that the problems they spoke of didn't exist. It had taken him several months to admit there was anything wrong at all, and now, when faced with a crisis, the regent's first instinct had been to lash out at his advisors and blame them for his own inadequacies when all they'd tried to do was point him to his duty.

Turilli had failed Luther's final test. The administrator was a tolerant man, but even he had limits. Rossi's legacy was being reviled by a sadistic tyrant, and Luther had heard and seen enough to know Turilli would never change. He could no longer serve a man devoid of honour and virtue, whose only talent was for inflicting pain on defenceless people. Luther knew that something had to be done, but Turilli's hold on power had not been weakened sufficiently for anyone to move against the regent.

Yet.

"If only the Chimera was ready," Turilli raged. "If only these infernal dust storms hadn't grounded my gunships then we'd have order restored in a day."

Luther didn't share Turilli's optimism. The regent had gorged himself like a wolf on the blood of Tanis, and was now surprised that people were fighting back. Rossi kept his finger on the pulse of the world, but Turilli seemed set on crushing it. The old regent had conducted purges to keep the population down, but these never coincided with tax hikes. By ignoring the people and turning Tanis into own his own personal plaything, Turilli had ensured his regency would be remembered as the nadir of his world's history.

"How long before the storms clear?" Turilli asked, a wild look in his eyes. "They're damaging trade as well as my calm."

Luther's chin came up. "We're still investigating, my lord. I wouldn't worry yourself too much; they're more a nuisance than anything. A bit of wind and sand won't topple buildings that have stood for millennia."

"Bring down houses, no," Turilli snarled. "My gunships, on the other hand..."

"Gunships aren't designed to fly through sandstorms," said Luther. "Had the fleet not been recalled, we might well have lost more."

Turilli buried his head in his hands and sighed in frustration. "And of course we can't replace them because we don't have the blueprints. Earth does."

"So ask them to send you six new gunships."

"I'm not going to waste my time," said Turilli. "I already know what their answer will be."

"Then let's not concern ourselves with matters beyond our control. Leave those on Earth to stew in their own paranoia - we've more than enough gunships left in reserve."

"And the storms?"

"Will blow themselves out like they always do."

"Your assurances leave me cold," said Turilli. "What shall we do in the meantime?"

"We should look into these reports of unrest among the villages. Send a force to investigate. The Phalanx, perhaps."

Turilli shifted his shoulders uneasily. The Phalanx was an elite unit comprising a thousand enforcers, dedicated to the protection of the regent and his ministers. The mere mention of their approach had been enough to avert rebellions in the past, but Turilli was reluctant to have his best troops leave Divinity and go off chasing shadows.

"It's time to send a message," Luther pressed. "Deploy the Phalanx and your enemies will melt away."

Turilli took a moment to consider Luther's proposal, blind to his true motives. The administrator was intrigued by the reports of a possible uprising, and wanted to uncover the truth for himself. If an army was coming against the regent, then it would be in his interest to aid the rebels, or at least meet with them. He could only do this if Turilli was distracted by some other crisis, and he'd already convinced him that the situation in undercity required his full attention. While the regent fretted over riots and storms, Luther aimed to take advantage by using others to help him seize power - granting friend and foe the illusion of control before shattering it completely when it was too late to stop him.

But such flawless manipulation took time, and demanded every ounce of his will and every aspect of his intellect.

"I'm certain we could put the Phalanx to better use," Turilli said eventually. "Why not send my enforcers to undercity instead?"

"And ignore the threat beyond the wall?" Luther countered, acutely aware that prolonging the riots would serve to keep Turilli's mind focused elsewhere.

The regent, though, was proving hard to convince. "What threat?" he scoffed, shooting Luther a derisive look. "What proof do we have that the townships have risen? The word of one spy, who's been out in the desert so long the heat has likely addled his brain. Yes, we should investigate, but let's send a squad of enforcers, not a whole regiment."

"And if this squad happens upon the rebels? What then? They'll be wiped out and we'll be no closer to determining the enemy force's strength and disposition. If your agent is speaking sense, then we have to stop this rebellion now before it's too late. What would those on Earth do if they learned we had the chance to act but didn't? Nothing pleasant, I'd wager. We wouldn't want to be remembered for our carelessness."

"You make a good point," said Turilli, "but even if the rumours are true, we've no idea where the rebels are. The thought of having my best troops stumbling around the desert looking for them doesn't particularly appeal to me."

A brief smile flashed over Luther's face. "We won't have to look for them, my lord. They will come to us."

"Oh?"

"Send the Phalanx north. Have your enforcers raid every village, take prisoners and kill if necessary. We're behind with this year's forced recruitment quota, and these storms should not deny you your pound of flesh. This action will either draw the rebel dogs out and into a confrontation they cannot win, or dishearten them to the point they'll give up and go home. The Phalanx *can* be put to better use, but its purpose is to smash your enemies, not dissect them. It is a sledgehammer, after all, not a scalpel. Allow me to wield it, and I will do so with great effect."

Turilli cleared his throat. "No, I need you in Divinity. The officers can lead them."

"Officers whose loyalty we cannot be sure of. Give command to one you trust, not some unscrupulous careerist. Let me be your eyes and ears and report back to you what I discover."

"You're of greater use to me here," said Turilli. "I need those who I can trust by my side."

Luther sensed his window of opportunity was getting smaller. "My lord underestimates himself," he said, letting a reverent tone play into his voice. "This is your moment - you shouldn't have to share it with anyone. Let Earth and all Tanis know and see that you are not a man to be trifled with. A man who shines under pressure. Rossi hadn't the heart to do what was necessary, but you have the strength and courage to succeed where he failed."

Turilli stood, brimming with confidence. Luther's words invigorated his spirit and quickened his heart. "Sound assembly," he rumbled, his mind steady once more. Were his troops to succeed, the glory would be his and his alone. Should they fail, he would have the perfect scapegoat.

But Luther didn't know that.

26

Kurt Steinsson tossed and turned in his bed, exhausted, but unable to sleep. Dark fears and thoughts conspired to keep him awake, and the harder he tried to calm his mind the more restless he became. The sound of Karlsen's incessant snoring drifted down from the bunk above. The steel floor plates vibrated to the hum of the crematoriums several floors below. Like death, rumour and hearsay had become staples of site life, but today he'd read something that warranted his attention whether he liked it or not.

He stirred again, and a voice growled from the neighbouring bunk.

"Shut it, the pair of you. Some of us are trying to sleep."

Steinsson threw back the bed-sheet, swung out his legs and sat up. The room was dark and stank of stale sweat. He stumbled over to where he knew the door was and opened it, drawing another harsh rebuke from Saul. Ignoring him, Steinsson donned his shirt and left without a word.

The corridor outside the dormitory was empty. A single lamp glowed dimly on the wall opposite. Steinsson followed the corridor round to the left and descended a flight of metal stairs, arriving at the workers' canteen. The dingy room with its plastic chairs was a welcome sight, providing him with a quiet space where he could sit alone with his thoughts. He stepped inside and flipped a switch, leaning lazily against the wall as the lights came on.

"Mind if I join you?" asked a voice from behind him.

Steinsson jumped. He hadn't been expecting company, but was relieved to see it wasn't Saul or Karlsen who'd followed him here this time. "Not at all," he said, taking a seat at the table closest to the door. Marcus Rathen hesitated, detecting a hint of sarcasm in his friend's voice. Steinsson smiled and gestured to the empty chair across the table. "Don't mind me. I'm getting old and cranky."

"I'll buy you a walking stick for your birthday," joked Marcus. "Or one of those tweed flat caps." He paused as if remembering something. "I take it you've had a chance to read the file?"

"I have," Steinsson replied evenly.

"And?"

"It asks more questions than it answers."

"Seemed pretty damning to me," said Marcus.

Steinsson shook his head. "The regime's top brass are greedy and cruel, but they're not monsters. I'm sure there's a perfectly rational explanation for all of this."

"Going to ask them for one, are you? They're not accountable to anyone." Marcus sighed and said, "Those on Earth don't give two shits about us. You know full well what they're capable of. I can't believe you're defending them after everything you've said."

"What's the alternative? Leave? Our families need the money we make to survive. Maybe you'd rather we tell the world the truth. Show me someone who'd believe us. To challenge the regime is to dig your own grave. They have spies and agents everywhere. You can't go up against those kinds of odds and live, let alone win."

"No, you're right," said Marcus. "Our lives are more important. Best pretend that file doesn't exist and the sun shines out of Turilli's arse."

"I didn't say that."

"Then what?"

Steinsson leaned forward, resting his arms on the table. "I don't know." Though outwardly calm and indifferent, his mind was in turmoil. The only logical thing to do was to forget what he'd read, but he hadn't been raised to shrink away in the face of evil. The regime weren't the benevolent saviours they'd made themselves out to be - they were a threat to him and his family. What they planned to do threatened the freedoms of every family in the galaxy.

"You can't turn away," said Marcus. "They won't stop this madness until someone stops them."

"Not us. We're welders, not soldiers. You'd need all the luck in the 'verse to make but the smallest chink in their armour. Their retribution would be swift and bloody - I've seen it before. You've got to pick your battles and fight them on your own terms. The regime won't let you do that. I'm no coward, but I can't provide for my family if I'm six feet under."

"And what'll they think knowing you had a hand in this, however small?"

"They'll understand."

"Maybe," said Marcus, "but this can only end one way. None of us will leave here alive."

"But the contract-"

"Isn't worth the paper it's printed on! Your rules and morals don't mean shit to thugs like Turilli. He butchers his own people readily enough - you think he'll have any qualms about murdering a handful of workers to save on relocation costs? This project completion bonus you're all waiting for isn't going to be an ample paycheck, it'll be poison gas pumped into your dormitories or a bloodbath at the assembly points. Knowing Turilli, I'd put my money on the latter."

Steinsson took a deep breath and exhaled slowly. By keeping his thoughts and emotions locked away for the last two years, he'd become a passenger in his own life. The regime told him how to think, how to act, and through his silence he'd complied. He wished he'd never come to Tanis - wished his wife was here to tell him what to do. He knew what he *should* do, but the thought of defying the regime filled him with fear.

"Leaving isn't an option, is it?" he asked eventually.

Marcus drew himself up tall in his seat. "Here's how it's going to go down."

Steinsson listened as Marcus outlined his plan in detail. Every once in a while he'd interrupt to voice his concerns, but Marcus stood firm and assured him that what he'd suggested was not only possible, but would work. Still, this wasn't good enough for Steinsson, who feared their actions would merely deal the regime a temporary setback.

"Stop them here and they'll just try again on another world," he argued. "One year from now or fifty, and this will all have been for nothing."

"No," Marcus smiled, shaking his head. "No, they won't. This'll be the beginning of the end for them, my friends will see to that."

Just as Steinsson was about to ask him what he meant, the supervisor appeared along with two enforcers and a short, stocky man he didn't recognise. He rolled his eyes, willing them to pass by, but his intuition told him that an already stressful day was about to get much worse.

"I thought I might find you two numbskulls here," the supervisor snarled, ordering the soldiers to wait outside.

"Well, there aren't many other places we're likely to be," Steinsson remarked sarcastically. He looked over at the burly individual who was standing by the door. "Who's your friend there, chief?"

The supervisor grabbed the man by the scruff of his neck and threw him forward. "This," he announced gleefully, "is Stanley's replacement."

Steinsson's blue eyes narrowed. "Give over. Earth wouldn't fill his position twice."

"Precisely," said the supervisor, scarcely able to contain his delight. "Which means we have an interloper on-site." He turned his gaze upon Marcus and said, "I'm treating this as a serious breach of security. Is there anything you'd like to get off your chest while you've the chance?"

"Don't be daft," Steinsson scoffed. "Why would anyone risk their life to infiltrate this shithole?"

"That's what I'm going to find out."

"You're wasting your time," said Steinsson. "I know you only want to impress the director, and that's lovely, but since when have clerical errors ever warranted a full investigation? So one of them got given the wrong papers. Big deal. Let's use the extra manpower to beat our quotas and show the director what we can do. You can say it was your idea and he'll praise you for showing initiative. Going off on a wild goose chase won't benefit anyone."

"Site protocols must be followed at all times," the supervisor insisted. "I won't be held responsible for leaving another team a man short - that's if both these cretins are actually meant to be here. Either way, it doesn't take a genius to see that something is amiss." Again, he turned to Marcus. "I don't recall you ever showing me your papers. We'll discuss this further in my office. Run some checks. Non-compliance will result in your immediate detention, and the implications for those you may have influenced could be severe."

Ignoring the supervisor's threats, Marcus stood. "Leave Steinsson and the others alone. I will come with you."

"And I," Steinsson declared. "I don't know what's going on here, but it's my responsibility to ensure any investigation is conducted without bias."

The supervisor scowled, angered by his failure to elicit a confession. Now he had to interrogate both men and consult his superiors - a process which could end up taking days if no-one took his accusations seriously. "Let's go," he fumed, storming out of the canteen with the enforcers in tow. Steinsson and Marcus followed, the latter's thoughts now focused solely on survival.

Muttering a string of curses and complaints, the supervisor led the party back to his office on the lowest level. With the site's lifts broken or being used for material transport, their route took them along narrow gangways and through areas that were normally off-limits to workers.

Noting this, Marcus reduced his pace, forcing the soldiers to slow down as well. The enforcers' passive response and weary movements told him they were tired, and he figured that a lack of sleep might make their reaction times a little slower than usual. He continued to vary his speed as they walked, testing them further. By deliberately hindering the group's progress he could better plan his next move, and look for ways out should the need to make a quick exit arise.

The supervisor, however, wasn't so lax. "Stop fucking around back there," he growled, eager to start his investigation.

It finally occurred to Marcus that this was one situation he couldn't talk his way out of. He had hoped to frustrate the supervisor by being as uncooperative as possible, but now realised the man's dogged persistence would ensure he uncovered the truth regardless of how long it took him. Marcus had no idea what would happen when he did, but couldn't imagine he'd be let off with just a warning. Still, he'd done everything Leo had asked of him and more, now had every right to try and save himself. If they made it back to the supervisor's office then the chance to escape could well have been lost, followed - he feared - by his life.

The group was halfway across a suspended footbridge when Marcus made his move. He stopped abruptly, reached out to grasp a railing and bent over, feigning illness. Steinsson went to check on his friend, and the man the supervisor claimed to be Stanley's actual replacement shouted for the others to stop. Aware of the commotion behind him, the supervisor whirled around, only to have his drowsy enforcer escort walk into him.

Pushing the pair of them aside, he stared angrily at the nearest soldier and gesticulated towards the man who'd alerted him to Marcus' condition. "You, take him back to my office. We'll be along in a minute." The enforcer obeyed without question and the supervisor glowered at Marcus. "The fuck's the matter with you?"

Marcus faked a cough and took several deep breaths. "I don't feel so good."

His patience exhausted, the supervisor drew his baton and marched up to him. "Here you go, boy. This'll help."

Without warning, he struck Marcus a mighty blow to his midriff. The impact should have caused him to double over, but Marcus only grunted. Surprised by his resistance, the supervisor hit him again, this time forcing him back against the railing. Still he refused to go down, and when the baton descended a third time, Marcus caught it in his strong left hand and wrenched it free from the supervisor's grip.

"The fuck-"

Before the supervisor could react, Marcus threw a punch with his other fist. The blow connected with the man's temple and sent him sprawling backwards. The supervisor tasted blood as he fell, stars dancing in his vision. Marcus was on him in a flash, striking him once across the face with the baton. Reaching down, he grabbed the supervisor's shirt with both hands and pulled the dazed man to his feet. It took all of Marcus' strength to lift him above the railing, but the moment he did he relaxed his grip and sent the supervisor plummeting some fifty feet to the level below.

Seconds passed before he hit the ground with a sickening thud.

Kurt Steinsson stood dumbfounded, but the enforcer who'd remained behind overcame his own shock and sprang into action. Pressing his panic button, he drew his sidearm and aimed it at Marcus, firing once before the weapon's targeter had acquired a lock. The bullet missed its mark by several inches, ricocheting harmlessly off a steel beam. Marcus snarled and launched himself at the enforcer, grabbing his legs in a flying tackle that sent both men crashing to the floor.

They wrestled furiously for control of the gun, Marcus' natural strength and agility matched by the enforcer's years of combat training. Slightly quicker than his opponent, Marcus twisted and turned, avoiding the enforcer's legs and elbows while managing to land several strikes of his own. He pulled mightily at the gun, but the enforcer responded by trying to straddle him and crush him under his weight.

Marcus offered only light resistance. He allowed the enforcer to pin him, seemingly handing him the advantage. Thinking the fight was over, the enforcer failed to anticipate Marcus' counter and was unable to block it when it came - a powerful neck scissor that almost entirely reversed their positions and gave Marcus control. Panicking, the enforcer relinquished his grip on the gun and fought valiantly to break the hold, but in less than a minute the struggle was over. Marcus squeezed with all his might, heard the enforcer's neck snap and felt his body go limp.

Steinsson found it hard not to gawp at the chaos unfolding before him.

Marcus got to his feet and steadied himself against a railing, breathing heavily. He peered down over his shoulder at the supervisor's lifeless form and smirked. "I think he missed his calling," he rasped in between breaths. "Bastard would have made a nice doorstop."

"You killed them," Steinsson stammered. "Why would you-"

"Sorry, no time," said Marcus, retrieving the enforcer's sidearm. "You'll have to finish this without me."

"Finish? We've barely started!"

Loud cries of alarm came from a group of enforcers who'd discovered the supervisor's body. Marcus looked up at Steinsson, the urgency in his voice clear. "Get back to the dormitory and keep that file safe. What happens now is up to you."

Steinsson swore loudly. "I can't do this alone."

"Then tell the others," said Marcus. "They'd want in if they knew."

"Saul and Karlsen?" A look of derision settled on Steinsson's face. "They wouldn't lift a finger."

"But this does involve them," Marcus pressed. "It involves all of us. You could at least try to argue the point."

"Alright. But you'll tell me everything the next time we meet."

"I will."

Steinsson managed a weak smile and sprinted off back the way they'd come. Marcus sighed mournfully, fearing he'd never see his friend again. He turned his attention to a metal stairwell up ahead, the sound of stomping boots growing ever closer.

Four enforcers stepped out and onto the footbridge, only to find Marcus already pointing his stolen pistol at them. Undaunted, the soldiers advanced, certain to defeat him with their superior numbers and training. Like a blur, the lead enforcer drew her own weapon, as did her cohorts.

Marcus squeezed the trigger.

27

Throughout the villages and hamlets of Tanis, support was growing for the Liberation League. United by their hatred of the regime, hundreds of townsfolk pledged themselves to Leo's cause, entranced by his strong words and the idea of standing up to those who had tormented them for so long. Where people hesitated, Kruger added his voice to Leo's. Luna's praise and encouragement kept Leo focused whenever he faltered. Doubters remained, but as soon as Leo or one of his captains divulged the regime's heinous plan, even they fell silent. Seven townships had joined the League in less than a month, and Leo intended to sway more. His ragtag army of freedom fighters - some ten thousand strong - snaked across the desert as it marched on Divinity, preparing for the battle that would decide Tanis' fate.

Turning nomads into soldiers proved a challenge. Leo spent hours imparting all he'd learned in the contingent to those willing to listen, but found he had to be quite severe and assertive when training peaceful townsfolk in the ways of war. Luna watched as Leo's charges grew in confidence, astonished at the effectiveness of his methods. He seemed to be everywhere at once, inspiring others and making time for everyone. When even the youths were able to grasp basic military strategies, Leo knew his persistence was paying off.

Now the League closed on Naissus, a small town nestled in a barren valley half-way between Arcana and Divinity. Their progress was slowed by the same sandstorms that kept Turilli's fleet of gunships grounded, but they pressed forward regardless. Leo willed the storms to continue, for as long as they did, the advantage lay with the League's gallant revolutionaries. The moment they cleared, the regime would be free to visit vengeance upon them in whatever manner Turilli deemed fit.

And yet, for all Leo's planning and foresight, neither sand nor steel could save Naissus from the regent's machinations.

The first anyone saw of the town was an orange glow through the storm, followed by a sound like thunder at the end of the world. Sensing danger, Leo called a halt to the League's march. He helped his captains set up a makeshift camp, seemingly unsure of his next move. They waited until a break in the storm allowed them to see a little clearer, and it was then that the reality of going to war with a ruthless enemy hit home.

All of Naissus was burning, though the fires that had consumed the town were now beginning to subside. Waves of fear and anger rippled through the League's ranks. Luna opened her mouth to speak, but the words caught in her throat. Battling his own emotions, Leo rallied a handful of people to help search for survivors. Expressionless, he stalked off into Naissus alone, furious with himself for having failed to prevent the town's destruction. Kruger warned him that the regiment responsible could still be nearby, but planning a defence was the last thing on Leo's mind.

He wanted revenge, and to get it, he vowed to be just as savage as the monsters he was fighting.

Leo walked the streets of Naissus' largest residential district, where the skeletons of burnt-out buildings still smoked. An eerie silence hung over the town, broken only by his footsteps and the occasional sound of flickering flames. He searched tirelessly among the rubble, but found neither signs of life nor death.

Being alone gave him time to think, and Leo wondered if the regime had enslaved the town's populace in an effort to dishearten him. He thought for a moment what he might have done, and why, were he in Turilli's position. Maybe this wanton act of violence was actually a stratagem - a ploy to bring the League to battle. The burning of Naissus had all the hallmarks of being a random attack, but the speed with which the regime had responded made Leo wary. Turilli was proving to be a most devious opponent. There was cold logic behind this move - logic that Leo himself would have applied were he regent. Had he in his arrogance underestimated Turilli? The thought was unimaginable.

Hours passed, and eventually Leo tired. The regime had done their work well, making an example of Naissus so as to demoralise their enemies, and were it not for Leo's iron resolve they might well have succeeded. He headed back to the League's camp, determined to hunt down the regiment that had torched Naissus and destroy it. Leo knew it was likely a trap, but the people desperately needed something to restore their flagging morale. Another victory - however small - would be the perfect remedy.

Leo took a shortcut through the ruins of a gutted building on his way back. The residence's roof had collapsed and the wooden ceiling supports were sagging badly. One had already fallen, and Leo clumsily tripped over it in his haste to reunite with the League. Muttering profusely, he aimed a kick at the beam before tossing it aside. A wrinkled hand immediately emerged from beneath the rubble. Leo cried out in alarm, stumbling backwards and falling over the same beam he'd just discarded.

He picked himself up and began clearing some of the wreckage, surprised to have found a survivor. Leo saw that the beam and part of the roof had come down on top of an elderly woman, who, despite her appalling injuries, was still alive. He did his best to comfort her, but there was nothing he could do to stop internal bleeding.

After binding her wounds, Leo sat down beside her and tried to strike up a conversation. The old woman looked over at him and smiled gently but said nothing. Leo carried on talking, telling her of the League and what they were trying to do. His words effected a sudden change in her features, and the old woman's blackened face glowed as if he were reciting a story she'd heard before.

Leo was in the middle of apologising for Naissus when Luna called to him. He stood and checked the woman's bandages, finding it hard not to think of the pain she must have been in. Swearing vengeance on the cowards responsible, Leo turned and went to leave.

"Wait," pleaded a weak voice from behind him. "Stay."

To Leo's surprise, the old woman had somehow found the strength to sit up. He returned to her side, offering to go and get help.

"Don't fuss so," she huffed.

Leo grinned, the old woman's indomitable spirit reminding him of his father. Then he remembered the atrocities Rossi had committed and his smile faded.

"I didn't think I'd live to see another war," the old woman remarked, resting her hands in her lap.

"Another war?" asked Leo. "The last battle was fought near three hundred years ago. There's not a person alive today who remembers it."

"For one who's seen so little, you sound awfully sure of that."

"Because it's true. People might be living longer, but not *that* long."

The old woman smiled. "My father told me all about the war. The one you're referring to. He used to say I had it easy - that I would never know true hardship until I'd fought and bled for something I believed in. But Karos wasn't so much a fight as a massacre. It was hard on all who were there that day."

"Karos?"

"You won't recognise the name. The regime crush rebellions, they don't commemorate them."

"Not this one," said Leo.

"I hope you're right. I really do."

Leo shifted his shoulders uneasily. "Will you tell me what happened?"

"I'll tell you of it," said the old woman, "but if you're looking for proof, know that I have none."

"I've learned to keep an open mind. Some things have to be taken on faith."

"Faith," the old woman sighed. "Faith can be misplaced." She coughed weakly, swallowed once and said, "From what I've gathered, Tanis was one of the last worlds to be subjugated by the regime. No-one knows where they came from, but their rise to power was meteoric. In less than two decades the war was over, and a new empire beginning to emerge from the ruins of the old. Planets were pacified then assimilated, every conquest feeding this nascent autocracy's insatiable hunger. Squabbling factions either swore fealty to the regime or were obliterated - there was no middle ground. Conflicts dragged on across the systems furthest from Earth, but these were oft petty disputes settled with words, not weapons. Initially, the regime had no interest in backwater planets. With the Core Worlds firmly under their control, they could consolidate their power and start rebuilding."

"So what changed?" Leo pressed impatiently. "And how exactly did the regime win? Who were they fighting?"

"I'm afraid that's about the extent of my knowledge on the subject," said the old woman. "There's a chance you'll have to look beyond Tanis for answers."

"But your father-"

"Liked a good story. His generation clung to tales spun and embellished by the previous five. I was born long after the conflict had ended. My parents and I knew of the regime - that they'd won the war and ruled from Earth - but never thought for one minute they'd come here. In a hundred years no regime official had ever set foot on Tanis, and these so-called saviours of ours had done nothing to help repair the damage done by the fighting."

"Establishing a tyranny takes time," said Leo, half to himself.

"That it does. And with their centre secure, the regime were quick to bring the rest of the galaxy to heel. I was eighteen when they set their sights on this sector - and Tanis."

"You fought against them?" asked Leo.

"In a manner of speaking. Up until then, I spent my days helping the construction crews build new homes and workshops in Divinity - the only city to have raised its shields in time to survive the bombing a century earlier. Might things have been different had the war not come to Tanis? Perhaps. But it doesn't do to dwell on the past and speculate. What's certain is that Divinity was already overcrowded, and with the land around the city irradiated, the only way to house a million refugees was to build up.

"There was a call for citizens to join the work teams and transform Divinity's skyline. People signed up in their thousands, and by the time I was old enough to help, the project was nearing completion. What made this enterprise so remarkable wasn't its scale, nor the speed with which buildings were erected, but the enduring cooperation between communities. Such a thing could not have been attempted had people let pride or fear get the better of them. Sixty massive high-rises and a wall to hold back the sands proved that everyone wanted to do the right thing, even if it still wasn't enough."

Leo listened dubiously, but he didn't voice his doubts. The old woman met his gaze and said, "I know you don't believe me. I can see it in your eyes. How could a city of cynics unite without some kind of incentive? But look at the League. Did you bribe or threaten these people into fighting for you? I think not. They draw strength and hope from the words of one man, just like we did all those years ago. It's funny, in some ways, you remind me of him.

"Pollux wasn't born into nobility, but his courage and clarity of mind served as inspiration to millions. He made a point of saying aloud what everyone else was thinking, asking questions others dared not, and while the nobility dithered over the post-war crisis, he was out there tackling it head-on. His eloquent and impassioned speeches carried us through the dark times, and when Pollux was elected first citizen we felt safer than ever."

"With the regime so far away, I'm guessing many backwater worlds did," said Leo.

The old woman nodded, her hands tightening into fists as long-buried memories swam to the surface. "I was naive to think this peace would last. Unknown to us, a storm was tearing through Carina and

Tanis lay directly in its path.

"The end began with a sector-wide blackout and garbled distress calls from tradeships and space stations. Then our listening posts in neighbouring systems went dark. Pollux ordered an investigation, but of all the ships dispatched only one managed to limp back to Tanis. From the crew, we learned that a massive regime fleet had emerged from the core and was subjugating every planet in the sector. Naturally, when people heard this armada was nearing Tanis, widespread panic and hysteria broke out, with some even choosing to end their lives rather than face a future under regime rule.

"Pollux refused to consider the notion. He declared the tyrants' advance would be halted at Tanis, using his verbal mastery to turn the population's fear of the regime into outright hatred. His confidence was such that we didn't just believe in victory, we expected it. We would topple these callous despots from their self-appointed rulership of the galaxy and send them running back to Earth like whipped dogs.

"Again you doubt me, but at this stage the regime's fleet of planet killers existed only on paper. Divinity's shield was strong enough to withstand any bombardment, and the city's army a superbly disciplined fighting force backed by tanks, gunships and artillery. Pollux urged ordinary citizens to enlist and overnight its ranks swelled. My parents tried to warn me against the idea - warned of the consequences his actions would bring - but I was young and let my romantic, rebellious heart rule my head. We trained during the day and at night watched columns of armour parade through the streets, buoyed by Pollux's praise and rhetoric. These shows of strength served to enthuse and inspire, but it was his will alone that made all of this possible, and we truly believed that with Pollux leading us we would not fail."

"Yet with his death your army would have been rendered helpless," said Leo. "He had no captains, no-one to help share the burden of command. Had I wanted to take Tanis without a fight, I'd have eliminated your figurehead."

"For one so young, you are extraordinarily perceptive," said the old woman. "When the regime's fleet arrived, we didn't meet it with violence. The army mobilised and we raised the city's shield, but nothing more. Divinity was self-sufficient and even a bloodless siege would not have been to the regime's advantage. Pollux expected them to offer terms instead, and while we'd trained for war, a diplomatic solution had always been preferred - provided any treaty was weighted in our favour. Of course, there were other options open to him, but you'd have chosen the safest one too, yes?"

"Most definitely," Leo agreed.

"We'd give them one chance to take us seriously. Pollux said that if diplomacy failed and the regime wanted to beat us then they would have to destroy Tanis. It was at best a reckless statement, but we all knew they didn't have anywhere near that kind of firepower on hand. Even if some of their ships had capital weapons, empire-builders don't go charging around the galaxy levelling dissident worlds from orbit - they find other ways to try and subdue them first.

"When the regime opened communications with Pollux, he gloated over his foresight and their weakness, haughtily presenting his list of demands. He declared that if Tanis was to join their burgeoning empire then it would continue to make its own laws and set its own taxes, remaining nominally independent. To our amazement, the regime agreed and sent emissaries to thrash out a deal with Pollux, seemingly keen to avoid bloodshed. The world held its breath as negotiations began, yet when Pollux emerged a day later he appeared changed.

"It came as no surprise when he announced the regime had betrayed us. While he'd been trying to find a peaceful solution, the cowards had landed their armies two hundred leagues away and were attacking every village beyond Divinity's protection. We immediately demanded he turn the city's guns on the regime ships in orbit, but Pollux wanted to concentrate our forces elsewhere. He made an impassioned plea to all citizens to mount a defence of the villages, and no sooner had he asked than everyone rallied behind him, utterly convinced that this was the right thing to do. We weren't about to abandon thousands of innocent families to the regime's marauders, but at the same time feared this was a ploy to draw us out and into the teeth of enemy fire. As ever, we looked to Pollux for direction, and like always, our quick-witted protector did not disappoint.

"Carefully, he planned his strategy. Under cover of darkness, civilian and military units would launch a two-pronged attack on the bulk of the regime forces massing at Karos, an old township not far from here. Both our armies would be accompanied by mobile radar jammers, ancient machines that blocked orbital scans and effectively rendered our units invisible. After testing and confirming that these devices did indeed work, Pollux led us out of Divinity and on to Karos."

"You followed this man blindly and without question," said Leo. "Trusted him on his word alone."

"It is faith," the old woman pointed out. "Though a politician first, Pollux was also a talented general who led from the front. His plan was sound. Civilian militias would engage the enemy first at close quarters, falling back when the regime's inevitable counterattack materialised. With their forces spread out and positions exposed, Pollux and the cream of our army would hammer them from afar with our mightiest weapons. We'd all witnessed the terrible power of these war engines in a series of demonstrations organised by Pollux, and knew they were capable of devastating anything the regime threw at us.

"We travelled at speed across the desert, abandoning our transports about a mile or so from Karos. A mounting sense of excitement had started to permeate our ranks, reaching fever pitch when Pollux finally gave the order to attack. We fell upon the town with fire in our hearts and curses on our lips, buoyed up with courage and our own sense of righteous purpose. Surprise was total, and we took Karos without a firing a shot. Our commanders claimed victory, but to others it was obvious the enemy had somehow managed to outwit us. The regime's strike force was nowhere to be seen. Men and women milled around in confusion, waiting for orders, unsure of what to do next. Then I looked to the sky and saw the first bombs beginning to fall. I don't think that even then we could bring ourselves to admit it was Pollux who had betrayed us. The regime had never landed on Tanis, and these so-called radar jammers were nothing more than the fabrications of a megalomaniac.

"Thousands died in a matter of seconds. Most of my unit tried to run, and those that didn't stood labouring under the delusion that Pollux was going to save them. I took cover in the basement of an old homestead, but the house above was flattened and collapsed into it. When I came to my senses, I started clawing my way up through the rubble."

The old woman paused and wiped the tears from her eyes before continuing.

"By the time I got out, the sun had already risen above the horizon. It's fair to say I wasn't prepared for the carnage that awaited me. I've never seen such devastation in all my life. Karos had been levelled and our army destroyed. Not routed or put to flight. Destroyed. I lay down in the sand and wept, paralysed by grief. My friends were gone and the man we'd idolised a traitor to his own people. When I couldn't cry anymore, I searched the battlefield for survivors. There were four of us in total, out of an army nearly a million strong. Nightfall came and we all said a few words in tribute to the fallen before setting off through the desert. We arrived at Naissus a day later and didn't look back."

"And what of Pollux?" Leo pressed. "Did he knowingly betray you or was he deceived?"

"Pollux knew exactly what he was doing," said the old woman. "He gave us up to our enemies and they gave him the world. In exchange for our lives the regime spared his, making their pawn the first regent of Tanis. They promised him wealth, status, power - rewards Pollux could not resist - and it was at Karos the cowards concluded their deal. In one stroke they eliminated those who would never accept regime control and simultaneously solved the world's population crisis.

"The people weren't told about Karos and accepted Pollux's version of events. His truth was very different to ours, but with no credible witnesses he could say what he liked. We agreed it was pointless trying to tell the world what had really happened. Who'd have believed four citizens over the man of the hour? Pollux could do no wrong in anyone's eyes, claiming to have driven the regime from Tanis exactly like he said he would. But they only departed when our technology was safely in their hands, leaving a sizeable garrison behind to keep the peace. Walls and purges followed, speeding our world's transition into a regime stronghold. We lost more than our friends that day at Karos, all because of one man's greed and desire to live."

"You said that I remind you of him," Leo interjected. "I'd like to know how. There's nothing the regime have that I want, and I wouldn't let them trick me into betraying the League either."

"Perhaps," said the old woman, "but you can't know for certain until you've been tested. The regime are relentless. They'll exploit any weakness and use your best qualities against you. It doesn't matter how strong or morally upstanding you are - if they can't get to you they'll go after your captains. Can they resist the lure of power or dodge an assassin's bullet? Can you? Pollux was a good, honest man before the regime went to work on him. I sense that you want only the best for your people, too. But if someone as principled as Pollux can fall, so might you. And whatever form the regime's attack takes, it's likely you won't see it coming."

Leo's brown eyes narrowed. "What are you saying exactly? That I can't beat them? I'm not so easily cowed by such displays."

"Then I hope you're prepared for the struggle ahead. This war won't be won by the faint-hearted, nor will it be decided here. It'll change you in ways that'll scare and appall you. Every step will be fraught with danger, every choice with uncertainty, and you'll forever teeter between triumph and disaster."

"I'll do whatever it takes," said Leo.

"Just don't lose sight of who you are. Pollux took the easy way out of a tough situation, abandoning his cause just to save himself. If you continue on this path, the regime will force you to face the same test.

They'll put you under pressure you've not known, blur the line between right and wrong and make you suffer to the point of madness."

"Well, luckily I know a few tricks of my own," Leo smiled, trying to lighten the mood. He weighed the old woman's words carefully, wondering if he was destined to share Pollux's fate or one far worse. Then he thought of Luna and Marcus, and knew that together they stood a better chance of resisting the regime than Pollux had.

Leo started to ask another question, but noticed the old woman's eyes were closed. She lay perfectly still with her lips parted slightly and head tilted to one side. He leaned over to check for a pulse, then sat back on his heels when he couldn't find one. A sense of sorrow came over him as he thought about everything she'd been through, all the hurt and lies she'd endured without being able to tell her story. He stood up slowly, saddened by the old woman's passing. Much of what she'd said resonated with him, though Leo was actually more afraid of his own mistakes than the regime's designs.

The sound of someone walking through the rubble drew his attention. Leo turned and was relieved to see a familiar face, even if Luna did look slightly vexed.

"So this is where you've been hiding," she said, sounding frustrated. "There's no time to mope. Pull yourself together and help me tend to the survivors."

Survivors? Leo felt his spirits lift. He followed Luna outside, pledging to return and give the old woman a proper burial.

"I've been looking everywhere for you," Luna continued. "The people were worried."

"How are they feeling?" asked Leo.

"Angry. They want to make the regime pay for this."

"Have the survivors told you what happened?"

"It was the Phalanx," said Luna. "They took prisoners and left the elderly and infirm here to die."

Anger surged in Leo, but he kept it in check. "Tell Kruger to break camp. We're going after them."

"Now?"

"Now," Leo affirmed. "The Phalanx didn't march all this way to burn one town. There'll be others. See if you can find me a map or someone who knows this area's topography. I need to figure out where we can intercept them."

"Anything else?" Luna asked sarcastically.

"Yes. You're going to stay here and look after the survivors. I can't fight the regime if I'm worried about you."

Luna stared at him in disbelief. "I'll pretend I didn't hear that," she scoffed angrily. "Captains lead from the front. Generals command. If anything, *you* should be the one who stays."

"A good captain follows her general's orders," said Leo. "If I'm sending people into battle, it is only right I go with them. It's not fair to ask of others what you are unwilling to do yourself."

"And is what you're asking of me fair?"

"No, but it makes tactical sense. Those who can't fight need someone to watch over them, and if things go badly then at least we'll have denied Turilli the satisfaction of wiping us out in a single battle."

Luna bit her lip and nodded. She wanted to continue the argument, but knew from experience that Leo wasn't going to back down. If she protested too vigorously, he might well have set people to watch her or caught onto her plan himself. As ever, she would have to be patient and bide her time. Luna turned and made her way back to the League's camp, happy to play the good captain for as long as it suited her.

Leo followed, pleasantly surprised that Luna hadn't pushed the issue further. Now he could devise a strategy to defeat the Phalanx, though he recognised that victory would be hollow if he didn't have enough of an army left to take Divinity. The battle might have been inevitable, but its outcome was far from certain.

28

The thought of defeat had never sat well with Lucas Turilli. A stubborn man with a restless spirit, he had always trusted himself to get things done without needing to call on others, and the project he'd been working on for the past week was no exception.

Turilli was trying to write an article that criticised Rossi's term as regent, but despite working through the night he was no closer to finishing it than when he started. Unwilling to give up and distracted by the sandstorm outside, Turilli continued to stare at the screen in front of him and read the same words over and over again, frustrated at his lack of progress. He should have shut his computer down and closed his eyes if only for an hour, but his fiercely combative nature prevented him from doing so. Now he was in danger of starting the day without having had any sleep at all, and his executors were already vying for assignments that would take them as far away from their temperamental master as possible.

So immersed was Turilli that he failed to notice a blinking red light on his touchpad, indicating an incoming transmission. A minute passed, then an audio alert sounded. This sudden noise startled the regent, causing him to flinch.

Turilli scowled in confusion as well as some annoyance. His train of thought had been derailed by the interruption. Never one to hide his feelings, Turilli hit the transmitter switch and started shouting into the void.

"This is a private channel," he fumed, "reserved for outbound calls. It was my express order that I was not to be disturbed. Whoever you are, you'd better have a damn good explanation for this impertinence."

A face appeared on the regent's monitor, partially obscured by the hood of a long black cloak. Turilli sat up straight in his chair, his eyes wide with fear.

From light-years away, on Earth, Lord Konstantin Artemov spoke. "I do hope this isn't a bad time, regent?" His words dripped with sarcasm and a certain amount of perverted joy.

"N-no, my lord," Turilli stammered, bowing his head. "Forgive my anger. I have no excuse."

The regent trembled before his master, afraid he'd overstepped the mark. Lord Artemov was one of the most feared men in the galaxy, possessing the power to elevate or condemn entire star systems. Though on different planets and separated by the vastness of space, the change in Turilli's demeanour was so spectacular that one could have assumed both he and Artemov were in the same room.

"This is an unexpected pleasure," Turilli continued, composing himself. "But I was under the impression that Earth would only contact my office through official channels, and with prior notice."

"You're not wrong," said Artemov, "but I have my reasons for wanting this conversation to be kept off the record."

Turilli shuffled uneasily. With the Chimera nearly operational, this must have been Earth's way of warning him against using it to further his own ambitions. Artemov was showing him a tiny glimpse of the power he had, and while Turilli feared his master's apparent omnipotence, he was entirely in awe of it, too.

But if the regent thought Artemov's sole purpose was to frighten him, then he was mistaken.

"Tell me truthfully," Artemov rumbled, fixing his vassal with a suspicious stare. "How is the project proceeding?"

"With pace and efficiency, my lord," said Turilli. "We are on schedule. No setbacks to speak of. You may rest assured that all is well here."

"And what about Tanis?" Artemov pressed. "Is the economy stable?

Are the people content?"

"Yes, yes. Output high. No signs of unrest. I am in complete control of the planet, from the spires to the dunes."

"You're certain of this?"

Turilli hesitated. Lord Artemov was a shrewd, perceptive man, but even he couldn't know everything. The regent sat back in his chair and thought for a moment. He had carefully managed the two men his master had sent to guard the Chimera, convinced they were spies instead. Only Luther knew the full extent of the crisis he was facing, and he couldn't well mention it to Artemov for fear of losing face. His silence might have indicated that something was amiss, but Turilli elected to raise a minor concern rather than come clean. He wasn't about to face Artemov's fury and suffer public humiliation when he could escape with a chiding.

"Actually," Turilli began, "come to think of it, there is something I feel you should be made aware of."

Artemov arched an eyebrow at him. "Go on."

"The nobles are growing restless. They want to know what their money is being spent on. Some are asking questions, but I've warned them against prying too intently. The situation is well under control."

"I should certainly hope so," said Artemov. "There's more at stake here than you think. If the nobility have taken a sudden interest in the project, I suspect that's down to the taxes you've imposed on them rather than natural curiosity. They all agreed to fund it at the outset, so why complain now? Because you've raised taxes. That works to a point, but even they have their limits." A mocking tone entered his voice. "You're not struggling to pay the workers and supervisors are you, regent? That would be embarrassing, given it was you who said that Tanis could sustain the project with funds from its own coffers."

Turilli seethed inwardly but held his tongue. *Yes*, he thought, *but Tanis wouldn't have been awarded the contract had I not pledged to do this.*

"I only mention it," the regent said eventually. "I'd be remiss if I did not."

"And for that I'm grateful," said Artemov. "You've done well, Lucas. You just need to control that temper of yours."

"I try, my lord."

"It detracts from your efforts and otherwise commendable performance as regent. Your idea to tax the people instead of forcing them to work on the project was ingenious, as was the strategy you employed to displace the villagers. Keep this up, and when your term as regent is done you may yet be invited to join the regime's inner circle."

"Thank you, my lord."

Turilli felt his anger subside, encouraged by his master's praise. Artemov, meanwhile, smirked inwardly. He knew exactly how to keep his puppet motivated, having chosen Turilli not because of the man's talents, but because he was easy to control. While a regent had to possess a degree of intelligence, Turilli wasn't smart enough to know if and when he was being manipulated or mollycoddled.

Content, Artemov was about to break contact when he noticed the bemused look on Turilli's face. "You have something you wish to say," he observed nonchalantly. "Say it, regent."

"I've been thinking about the project," said Turilli.

"Yes?" Artemov pressed when he did not continue. "Speak freely or don't speak at all."

"Is it really necessary? You already have complete control of the galaxy. If the existing strategy is so successful, why change it?"

Artemov smiled stiffly. "You think it's a vanity project. A demonstration of our wealth and power. But from an economic standpoint it makes perfect sense. The galaxy is far too big for the fleet to police effectively, and in time more Chimeras will follow. One on every world. We can then reduce the number of ships at anchor and dispense with the crews manning them. Their upkeep is considerable."

"But surely-"

"I haven't finished," Artemov snarled, visibly irked by the interruption. "The planet killers were built for one purpose. Now that purpose is fulfilled, we can prepare the galaxy for what is coming.

Contrary to what you may have heard, our resources aren't infinite. If we were to destroy every planet that rebelled against us, then the number of taxable worlds would diminish. Any regent worth their salt knows this. Fortunately, we have already achieved our primary objective. Now there is nothing left to remind the people of their decadent past and the folly that was religion."

"Religion?" Turilli queried.

"My master is both wise and powerful," said Artemov. "Far better to venerate the one who ended the war, not that which caused it. People have refuted the supernatural, and are ready to put their faith in a real person instead of fictional deities. My master intends to fill this void. We do not seek to deny people their right to believe in something greater than themselves - just to direct and instruct them. The galaxy needs to be united."

"I concur," said Turilli. The regent was baffled by Artemov's reasoning, but found himself imitating his master in an effort to appear cleverer than he was. This made for an amusing scene as he copied everything from Artemov's accent to his mannerisms, though if the High Lord had noticed this odd behaviour then he didn't show it. "Going back to my original point," Turilli continued, "I'm not against the project, but I am worried that someone might try to sabotage it."

"You're referring to the nobles, of course," said Artemov. "Well, if you've followed the directives we set then you have nothing to fear. Vast amounts of time and money have gone into securing the Chimera, and we've taken every precaution. Insurgents aren't going to exploit some hidden weakness or flaw that we weren't aware of when we designed it. If a noble is giving you cause for concern, punish them, but not excessively so. You want to deter, not humiliate."

"Yes, my lord. And we have been careful not to deviate from your instructions. Tell me, will you be honouring us with your presence at the demonstration?"

"I'm afraid not," said Artemov. "I couldn't stomach a six-month voyage, even on my luxury liner. No, regime agents will observe it instead and report back to me with their findings. Have you selected a target?"

"I have," Turilli crowed, secretly relieved that he wouldn't have to meet his master in person. "Undercity will serve as a suitable test site. There are no military bases in the area, and I've already taken the liberty of closing several traders and securing their stock for the regime."

Turilli sat tall in his chair feeling very proud of himself, expecting his master to praise him for showing initiative. This was one of the regent's bolder ideas, due in part to the fact he hadn't stolen it, but also because he hoped to use Earth's new toy to further his own agenda. He looked at Artemov expectantly, anticipating his approval, but the High Lord's expression remained unchanged, and Turilli couldn't tell whether his idea had been well received or not.

"A sound plan," Artemov said eventually. "Except for one thing."

"What's that?"

"You're an incompetent, egotistical whelp with the subtlety of a sledgehammer." Artemov's voice crackled with anger. "Do you not see that your reckless actions could have jeopardised the entire project? You may as well open the site for public tours, or just broadcast our intentions to all and sundry. I know exactly why you're securing the traders' stock, and it isn't for any cause greater than yourself. You want to make Tanis the capital of your own little empire, and think that with the Chimera under your control you can do as you please. An amusing fantasy, but has it occurred to you that these sudden closures might make people suspicious? The lower classes understand more than you think. I just hope your security is as good as you say it is - for your sake."

Turilli cowered in his chair, reeling from Artemov's verbal assault. The previously unflappable regent suddenly felt very small. "I don't know what to say," he stammered. "But why should we care what people think?"

"Nothing is more important," Artemov scolded. "You need to convince the people that the Chimera is there to protect them, not control. Testing it on a major population centre could well have the opposite effect."

"Better they witness its awesome power first hand," said Turilli. "Fear will keep them in line."

"Perhaps, but until the Chimera is ready it is vulnerable. If someone discovers its purpose then the people could unite against you, or the nobility may opt to pull the project's funding. I can't predict how Tanis might react, but I do know the Chimera wouldn't survive a full-on assault in its current state. We're relying on secrecy and the ignorance of others for now, unless there's some higher method behind your drive to turn the whole world against you?"

"No, my lord."

"Then try to see the bigger picture here. There's a fine line between confidence and arrogance, but it'll be your hubris that dooms you long before your humility. If you push people too far then they'll have no choice but to oppose you. Why do you think we let each world celebrate its Landfall Day?"

"I'd take that away from them too if I thought they wouldn't riot," said Turilli.

"My point exactly. You have to make the odd concession just to keep people happy. Give them one luxury, however small, and they'll love you for it. But if you remove that as well, be prepared to face a furious reaction. In your mind you've closed a few shops, but to others this is their livelihood. The traders and their customers will start talking. They'll want to know why. Some may try to investigate, while others might want to confront you. We don't need either."

"I only closed the stores because of the nature of their stock," Turilli argued. "Surely you want these relics preserving?"

Artemov smiled. "We wouldn't let the traders acquire anything of value. They can help themselves to fakes, replicas or trinkets, and sell any item we cannot prove to be a genuine artifact. Only authentic, spectacular finds deserve to be protected. Look at this."

The High Lord activated a live video feed from one of his cameras inside his private storehouse. Turilli leaned forward, gazing intently at the image of an ancient machine from another time.

"The first Lunar lander," Artemov declared, allowing Turilli the briefest of glimpses before cycling to another feed. "And this skeleton is the only proof we have that great beasts once stalked the frozen wastes around Earth's north pole. For as long as the regime endures, we can take comfort in the fact that treasures like these will never fall into uncultured hands."

Turilli continued to stare at the screen long after Artemov had cut the feed. "What would you have me do, my lord?" he asked eventually, mesmerised by his master's knowledge and power.

"Return the stock and choose another target. One of the villages, perhaps? Undercity represents a major source of tax revenue, and I doubt the nobility would look too kindly on losing it. If their hideous wailing doesn't drive you insane, then the clamour from those good-for-nothing firebrands and altruists on Gethsemane will. You may think your forces capable of quashing any rebellion, but you'd do well to heed my words."

"Yes, my lord."

"Don't forget that it was I who awarded you the contract," Artemov continued. "I've been more than generous already, sending two of my own operatives to help secure the site. You also asked me to provide you with an off-world labour force, and I obliged."

Turilli listened as Artemov reeled off a list of favours he'd done for him. Though he valued his master's guidance, the regent stubbornly believed he had come this far based solely on his own merits - never once relying upon the actions of others. If Artemov couldn't see it, then the High Lord would be made to.

"About the workers," Turilli ventured. "May I have your leave to 'take care' of them when the project is finished?"

"Make it quick," said Artemov, well aware of what Turilli had in mind. "You are to be congratulated on yet another excellent idea."

"Thank you, my lord."

"There can be no loose ends. The Chimera project will change the face of the galaxy, but do not think yourself invincible with one of these fierce machines at your side. You'd be foolish to think we haven't anticipated all eventualities. Go now and oversee its completion. We'll speak again very soon."

In an instant, Artemov's menacing stare was gone. Turilli slouched back in his chair, glad to be free from his master's taunts and put-downs.

Who does that pompous toff think he is? Addressing me in such a manner.

Feeling aggrieved and angry, the regent decided that he wouldn't give the people anything, nor would he return the trinkets. He would add them to his own collection instead.

Turilli began ranting to himself, swearing vengeance on all those who'd defied him, entirely unaware that Artemov had anticipated every scheme he planned long before he'd even conceived it.

29

To the people of Tanis, the Phalanx was more than just a unit of veteran enforcers. Its soldiers embodied the regime's military doctrine, relying on fear and force to keep Lucas Turilli's subjects in line. Utterly loyal to the regent and with souls as black as their armour, the enforcers never stopped to question their orders, nor did they feel remorse for their brutal actions. Now this weapon of terror had been unleashed on the northern villages, catching Leo off-guard and outmanoeuvring the Liberation League at every turn.

The soldiers moved at a pace Leo had thought to be impossible. Pausing only to raze yet another village, Turilli's enforcers were so far ahead of the League they hadn't even realised they were being followed. Unwilling to force-march his army across the burning desert, Leo called off the pursuit while he rethought his strategy.

Furious with Leo's decision, some of the more extreme elements in the League went to Kruger with their grievances. Ignoring them at first, Kruger became increasingly riled by their mindless provocations and Leo's apparent inaction. When one outspoken upstart branded him a coward, Kruger's already thin patience finally snapped. After laying the man out cold with one clean punch, he confronted Leo in a fit of rage, firing questions and insults at him in equal measure.

Undaunted, Leo cooled his captain's anger by admitting he had made a mistake, calmly asking Kruger to help rectify it. "Then you'll have the fight you seek," he promised, sensing the man's lust for vengeance. "Maybe you can turn that fire and zeal against our enemies instead of wasting it on me."

"If we ever catch them," Kruger scoffed. "But I see you've given up on that idea. Turilli's thugs are busy giving us the run around, and what have we to show for our efforts? Fuck all, that's what. We're out here sweltering away in this infernal heat, and you've gone and buried your head in the sand like a fucking ostrich. I must have been mad to leave Arcana. You don't know what you're doing, do you?"

"I know *exactly* what I'm doing," Leo rumbled, the conviction in his voice making Kruger take an instinctive step back. "But I'm not infallible. Nor am I too proud to ask for your help."

Kruger folded his arms across his chest. "When have you ever listened to anything I've said?"

"Look around. We're here because I listened to you. But I've got a thousand people suggesting ten times that many strategies and I can't act on all of them. Not all of what you say makes tactical sense, but I won't hide my feelings just to spare yours. It's not right. Would you rather have the truth or some twisted version of it? You're always frank and honest with me, so it's only fair that I'm equally candid with you." Leo glared at Kruger and said, "If you want to help, tell me where you would go from here."

Kruger thought for a moment, determined to prove to Leo that he was equally skilled in the art of war. "Let the Phalanx come to us," he said confidently. "We outnumber them ten to one. Meet them in force and they can't possibly stand before us."

"You want to fight a pitched battle? Give up the element of surprise?"

"Honour demands that we do."

Leo shook his head. "Half our number can't fight. There goes our numerical advantage. And charging wildly across open desert might sound heroic, but we'd be cut to ribbons by a couple of decent volleys."

"You don't know that," said Kruger.

"I do, as it happens. We can't worry about honour when our enemies have none. They won't stop to follow the tenets of war even if we do. Still, you make a good point."

"Regarding what, exactly?"

"About having the Phalanx come to us." Leo unfurled a battered old map and pinned its corners to the ground with small pieces of rock. "There," he said, pointing at a range of mountains to the north of Divinity. "Monarch Pass. It's the only way through that formation, and the quickest route back to the city."

Kruger crouched down beside him. "So what's to stop them from going around?"

"The mountains," said Leo. "The Phalanx won't take a fifty mile detour - not when there's a passage through." He took two pebbles and placed one on either side of the pass. "We set an ambush. Wait until they've reached the middle of the pass, then strike. Two armies of equal strength; mine from the east, yours, the west. The soldiers will be out of battle formation and tired."

"And all the more dangerous for it," said Kruger. "Surround them and they'll fight to the death."

"Which is why we leave a gap. Let some of them escape."

"To what end?" Kruger scoffed. "They'll go straight to the regent and tell him everything."

"I wonder how he'll take the news," Leo said with a smile.

"Oh, I see. Very clever."

"We'll be off to the pass before long," said Leo. "Tell your overzealous friends they'll get to face the Phalanx first. That'll brighten their day." *And rid me of their extremist beliefs and ideals at the same time.*

The Phalanx entered Monarch Pass exactly as Leo had predicted. As dusk fell, he could see the armour-clad enforcers approaching - and feel the anxiety building within the League's ranks.

From his vantage point high in the mountains, Leo watched the steel column advance towards him. Two blocks of enforcers trudged forward with their prisoners - numbering roughly three thousand - packed safely in between. The soldiers marched mechanically and in loose formation, paying more attention to the ground than their surroundings.

Leo edged slightly closer, hoping to identify the small cadre of men and women leading the Phalanx. The unit's commanders posed the greatest threat to his forces, but it surprised him to learn that these elite officers had failed to adequately scout the pass. Any diligent captain would have sent patrols ahead of their main army, so to both Leo and Kruger it appeared that these four had either grown careless or complacent.

Then again, Leo thought, staring dumbly at the soldiers' weapons, *with that much firepower on hand, perhaps they didn't need to.*

With the Phalanx drawing near, Leo signalled his fighters to move quietly down the mountain. Hard to spot among the rocks and letting darkness hide their approach, he knew that every metre they made here was one less to cover in the open under fire.

Kruger's host followed suit and descended the precipice opposite. From above, Luna watched both armies moving into position, afraid for Leo but certain he would win. If he was ever going to beat the Phalanx, then this was the time and place to do it. She looked on as Leo gave the order to attack, and as one the League's fighters surged toward their foes.

The battle for Tanis had begun.

Plans and tactics went out of the window as the charge gathered momentum. Men and women barrelled down the mountainside screaming war cries and waving sticks, batons and other makeshift weapons above their heads. The thousand soldiers of the Phalanx halted, looking to their shell-shocked officers for guidance. Like mindless drones, the enforcers set about forming ranks when ordered to, preparing to repel the attack with extreme prejudice.

Leo urged his fighters onwards, counting on their charge to cause as much chaos as possible. The regent's soldiers had already locked shields and were readying their weapons, standing firm in hollow squares so they could defend all sides effectively. Aware of the danger and willing to face it, the League had covered nearly three hundred yards when the enforcers shouldered their guns and opened fire.

Scores of fighters were killed outright, while others had arms or legs blown off and fell screaming to the ground. Still the League came on, undaunted and getting ever closer. Another volley tore into their ranks, but tiredness meant the enforcers' aim was not as accurate as it should have been. With the League almost upon them, some soldiers drew their batons while others snapped off shots from their sidearms. Leo and Kruger fired back with the weapons they'd taken from Luna's stash, managing to down several enforcers before their charge crashed home.

The fighting that ensued was savage and chaotic. Leo's forces fought hard to break the line, only to be repulsed time and time again by fierce regime resistance. Kruger fared little better, finding that the soldiers' ordered discipline was more than a match for the League's frenzied attacks. His fighters' strikes were too predictable; easy to block or slow enough to dodge. Every miss was punished by a sickening blow from a baton or shield, and when an enforcer retreated it was only to let another take his place.

Kruger watched in horror as the Phalanx started to gain the advantage. The soldiers had stopped firing for fear of hitting their own, but were equally proficient in hand-to-hand combat. They had the best weapons and training, able to fight as a unit and wear an enemy down. Over to his right, Kruger saw some of his men trying to free the regime's prisoners. The enforcers didn't even try to stop them, knowing that their chains could not be broken. Kruger shouted Leo's name, furious he'd led them to this pass and now seemed incapable of action.

So much for the regime's brightest.

With the battle going against him, Leo finally played his hand. He'd learned all about the Phalanx at the academy - everything from the unit's command structure to how its captains would respond to an ambush. As the soldiers tightened their ranks, Leo powered up the torch he'd taken from Luna and shone it at the foot of the mountain.

Kruger heard a quick succession of muffled thumps above the tumult. He turned to see four missiles streaking skyward, watching as the warheads corkscrewed high above the battlefield. They hung there for what seemed an eternity before beginning their descent, plunging to the ground like comets into the heart of the enforcers' ranks.

The missiles detonated on impact, incinerating men where they stood and knocking Kruger off his feet. For the briefest of moments, the battle stopped. Neither side knew what had happened, nor the condition of the other. When the smoke cleared, Kruger saw dozens of enforcers lying dead and that the regime's formation had been broken. He stood unsteadily, aware that someone had to seize the initiative while the soldiers were still recovering.

"What are you waiting for?" he shouted to his fighters. "Get after them!"

Dispersed and slow to act, the enforcers were not as formidable as the League had found them before. Their officers fought on, but noticed they were losing ground to a revitalised opponent and began to contemplate retreat.

The League's left flank found the going much tougher. Separated from his fighters, Leo fought like a man possessed until he was surrounded by five baton-wielding enforcers. He bested two before a hefty blow to the back of his head knocked him to the ground. As his enemies advanced, three shots rang out and the soldiers fell beside him, dead. Leo instantly recognised the sound of a bolt-action sniper rifle, silently thanking Luna for saving his life.

Reloading quickly, Luna chose another target and fired again. The rifle only took five bullets at a time, but she'd been learning how to use it ever since she'd lifted it from the contingent's armoury.

The weapon's targeter and laser sight helped her score a kill with every shot. Using the sight, she located the Phalanx's commanders and set about eliminating them, acutely aware of what their loss would mean to the rest of the unit.

Radio contact between the enforcers and their captains stopped. Too late the soldiers realised what was happening, and by the time the last commander fell they were disoriented and in danger of being overwhelmed.

Without their captains' orders, discipline collapsed. Leo's fighters were everywhere, pressing home their relentless attack. To the exhausted men and women of the Phalanx, there was but one option left. Spotting a gap in the League's ranks, the remaining enforcers broke out and into the pass, fleeing back to Divinity as fast as they could.

Kruger let them go as Leo had instructed, raising his arms in victory. His fighters did the same, cheering loudly as the scale of what they'd achieved became clear. The Phalanx was routed, and the League's own casualties light by comparison. Kruger shouldered his way through the crowd, coming face to face with Leo for the first time since their argument four days earlier.

Instead of shouting at him, Kruger surprised everyone by embracing Leo warmly, but his friend did not return the gesture. Kruger was about to admonish him for his rudeness, then he felt the faint vibrations in the ground too.

Leo looked back down the pass but couldn't see anything.

"What is it?" asked Kruger, concern evident in his voice.

Leo shook his head. "I don't know."

The vibrations got louder. Kruger loaded his gun. Then a brilliant white flash lit the pass and two shells screamed through the air, slamming into the ground only metres away. The blast was so strong it sent both men flying in opposite directions.

When Leo came to his senses, he saw Kruger lying face down in a pool of blood. He lifted his head, scanning the pass for signs of movement. Through the darkness, a pair of glowing red eyes stared back at him.

Leo staggered to his feet. Something large loomed up before him, something that belonged in his nightmares and not the real world. It had the rough shape of a man - a man magnified until it was over fifty feet tall. Leo froze, remembering a story he'd once heard about the war-engines of old and their awesome power. Even now he could not understand what had driven men to build such things. He rubbed his eyes, convinced they were playing tricks on him.

Then the engine opened fire.

30

The mid-afternoon glow from the open windows spilled into the regent's palace, as Elena lounged about her apartment sipping a glass of red wine. With Luther away, she'd made a conscious effort to mingle with her peers, hosting nightly balls and galas to alleviate the boredom caused by her husband's absence - and remind the elite of her undiminished wealth and power.

Maria van Dyck and Lady Chiara were her honoured guests today. She'd invited them over under the pretence of friendship, with neither woman wise to her true motives. Ever the schemer, Elena saw their visit as an opportunity - one where she might try to gauge their loyalty to the regent while advancing Luther's cause.

Now began her game in earnest.

"It's excellent, this," Maria remarked, sampling the wine. "Might I ask where you got it?"

"A gift from Rossi," said Elena. "I forget why."

"Lucky you. The old codger never got me anything."

Elena tried to stifle her annoyance. Crass and uncouth, it was her inferiors' brazen sense of entitlement that irked her the most.

"Don't expect our new regent to show you such charity," Chiara snorted. "Blood and taxes are his only 'gifts' to us."

"I heard that he wants to expand the industrial zone," said Maria. "We'll have swarms of unwashed plebs on our doorsteps before you know it."

Elena nodded absently, content to watch her guests and learn a little more about them before she made her move. Her razor-sharp mind was already at work, honing in on Chiara and the throwaway remarks she liked to make when discussing Turilli. Openly slating the man's behaviour and policies, Elena sensed that she harboured a degree of mistrust - maybe even resentment - towards him, and was not the loyal subject she made herself out to be.

Making my task all the easier.

Maria, however, kept her tone level and her opinions to herself. The young brunette was the opposite of Chiara; reserved, calculating and near impossible to read. Her toothy grin and obsequious manners might well have fooled others, but Elena knew that behind this amiable facade lurked a formidable intellect that rivalled her own.

"I doubt there's ever been a more despised regent," Chiara snorted. "Turilli isn't fit to run a bath, let alone a planet. The man's stark raving mad. Just the other day he barked at one of my servants, then went and chased another down five flights of stairs."

"Clearly he's insane," said Maria, taking another sip of her drink. "That, or it's all part of an elaborate charade designed to fool us into underestimating him."

"Call it what you like," said Chiara, "but his ineptitude is staggering. There's still no strategy in place to deal with the workers when this so-called Chimera project is over. He can't well send them back without bankrupting himself, so the only thing to do is resettle them here."

Maria scowled and shook her head. "Half a million people? And where will they go, exactly? The city's overcrowded as it is. These vermin breed - give it five years and we'll be in the minority. Our laws and values gone, while we're hounded out of our own homes by a swarm of foreign vagrants."

"Perhaps," Elena ventured, "we should do the decent thing and put Turilli out of his misery."

Her bold suggestion shocked Maria and Chiara into silence. The two women exchanged a worried look, unsure whose side Elena was on. Those loyal to the regent often found themselves in positions of power - or knew someone who was. Luther served Turilli, and it had always been assumed Elena did too.

But what if Luther only served him out of fear? What if Elena had meant every word?

"That's treason," Chiara said after a while, unwilling to commit until Elena had made her position clear.

"Is it?" Elena set her glass down and leaned forward. "The constitution states that if a regent acts against Earth's interests then he should be removed from office."

"Turilli isn't stupid," Maria scoffed. "Deluded, yes, but even he wouldn't dare tempt their wrath."

"No?" Elena took a small recording device from her pocket and let it play. Her guests listened closely, their eyes widening as they heard Turilli reveal his intentions to Hauser.

"Well," said Chiara, "I'd say that changes things a little."

Elena nodded. "Best we strike before Earth finds out."

"How?"

"You can start by dropping the act, my dear. I'm no friend of Turilli, and I would like to think Maria has her family's best interests at heart as well. Come now. Why the long face? Don't tell me you haven't at least considered moving against him."

Elena's words helped put Chiara's mind at ease. "We all have dreams," she admitted. "One of mine is a world without Turilli."

"And why is that?"

"How long have you got?"

Elena listened as Chiara reeled off a lengthy list of grievances, stunned by the ferocity of her words. If she truly hated Turilli, then converting the disgruntled minister to her way of thinking wouldn't be hard.

"He's impossible to work with," Chiara ranted, continuing her attack. "Hypocritical. Arrogant. Then there was that business with the ministers."

"Yes, I had heard about that," said Elena. "Was it very upsetting?"

"I've never been more humiliated in my life. Thrown out of council then suspended for a week. I'll bet Turilli enjoyed it, though. Setting one of his thugs to beat me like I was some common tart. Me - a minister of Tanis. The man has no respect. He's the one who asked for my input on the project in the first place."

"It's strange," Elena remarked, motioning for a servant to refill their drinks. "Of all the things a regent can do, that ours should take an interest in construction."

"What do you mean by that?"

"Well, it's hardly very exciting, is it? Analysing graphs and charts. I thought Turilli considered himself above such trivia."

"That 'trivia' is my job," growled Chiara. "A job I'm very good at."

Elena blinked and held up her hands. "Forgive me. I didn't mean to diminish the importance of the work you do."

"Think nothing of it. Turilli's insults are far worse."

"Has he ever interfered before?" asked Elena.

"Never. I have to say, something about this project didn't feel right from the start. The transmissions from Earth, the secrecy. Turilli asked me how long I thought it would take, but the files and blueprints were all locked. He kept pressing me for an answer, so I guessed. I just wanted to get the man off my case."

"You couldn't have won either way," said Elena. "He was always going to make an example of you."

"To warn others against prying? I'd say the whole thing was a test to see what I knew. But I'm still none the wiser. In truth, Turilli knows more about this project than any of us."

"Is that a bad thing?"

"Until he divulges its purpose, yes," said Chiara. "I've no idea what's happening there, and I'm the director of engineering. He could be building some kind of doomsday machine for all I know."

Elena shuffled uneasily. "I doubt it." For a fleeting moment she thought about telling her guests what she'd discovered, then decided against it. She wasn't here to make friends, only to strengthen Luther's cause. With this in mind, Elena finished her drink, looked over at

Chiara and said, "What if I can make your dream a reality?"

The minister's brown eyes narrowed. "Explain."

"Turilli's actions pose a direct threat to Tanis. He's set on a path that'll lead us to destruction, and we owe it to our children to stop him. Luther wants what you want. An end to suffering and fear. A return to the glory days of old. Were you to back him, then the rewards when he becomes regent would be very handsome indeed."

"How handsome?"

Elena smiled inwardly. "No more threats and jibes. A bigger budget for construction. Autonomy. You shall make your own appointments and have a job for life should you want it. We can think of no-one better to head such an important division. Of course, your loyalty to Luther would be deserving of a substantial monetary bonus - one that you can set."

"Dear me," Chiara stammered, taken aback by Elena's offer. "That is most kind of you."

"Would you like some time to think about it?"

"No, no. I accept your terms wholeheartedly. You can count on my support."

"Excellent." Elena leaned back in her chair, content. She turned to Maria, hoping she would follow suit. "And where do the van Dycks stand on this?" she asked nonchalantly. "Are they happy toeing the line, or do they want something more?"

Maria didn't answer immediately. The young aristo had been biding her time, watching as Chiara squandered the chance to press for further concessions.

She was not about to do the same.

"I have no quarrel with Turilli," Maria remarked after a while. "In fact, I'd say he's been rather good to us. Awarding my Arturo rank and status. He's a little odd, I'll grant you, but I've never had reason to fear or despise him."

Elena frowned. A deal was still on the cards, but Maria was holding out for more favourable terms. Elena knew she had to be careful.

Give her what she wants and others will start making demands of their own. Refuse, and the deceitful little leech might tell Turilli everything.

With Maria, she would have to change tack.

"It is most unfortunate," Elena began, "that Turilli saw fit to condemn your youngest to death."

"She meant to kill him," said Maria. "Turilli could not honourably do other than he did."

"Oh, please. No-one believes that. He made you denounce your own daughter and you hate him for it."

"No, I-"

"Look, you might have fooled Turilli, but no real mother stops loving her child overnight. Here's what I think happened. You somehow managed to talk Turilli out of mounting a full-scale search for her, letting him believe the decision was his. My executors only saw five gunships leave the city that week. This would give your daughter a fighting chance, assuming she was still alive." Elena sat up straight and said, "Luther wouldn't make you choose between him and one of your children. Any man who does is no man at all."

"Be that as it may," said Maria, "I like my life the way it is. Change makes me nervous."

"Then let me deal with Turilli. You don't have to say or do anything. A simple show of unity when Luther is regent will suffice."

"And what of Earth? Our masters chose Turilli to do their bidding. Can you predict how they'll react when they learn what has transpired here?"

Elena shrugged. "They'll be pleased that we exposed Turilli's treachery before it could spread."

"If you say so," said Maria. "I'm still not convinced."

"Then I guess we've no more business."

"Hold on a minute," Maria exclaimed, worried she might now end up with nothing. "I'm sure we can reach an agreement. You just have to persuade me, is all."

"And how might I do that?"

"I, uh..." Maria knew she would not get a better chance to extend her influence, but Elena's manoeuvring had caught her off-guard. "I don't want to pay any more tax," she stammered, struggling to impose her terms. "My husband is to be vice-regent *and* administrator. Our children's careers fast-tracked. And rooms. We shall all have rooms in the palace."

Elena sighed, pretending to appear hard done by. "Agreed," she said eventually, happy to let Maria think that she was in control. There would be ample time to placate her later.

"One question," said Maria, annoyed she hadn't asked for more. "What'll become of Turilli?"

"Feed him to the dogs," Chiara suggested with a smirk.

Elena smiled. "There are no dogs here. But I've heard the wolves on Earth are always hungry."

Chiara raised her glass. "Then let us prepare a great feast."

Their deal done, Elena and Maria joined their glasses with hers.

William Marshall was no stranger to hardship. The old tradesman had survived his years in the contingent and the wounds that time had inflicted, but the stresses of recent months had taken their toll and left him feeling weak and worthless. He was tired now, and after putting his affairs in order headed out into the late afternoon heat with only his gloomy thoughts for company.

The howling wind slowed Marshall's journey across the city. His body ached as he battled through the storm that had returned to lash Divinity, his ankles screaming with every step as if the bones there had been replaced by shards of broken glass. Yet despite the pain, Marshall willed himself on. He'd weathered far worse storms than this, and wasn't going to rest until he'd seen his cherished store one last time.

As he walked, Marshall couldn't help but wonder what he might find. Two months was time enough for the regime to level the building, sell it or move new tenants in. Marshall girded on his old enforcer baton at the thought these 'tenants' might be squatters, or worse. Even though he'd been pushed into retirement, Marshall felt he still had a duty of care towards the small piece of land that had been his for over fifty years.

Victoriam Plaza was deserted. Empty stores lined streets where children once played and traders met to do business, a stark reminder that nothing here was constant. Marshall remembered the boom years as if they were only yesterday. He'd seen things change for the better and for the worse, but was thankful to have memories of the good times.

Marshall headed straight for his store, relieved to see it was still standing. He took a silver key out of his pocket, congratulating himself for having made a spare, then waited. Enforcers weren't known to spend their days guarding vacant shops, but Marshall wasn't taking any chances. Though he didn't consider what he was about to do a crime, he'd known people who had died for less.

Certain that no-one was watching, Marshall put the key in the lock and turned it. The wooden door stuck at first, but he nudged it open with his shoulder and stepped inside, closing it behind him as quickly as he could. Marshall conducted a thorough search of the property but found no intruders nor any sign of a break-in.

He was alone.

Though the regime had removed everything of value, Marshall's shabby old desk remained bolted to the floor. He ran his hand over its smooth oak surface, sighed and looked up at the door, remembering the sights and sounds of another time. Customers thronged his store, from clients waiting to trade to children comparing their recently purchased gems and trinkets. Marshall revelled in the carnival-like atmosphere, hoping that he might find peace here after all. But some things just weren't meant to be. Those golden days were gone, and this time no-one was coming.

Marshall lowered his gaze and leaned back against the desk. Given everything he'd done, perhaps he didn't deserve happiness.

He was staring dumbly at the floor when something caught his eye.

Reaching down, Marshall grasped what looked like a corner of paper stuck between the floorboards.

The object proved to be a photo - one from Marshall's personal collection. It had come to him by way of an exchange; from a boy who'd wanted to buy a ring for his intended but hadn't the money. The youth had offered the photo and album it was part of to help make up the difference, much to the amusement of everyone watching. Under normal circumstances, Marshall would have refused, but he empathised with the boy's plight and took pity on him.

He smiled suddenly, remembering the look of surprise on the boy's face when he agreed. He'd perused the album later that night, and out of the hundreds of photos only one had stood out. This one. A family was sat in front of a strange-looking tree, surrounded by gifts and presents. Marshall scratched his head. He'd never asked the boy what the occasion was, nor had he managed to find out what they were celebrating in the years since. It had been a source of great frustration for him, but also great joy. Even though he didn't know its meaning, the people in the photo looked like they were having a wonderful time. More importantly, they looked happy.

Marshall set the photo down on his desk and sighed. He wondered what had become of the boy and his intended - whether they'd married and had children or left Tanis for pastures new. These were all things Marshall wished he'd done years ago, but he'd lost himself in his work and done nothing remarkable with his life - nothing worthy of remembrance. He would die a nameless, faceless footnote, one who'd left it far too late to do anything about his regrets, his name and achievements forgotten like so many others.

Maybe it was for the best.

No-one would remember Victoriam Plaza, nor the old man who used to sell trinkets out of his humble store. In time, people would forget that there had even been a shop here. Marshall slumped to the floor, reflecting on how meaningless his life had been. Dreams of home occupied his thoughts, and a single tear ran down his cheek. He recalled his youth and happier days when he'd been surrounded by loving people - his brothers, sisters and parents - and contented himself with the thought that he would see them all again very soon.

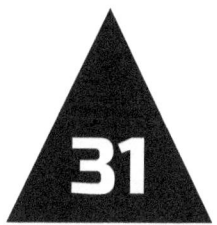

31

The freedom fighters of the Liberation League ran for their lives. Leo dived for cover as two more shells whistled past and exploded just behind him, showering his position with rocks and sand.

The engine took a step, and the ground trembled. It let out a terrible blast from its warhorn, provoking fear and panic in the League's ranks. Those who'd survived its first volley broke and ran, fighting each other for an avenue of escape. The dread machine stalked after them, regarding the tiny, fleeing men and women as one might do a swarm of ants. Eager to avenge the Phalanx, it levelled out its weapons, locked on and fired.

Hundreds died as the searing hellstorm overtook them. The engine hammered its foes with salvo after salvo, tearing through the League with brutal efficiency.

Luna swung her rifle around and fixed the metal monster squarely in her sights. Bullets pinged harmlessly off the engine's armour, grazing its jet black paintwork but doing nothing to slow it. Like Leo, Luna had never seen a war-engine before, nor did she have the first idea about how to fight one.

Massive gears groaned and clanked as the engine continued to advance. Flights of shrieking rockets rained down on the League, gouging out deep craters in the landscape and bursting men apart like wet sacks. Some were trampled underfoot by the rampaging behemoth, while others turned and lobbed grenades that detonated at its feet. The engine was unimpressed. It launched a full spread of rockets from the mount atop its back, then moved in to pick off the survivors with its cannons.

Leo hid behind a rock, watching the carnage unfold before him. Surprise and terror chained him to the spot, clouding his mind and robbing him of his senses. He knew the battle was slipping away, but there was nothing he or Luna could do about it. Their stratagems were useless against such awesome power, and they hadn't a weapon between them that was capable of piercing the engine's armoured hide.

Leo began to question himself, afraid he wasn't as clever as he thought he was. The League's apparent victory was turning into a rout, and he was the one responsible for it. He'd led these people to their deaths instead of the freedom he'd promised them. Through his arrogance he'd failed them all, and, even if he survived, Leo knew it would be better for him to take his own life than live with the shame.

He told himself that Luna would have made a better leader - that she'd have kept her head and not made the same mistakes he had. *What would she have thought if she saw him like this?* Leo wanted the ground to open and swallow him up. *How had this happened? How had the regime managed to conceal such a thing, and what other horrors were they hiding?* If he'd really been so blind, then maybe this was just punishment for his laxity. Incredibly, people were still looking to him to save them, but Leo was thinking only of saving himself.

A sudden burst of cannon fire prevented him from running. The engine had turned and was heading his way, the bloodied remnants of his army scattering in its wake. Its weapon mounts lit up with vivid muzzle flashes, every salvo sounding like thunder.

Leo turned away, the screams of dying men and women ringing in his ears. This wasn't war - at least not as he knew it - this was mechanised butchery. Even those who escaped would wish they hadn't when Turilli was through with them, and with no League left to stop him, the regent would unleash the Chimera on an unsuspecting populace and plunge the world into darkness. Leo came to realise that all these things would come to pass because of his weakness, and with that thought held firmly in his mind, he admitted to himself that death wasn't such a frightening prospect after all.

Heavy weapon discharge snapped him from his ruminations. The engine had paused to survey the battlefield, sporadically belting out gunfire across the desert at Leo's retreating fighters.

Again, Leo thought of running. He decided that if he was going to die, then it would be on his own terms and not the regime's. He'd barely made it to his feet when he noticed a young woman staring at him, her legs cut and bruised, yet the look on her face was not one of fear, but disappointment. In that moment, Leo knew what true failure was. He'd let himself down, betrayed everyone who'd had the courage to believe in his vision, and ensured at least one brave woman's defining memory of her captain was of him cowering behind a rock.

He couldn't let that stand.

Leo burst from cover, heading towards a pile of regime dead. "Go!" he shouted at the woman, who turned on her heel and took off down the pass. Searching the bodies for weapons, Leo grabbed a rifle, cocked it and advanced on the engine.

It didn't take him long to get in range. He set the rifle to full auto and sprayed the monster's lower chassis, lengthening his stride as he got closer. "Over here, you piece of shit!"

The engine swung its head around and seemed to gaze down with mute amusement. "Ugly fucker, aren't you?" Leo shouted. "Come on then! What are you waiting for?" He emptied the clip, slapped in a second and opened up again. The engine's weapon limbs auto-loaded as it turned to face him. His ammunition spent, Leo dropped the rifle and drew his sidearm, firing up at the engine's cockpit. He continued to advance, expecting at any moment to hear the roar of the cannons and feel the heat of a thousand suns on his skin.

But the killing shot never came. Towering above him, the engine lurched as an internal shockwave rippled through it. Leo saw smoke venting from a hole in the beast's back, then the blood-red lights that shone out of its cockpit flickered and died. There was a grinding rumble as the engine slowly toppled backwards, landing with an impact so heavy that even Luna felt it.

Leo stood in sullen silence, staring dumbly at the fallen giant. Smoke continued to pour from its ruptured boiler, and the weapons that had devastated his army lay broken beyond repair.

The day was his, though Leo sensed there was more to it than one lucky shot.

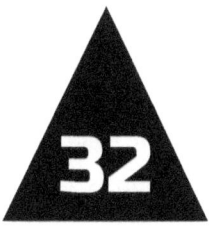

32

They were calling it the Battle of the Dunes.

As smoke from the regime's fallen engine drifted across the battlefield, groups of exhausted fighters began to return to the scene of their greatest triumph. Daylight revealed a blasted wasteland strewn with craters and bodies, while the only sounds were the desperate cries of the wounded and dying.

Though the outcome of the battle wasn't immediately clear, Leo's spirits soared as more and more of his fighters congregated at the mouth of Monarch Pass. The League's ranks had been thinned beyond measure, but the Phalanx was routed and their war machine destroyed. Leo calculated that enough of his army remained to take Divinity, and after besting the regime's elite, even he started to believe they actually could.

The smoke helped guide hundreds of weary men and women back to where the League was gathering. Marcus Rathen had seen it too, setting off in search of its source having fled Divinity days earlier. Starving and dehydrated, he wasn't sure if the sight before him was real or just another hallucination. The desert heat had wilted his mind, and he didn't trust any member of the League to tell him whether Leo had survived the battle or not. He would find his friend himself and only then tend to his own injuries.

Leo walked among his army, helping where he could. The celebrations were more muted this time, but that wasn't down to anything the regime had done, nor the hardships the League had endured. Everyone was staring at Leo, no longer regarding him with mere respect, but reverence. In the people's eyes, he'd saved them from destruction and won the battle with a single shot - feats that no ordinary man could have possibly achieved. Wherever he went, people gazed upon him as if he was divine, though Leo knew better. His response was to grin sheepishly, shake his head and turn away, walking out of the spotlight and straight into Luna's arms.

The two of them embraced as if they'd been apart for years. Again, Leo thought about taking Luna's hand and leaving everything behind, but once again he hesitated. He would just have to deal with the fear of losing her until they'd beaten the regime, aware that nothing he said would ever stop her from following him. Leo couldn't keep Luna safe and happy at the same time, but neither could he act on his own feelings for her without compromising his commitment to the League.

Luna had none of these concerns. She was living in the now, holding Leo tightly and enjoying every moment. Following her heart, she leaned in to kiss him but Leo pulled away.

"Don't," he pleaded, unable to look at her. "Not now."

Surprise and anger sparked in Luna's eyes. "When?"

"When this is over. When I've rid the world of those who'd come after you to get to me."

Frustrated, Luna took a step back and folded her arms. She knew Leo was right, but that didn't make his rejection any easier to bear.

"I can wait," she said, forcing a smile. "I guess your people can't."

Leo hung his head. "If only they knew the truth."

"You think they need to know what happened?" Luna scoffed. "What might have been? None of that matters."

"It does to me."

"Then let me tell you the truth as I see it. You could have run, you didn't. We might have died, we lived. We won. Luck, fate, let the people call it what they want. Be whoever they need you to be."

"I will," said Leo, meeting her gaze at last. "How's Kruger?"

"He'll be fine. Tough as old nails, that one. Give it a day and-" Luna noticed that Leo was staring past her and off into the distance. "Anyone home?" she snapped, waving a hand in front of his face.

Leo pushed her aside and caught Marcus before he could fall. "A little help wouldn't go amiss," Leo rasped, scowling at Luna, and together they gently lowered their friend to the ground. Marcus looked like death itself, desperately dehydrated and bleeding from at least four gunshot wounds, but none of that seemed to bother him.

"Don't tell me I missed another fight," he quipped before allowing himself the luxury of passing out.

Leo sent Luna to get some water while he waved the stretcher-bearers over. When they asked him if he wanted Marcus to be treated first, Leo shook his head and ordered them to do their best for him, but not at the expense of others. He would have tended to his friend's injuries himself had not an animated group of fighters surrounded him, chattering away excitedly and talking over one another.

They all bowed before him but Leo reprimanded them sharply, insisting they stand.

"We have something for you, my lord," a short, bearded man babbled, his weathered face glowing with pride. "This way."

They headed back to where the engine had fallen, attracting a sizeable crowd along the way. Curious, Leo shouldered his way to the front of the group, keen to see what all the fuss was about. His fighters continued to jostle for position, preferring to appoint themselves his captains and advisors instead of passing him useful information - much to Leo's dismay. He had hoped to learn what he was dealing with beforehand, but any voices of reason were lost amid the tumult leaving him none the wiser.

"There, my lord," the bearded man called out, pointing at another group of fighters. Leo saw that they were holding someone captive - someone he'd heard his father talk about often enough but had never spoken to at length himself.

Administrator Luther seemed to be relaxed and in good spirits despite his predicament. He was talking to his captors and smiling away, unfazed by the number of weapons being trained on him. His casual demeanour unsettled Leo, who quickly figured that Luther had come here to pursue his own agenda - whatever that was.

"This one surrendered to us," another man beamed, eagerly awaiting Leo's approval. "Says he's the commander of the regime forces. Asked to speak with you. Have we served you well, my lord?"

"You have," said Leo, eying Luther suspiciously. "Now leave us."

His fighters hesitated and exchanged worried looks.

"It's alright," Leo assured them, "I don't think the administrator has any ill designs on me. Do you?"

"Not under present circumstances," Luther grinned.

Again, Leo bade his men leave, and this time they obeyed without question. Luther looked on as they withdrew a respectful distance still holding their guns, ever watchful and wary.

"A sterling performance," he remarked, his gaze shifting to Leo. "Though admittedly, I can't take all the credit."

Leo ignored him and spoke in a quiet, icy tone. "I trust you have been treated well, administrator?"

"I have."

"Then walk with me."

The two men ambled off away from Leo's army, silently trying to figure each other out. Confident in his ability to control Leo and bend him to his will, Luther put his well-rehearsed plan into action.

"You'll find the people are as changeable as the wind," he began nonchalantly. "One day they love you, the next, they're lining up to tear you down."

"Depends on how you treat them," said Leo.

"It does. Honesty goes a long way."

"They say politicians speak of honesty as fish talk of flying."

Despite himself, Luther laughed. "Touché, but I wonder if one so young can meet their rising expectations."

"Stick around and you'll find out."

"I'm sorely tempted," said Luther, "and I know you'll welcome the challenge. Still, I fear I may have handed you an impossible task, and for that I apologise."

Leo's brown eyes narrowed. "For what, exactly?"

"For turning you into something you're not."

"You destroyed the engine?" Leo asked, trying not to sound surprised. "To what end?"

"I wanted to meet you."

"Why? Your master wants me dead. Were you a loyal subject, you should too."

Luther smiled. The boy was smarter than he'd thought, but too naive to pose a threat to him. "I owe Turilli no more loyalty," he said, stopping suddenly. "His arrogance will bring Earth's wrath down upon us - should anyone survive his pogroms and purges, that is. Our world deserves better, Leo. The people deserve better. The natural order of things must be restored, but I can't topple the tyrant alone. Will you help me?"

Leo looked into Luther's eyes, seeing past the glamours and the bravado to the heart of an individual who desired nothing more than power. His offer seemed genuine enough, but Leo had seen the ruthless ambition and capacity for violence at Luther's core. Men like him had kept entire generations down with bribes and myths of opportunity, only to turn on their so-called friends and allies when they had achieved their goals. Leo wasn't going to sell anyone out, nor would he let Luther use him as a pawn against Turilli.

If there was a deal to be made, it would be on Leo's terms and not the regime's.

"It was good of you to help us last night," Leo remarked, "and I'm sure you have your reasons for doing so."

"I only want what's best for Tanis," said Luther.

"I think you do, though I doubt that your idea of what's 'best for Tanis' is the same as mine."

Luther looked confused. "Why so?"

"You're quick to blame Turilli," said Leo, "but he isn't solely responsible for all the world's woes. You only criticise him when he raises taxes or makes a law that affects you directly, but the real object of your ire should be a council of kingmakers orbiting a distant star. Earth's autocrats and despots gave Turilli the power you crave. How can you, they or any noble presume to know what the people want? Our leaders aren't even elected. You strut about your palaces and penthouses while millions struggle to make ends meet, feathering your own nests instead of doing right by those who need your help."

"Remember who you're talking to, boy," Luther snapped, stung by Leo's words. "Show some damned respect!"

"Why should I?" said Leo. "Why do the nobility require special treatment? You're flesh and blood, the same as me. No-one here gives a damn about your titles or how vast your fortune is. You're just another elitist with an over-inflated sense of self-importance, here to enlist me in your quest against Turilli, though it isn't for any cause so noble as the people."

"You've enjoyed a pretty comfy life yourself," said Luther, struggling to maintain his composure in the face of Leo's accusations. "Had you inherited your father's wealth, would you have lived any differently?"

"I'd have given away that which I did not need."

"Truly?"

"Truly. Didn't you learn anything from Rossi? He made you, after all. You might have started out with nothing and worked long and hard to get to where you are today, but somewhere down the line you fell in love with power and all the things that drive men mad. You didn't just forget his teachings, you forgot yourself. Now you think the world owes you a favour because you had it hard early on, living off your past glories and resting on your laurels when in fact it is you who should be giving something back to those far less fortunate than yourself."

"I've done more for Tanis than most," hissed Luther. "Why can't I enjoy the fruits of my labour after all the hardships I've endured? And I got this far on my own - it wasn't all Rossi."

"Oh, I'm not questioning your intellect," said Leo. "In fact, I'm quite impressed. I bet it took all your wits and patience to convince Turilli that you should lead the Phalanx into battle. So what was the plan, Luther? You'd never kill anyone yourself, let alone a regent, so I'm guessing you came here looking for someone who would - someone you could crush when the deed was done. You'd be the obvious choice to replace Turilli, lauded by the nobility for restoring order and made regent by popular acclaim. But there's a problem. Even if the nobles didn't suspect anything, those on Earth might. How did you intend to convince them you weren't behind the whole thing when you can't even fool me?"

"I see now that coming here was a mistake," said Luther, unable to refute Leo's claims. He'd underestimated the boy, but that didn't mean he was going to give up and walk away from their debate empty-handed. "Maybe you're starting to believe your own hype," he continued, "but you still need me. Turilli's forces can beat you so easily, and you've no way of breaching Divinity's walls. Even if you did - if the city fell - you must know that Earth would retaliate."

Leo smiled, acutely aware of Luther's importance. "We need each other. I'm happy to admit that, but are you?"

"I am."

"Then let us work together as my father would have wanted. I can help you take the regency, but only if you renounce the regime and agree to help the people."

"You don't want to be regent?" Luther queried.

"Of course not. I have other matters to attend to far beyond Tanis."

"Leaving me in the firing line," said Luther. "I don't have the means to resist Earth's armies, Leo. They'll wipe this planet clean when they learn what has transpired here."

"Then you'd better work on your story," Leo stated calmly. "I'll help. Turilli isn't just insane, he's ambitious, so what if *he* rebelled - against Earth? Claim his madness as his motive and the Chimera as his means. You can play the hero if you like and say you stopped him, and that he took his own life when faced with defeat. A far more plausible scenario than yours, especially if you have some evidence to support it. A recording, perhaps."

Luther's eyes narrowed. "So I become regent. What do you want from me?"

"I want you to get the League inside Divinity. To deactivate the defences on and above the nineteenth level. To keep stringing Turilli along. There will be no looting by my forces nor any violence against the nobility, but if more isn't done for the people when you are regent, that can change."

Luther had to remind himself that it was Leo he was speaking to and not Rossi. The boy had inherited his adoptive father's talent for diplomacy, but his powers of deduction were unlike anything he'd known.

"Say I do all that," Luther offered, "you'll still be up against it. You've roused your rabble, but Divinity's a different beast. The people won't follow you so long as they live in fear of Turilli, and you'll need their help to overcome his enforcers and gunships."

"They'll be queuing up to join me," said Leo, "if you continue to manipulate Turilli. Destroy his mind and you destroy him. We will use the regime's greatest weapon against them and shake the people from their apathy. There's no catch, Luther, but I do have one more favour to ask of you."

"Which is?"

"I need you to get thirty Crusader-class transports here without alerting Turilli."

"For what purpose?" asked Luther.

"Just tell me if you can do it."

The administrator folded his arms and sighed, giving Leo the impression that such a thing would require great effort.

"I can handle Turilli," said Luther, "but it won't be easy getting so many ships here on short notice."

"Don't give me that," Leo scowled. "There's a fleet staging area at Gehenna two sectors away. You could have those ships here within a week if you pushed through the paperwork. Those vessels stand at constant readiness if the regime need to move large numbers of people in a hurry."

"How do you know about Gehenna?"

"Because I know things," said Leo.

"Then you're aware that I can action your request without Turilli's knowledge or approval. And that he'll start asking questions the moment those ships arrive in-system."

Leo nodded and said, "It's up to you to keep him in the dark."

"You're asking a lot of me," Luther grumbled, "and putting a great deal of trust in someone you barely know."

"I have faith in you, Luther. The same faith my father did. Stand with me against the regime and be part of something incredible."

Luther hesitated, recognising that he wouldn't get a better chance to save Rossi's legacy. "I'll help you, but in return I expect you to keep your word," he warned.

"As we agreed," said Leo, "you become regent and make Tanis a safer, fairer place for all. Now, tell me, can you resettle three million people?"

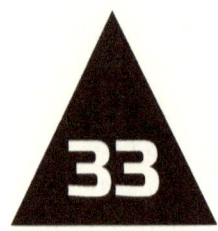

33

"Idiots! Traitors! Morons!"

Once again Lucas Turilli had worked himself up into an uncontrollable rage. No sooner had the Phalanx returned than he was storming over to the unit's barracks set on punishing those who had survived the battle, his cries of anguish striking fear into the hearts of even the most disciplined and hardened enforcers.

The mad regent berated his soldiers, subjecting them to an hour-long tirade of verbal abuse and indiscriminate beatings. Menials fled or bolted their doors as Turilli's screams echoed around the assembly yard, terrified he'd make good his threats then turn on them. None dared take responsibility for the Phalanx's failure, but the enforcers' silence merely enraged Turilli further.

"It seems the universe itself conspires against me. You had a fucking war-engine with you - how did you lose? I'll have the truth or your lives! I'm the master here and you'll all dance to whatever tune I play!"

Any demons Turilli had been suppressing now burst forth in spectacular fashion. He had waited patiently for the messengers and heralds to bring news of his victory, dreaming up a number of titles he intended to bestow upon himself the moment the Phalanx returned.

Warlord. Master strategist. Emperor.

Then he'd learned the truth. A truth laid bare before the eyes of all as a handful of soldiers traipsed solemnly through the city streets. For one as prideful as Turilli, the humiliation proved unbearable.

"These rebel dogs have won nothing but a slow and violent death. I'll have each of them hung, flayed and shot - in that order! All they've done is seal their fates." Turilli pulled the nearest enforcer to his feet and bellowed, "Stand up, ready the gunships and tear this city apart until you've found Luther! I want to see him squirm before he dies."

Luther was watching Turilli's meltdown from a window overlooking the compound. He considered letting the regent simmer a while, but knew that he would have to face him sooner or later if he really wanted what Leo had promised.

"There!" Turilli screeched, finally spotting Luther at the window. "Arrest him for treason!"

The regent's soldiers were in no mood to arrest anyone. Angered by his taunts and callous behaviour, they remained seated and refused to carry out his order. Turilli stood foaming at the mouth like a chafed panther, barely able to accuse the enforcers of treachery before marching off to confront Luther himself, muttering a string of profanities as he went.

His soldiers might have suffered enough, but Luther's pain was just beginning.

"Let's see you talk your way out of this," Turilli raved, booting open the door to the room where Luther was skulking. "You'd be wasting your time. I've not come to hear your excuses, I'm going to pull your spine out - if I can find it." The regent's eyes bulged as he tried in vain to compose himself. "I indulged your little game, but no longer. Gave you men, money, weapons... our only war engine. That machine could decimate an army! How the fuck did you lose?"

"My lord, I-"

"No excuses! You're finished, Luther. Why not do the decent thing a put a bullet in your brain? You should have let that filthy rabble do what you could not. They might have made it quick, but now my torturers will ensure your end is anything but."

Luther wisely held his tongue, keeping his expression bland for fear of angering Turilli further. The regent's mind had gone and it was up to Luther to try and bring him back - to somehow convince him that he'd invested too much time and trust in his loyal administrator to kill him now. Luther backed himself to do it, but the loaded gun he'd concealed beneath his tunic said otherwise. He had no way of knowing what Turilli was going to do, though after half an hour of shrieking hysterically and punching walls the regent was starting to run out of steam.

"Luther," he murmured, his rage subsiding, "give me back my soldiers."

"I can't do that," said the administrator, "but let me try to make amends. There is some cause for optimism." Turilli stood in stony silence, too furious to respond. Sensing the regent would rather kill him than hear him out, Luther shuffled nervously and said, "your wrath is understandable, given my failure. However, the campaign wasn't a total disaster. We managed to inflict heavy casualties on the rebels. We know who their leaders are and how to hurt them."

"I don't want to hurt them," Turilli snarled, "I want them dead. That is why I sent you. To teach those bastard ingrates the folly of standing against me. Were my orders unclear? I should be dancing on their graves instead of having this conversation, so don't you come to me with names, numbers and weaknesses."

"But I have a solution. Will you not hear it?"

"No."

"Look, the city's walls cannot be breached. Raise some enforcers from the ranks and you'll have the Phalanx back up to full strength in a day. Pin everything on me - destroy my reputation and tear me limb from limb, but give me leave to put things right first."

"Traitors don't get second chances," said Turilli. "They die screaming."

"A traitor would not have come back."

Turilli paused to dissect Luther's claim. He reasoned that if the administrator was going to betray him then he would have done it long ago. Luther was a clever man and knew the penalty for failure, so his attempts to resolve matters must have been sincere. He had returned when it was safer and easier to defect or find a remote village out in the desert and stay there. Yet despite his laudable actions, Turilli had a vague but nagging feeling that this was all part of an elaborate ruse he had somehow failed to anticipate.

"No-one plays me and lives," the regent hissed, turning to leave. "You'll stay here under guard until I can figure out what to do with you. Now the storms have cleared I'm going to take the gunships and hunt these rebels down myself."

"Alas, the fleet is grounded, my lord," said Luther, with the faintest hint of a smile. "They're in for maintenance at the high command's request."

"All of them?"

"I'm afraid so."

"And which idiot signed that off?"

"You did," Luther mumbled casually.

"What?"

"I said that there's another way to sate your thirst for vengeance."

"Oh? And what way is that?"

Luther sighed inwardly, annoyed Turilli hadn't caught onto what he was implying. The regent wasn't listening to reason, so Luther opted to repay his madness in kind. "The Chimera," he said eventually, well aware that his audacity would either save or damn him.

"What did you say?" Turilli spat. The regent's face began to turn crimson.

"The Chimera, my lord. Fate has presented us with the perfect opportunity to test it."

Turilli looked like he was going to explode. *Just how much did Luther know about the Chimera? Its design was meant to be classified. If he'd divined its purpose then others might have, too. What if one of the supervisors was passing him information? The entire project could be compromised. Maybe Luther was bluffing. But calling him on it would have been too easy. How, then, had a lowly administrator managed to crack his safeguards and uncover the truth about one of the galaxy's most closely guarded secrets?* Turilli was furious Luther would put his standing with Earth at risk, but couldn't escape the fact that his administrator made a valid point.

"Don't worry," Luther assured him, "it took much more than guesswork or a lucky break. The best part of a year, in fact. You see, your ministers never held all the pieces of the puzzle at once, but I did. Their reports and statements are vetted by my office because you pay me to ensure that they are all above board. Well, I found some anomalies. My intuition told me the rest. You've nothing to fear; it's my job to be discreet. No-one else knows. All I want is a chance at revenge, then you can take yours."

"You're a good talker, Luther," said Turilli, "and loyal to a fault."

"Thank you, my lord."

"There might be hope for you yet. A few more days and the Chimera will be ready. Use it to destroy my enemies and we can pretend this pointless rebellion never happened." Turilli was imagining a trouble-free future when he saw the look of disapproval on Luther's face. "What now?" he snapped, having anticipated his support.

"You'd test it on a handful of traitors?"

"What else?"

Luther looked up at the moon.

"Gethsemane?" Turilli exclaimed. "Are you mad? Earth would have my head for even considering it."

"Forget Earth. The whole planet is just one big retirement home. Why should you have to worry about what some doddering old men think? A regent isn't answerable to anyone. Target Gethsemane and show everyone what you're about - give the world a demonstration that will be remembered for years. The rebels would be foolish not to give themselves up when they witness the full extent of your power."

"And if they don't?"

"Then turn the Chimera on them. But testing it on millions of people instead of a few hundred would send a much stronger message. Besides, we have no assets on Gethsemane, and those arrogant traders have always thought themselves above you - *beyond* you. It's time to prove them wrong."

"Yes... yes." Turilli nodded in excitement, completely taken by Luther's plan. "Then we'll cleanse undercity as I'd originally intended. If those codgers on Earth thought they could control me, they're wrong."

"Always telling you what to do," Luther added, "and undermining your position. You don't need them anymore."

"You'll be amply rewarded should this plan of yours succeed," said Turilli. "I need not remind you what will happen if it fails."

"It won't."

"Then let us begin. Round up the workers so that we may 'congratulate' them. I don't want anything left to chance."

"Yes, my lord. And what of the supervisors and foremen?"

"Suggest they join the celebrations. Now go. You're wasting valuable time talking to me."

Luther hurried away to carry out Turilli's instructions, weighing the benefits of what the regent had promised against the deal he'd cut with Leo.

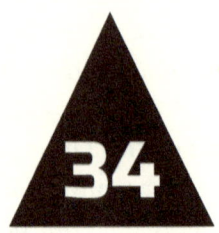

34

Workers are to cease construction and proceed to their designated assembly points. Compliance is mandatory. Failure to do so will result in forfeiture of earnings.

Across the Chimera site, all building work stopped at the director's command. Bemused workers paused to lay down their tools, exchanging cheery looks with one another and gossiping excitedly. Some joked that the regime had lined up one of their ministers to help 'motivate' them, while others looked forward to an unexpected but well-earned break. Following their supervisors, they began to gather at the assembly points; gloomy, windowless rooms with only one way in and out.

It was the moment Kurt Steinsson had been waiting for. Fully aware of the regime's true intentions, he grabbed the file that Marcus had left him before catching up to the rest of his team.

A lighter workload should have told them something was amiss, but there were none who shared Steinsson's concerns. With no new quotas to meet and the supervisors tasking them with trivial or irrelevant jobs, he figured the Chimera would soon be operational - if it wasn't already. Intuition coupled with Marcus' warning told him what would come next, and as the welders made their way to the assembly points, Steinsson quietly slipped away when no-one was looking.

Saul and Karlsen had the same idea. Having ridiculed Steinsson at first, now the bickering pair chose to join him - though Saul was keen to stress this was only because they valued their lives more than their paychecks. Evading supervisors and enforcers, they found Steinsson hiding in a dimly-lit stairwell - exactly where he said he would be.

"You could have chosen a better place for us to put our feet up," Saul grumbled. "Now what? We going to hide here forever?"

"I'll get the fucking tea and biscuits," said Karlsen.

Steinsson rolled his eyes. "Muppets," he scowled, hitting Saul once over his head with the file. "We use this. The blueprints are our map. If we make it to the control room then we can shut this thing down."

"The control room, he says," Saul hissed, rubbing his head. "I thought you'd found a way out. You never said anything about this have-a-go hero bullshit. Do you even know how to use a computer?"

"Maybe we'll find the manual," joked Karlsen. "Or the 'off' switch."

"Get your shit together," Steinsson snapped as he started to climb the stairs. "We've work to do."

The three welders pressed on, through storage areas and down a labyrinth of narrow, winding corridors. Steinsson led the way, but had trouble deciphering the blueprints. After making several wrong turns, Saul's frustration boiled over and he took off, adamant that he could find the control room himself.

"What good's a map if you can't read it?" he muttered, ignoring Steinsson's advice about proceeding cautiously.

Saul was so determined to prove himself right that he quickly lost track of his surroundings. Storming round a corner, he didn't see the automated sentry gun hanging from the ceiling above him. Only when the weapon's targeting laser lit him up did he realise his predicament, but by then it was too late.

A strong hand pulled him back as bullets ripped apart the spot where he'd been standing half a second before. Saul lost his balance and tumbled over, swearing loudly as he went and ended up in an undignified heap on the floor.

Steinsson looked down at the disgruntled welder and shook his head. "You're welcome."

"The fuck was that?" Saul wheezed, more surprised at Steinsson's strength than the fact that he was still alive.

Steinsson hauled him back to his feet and said, "I lead, you follow.

Questions? Good."

"I've a question for you," said Karlsen, walking over. "Why doesn't that sentry gun show up on the blueprints?"

"Whatever the reason," Steinsson replied, "I wouldn't bet against there being more of them. It's pretty obvious the regime don't want us getting anywhere near that control room."

Saul looked both annoyed and relieved. "That's it, then," he sighed, grudgingly accepting defeat. "We can't get any further with those guns everywhere. Might as well call it a day. Let's go back and see if there's a way out of here."

"What did you expect?" Steinsson scoffed, "a walk in the park? This was never going to be easy."

"The control room isn't far," said Karlsen, showing a little more enthusiasm. "We could make a run for it. Damned guns can't be that quick."

Saul folded his arms and said, "Off you go, then. I'll wait here while the pair of you test that theory." He went on to slate Karlsen's plan, accusing him of mindless optimism and wanting to get them all killed. Karlsen laughed off his remarks and called Saul a coward. They argued back and forth, both so intent on having the last word that they forgot why they were there.

The distant sound of gunfire reminded them and brought their argument to an abrupt halt.

"It's started," said Steinsson, drawing an enforcer's sidearm.

"Where did you get that?" Saul exclaimed, fearing he'd lost his patience with them and was going to put an end to their incessant bickering himself.

"Our friend made quite a mess when he cut fence," said Steinsson. "So many dead enforcers, no-one bothered to check if all their weapons had been accounted for."

Karlsen grinned. "I never did get to thank him for offing that bastard supervisor. Still, our situation has not improved. That peashooter you're holding doesn't change anything."

"Does it not?" Steinsson took the safety off and smiled. "Those automated guns don't react well to bullets. Too many wires and fragile components. If I can hit one of the sensors then that'll disable the gun."

"So you know your shit," said Saul. "Doesn't make you a crack shot."

Steinsson offered him the gun. "Are you?" Saul put his hands in his pockets and sheepishly backed away. "Then here's what we'll do. You and Karlsen are going to give that sentry gun something to shoot at. Keep it occupied long enough and I'll take it down from here."

Saul couldn't believe what he was hearing. "I'm not going through that again," he scoffed. "Karlsen can do it. He's mad enough."

"You can hold his hand if you like," said Steinsson. "I need five seconds. If you're not up for it, then leave."

"But why not-"

Quick as lightning, Karlsen grabbed Saul by the scruff of his neck and threw him back into the corridor. Again, the automated sentry gun powered up, but this time it struggled to lock on. With Karlsen behind him, Saul could only run towards the gun, weaving from side to side and screaming incomprehensively. Making the most of the opportunity they had provided, Steinsson took careful aim and fired.

His first shot deflected off the sentry gun's inch-thick armour plating. The second missed completely. His third hit the target acquisition sensor just as the gun had swivelled to face him, disabling it only a fraction of a second before it could fire. Wiping the sweat off his forehead, Steinsson lowered his sidearm and breathed a sigh of relief as the sentry gun fell silent.

"All clear," he shouted, stepping out into the corridor.

"Get over here, you idiots," Saul snapped, holding his arm. "I've been shot!"

Karlsen ambled over to take a look. "There, there," he soothed, trying his hardest not to laugh. "It's only a scratch."

"But I'm bleeding. See?"

"Oh, I think you'll live."

Saul lifted his arm, trying to examine the wound himself. "Help me bandage it," he rasped, convinced that Karlsen was lying. "I'm done for."

"Get a grip," said Steinsson, looking unimpressed. "Karlsen's right. Now give me a hand with this gun. It'll take all three of us to move it."

Saul and Karlsen helped him pull the sentry gun down, setting the firing mode to manual.

"Thing weighs a bloody tonne," Saul complained. "I shouldn't be doing this in my condition."

The three of them continued on, using the gun to neutralise the defences around the control room. Every so often an alarm would sound, but no enforcers came to investigate.

"Do you think anyone else made it out?" asked Karlsen.

Steinsson shook his head.

The control room lay at the end of a dingy, narrow corridor. There were no guards, but the way was blocked by a steel door that looked nigh-on unbreachable.

"Leave that," said Steinsson, abandoning the gun. "Won't fit. The door's not wide enough."

"The fuck you on about?" scoffed Saul. "How are you planning on getting inside?"

Steinsson walked up to the door and pushed it open. Saul's face reddened.

"Hang on," said Karlsen, "what if there are more of those guns in there?"

Saul stepped forward and said, "Only one way to find out."

Scanning the interior for threats, he cautiously inched his way into the control room. Once inside, Saul unlaced one of his boots, yanked it off and threw it as far as he could. He listened carefully for the sound of an auto-gun activating, but heard nothing.

"Looks clear," he called back to Steinsson.

He'd barely had time to turn his head when a missile blew him across the control room and into a wall. Saul crumpled into a dazed heap, blood pouring from his broken nose and a deep gash on his leg. The launcher that had fired the missile reloaded, clicked twice, then powered down. Karlsen stood in shock, staring dumbly at Saul's mangled form.

"Just wait," said Steinsson, warning him against helping his friend.

A minute passed and Saul started to come round. "Today can go fuck itself," he groaned, wiping the blood from his nose and applying pressure to his injured leg. He sat up with his back against the wall and saw the missile launcher trained on him, wondering why it hadn't finished him off. This respite gave Saul the confidence to take a chance, and he slowly got to his feet.

Nothing happened.

"It's alright," he shouted after a few seconds. "The launcher's jammed." Saul steadied himself against a chair and laughed. "You think they'd learn. Fancy tech and machines can't beat the real thing."

Steinsson breathed a sigh of relief. He and Karlsen entered the control room, cautiously at first, wary of unseen traps and turrets. When it became clear there were none, they ran over to check on Saul.

"Oh, so now you care," he grinned. "Where to next?"

"There," said Steinsson, pointing at a giant screen and the computers sitting beneath it.

The three welders headed over to the control room's main workstation. Saul started hitting buttons on keyboards while Karlsen looked for a way to shut the computers down. Steinsson stared up at the screen, trying to make sense of the dizzying array of data displayed before him, but lacked the technical nous needed to decipher it.

After several minutes of getting nowhere, Saul turned to him and said, "This isn't going to work."

Steinsson nodded grimly. "Agreed. We should spread out." He motioned towards a staircase at the back of the control room. "I'll go check the lower levels. You and Karlsen stay here - see if we've missed anything."

Saul began searching the room as instructed, but Karlsen had other ideas. "I don't care if it's dangerous," he said, following Steinsson over to the staircase. "I'm coming with you."

They descended the stairs together, ending up in what Steinsson presumed to be a dark vault some fifty feet below the control room. The lights came on automatically, revealing not a vault but a storehouse filled with artillery shells, each four times the size of an average man.

If either of them had doubted it, now the Chimera's purpose was clear.

For once in his life, Karlsen was speechless. He couldn't believe the regime would build such a thing, nor come to terms with the fact that he'd had a hand in its construction.

"What have we done?" he mumbled, looking up at Steinsson. His face was expressionless and cold.

With no answer forthcoming, Karlsen followed his gaze over to a cluster of shells labelled 'massive ordnance'. It took him less than a second to see what Steinsson had, though he wished he hadn't.

The shells were sitting next to an automated crane and loader, and one of them was missing.

35

Leo stood alone atop a small sand dune, scanning the surround. Behind him, dawn was breaking in the east, while ahead, the gloomy spires of Divinity were visible on the horizon.

Though Leo's mind was elsewhere, the significance of the day was not lost on him. He had struck a blow against the regime by defeating their strongest enforcers, but this conflict would only truly be settled in the coming hours on the streets of Divinity.

Slowly, the long, winding column that was his army began to pass by. Leo looked on proudly, delighted that so many were here today in defiance of tyranny. He wouldn't have traded any of his fighters for an entire battalion of regime soldiers. They might have lacked the training and ruthlessness of their enemies, but their collective will was stronger than the mightiest war machine.

As the sun continued to climb, Leo found himself reminiscing about his early years on Tanis. Back then, he'd assumed the regime was a force for good and that his adoptive father could do no wrong. Everything was what it seemed - every day the start of a new adventure. For a moment, Leo wished that he was back there now, at play, enjoying simpler times. He even considered forgiving Rossi, for the old regent had given him the childhood he had such fond memories of. Leo could see him now, watching on as he returned from yet another training camp, resplendent in full regalia. Reuniting with his father was the best feeling in the world then, but he wouldn't be there to welcome him home this time.

"All comes down to this," said a familiar voice over to Leo's right. "Don't think I've ever been so nervous. How about you?"

Leo had been so lost in his memories that he hadn't noticed Marcus standing beside him. "Something like that," he mumbled clumsily. "I was far away."

Marcus grinned. "Always planning, you. Listen, I don't want to make a fuss, but we have a problem."

"Which is?" Leo asked when he did not continue.

Marcus motioned towards the marching column and said, "It's all very impressive, to be sure, but Turilli isn't going to look upon your army and surrender. He doesn't even have to fight. The wall around Divinity is four hundred metres high and can't be scaled. The city's gates are made of steel. It may have escaped your notice, but we've no way of breaching either."

"Nothing escapes my notice," Leo snapped, annoyed Marcus still doubted him. "I never said anything about scaling walls and breaching gates."

"Then why bother dragging those rocket pods all the way here if they're no use to us? None of this makes any sense. Everyone thinks we're going to blast our way in, but that isn't your intention at all, is it? What are you planning?"

"You'll see soon enough," said Leo.

"I want to know now. You've no reason to hold anything back."

"And you have no reason to question my judgement."

Marcus frowned. "Then I'm free to draw my own conclusions. You don't trust me."

"I trust you completely," Leo assured him. "I'll tell you everything, but only when the time is right."

"If you say so." Marcus shook his head and turned away. All Leo ever talked about these days was toppling the regime, but when anyone pressed him on how he intended to do it he clammed up. Marcus had come to suspect he didn't have a plan at all, or worse, had struck a deal with Turilli that would see him spared and given rank and wealth in return for the League's destruction. He didn't want to believe it, but such a thing was not without precedent. Something had to be said.

"If that's the way it's going to be," Marcus sighed, "then I don't want any part of this game. Something's very wrong if you can tell that arch-manipulator Luther what you're about but not me. How long have we known each other? Twelve, thirteen years? You might have fooled everyone here into thinking you're infallible, but I'm not so easily awed. Don't expect me to quake and bow down like these people - I you know better than they do. I know that for all your bravado you're just as scared as the rest of us. Scared enough to cut a deal with Turilli."

Leo looked genuinely shocked by what he was hearing. Having always been honest with Marcus, his friend's remarks and accusations hurt. "Of course I'm scared," he shot back. "Terrified. But 'these people' are counting on me and I can't afford to show it. I only want what's best for them. Maybe you don't know me as well as you think you do."

"Oh, I do," said Marcus. "I know all about your cosy little chat with Luther. So what deal did he offer? How much to sell us out? I bet you bit his hand off."

"Don't be stupid. The Liberation League isn't just a carefree band of sycophants who follow me wherever I go. There are factions forming, and I've got to placate them. Daily. What do you think will happen if I tell the League I've made a deal with Luther? The hardliners will grumble, call me weak and accuse me of favouring the moderates, who in turn would want to know every detail and could end up jeopardising the agreement. We'd be at each other's throats in no time, all because I was open and honest. I'd like to think it wouldn't come to that, but if your reaction is anything to go by then I was right to keep it to myself."

"So Luther *did* offer you a deal," Marcus declared triumphantly. "And you took it. What were the terms? Our lives for yours?"

Leo's expression tightened. "I'd never consider such an offer and you know it. Everything I do is for the greater good and the advancement of our cause. Yes, I made a deal with Luther, but I don't want the people worrying about whether he'll honour his word or not. That's my burden. They don't need something like that playing on their minds."

"You didn't even ask," said Marcus, "just assumed you spoke for everyone. You made this pact alone - none of us had a say. So you beat the regime a couple of times. Does that give you the right to make decisions for us? Is this how it's going to be from now on?"

"So what if it is," Leo retorted. "I'm done arguing. Think what you like, go ahead and tell the League what I've done if it makes you feel better. It's not like they'll listen. I've got better things to do than stand here listening to your drivel."

At this, Marcus turned and stormed off, muttering furiously. Leo watched him go, wondering if he could be counted on in the coming battle - a concern he could have done without. As he rejoined his army, Leo decided that unless Marcus apologised he would make Kruger his number two, but would wait until after the battle before issuing ultimatums.

He'll see sense soon enough, Leo assured himself.

Hours passed, and by mid-afternoon the League was less than a mile from Divinity. Leo called a brief halt to strategise, frustrating Kruger and those who wanted to attack immediately. While his army rested, Leo donned his armour before taking Luna and Kruger aside to ensure they knew what was expected of them.

"We've been over this a hundred times," Kruger complained. "Isolate and destroy regime assets. No looting. No violence against the nobility - though why you think they should be spared is anyone's guess."

"The nobility will ensure a smooth transition of power," said Leo, "and support our new regent. We're not staying on Tanis to await the regime's retribution - we'll take the fight to them."

Kruger looked annoyed. "And what of Turilli? Surely you're not thinking of sparing him too?"

"Only from death," Leo smirked. "War crimes shouldn't go unpunished. I want him tried and held to account for all the suffering he's caused."

"You underestimate the man," said Kruger, "and risk turning him into a figurehead behind whom our enemies could rally. If he ever got free the consequences would be dire. Trust me on this one, Leo. He's too dangerous to be left alive."

Luna nodded thoughtfully. "Kruger has a point. Even the worst regents have their sympathisers and apologists. Besides, it's not a crime to be mad. Turilli isn't guilty of mass murder or genocide."

"Yet," Leo insisted. "And killing a man in cold blood would look ill with the people."

"Then make up a story," said Kruger. "Say he died in the battle. I'll kill him myself if you don't want to get your hands dirty."

"No. We're not the regime. I won't have anyone label us butchers."

"Alright," said Luna, "you've got a plan and don't want to share it with us, that's fine. We've no reason to doubt you. But at least tell us what we *can* do."

Leo straightened up and smiled. "You can help me infiltrate the regent's palace."

"And miss out on the fighting?" Kruger scoffed. "How can we influence the battle if we're so far from it?"

"By capturing Turilli," said Leo. "With him detained, regime resistance will crumble. The Royal Guard won't be expecting an attack on the palace and may even be committed elsewhere. Let's see how tough those enforcers are when they're full of holes." He paused a moment to let his words sink in then said, "Turilli is not to be harmed. If either of you have a problem with that then you'll sit the whole thing out. Do I make myself clear?"

Luna voiced her assent immediately, and after some grumbling Kruger followed suit.

"Good." Leo sounded pleased. "This is just the beginning, so we watch each other's backs out there. Don't get careless."

"And here was me thinking you didn't care," Kruger grinned.

"Of course I care," said Leo. "You've both helped make this possible. Without you there would be no League. Ten thousand people are here willing to fight and die so the things they believe in don't."

Kruger smiled and nodded acknowledgement, then noticed Luna staring off into the distance. "Unbelievable," he scoffed, nudging her arm. "We get some praise for once and you're not listening."

Leo followed Luna's gaze to the highest point of Divinity, where the skyline was starting to change. A terrible screeching sound echoed through the city as the Chimera site transformed into a weapon of unimaginable power, prompting gasps and cries of anger from among the League's ranks. They stood and watched in horror as the massive cannon began to rotate, its single barrel elevating higher and higher until it had Gethsemane in its sights. And fired.

A blinding flash of light burst from the cannon's maw, its report louder than thunder. As the shell sped towards its target, a deathly silence fell over the League until someone shouted that the gates of Divinity were open. For the briefest of moments, Leo's army stood stunned and immobile. Then, as if a spell had been broken, the League erupted into a frenzy, every man and woman clamouring for vengeance and demanding Leo give the order to attack.

With a word he obliged.

So loud was the Chimera's discharge that it could be heard a thousand miles away in Arcana. At last the people of Tanis saw what Turilli and the regime were about and terror settled upon them, but with the League closing in they wouldn't have to be afraid for long.

Inside the control room, the proximity of the blast knocked Saul off his feet and sent Steinsson and Karlsen staggering around like a pair of drunks, their ears ringing and vision blurred.

"The fuck is happening?" yelled Karlsen, fighting to regain his senses.

"Have a guess!" Steinsson shouted back. "They've done it. The regime. They've fired the weapon."

"At what?"

"I don't know," said Steinsson. "Can't see shit from down here."

As the ringing in their ears subsided, Karlsen shouted for Saul to join them. He turned to Steinsson and said, "If your friend was right about what this thing can do, we can't let it fire again."

Steinsson nodded grimly. He and Karlsen started to explore the storehouse, looking for anything they could use to disable the weapon. Karlsen set about emptying crates and boxes all over the floor, while Steinsson was more methodical in his approach. He re-read certain sections of the file, hoping the regime had built in a failsafe or self-destruct mechanism, but couldn't find any reference to one. Frustrated, Steinsson scanned the room for inspiration. He saw that there were three shell types, and that the firing system was fully automated. Added to what he already knew, he theorised the Chimera could be aimed and fired remotely, able to strike even a moving target anywhere within the system. Then he saw the yellow crane that loaded shells into the weapon's breech move, and this gave him an idea.

Karlsen, meanwhile, had given up rummaging through boxes and was pacing back and forth. "What's he doing up there?" he muttered, still waiting for Saul. "Deaf bastard. I'll go get him myself."

Before Steinsson could object, Karlsen had disappeared up the stairs. Sensing that something was wrong, Steinsson followed, shouting for him to wait.

"I've got this," Karlsen snapped, entering the control room. "You stay put."

Steinsson had almost reached the top of the stairs when he heard a heavy thud from above. Running the last few steps, he was greeted by a gruesome scene. Karlsen lay dead on the floor, his throat cut. Three metres away, Saul's lifeless body was slumped against the wall in a pool of blood. The man responsible stood next to Karlsen's corpse, knife in hand, surprised by Steinsson's sudden appearance.

"Always someone or something in the way," Steinsson grumbled.

The balaclava-clad man reacted quickly, closing the distance between them in a heartbeat. Barely shorter than Steinsson, he wore a modified suit of enforcer armour yet moved with a speed that defied logic. The man lashed out with his knife, missed, then struck again. Steinsson dodged each attack by the narrowest of margins, quickly realising that this was no mere enforcer he faced. The man continued to come forward and Steinsson continued to give ground. Instinct told him to fight back, but he couldn't think about anything other than evading his opponent's attacks.

The man kicked out with his foot, catching Steinsson on the shin. Pain flared in his leg. Steinsson believed that if he'd had a weapon he would just about have been his equal, but he didn't and that was making the difference. The man allowed himself a snarl of satisfaction as he pinked Steinsson's arm. It turned into a smile as he opened a nasty cut above his right eye. This spurred Steinsson into action, and as the knife flicked out again this time he managed to catch his attacker's wrist in mid-swing. The man punched him across the face with his free hand, but Steinsson didn't let go and struck back with a right hook of his own.

The two men traded blows as they grappled, oblivious to their surroundings. Steinsson tried to work an opening for another clean strike, but his adversary was too quick. They sought to destroy each other, so focused on winning - on surviving - that neither man saw how close they were to the stairs. As Steinsson fended off a flurry of jabs, he lost his footing and fell, dragging the man back down to the storehouse with him. Contact with the metal stairs sent the knife flying from his grasp and it clattered to the floor below.

Steinsson landed awkwardly, hitting his head on one of the steps. He could taste blood as he scrambled back to his feet. The man was right behind him, rolling with the fall to avoid injury. He righted himself with a tumbler's grace, drawing another blade in a single motion. Steinsson cursed his luck and sighed in annoyance. Blood was now starting to drip down into his eye from the cut the man had inflicted, hindering his vision. He glanced around for a weapon but the only thing he saw was the crane preparing to load another shell into the Chimera's breech.

Again the man advanced, his knife raised. Steinsson backed away, hoping to frustrate him into making a mistake, but in doing so failed to spot the crates that Karlsen had emptied onto the floor. He tripped and fell backwards, landing hard on his side. The man was on him in a flash and brought the knife down in a sweeping arc, aiming for Steinsson's heart.

At the last moment, Steinsson pulled left. The knife missed its mark by an inch. Denied a clean kill, the man's lips curled back in a feral snarl. Now he had to wait. But the wound was still fatal and in time Steinsson would weaken to the point he could no longer fight back. Even if the knife didn't end up killing him, blood loss would.

Steinsson had nothing left to lose. He reached up and drove his thumbs into the man's eye sockets, gripping his head tightly. The man screamed in pain and let go of the knife, desperately trying to fight Steinsson off, but hadn't counted on the welder's strength.

With one quick twist, Steinsson broke his neck and let the man's limp body slump to the floor beside him. Exhausted, all Steinsson wanted to do was lie there and let darkness take him, but he wasn't going to let the regime win.

Not now.

Somehow, Steinsson found the strength to rise. He rummaged through the dead man's pockets, finding a loaded handgun and five grenades and wondered why he hadn't shot him instead.

Too easy, he mused.

Taking the grenades, Steinsson stumbled over to the crane. He strapped them to the shell that was being loaded, unsure if his idea would work. When the Chimera fired again, the grenades would detonate the shell and tear the weapon apart, forever ending its threat. He hoped. Steinsson stayed on his feet long enough to see the shell disappear, then fell back to the floor.

As the battle for Divinity raged outside, Kurt Steinsson died alone and unremembered, having broken the only promise he had ever made.

36

The destruction of Gethsemane warmed Lucas Turilli's black heart. Dismissing his lackeys, the mad regent had locked himself in his office to witness the event alone, pulling up a chair and opening a bottle of wine he'd been saving for the occasion. Years of toil were coming to an end, and Turilli wasn't going to let anyone spoil his moment. He'd already sent the nobles and their servants away, labelling them narrow-minded fools incapable of sharing his vision, but in reality wanted to avoid any embarrassment if the weapon didn't work as intended.

"A masterstroke!" Turilli crowed. He raised his glass to toast himself then gave the order to fire.

Turilli watched as the shockwave from the explosion toppled city spires, then laughed when the fireball that followed engulfed them completely. It expanded outward in every direction from the point of impact, consuming Gethsemane in flame. The small moon burned but wasn't destroyed, exactly as Turilli had hoped. Now everyone on Tanis could witness true beauty. The old masters had written poems that stirred the soul and composed great symphonies, but in the present day only he was capable of creating real art.

So great was the devastation that Turilli publically declared his enemies' defeat. The traitors and rebels who had defied him would now realise their mistake and come before him to surrender, or beg for mercy. Turilli sat aloof in his chair, sniggering away, his victory certain.

But when the first reports from undercity reached his ears there was no mention of surrender. Far from cowing Divinity into submission, Turilli's genocidal act had inspired a city-wide uprising that his enforcers could not suppress. Pushing his servants aside, Turilli took off like a man possessed, not waiting - nor wanting - to hear any more about the threat to his rule.

The regent's ministers, however, had heard and seen enough. They gathered their effects and fled the palace in short order, hoping to distance themselves from Turilli and avoid taking any blame for his folly. Having seen him lose the Phalanx, many doubted his ability to bring the situation under control. Though Turilli's power was still great, the nobility feared an angry mob with retribution on their minds more.

Their cowardice enraged Turilli to the point of madness. He stalked the corridors of the palace in a blind rage, swearing vengeance on those who had abandoned him, blaming everyone but himself. The ministers and nobles would be his scapegoats, he decided, convinced that one of their number was responsible for all of his misfortune. Turilli knew his list of allies was short, but there was still one man he could rely on and trust to save him.

Luther's gaze flitted between the lower levels of Divinity and the burning rock that had once been Gethsemane. The city he loved was tearing itself apart, but he kept telling himself that he had done right by its people, and any suffering or loss of life was for the greater good.

Elena had more pressing concerns to contend with. Her servants had somehow managed to crease Luther's new tunic - one that she'd chosen and ordered - and now seemed incapable of performing the most menial of tasks. Dismissing them with a wave of her hand, Elena finished buttoning the tunic herself, adamant that everything had to be perfect.

"There," she beamed, flicking imaginary specks of dust off Luther's shoulders. "Now you look the part."

Luther turned to view himself in a full-length freestanding mirror. He noticed the tunic was white with gold buttons, much like Rossi's had been, and wondered what the old regent would have said if he could have seen him now.

Sensing the unrest in him, Elena smiled and clicked her fingers. Two more of her servants entered the room, carrying a large brown box. Luther watched them suspiciously as they set it down, opened it and presented him with an oversized claymore sword, mounting it on the wall at Elena's command.

"What in the name of sanity is that?" Luther sighed, looking bemused. *Something she'll get far more 'use' out of than me.*

"Don't be like that," said Elena. "It's a gift."

"Yes, but for who?"

Elena looked at him and smiled. "Can't I spend a little on my loving husband every now and again? You've worked so hard for this. The biggest moments should always be marked and remembered."

"Well, I'll certainly remember today," said Luther, "but if you wanted to buy me something, a pendant would have sufficed."

"Only the best for you from now on," Elena insisted. "No more trinkets. A regent is above such things."

"Perhaps, but not this regent. I don't want anything, other than the chance to lead."

Now it was Elena's turn to scowl and sigh. "Very noble of you," she remarked, "but can you actually engender change? Do you even want to?"

"Yes," said Luther, "I do."

Elena smiled. "Ever the idealist. There's nothing wrong with the world, dear husband. Nothing needs to change."

"It will," said Luther, shaking his head. "It has to. Leo was right - the system is broken."

Elena shrugged. "Works fine for us."

"Of course it does. The people get poorer while our wealth grows. Tell me, is it right we earn more in an hour than a surgeon does a year?"

Elena shuffled uneasily and said, "Can't say as I've ever thought about it." For once she had no idea what Luther was thinking, but his unbridled optimism and talk of change made her nervous.

"It's time the privileged few gave something back," Luther continued, recalling his unhappy childhood and fierce hatred of the nobility. "If Leo wants to go fix the galaxy then good for him, but my interests are purely local."

"And if the nobles refuse?" asked Elena.

"Then Leo's fighters will finish what he started. You forget that it's only by his grace we're all going to be spared."

"Apparently," Elena mumbled, aware that the deal Luther had cut with Leo, though not ideal, was still to her benefit. "But what if-"

She was cut off mid-sentence as the doors to their apartment were flung open and Lucas Turilli burst in, looking somewhat worse for wear. The regent paused to catch his breath, standing there with wild eyes and a deranged look on his face, relieved to see that Luther hadn't abandoned him like everyone else.

"Luther, the rebels," Turilli rasped, "they're here. Inside my city. Our forces can't hold while the Chimera is recharging. The gates-"

"Are open," Luther finished for him. "And the defences offline."

His icy tone sent a shiver down Turilli's spine. The regent saw that Luther had been modelling a new tunic and was dressed more appropriately for a banquet or ball than a military campaign. Gradually it dawned on Turilli that the real traitor was standing before him, though the horrified regent didn't want to believe it.

"You," Turilli stammered, more shocked than angry. "Why?"

Luther bade Elena leave before replying. Confident her husband could handle Turilli - though equally afraid of what the mad regent's response might be - she was only too happy to oblige, leaving them alone in the foyer of her penthouse. The two men regarded each other in silence, a sardonic smile playing at the corners of Luther's mouth.

"Why?" Turilli repeated, desperate for answers.

Luther's expression turned serious. "You know why."

"No," said Turilli, "but I can guess."

"Elena had nothing to do with it. My actions were my own."

Turilli shook his head. "You, Luther. You to whom I gave everything.

Wasn't it all enough?"

"A pity you weren't so generous to the people. They needed your help far more than I did."

"The plebs? Who gives a fuck about the plebs?"

"Their new regent." Luther straightened his tunic and drew himself up to his full height. "You think I want power for power's sake, but I've never abused my position for personal gain. A regent has to work, and work hard - it isn't a ceremonial title with no responsibilities attached. You could have made a difference like I'm going to, but instead you chose to fight and oppress the very people you swore to protect until they couldn't take any more."

"Utter cack," Turilli scoffed. "Where did these vermin find the strength to fight back? We've kept them down for years - what makes this purge any different?"

"It's not a purge, though, is it? You've destroyed a moon, not a village."

"So?"

"If you were paying attention," said Luther, "you would see that people are happy to ignore violence perpetrated on a smaller scale so long as it doesn't directly affect them, but what you've done cannot be overlooked. That permanent reminder orbiting our world means the Chimera isn't something they can pretend doesn't exist or will go away. They don't fear your weapon, Turilli, they abhor it. What you thought would crush the fight out of them merely roused Tanis to anger. But you played your part superbly, I'll admit. Got everyone's attention as I'd hoped. Just like the Phalanx."

Turilli re-ran some of their conversations in his mind and realised he had been duped. He'd sent the Phalanx to crush the rebels and made an example of Gethsemane, always following Luther's advice. His suggestions made sense at the time, but now Turilli began to see the bigger picture. Luther had exploited every crisis and played him very well indeed. Worse, he'd likely revelled in his pain and enjoyed a good laugh at his expense along the way, but that ended now.

"Alright," the regent snarled, "you've had your fun. It's over. All of your silly little tricks and games, for what? To rule a fractured city for all the time it takes that mob to storm the palace? What's the plan, Luther? You're going to convince a million angry illiterates to spare you and let you rule?"

Luther smiled broadly. "I already have. They drove a hard bargain, admittedly, but even illiterates recognise the need for stability."

"You shame yourself by kowtowing to those animals. It makes me sick to think we breathe the same air."

"Come now, it wasn't nearly so bad. In the end I only had to convince one man. Any guesses who?"

Turilli raised his hands in exasperation. "Rossi's fucking ghost?"

"In a manner of speaking. He's not about to kill anyone unnecessarily, but he does need to hold someone to account for Gethsemane. His people demand it. As regent, the buck stops with you. You're the only one who could give that order. The only one they want."

"You think you're so clever," said Turilli, "plotting behind my back. What makes you think you can do any better - what can you give Tanis that I can't?"

"A voice. A vote. Democracy. I'm going to empower the same people you suppressed and become all the stronger for it."

Turilli shook his head. "You're a fool, Luther. People are better when they've been told how to think and what to do. They should be grateful for what they have. Let them dream and soon enough they'll be holding you to account, challenging your decisions and laws, a nation of spineless cravens who take offense at every opportunity and think themselves entitled to all the riches in the world."

"And you're afraid of that prospect," said Luther, "since you've never had to explain yourself to anyone. Loafing about up here in your lavish palace while the people struggle. They need to know there's more to life than work and taxes. What if they could learn to enjoy it? If families had more time together and the most demanding jobs paid best? I'd make a fairer system for all, one where the more you put in the more you get back. Who you are counts for nothing in my world - it's what you do. I doubt the nobility will like it, but the days of living off a pretty smile and a famous name are over."

"You really are priceless," Turilli sneered, angered by Luther's constant accusations and sanctimonious prattle. "Earth won't give you the chance to build your little utopia, let alone live in it."

"I can be very convincing - should it come to that. Your masters will never know the truth."

"But they will," Turilli raved, becoming more and more irate. "They will know from me."

"A clumsy threat," said Luther, "considering your position. You'd never risk your reputation to spite me, not if there's a chance you could one day return to power. For that reason alone, they'll let you live."

The thought of seeing out his days in a cell stung Turilli into action. He reached inside his tunic, pulled out a small handgun and pointed it at Luther's head. The administrator took a step back and opened his hands, trying not to show any fear. He had no way of knowing what Turilli would do next, but twisted a smile onto his face to hide his consternation.

"No," Turilli said after a while. "It's too quick. I want you to think on your failure a moment."

"What failure?" Luther scoffed, his eyes fixed on the gun.

"Your inability to save the people you love. I might not be as smart as you, Luther, but I have this." With his free hand, Turilli produced a portable datapad from one of his pockets and started pressing buttons. "The remote firing mechanism for the Chimera," he explained. "Didn't know about that, did you? Neither would your friend. I think another demonstration is in order, and I have the perfect target in mind."

Luther's heart filled with dread. He hadn't anticipated this, and didn't doubt for one moment Turilli's resolve to make good his threats.

"Do not pursue me," said Turilli, backing out into the corridor. "Go and seek comfort in your harpy's arms. This is the end for all of us, so make your peace with the world you've condemned." The regent turned to leave before looking back over his shoulder and adding, "Die screaming."

Turilli made for the council chamber, priming the weapon as he went. A moment passed before Luther retrieved his own sidearm and took off down the corridor after him.

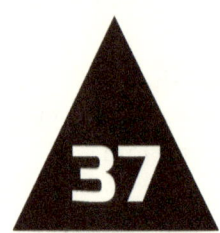

37

Leo Rossi was home. Stepping silently into the palace's main lobby, he took in the huge room with a sweeping scan, his right hand hovering above his holstered sidearm. He hoped he wouldn't have to use it, but a small, savage part of him relished the thought of facing down the same enforcers who had chased him out of the palace a little over a year ago.

The injustice of it all still rankled. Turilli had set his soldiers on him as if he were some kind of criminal, and Leo had been sorely tempted to return the favour. But he wasn't going to kill anyone out of revenge, not when he knew that passing judgement on Turilli would be infinitely more satisfying than putting a bullet in him.

Time seemed to slow as Luna drew up beside him, holding a rifle loaded with armour piercing rounds. Leo watched as Kruger moved ahead to take point, his own weapon raised and ready. The palace was eerily quiet, save for their footsteps on the marble floor. If Turilli's royal guards had chosen to stay and defend their master, they were keeping a low profile.

With the lobby clear, Leo knelt and brushed his hand over a blemish on the floor. Much had changed since he'd last been here. The palace hadn't, but Leo felt as if he no longer recognised it at all. Now everything took on a darker meaning. The tapestries and statues he'd once admired were symptomatic of an unelected, unaccountable caste who had been putting their own wealth and status first for far too long. Turilli wasn't just some pantomime villain he could mock from afar, he'd become a very real threat who needed stopping. Leo had imagined this moment a hundred times, and while he hadn't expected fanfares or trumpets, his return seemed strangely anti-climactic.

Luna was equally disappointed. Though Leo had noted her proficiency with a rifle, she wanted to prove that her showing against the Phalanx wasn't a fluke. Kruger liked to provoke her by saying it was, or that she'd just imagined the whole thing, but she couldn't silence him nor experience the thrill of another firefight unless the Royal Guard challenged them. In her mind, she was here to do a job, nothing more.

She glanced over at Leo and then Kruger. It pained her to see him staring up at the opulence that surrounded them, seemingly captivated by its allure. Having never felt emotionally attached to her birthplace, Luna couldn't stand and gawp at such grandeur but understood how easily one could fall in love with it. But Kruger should have known better. A few choice words brought him back to reality, though he was quick to deny he'd been distracted.

"Luna's right," Leo affirmed. "Focus. There's no mysterious force protecting us, and I can't beam you out if things prove more than you can handle."

"No danger of that," said Kruger, cocking his rifle.

"I'd have felt better if Marcus was here," Luna added. "He's a good shot, if nothing else."

Leo shook his head, seeing no reason to concern them with the truth. "Someone had to lead the main assault."

This response was good enough for Kruger, who had taken an instant dislike to Marcus on account of his closeness to Leo. With his rival elsewhere, Kruger could focus on convincing Leo that he would make a better number two - a position that he believed should have been his from the start.

"Let's move," he said, leading the way out of the lobby and down a corridor lined with windows and pillars. Leo followed, and after a moment so did Luna, who sensed there was more to Marcus' absence than Leo was letting on.

Kruger swaggered along, brimming with confidence. Leo asked him to wait, but it was clear he was spoiling for a fight and out to prove himself, full of piss and vinegar. As he neared a flight of stairs at the end of the corridor, a single shot rang out and Kruger fell back behind a pillar, holding his arm. Taken by surprise, he'd nearly dropped his gun and had failed to spot the shooter, trying to regain a shred of dignity by spraying the entire area with return fire.

"Careless," Leo tutted, falling in behind him as more bullets zipped past. "You won't hit anything unless you aim. Besides, there's only two of them."

"How can you know that?" Luna grinned, impressed by Leo's visual perception when she hadn't seen anyone.

Leo risked a brief glance out from behind the pillar. He turned to Luna and said, "Two royal guards using automatic rifles at twenty-three metres. One behind either column at the top of the stairs. Standard rounds loaded, marksmanship poor and a maximum of five years combat training between them."

"Again, how?" asked Luna.

"Kruger's still breathing. Should have been a kill shot from that kind of range. Hear their rate of fire drop? They've been to warzones but aren't used to people firing back."

"How is this helping?" Kruger shouted, unsure what Leo was trying to accomplish. "Is there anything useful you'd like to share with us?"

"Naturally," Leo continued, "both are in full battle dress, so the most expedient solution would be two well-placed shots from any weapon loaded with armour piercing rounds."

Leo drew his gun, and at that point everything seemed to slow down around him. He knew exactly where the enforcers were and what they were going to do, zeroing in on them with speed and precision. Leaning out just enough to see past the pillar, Leo fired twice, his aim true. They were shots no other would have attempted - impossible shots - but Leo executed them to perfection.

The next thing he heard was the sound of a gun clattering to the floor followed by two soft thuds. Leo waited a few seconds. No more gunfire. He stepped out into the corridor, his pistol still raised. Luna looked at him, not knowing what to say, her expression a comical mixture of shock and delight.

"Laser sight," said Leo, tapping his gun. Luna nodded, even though she'd never seen him use it. They were about to move forward when she heard boots running towards them and dragged Leo back into cover. More royal guards swarmed the corridor ahead, taking up position where their comrades had fallen.

"Now the whole garrison knows we're here," Kruger hissed as the enforcers opened fire.

"Good," Luna smiled, readying her rifle. "Wouldn't be fair otherwise."

Leo wasn't as optimistic, knowing full well he couldn't take them all. "We don't have time for this," he scowled.

"Just do that trick with your gun again," said Kruger.

"It's called aiming," Leo snapped. "You try it. I've got to find Turilli. You hold them here and I'll take the long way."

By the time Kruger had turned to voice his objections, Leo was half way back to the lobby. He reasoned Turilli would never flee the palace - being too proud to leave willingly - but the regent's volatile nature gave him cause for concern. There was no telling what he would do when faced with defeat, and Leo didn't have time to turn over every room looking for him. Still, if Turilli was set on making some kind of stand then Leo knew he wouldn't be hiding at all, and this gave him an idea where to start.

As the sun began to set, Leo made his way through offices and staterooms where nobles would lounge, avoiding areas the Royal Guard were assigned to patrol. The hours he'd spent exploring these rooms as a boy made navigating the palace easier, though progress was still painfully slow. He saw danger everywhere he looked, every sound fraying his nerves. Leo told himself that the nobles and ministers had left the palace for their estates and all enforcers were committed to the battle, pressing on despite his trepidations.

Then the great wooden doors of the council chamber loomed before him, and Leo hesitated. The thought of failure crossed his mind, as did doubts over his plan. He was going in alone and unprepared, but none of that mattered with the future of Tanis hanging in the balance.

Leo pushed the doors open and stepped inside.

The council chamber was much larger than he'd imagined. Rows of wooden pews ringed the oval room's periphery in ascending tiers, and banners of Divinity's oldest noble houses hung from the ceiling. Leo figured the chamber could hold up to three hundred dignitaries, though he was more intrigued by its centrepiece - an elaborate golden throne on which rested the royal sceptre. But of Turilli there was no sign. Leo cursed inwardly, afraid his hunt for the regent would prove fruitless.

As he turned to leave, a short, mirthless laugh echoed through the room. Leo looked back and saw Turilli step out from behind the throne, grinning maniacally. The regent threw the royal sceptre to the floor and calmly seated himself, tinkering around with a customised datapad. Leo closed the chamber's doors, his pistol still drawn, noting that Turilli seemed almost dismissive of him, as if he'd been expecting an angry mob instead.

"Rossi's ghost indeed," the regent mumbled, sounding mildly amused. His gaze settled on Leo's sidearm. "Dispensing justice from the barrel of a gun."

Leo holstered his weapon without a word. Turilli smiled. Rules and codes made his enemies weak, and this pretentious upstart was no exception. "So predictable," he snarled, pulling a gun of his own. He felt a sudden surge of power as he pointed it at Leo. The boy would pay for his arrogance, but not until he'd grasped the true depth of the regent's genius.

"Killing me won't change anything," said Leo, pacing the room. "Events are in motion that you cannot stop."

"I don't need to kill you, boy," Turilli snapped. "You're no threat to me." He held the datapad aloft and said, "Do you know what this is?"

Leo shook his head. "Enlighten me."

"A remote, of sorts. This device has a direct link to the Chimera, meaning that from here I can control the most powerful weapon ever built. I could obliterate a village, a moon, individual districts of a city or even the city itself." A slight smirk tugged at the corners of Turilli's mouth. "I've already chosen my next target."

"Get on with it, then," Leo shrugged.

His measured response caught Turilli off-guard. The regent had expected Leo to panic and beg him not to follow through, but he didn't seem overly concerned by his threats. That, or he wasn't taking them seriously. Feeling he could regain the initiative without using the Chimera, Turilli changed tack.

"Perhaps," the regent sighed, "I spoke too hot. There's no need for further bloodshed. Just tell me what it would take for you to call off this attack. Land? Titles? I can make you monstrously rich. Restore your name and rank, too. The finest clothes, the most diligent servants - all of this could be yours. Just ask and I shall make it so."

"These things are no longer yours to give," said Leo. "You should consider yourself a prisoner of the League. You'll be tried, convicted and locked away, never witnessing another sunrise, remembered only as the drunken fool in plays for years to come."

Turilli couldn't suppress his anger any longer. "Fool?" he roared, furious that Leo would refuse his gifts. "There is no law but that which I make. Who will try me when I have no equal? You? You're just some low-born prole the old regent was fond of. A fantasist with no talents of his own out to make a name for himself by challenging me. Well, I've indulged your game long enough and I won't buttress your ego and self-righteousness by playing along anymore." Turilli tapped the screen of the datapad and said, "You've left me no choice. This world is mine, and I'm not about to lose it. What happens now is on you."

The regent swiped his finger across the datapad's screen and tapped once. His command reached the Chimera's central computer in seconds, prompting it to activate the weapon and discharge another shell. It was the act of a madman, one taken without a moment's thought and only possible when the horror of life entombed outweighed the fear of death. Turilli stood, his arms outstretched, but the ensuing explosion was far louder than he'd expected. More detonations followed, and Leo's growing smile told him something was wrong. He grasped the datapad and started pressing buttons, only to find his link to the Chimera cut. Exasperated, Turilli looked up and fixed Leo with his most threatening stare.

"What have you done?"

Leo's smile disappeared and his gaze met Turilli's own. "The Chimera project is over," he declared coldly. "Along with your rule."

"Nothing is over until I say it is!" Turilli raged, tightening his grip on his gun.

"You no longer have the means to hurt anyone," said Leo. "No more soldiers to call on, no doomsday weapon to hide behind and no words that can save you."

"Is that so?"

"I'm not wrong," Leo continued. "Given how much you crave power, it was obvious you would have some kind of contingency, and your contempt for life meant you'd certainly execute it before you ever lost control. I was never going to leave anything to chance when I learned what the Chimera could do, which is why I had someone infiltrate and destroy it."

"Not in time to save Gethsemane," Turilli smirked.

"That was never my intention. Think about it. Only the most unspeakable act could have shaken the people from their apathy. Had you turned the weapon on the League and not Gethsemane, Divinity would still be yours. Those people had to die to ensure this movement's success, and a few choice words from Luther ensured your compliance."

Turilli's smug expression turned to one of disbelief. "You didn't just stand by, did you? You licensed it."

"A small price to pay," said Leo, "given what was at stake. I might have influenced the outcome, but you'll forever be remembered as the man who pulled the trigger."

"No, no, no," Turilli rasped, waving his hands. "You're not going to come out of this unscathed. I'll see to it that everyone on Tanis learns the truth."

"And who will believe you? The people you oppressed? I think they'll be far more interested in what I've got to say."

"Nothing you say is going to save you from Earth's wrath."

Leo smiled easily. "No empire lasts forever. Those built on lies and sustained through violence invariably fall. Luther's assurances will keep the regime blind to events here, and by the time they figure out what really happened I'll be on my way to Earth with an army at my back."

"Luther," Turilli stammered, "will turn on you as he did me."

"It's possible," said Leo, "but for now our interests are conjoined. I have no doubt that Luther will build a better world, and in time we will share our vision with others. If he doesn't stay true then that's his decision, but know that I've considered every eventuality."

Turilli tossed the datapad aside and pointed his gun at Leo. The regent's face started to twitch and his hand was shaking. Defeat was inconceivable. He'd been outmanoeuvred by a child, one who intended to destroy him along with his name - the only thing he had left. The boy couldn't be reasoned with, so he had to die. Turilli composed himself and steadied the gun, so focused on Leo that he didn't see one of the chamber's doors open.

"Every eventuality?" Turilli snarled, his finger on the trigger.

"Don't embarrass yourself," said Leo. "Put that down and come with me. There's a cell waiting with your name on it."

This last remark struck home, pushing Turilli over the edge. He squeezed the trigger and two shots rang out, then he felt himself falling forward onto his knees. Peering down, he saw blood bubbling from two holes in his tunic, which had now started to seep into his trousers. He looked up at Leo with hate-filled eyes, trying to lift and aim his gun once more. Then the third shot caught him squarely in the stomach and he felt nothing at all.

Leo holstered his sidearm as Marcus Rathen entered the chamber with his own weapon still raised. Having assumed Turilli would listen, Leo was grateful his friend had intervened when he had.

"Shame on you, Marcus," he scowled in mock censure. "Look at the mess you've made."

Marcus managed a smile and said, "You're lucky I got here when I did. From what I heard, it sounded like you wanted him to shoot."

"Don't be so dramatic. I doubt Turilli had ever fired a gun in his life, and this armour is bulletproof."

"You were goading him."

"No I wasn't," Leo scoffed. "Humiliating, perhaps. It was the least he deserved. Anyway, forget Turilli, don't you have something you'd like to say?"

"I don't think so," said Marcus. "Do you?"

"About Gethsemane," Leo offered, guessing that Marcus had heard most of his exchange with Turilli. "You're right to ask, but know that I wouldn't sacrifice any number of people whatever the circumstances. They're safe, and being brought to Tanis as we speak."

"I see."

"Luther arranged it. Made the whole thing look very convincing, I'll give him that."

Marcus nodded once. Leo forced a frown into a faint smile, annoyed Marcus had still not apologised and was unrepentant for killing Turilli - something he'd never wanted to happen. Now he had to decide whether or not to demote him, but that was a decision for another day.

"Come on," Leo said eventually, heading towards the doors. "Let's get out of here."

Marcus followed, worried the conflict had already changed them for the worse.

Luna sat exhausted in the lobby, watching Kruger and the city's administrator exchange pleasantries. The few remaining royal guards stood nearby, having elected to serve the new regent rather than face destruction at the League's hands. When Leo and Marcus appeared, Luther was quick to congratulate them before taking his leave, recognising that this was their moment and all they required of him was to oversee preparations for his swearing-in ceremony.

"Simply brilliant," he remarked, still stunned by their triumph.

Stifling a yawn, Kruger turned to Leo and said, "You and your politician friend can take it from here. I feel like I could sleep for a week."

"No time for that," Leo smiled. "We'd be naive to think the regime won't learn what happened. They'll respond in the only way they know how, so I say we drive home our advantage and bring the fight to them."

"How?" asked Marcus and Kruger in unison.

"We'll use the transports Luther requisitioned to get off-world and strike at Gehenna. It's the regime's primary naval base in the sector so there will be plenty of ships at anchor - ships that we're going to take."

"And then?" Kruger pressed, keen to learn just how far Leo had planned ahead.

"Then we'll sway those worlds closest to Tanis to our cause. Rossi maintained favourable ties with at least a dozen other regents, so that's where we'll start. I know them, and the very least they'll do is hear us out." Leo thought for a moment before saying, "I won't force anyone to fight who doesn't want to. Those who stay can either keep the peace and ensure our new regent honours his word, or just live long, prosperous lives. This is how it should be, and how it will be when Luther distributes the nobility's wealth."

"Some of which we should keep for ourselves," said Kruger. "I'll take a couple of Turilli's old chambers as my reward and sleep very well tonight in a comfy bed."

With that, Kruger disappeared off into the palace, whistling as he went. Leo asked Marcus to go with him, if only to keep his exuberance in check.

"You want to watch that one," Marcus warned. "He has a

temperamental streak."

Leo nodded and seated himself next to Luna. "I don't know how much more of this bickering I can take," he grinned.

She managed a tired smile. "Send them off to Gehenna and we can stay here."

"Would you like to? Stay, I mean."

Luna shrugged. "I don't know. Maybe. If all I've got to look forward to is a lifetime of war."

"Trust me," said Leo, "I'll be through with the regime much sooner than you think."

"And what then? Look at Divinity. The city's a mess, and now you want to start fixing the rest of the galaxy? How many years will that take?"

"You can't put a timescale on it," said Leo, "but I have to try. And Divinity is in good hands, so don't worry."

"Because Luther loves the people so," Luna mumbled. "With you gone, who's going to look out for them?"

Leo stood up and gently pulled her to her feet. "Then we'll leave only when you're ready."

"Do you mean that?"

"There'll be no more talk about leaving until we've improved every citizen's quality of life. If this matters to you, then it does to me."

Luna playfully wrapped her arms around Leo's waist and hugged him as hard as she could. As he held her tightly, she looked up into his eyes and wondered if her dream of a bright future was really so far away after all.

www.ingramcontent.com/pod-product-compliance
Lightning Source LLC
Chambersburg PA
CBHW021943170626
46808CB00001B/12
9781910223970